audience participation
THEATRE FOR YOUNG PEOPLE

brian way

Walter H. Baker Co./Boston, MA. 02111

Walter H. Baker Co., Inc.
100 Chauncy Street
Boston, Mass. 02111

ISBN 0-87440-000-7

Book and Cover Design, Teresa Power

Dedicated to

G. LAURENCE HARBOTTLE

in appreciation of 25 years support of
Theatre for Children and Young People.

Foreword

It is a privilege and a pleasure to write a Foreword to this book. In spite of wide interest in participatory theatre, and experimentation with its techniques in recent years, very little has actually been written about it. An authoritative text is, therefore, long overdue and Brian Way is the obvious one to write it. His thirty years of experience as director of the Theatre Centre in London and his extensive travels as a workshop leader in Britain, the United States, Canada and the continent of Europe, qualify him to speak with authority on the subject of producing plays for children.

His format for a play that invites total audience involvement further identifies him as an innovator, whose work is admired and emulated on both sides of the Atlantic. He makes the point early in the text, however, that he did not "invent" participation. Children are naturally involved in a performance, Way explains; therefore actors, working in children's theatre, are able to "explore, develop and extend" their reactions as a way of deepening the experience.

Way's book is rich in detail and filled with anecdotes and examples from his own experiences. It is the text we have been waiting for, and it does not disappoint us. The author describes his early years at the Old Vic, during which time he played many performances for school children. His sensitivity to their interests, and the causes of their occasional restlessness brought discoveries that led eventually to the creation of some new and radical methods. He also found that they accomplished what conventional production techniques failed to achieve in many instances. Since then directors have used and incorporated his methods; sometimes successfully, sometimes not.

Brian Way was a pioneer. As he himself explains, there was no area of experience to study or be influenced by at that time. The producer was forced to discover for himself the most effective means of bringing children and theatre together. Way's basic principle from the beginning was to do only plays that he believed to be valid and appropriate. He was convinced then, as now, that children's theatre, together with the other arts, should be accorded a priority in fostering human development. He also believed, as a corollary, that theatre for children needed no further justification for its existence.

To Brian Way, the spiritual and emotional nature of theatre is connected with the stretching of a child's horizons. The immediacy of the experience he believes to be of greater value than special preparation preceding the event. Likewise, he is convinced that tranquility and privacy after the experience is far preferable to an academic follow-up. "Theatre is much more than another audio-visual aid to the teaching of subjects in school," he says, although he agrees that it is an area where the academic and the performing arts do overlap.

He explains that his understanding of approaches to participatory theatre came equally from working with children in school and working in theatre. In both cases he tries constantly to keep the children at the center of the situation, rather than allowing either interest to dominate. Thus the child remains whole.

Way discusses in detail the creation of a participation play, including form, content and the opportunity for audience input. Whereas, in our society participation is normally confined to an intellectual, emotional and spiritual response, children will add verbal and physical responses, if permitted. Why not, Way argues, involve them as completely as possible by encouraging them to offer suggestions and help to the actors in the form of spontaneous dialogue and improvised action? In subsequent chapters Way describes three kinds of audience participation: spontaneus, stimulated, and directed. He distinguishes among them, explaining their legitimacy and place. Using as illustrations a number of plays produced at the Theatre Centre, he tells in detail how the plays were written, produced, and received by a variety of audiences.

He warns the inexperienced director however, of the difficulties he will encounter. Actors must be schooled to work in this kind of theatre and it is not an easy assignment. Indeed, the best of actors, trained for the proscenium stage, need a period of apprenticeship before they are ready to step into the arena, where they will be in direct communication with the child audience. Way stresses sincerity as the key to successful acting in a participatory play. The actor must be able to ask for help from the audience and then accept and use whatever is offered. True participation is, therefore, not a gratuitous gimmick, which, incidentally, children are quick to detect; but an integral part of the play and performance. Way warns also against "campy" effects, the cheap laugh and the temptation to overexcite the audience. Sensitivity to and respect for the child are as basic for the actor as schooling in special techniques.

The playing space for this kind of performance is described in detail. One of the author's first observations was that in taking theatre to children, adaptability as to the shape and form of staging was essential. Here Way explains what he means by the open stage. It is an avenue area, which may be a combination of proscenium arch and arena, half arena, or a playing space completely in the round. The action takes place everywhere, for the stage and the audience are one. Indeed, the sharing of physical and psychological space is essential for true participation to happen. The child audience, ideally numbering no more than 200, is seated on three or four sides, thus enabling each spectator to establish eye contact with the actors. Because younger children respond more readily to this kind of theatre, Way recommends an age level audience of boys and girls from six to ten, rather than an older group or a group composed of a wide age range. In later chapters, however, he discusses Shakespeare and other plays with interest for teen-agers as having proved highly effective when produced in this way. As to entertainment that spans all ages, he believes the circus to be the only form capable of doing it successfully.

Way disagrees with those who would discard the folk and fairy tale in favor of stories of the here and now. He sees in the traditional play beauty, narrative and psychological values, without which children's literature and children's theatre would be impoverished. Most of the examples he uses throughout this text are taken from such well-known tales as *The Sleeping Beauty, Puss In Boots,* and *Pinocchio.* Contemporary life, social values not withstanding, dulls by comparison with the magic and color of fantasy.

Way's more than sixty participatory plays are the legacy of his years of experience; they are to be read, studied and produced by directors interested in his techniques and point of view. His commitment to children's theatre and his innovative methods have made Brian Way one of the most important leaders in the field. With the publication of *Audience Participation* he has given us a welcome and important text.

Nellie McCaslin
New York City

Preface

Children's Theatre is, in many ways, the youngest of the theatre arts.

This book is an attempt to share the detail of discoveries from experiments I have been involved in for over 30 years, and for this reason it is a personal statement of one very particular aspect of Children's Theatre: scripted theatre with intended and constructive participation by audiences of children and young people in attendance at performances by adults.

Readers who are not interested in this particular form of theatre for children and young people may save themselves disappointment by not reading any farther. The book is about:

Family audiences in conventional theatres with fixed seating;

Approaches to many different forms of open staging;

Details of participation for confined age-groups and controlled numbers in the open stage;

The approach of the actor and the director to Children's Theatre with audience participation.

However, for one director to tell another what to do in any kind of theatre is both impertinent and a betrayal of the right to individual creativity. I have tried not to do this, but simply to share the fruits of a lifetime of experimental opportunity. And I have always had only one goal — to find out what is appropriate for children and young people.

It is important to make clear that this is not a history of Children's Theatre, with an outline of the work of different people and groups, nor is any attempt made to evaluate the endeavors of others in the field. The reader will find no information about: Theatre in streets, parks, leisure centers, play centers, playgrounds or other environments; no mention of Improvised Children's Theatre as such, nor of Dance Theatre, Media Theatre or Puppetry; no in depth references to Theatre in Education, political theatre, social theatre or religious theatre; and no mention of theatre performed by children for children, though suggestions are made regarding teen-agers performing children's theatre plays with audience participation. That I should not mention any of these is neither through lack of interest, admiration or even partial involvement in almost all of them. I simply have not been involved for long enough in sufficient depth in any of them to be so impertinent as to write a book about them. Others will do that.

However, what all of these activities, many and varied as they are, do have in common is the child or young person, and such is the very heart of this book.

Many people speak of their good fortune in having work that is also a hobby. From this point of view I am doubly blessed, for I have had two distinct yet ever interweaving occupations — Children's Theatre and Drama in Education. Both have absorbed work and leisure time, and both have had one golden thread running through them, joining them — children and young people. Because of this, I make no apology that, although fundamentally concerned with theatre, the pages of this book return again and again to a concern for youngsters, whether it be in school or the home, whether about young children or teen-agers, whether concerned with education or recreation. Perhaps, therefore, colleagues with specialized interests other than Children's Theatre may find some thoughts that can be shared.

At one stage in the preparation and writing of this book, it became a kind of autobiographical romp. This had many disadvantages as it was too long and very boring, and its essential substance became diffused by nostalgic meandering. But it had one advantage that this finished product does not have: it was able to trace my indebtedness to so many fine people with whom I had the pleasure and privilege of working in detail, and others with whom I had a contact that was momentary, ephemeral, and yet deeply important to my own thinking and the development of any work I have been about to do in the field. If per chance they should read these words, they will know I mean them, and they will know of my respect, admiration and gratitude. Many will claim that they were able to offer no more than "encouragement"; but,more often than not, encouragement was the most important offering of all. However, I should like to say very particular thanks to:

-   the many people who gave time, advice and energy as members of Theatre Centre's Board of Governors from 1953 onwards;
-   the hundreds of actors and actresses, who so readily and trustingly joined in this "adventure of discovery," and the administrative staff who organized tours all over England, Scotland and Wales;
-   the many drama advisers who encouraged and supported so much of the work described in these pages, and particularly those who went out on a limb to encourage experiments of many different kinds;
-   Stanley Evernden, lifelong friend, counsellor and adviser, who eventually wrote plays for and worked very closely with Theatre Centre;
-   Len Dixon, for his wisdom and understanding;
-   Ralph Kunkel for his help and advice on preparation of this manuscript.

Most of all, I wish to acknowledge my indebtedness to Margaret Faulkes-Jendyk, who co-founded Theatre Centre in 1953 and was joint-director for fifteen years. She built up the administration of Theatre Centre's tours to schools from a mere few weeks with a single company, to a peak when 7 companies visited over 3,000 schools and performed to about one million children and young people in a single year. In addition to this administrative work, she also helped to plan and develop the long term experiments with audience participation for all age groups, drawing on her own expertise as a teacher of drama. She also designed costumes for the majority of the plays, directed many productions, and was responsible for all choregraphy. She was one of the most significant pioneers of Children's Theatre, the open stage, audience participation and Theatre in Education and leisure, and she has continued similar work in North America, particularly in terms of training University students.

1

A Natural Phenomenon

Audience Participation in Children's Theatre — particularly with younger children — is a phenomenon that exists within the children themselves. The phenomenon is observable even by inexperienced observers, and an important truth is that nobody invented the phenomenon. Some people observed it, and then, within a special area of study and experiment, explored and developed it, as part of a detailed interest in Theatre for Children. These activities were often closely linked with the educational development of child drama, creative dramatics and intergrated arts, within both school and the leisure life of children and young people.

This book arises from my personal involvement in the observation, exploration and development of audience participation. But I cannot reiterate too often, that neither I nor anyone else sat down to invent — in theory or in practice — the notion of audience participation. As a member of a professional theatre company I, like others, noticed that it was happening. I then moved from mere noticing to detailed observation, and thus to continuous and constantly changing experimentation over a period of thirty years.

I emphasize this factor of an "observable existing phenomenon" partly for the sake of those who state that they "do not believe in audience participation." Many such people have probably had unhappy experiences of uncontrolled and chaotic audiences ruining the produce of precious weeks of rehearsal. I sympathize with such people and have myself reached moments bordering on despair when I have witnessed the totally wrong approach to audience participation. At such moments, I remind myself that we are concerned with *a phenomenon that is,* not one that was invented.

Perhaps we need constantly to remind ourselves that *all theatre,* for whatever age group or kind of audience, calls for and even depends upon the participation of the audience. For the majority of theatre experiences, the main areas of participation, however, are intellectual, emotional and spiritual,

1

not necessarily in equal proportions — perhaps not always all three. And on occasion these may be contrary to the intentions and expectations of the author, the actors or the director. Whatever the motivations and objectives of the author, or the method of procedure of the cast and the director, the factor of the live audience will have some kind of bearing, through participation of the mind and/or the emotions, and/or the spirit. Again, we can, if we wish, observe, explore and develop, but we cannot *ignore* the actual existence of these forms of participation. They are part of "the theatre experience."

Every culture in every civilization slowly evolves its own "rules" for all aspects of life, including response to theatre, and one of the rules of theatre in Western Civilization is: "However much you may participate intellectually, emotionally and spiritually, please do *not* participate *physically or vocally.*" The rule does not apply to laughter, clapping and cheering and calling "encore." Generally speaking, however, tears and sobs should be suppressed.

The rule is aided and abetted among adults in Western Societies by natural human traits of reserve, self-consciousness or inhibition, so that even some of the few intended exceptions to the rule have to be handled carefully and skillfully by the cast, particularly with an audience that is unfamiliar with the particular *genre* in question. Melodrama, for example, may call for planned and intended "boos and hisses" of the villain, but this participation may not come without some subtle stimulation from a member of the cast, and even then, will come only when an actor's lead is taken up by a few "courageous" members of the audience. "Joining in a song" with voice or hand-claps also often calls for some encouragement and stimulation.

For the majority of adult audiences, the rule, consciously or unconsciously assimilated, is so entrenched that it is difficult for people to break away from it, even when "required" to do so by a particular form of theatre. We are simply not used to giving vocal or physical reaction to our intellectual, emotional and spiritual participation.

Now, the straightforward fact is that young children *do not know* the rule of this particular game, so that when they attend a play that is well done, in the right environment, not only do they, like adults, participate with their mind, their heart and their spirit, but also give vent to the inner reactions of those experiences through additional vocal and physical participation. They do so directly and with total simplicity — providing circumstances permit. And when they are young, i.e. pre-puberty, they are in no way governed by the natural growth factors of self-consciousness and inhibition.

These physical and vocal reactions form the basis of the phenomenon of audience participation in Children's Theatre — a thing that *is*, that has not been invented by grown-ups, but can be explored, developed and extended by adults as an enrichment to almost a new form of theatre — Children's Theatre.

This book is, in part, an attempt to answer many of the fundamental questions associated with this development.

1. What exactly is meant by "young children?" The question of audience age group is of utmost importance for certain kinds of Children's Theatre and will constantly be referred to. In general, I mean children up to the age of 9 or 10 years, the maximum age where the natural phenomenon of vocal and physical participation is observable. This, too, is the age when the youngster's own play, having moved from unconscious to conscious drama, begins to move to an awareness of conscious theatre, an important factor with great bearings on audience participation.

2. If children "do not know the rule of this particular game," then can we not, should we not, *teach* them, so that they do know, and consequently will *behave* as an audience in the *correct* manner? Indeed we can — or, at least, we can *try* to do so. I have attended many performances when the authority in charge of the young audience has given, by way of introduction to the performance of a play, the following type of speech:

"Right, listen to me all of you. You're going to see a play. Some of you may not have seen a play before, so let me tell you how to behave during the performance. It's very simple really. All you have to do is to sit up and shut up — and enjoy yourselves. But I don't want to hear a word or see a movement from any of you. That way we can all enjoy ourselves, and the actors will be able to do so as well."

With a play that includes planned, intended, constructive, controlled and purposeful participation, this speech does not make for the easiest of conditions — but invariably, if the participation is integrated within the play itself, because it is a natural phenomenon, it will flow quite easily and simply.

(In East Berlin, the actors at one children's theatre toured the schools to instruct the children on their behavior, and the teachers followed up with further details of the rules. However, at each of the performances I observed, there were moments when almost the entire audience took in the necessary breath for some simple vocal participation — but the teachers' "Ssssshh!" and the actors' speed of continuity with the action and dialogue managed to avert the participation just in time. It would seem, therefore, that the rule can be not only taught, but also very simply enforced.)

Much of this book is concerned with audience participation that is *planned, intended, constructive, controlled, purposeful and integrated within the play.*

3. "...a play that is well done...?" This factor will be looked at over and over again. Fundamentally I am referring to the kind of integrity of writing and sincerity of directing and acting that removes children's theatre hrom the notion that "almost anything will do for kids, as long as they can shriek with laughter and generally raise the roof." We need to look squarely at the fact that "playing down to kids," whether it be by the author, the actors or the directors, is first and foremost going to undermine the genuine basis of the intellectual, emotional and spiritual participation, and if the factors are even partially destroyed, then any physical or vocal participation will bear the scars of insincerity leading to forms of participation that range from mockery to anarchy.

4. "...in the right environment...?" Shape of playing area, use of space, etc., are all important factors in children's theatre with audience participation, and will be considered in detail. At the same time, the fact is that most of us are unlikely ever to have what might be considered "ideal conditions" of environment. If we all had to wait for "the ideal," there would be very little theatre for children to experience.

5. "...providing circumstances permit...?" Many of the barriers to successful, exciting, vital and often intensely moving audience participation invariably arise from the wrong "attitude" to either children or theatre or, at its saddest, to both. This is not meant to be the pompous statement it might appear to be. Indeed, I am constantly enthused by

the genuine dedication of many people who want to provide theatre — the activity they themselves love — for children. It is seldom the fault of such people that they have had neither the time nor the opportunity — nor perhaps even felt the need — to study children in relation to theatre. I hope this book may perhaps help such people to find even more interest and excitement in the work they do. But this again entails the necessity of looking at the basis of the phenomenon of audience participation as a *natural* vocal and physical expression of the participation of the heart, the mind and the spirit. The phenomenon is no less serious or challenging than that. But the challenge is not boringly intellectual and theoretical. It is the very stuff of exciting and exacting creative theatre, and brings about that extraordinary inner satisfaction that is the reward of all such genuine endeavor.

In one sense, this book is the result of a series of intuitive leaps in the dark. I had the great good fortune to be a pioneer working alongside many other pioneers. Our mutual blessing lay in the fact that there was no area of experience (at least, that we knew of) for us to look back on or be influenced by. Nobody before us had set up rules that we should slavishly follow. We simply had to discover for ourselves through trial and error. One of the curses for people following us, three decades later, is that they have to contend with the body of knowledge unfolded in that time. It can be a mill stone around their necks, or it can be some kind of helpful stimulation and guide, no matter how small, perhaps at least saving them the necessity of having to cover the same ground again, thus perhaps saving time for new discoveries and experiments.

The one cardinal yardstick that I have used throughout a long period of experiment has been "what is right and appropriate for children and young people." This has been an unswerving basic principle.

It sometimes helps people to know how I came to be involved in Children's Theatre. My first job in theatre was as a *very* junior member of the Old Vic Company from 1941-43, touring villages and towns in England and Scotland, playing small parts and assisting with all aspects of stage management. This proved to be a thorough apprenticeship in every aspect of theatre, all of which has served me well in subsequent years, as actor, stage manager, producer and administrator.

One of my stage management functions at the time was that of prompting, and one of the advantages of prompting was that I had immediate access to the small and concealed "peep hole" that enables direct observation of the auditorium and the audience. It was, I believe, from such observational opportunities that the first seeds of interest in specialized children's theatre work were born in me — not that I had the slightest *conscious* awareness of any such happening.

Twice a week, usually on Wednesday and Saturday, there was a matinee of a Shakespeare play, and the mid-week performance was exclusively for school parties. The youngsters came in hundreds, by bus and coach, by car and on foot, and they crowded the theatre with an overexcited festive expectancy. They filled to capacity each theatre or cinema or hall, according to our venue in the many small towns and villages, which meant they could number anything from four or five hundred to, on at least one occasion, 2000. They invariably covered the whole age span of compulsory education, which at the time was from 5 to 14 years, and when there were "private" schools nearby, the upper age would extend to include some aged up to 17 plus. They outnumbered adults in the audience (usually their own teachers) by 45 or 50 to one.

I doubt that many had been to the theatre before, except perhaps for the traditional "Christmas Pantomime," so curiosity was high, particularly when the performance was held in what was for them their local cinema. Arrangements were usually made for their arrival to be staggered over a period of half-an-hour, which meant that a high proportion had to wait almost that amount of time before the curtain went up, and it seemed beyond the power of the teachers to control the excesses of excitable energy, which usually took the form of rushing up and down the aisles.

Through the peep hole in the prompt corner, the stage management team would see the house manager's signal that all were assembled — not that they all were, for there was invariably one school that arrived late, but it was unwise to wait any longer, no matter how much confusion the late arrival would cause.

The house-lights would go out to a tremendous pent-up roar, which is still the lot actors have to put up with, and always will be until directors accept the fact that to plunge any audience of children into sudden darkness is both unwise and unnecessary (often the same applies to adult theatre). The roar would change to laughter as soon as the youngsters saw actors dressed in Elizabethan costume, but as the dialogue started there would come a hopeful silence. Sadly this was short lived, and the momentum of private conversation, observation and comment would soon begin to spread through the audience. The entrance of a new character generally brought another few moments' hiatus, but the end of the scene was usually greeted with cheering, booing, catcalling, and the first hesitant throwing of missiles.

The Old Vic managers and directors were deeply concerned about the situation and, during the next year, two entirely different programs were specially written and devised for the younger part of the audience, and steps were taken to try to confine the Shakespeare matinees to Secondary school audiences.

These programs made a considerable difference, bringing a note of hope and gladness to the weekly matinee. For many reasons, there were still moments of chaos, still the need for the actors to battle against general chatter and other vocal noise, and still the occasional throwing of missiles.

From the peep hole in the prompt corner I tried to study and understand some of the reasons for these reactions. Occasionally I was also allowed to sit out front among the audience so that I could obtain a more detailed view, but again I must hasten to add that there was no conscious or planned intention behind any of this growing concern and interest — my curiosity was intuitively based.

My observation, both from the peep hole and from sitting among the audience included the following:

1. The deepest and most sustained interest in the performance came from those sitting closest to the stage. This often included the first six to ten rows, but the number of rows was relative to the width of the aisle in front of the first row, the additional width of the orchestra pit (if any), and the depth of apron stage (if any) extending from the proscenium opening. Interest was also affected by when the actors were well down stage, thus "front cloth" scenes often held more attention than centrally staged scenes, even though the latter were pictorially more interesting. Indeed, it often seemed clear that the less distraction there was in the way of scenery the more interest the youngsters took in the actors themselves.

Absorption and sustained interest generally decreased the farther back one sat from the stage, despite the fact that those often nearest to the back of the theatre were the right age group for understanding the language and content of the play.

2. The inter-action of older age groups to younger age groups was most marked. For seniors to be present at the same performance as 8-11's was clearly *infra dig*, as it was for 8-11's to be among the 5-7's, although because there were many 5-11 schools, this latter separation was less marked.

3. Much of the overexcitement before the start of a performance arose from the fact that the journey to the theatre, with its many accompanying sidelines, was an adventure in its own right, often creating more interest and delight than the fare at the theatre itself, leading to some disappointment and frustration, and a consequent looking forward to the return journey. Food for the journey and the performance — though limited in scope because of rationing — was also a distraction.

4. No matter what program material was tried, the age range was too wide and the numbers too great.

5. Much of every performance included a continuous babble of chatter from the audience, for many different reasons, often happening in parallel and often based on a kind of social helpfulness where some would try to help their friends catch up on what had been happening while those friends had been trying to help someone else. This helpfulness factor often involved quite lengthy and heated discussions and arguments. A good example, in the Shakespeare matinees, was the heated exchange among boys as to whether Shylock's knife was real or fake, whether chains worn by Antonio were real or fake. By the time some had resolved this, a whole scene would have passed, so they would now turn to their other nearest neighbours and ask to be brought up to date. By the time the explanation had been given, often involving much searching for words and contradictions by nearby friends, the helpful ones had in their turn lost track of what was going on, so they would find yet other people — perhaps some rows away — who could bring them up to date. Meanwhile, for some, and almost inevitably because of these lengthy procedures, interest would have died altogether, so they would start entirely new activities, such as kicking or punching the person in front of them; or, if not too far away, throwing something at the stage, and this would often catch on as an activity of great rivalry and competition, until such time as teachers could contain it — at least, for a while.

6. Among those closest to the action, within the few front rows, some of their chatter took a quite different form, however, including various things said directly to the actors on stage. What they said was often sincere, indeed sometimes even desperately anxious, and much was meant as quite genuine advice based on their foreknowledge of what was to come. Thus, Antonio often received information about what Shylock was going to do to him—and the words would be called in everything from strangulated whispers to almost bold shouts, usually at the time when the main protagonists were assembling for the formal beginnings of the trial scene. Or, again, the youngsters would try to reassure Bassanio and Gratiano that Portia and Nerissa were really

"only kidding" when accusations were made about giving their precious rings to other women. The advice, of course, was totally ignored by the actors, who, to their credit tried very hard to keep a straight face, but the youngsters were often ready with a scornful "There, I told you so" when a later stage of the action proved them to have been right. Their scorn and derision contained a feeling of "if only you'd listened to us, then none of this need have happened!"

These were some of my first experiences of "spontaneous audience participation," and, while it would be foolish to suggest too detailed a practical concern about it over thirty years ago, there is no doubt that these experiences were also "seedlings" that were to be of tremendous significance for me a few years after the event. They have been the root of experiment and discovery from that time (1942) to the present (1980). The main concerns, everyone of them fundamental to serious children's theatre and audience participation, are:

1. *Form and shape of presentation,* including the theatre environment itself, and approaches to the use of scenery, lighting, costumes, properties, media, music, etc.
2. *Content,* or the subject matter of plays, but with particular reference to plays written or adapted as experiments.
3. *Age groups,* and the development made possible by being able to have some control over the age groups attending Children's Theatre.
4. *Size of audience,* and the potential developments that are opened up for the work itself when the size of the audience can be controlled without losing sight of the economic problems that can arise from such control.
5. *Audience participation,* with family audiences in rather large and conventional auditoria to the potential developments when age groups and size of audiences are controlled in flexible shapes of open stage theatre. Also, the approach to the development of conscious theatre creation of crowd scenes with teen-agers.

Interlinking, and to an extent, the overriding factor, is the youngster himself. Whatever may be our particular concern or factual and practical problems in Children's Theatre, all five of the basic points mentioned above are viable for any type of theatre for any age group.

For those of us concerned with theatre for children or young people, life can seldom be organized into cozy sequences that exactly fulfil requirements for this, that or the other pieces of research. Indeed, it is often because one is working with impossible difficulties that genuine discoveries are made without the slightest realization that they lie just around the corner. I would go so far as to add the suggestion that what does frequently go wrong with long term study periods in universities and other places of training is the careful elimination of the circumstances whereby "accidents can happen" — hence losing the balance between intellectual certainty and intuitive happenings. Thus, for example, the detail of the uses to which I have put the open stage in theatre for young people owes most of its origin to experiments in open stage theatre *as such,* without reference to children or young people as a specific audience; further, many experiments regarding content arose from being in the open stage rather than in the proscenium; and a number of experiments regarding audience participation arose from the accidental but enforced limitation suddenly placed on age groups and numbers in the audience. The paradox of "which came first, the chicken or the egg?" has as much relevance to Children's

7

Theatre as to any other factor in life. As a final example, I would mention that a great deal of drama in education today owes its beginning to observation of audience participation in performances of Children's Theatre, but that very participation has probably arisen from observation of youngsters doing their own creative drama in school.

I believe there are hundreds of actors and theatre groups, professional and non-professional, who have had a wealth of other theatre experiences who could be interested in the immense potential of theatre for children and young people. For many of them, a "specialist" book such as this might be very off-putting. That would be sad, because the ultimate hope is to encourage such people to provide the means for more youngsters to have more opportunities of the experience of theatre. There is no need for anyone to make a sudden and totally abrupt change from past experience, if their interest is genuinely concerned with youngsters. For this reason I feel it important to start from the point of view of the conditions of theatre that are possibly common to most of us — conditions similar to those I experienced with the Old Vic, and to work outwards from there to whatever is possible or within our interests. But we need to start from where we are...

2
Start From Where You Are
The Traditional Theatre Environment

The old adage — *start from where you are* — is probably as applicable to Children's Theatre as it is to most other developmental activities in life.

The straightforward fact is that, whatever "theories" may have validity or be of interest, very large numbers of people who would like to be involved in or with Participatory Theatre are confronted with the following realities:
— having to work on a picture frame stage;
— an auditorium with fixed seating, often tiered;
— need to accomodate "family audiences" rather than audiences of children only;
— little opportunity to break down age groups;
— a budget which necessitates audiences of 400 to 500, sometimes even larger;
— a majority of actors who have never been involved with the idea of "seriously intended" audience participation, perhaps with a majority who have never been exposed to children at all;
— a majority of actors who have never before "come through" the proscenium arch to make use of the auditorium;
— little or no experience of purposefully and needfully making any kind of departure from a rehearsed script, i.e. a practical use of improvisation.

Can Participatory Theatre for Children work in such conditions? The degree to which it *will* work as a rich experience for the audience will depend largely on the attitude of the cast, director and all others involved in the production. Certain basic adjustments have to be made compared to an approach to non-participatory theatre.

The Play
There are obvious advantages to choosing a play in which the author has

already integrated the idea of participation into the story so that it has purpose, intention and logical development. It can be unwise, both for actors and audience, to impose participation on a play for which it was NOT intended; so often the results are artificial gimmicks. For this reason I shall quote many examples from plays I know well as author, director and in some cases as an actor. I have directed some of the plays with groups that have never before been involved in participatory theatre, even directed groups that have never before done any work deliberately intended for a family audience or for audiences of children only. Many of the people involved were genuinely sceptical about participation, but in the majority of cases ultimately became intrigued with a form of theatre that was totally new to them. I should mention that many groups, both professional and amateur, have performed in other countries, including performance in translation to other languages. Indeed, one of the joyous experiences of this type of theatre, certainly with youngsters up to 12 years of age, is the constant rediscovery that "children are children are children," whatever their nationality or cultural heritage.

"The Stage"

Possibly the main adjustment in approach to participatory theatre concerns the question: Where does the action take place? The answer is — *everywhere.* The stage and the auditorium need to be thought of as one, not as comprising one place for the actors and another for the viewers. The actors and audience share the same physical space together, with the sole exception that, although the actors make use of the area occupied by the audience, no one from the audience is invited on to the stage. Participation by the audience in these circumstances involves the whole audience participating at the same time, not just one or two going up "on to the stage," where they will feel exposed and self conscious, resulting in either exhibitionism or acute embarrassment, both alien to the absorbed sincerity that is achieved when they remain off the stage.

As soon as we think of the "stage area" and the "auditorium" as one — *as a space in which anything can happen* — and as soon as the actors begin freely to use all of that space, then a whole new relationship is fostered between actor and audience as they share together the same psychological space, arising from a mutual sharing of the same physical space. It is this relationship between actor and audience that is a vital necessity for genuine audience participation to take place. I know of no cases when participation has been wholly successful if the actors and audience have remained in their entirely separate locations throughout a whole play.

This does not mean that theatre loses its capacity for "creating illusion" and remarkable moments of "sheer magic." On the contrary, though a paradox for many, where children are concerned, this new and close relationship can actually aid such capacities and such moments.

We can use the same amount of scenery and lighting, costume and props, music and effects, but we reinforce the potential through the close and intimate involvement. We are all a part of what is happening. Everybody involved drops the pretend game, in which actors pretend the audience is not there, and the audience pretends the actors don't know they are there, while they become a kind of secret watcher of what is happening beyond the "fourth wall of the stage." Tyrone Guthrie spoke many times on the need for giving up this particular game of pretense. "Why," he asked, "cannot we openly enjoy going to see the actors play a play and the actors enjoy saying 'we have come to play a play'?" He foresaw a healthier form of theatre arising from such an approach. "And," he added, "we need not fear, for if the play is sufficiently interesting to capture our interest, and the acting such as to absorb our faculties, then we shall still be 'transported', still experience moments that transcend our own ordinary lives, which is one of our principle reasons for going to the theatre."

It is fear of losing such moments of theatre that makes many actors reluctant to look on the whole theatre as the place in which the action takes place, including the involvement and participation of the audience. There are many actors who, having overcome that fear, have been astonished that not only have they lost nothing, but have gained much.

So in considering the necessities of staging for participatory theatre, we already arrive at a few simple prerequisites:

1. The use of doorways and aisles from all parts of the auditorium.
2. Ease of access from auditorium to stage and stage to auditorium — I have never known a theatre unable to meet these requirements. The "bridging" between stage and auditorium can take many different forms. There can be steps on one or both sides of the stage; sometimes, particularly where there is a central aisle in the auditorium, additional or alternative steps can be arranged from the centre of the stage. Many stages already have some kind of apron stage, extending the stage area outside of the proscenium arch, a most useful asset. On occasion such a forestage has been built by covering over the whole or part of the orchestra pit.
3. The front curtains should be open when the audience arrives, even if there is a quite elaborate set on the stage. Closed curtains establish a firm division between "actors' world" and the audience. When they are open, a feeling of oneness of the space is established from the outset, and the audience also has time to become familiar with any setting so that it is not a distraction, as so often is the case when it is suddenly revealed. **(See Section on Scenery — Pp. 201-231)**.
4. The houselights need to be a careful part of the lighting plot, so that whenever the stage only is being used the houselights can be taken out, and when the whole theatre is being used they can be brought in. Control on dimmer is of course ideal as there is seldom need for houselights to be fully on. If they are not on dimmers, then bringing in just one or two sections can be equally helpful. I have known occasions when the houselight control has been from switches at the back of the auditorium instead of from the main stage-lighting control or from the stage itself. In such cases, the use of the houselights has had to be carefully rehearsed.

When these four simple adjustments to staging are made, then the environmental conditions are right for many facets of participatory theatre, depending now on the requirements of the play.

The Use of the Aisles and the Auditorium.

Just as leaving open the front curtain when the audience is assembling helps to establish the lack of division between stage and auditorium, so, too, does the earliest use of the aisles help to confirm that all of the theatre is the place in which the play is going to happen. Indeed, *to open and start* the play in the auditorium can totally establish the convention of playing, making for both the actors and the audience the first "breaking of the ice" of their closely

11

knit relationship. Let us consider some examples of this early use of aisles. The author's stage directions at the beginning of Act 1 of **Pinocchio** read as follows:

> On the stage area we see Gepetto's house and the house and workshop of Fire-Eater, the Puppet showman. About five minutes before the advertised time of the performance, as many of the company as can be spared mingle with the audience selling imaginary tickets or programs for the "GREAT FIRE-EATER'S PUPPET SHOW."Some of them have boards announcing that the show can be seen "IN THIS CITY IN THREE DAYS TIME." A few minutes later (i.e. just prior to opening of the play itself), GEPETTO the puppet-maker comes from his house (stage area) and stands listening to the ticket sellers. He moves down into the auditorium and makes his way through to one of the ticket sellers.

Then starts the first dialogue of the play.

In production, the development of simple openings may show many differences, dependent on the imagination of the director, the number of actors, the confidence and experience of the actors and, of course, the detailed environment of the theatre itself. In theatres with circle, upper circle and gallery, it has naturally been necessary to have some of the cast upstairs in each area, involved in similar activities.

The minimum character requirements for this opening are: Mr. Fire-Eater, his three live human puppets — Harlequin, Pantalone, and Columbine — each accompanied by a controlling puppeteer with rod and connecting strings to the puppets' wrists and ankles, a clown with a large drum, and eventually, Mr. Gepetto. If there are other people available, then the opening can easily embrace many others.

But even with the above eight people it has been possible to develop the author's original suggestion in order to open the play with a gay, exciting, circus-like processional entrance, headed by Mr. Fire-Eater and ending with Clown, and all going to all parts of the auditorium calling out information about Mr. Fire-Eater's famous puppets. With strong, gay, festival music accompanying the entrance, the whole theatre is suddenly alive with vitality and excitement. When all parts of the auditorium have been covered, then the puppeteers, each in a different section of the audience, can give their puppet-rods to a youngster in the audience with the request that the Puppet be looked after very carefully, and continue with "selling tickets" for the big show in three days time (the tickets are entirely imaginary — so the youngsters know they they can hand over imaginary money). Attracted by all the hullabaloo, Gepetto comes from his house (note, the stage area now, so that, without fuss, we realize that all of the space is to be used, stage as well as auditorium) and comes into the auditorium or, if this would create problems of vision for the audience in theatres with a circle, upper circle, etc., the very front edge of the stage. The music fades right down to dialogue level, so that as Gepetto speaks, he can clearly be heard, *and all of the members of the company in the auditorium draw attention to his presence* so that activity and conversations cease and the opening dialogue of the play is clear to all.

Within the space of eleven lines of dialogue, it is established that these are Mr. Fire-Eater's puppets, that they are going around performing a short trailer or preview of their famous puppet show which they will be showing in three days time, and that the person asking all the questions is the famous

---

Publisher's Footnote: Brian Way's version of **Pinocchio** was written — with the collaboration of Warren Jenkins — for John English's Arena Theatre Co. in 1953. It has subsequently been performed all over the world both on proscenium and open stages. It was first published in 1954 by Dennis Dobson, London, and is now available through Baker's Plays, Boston, MA.

puppet maker, Gepetto. Then, at Fire-Eater's command, the puppeteers collect their puppets, Clown sets up two painter's ladders with a trestle board — accompanied by a great deal of clowning — and everyone, except Gepetto who finds a seat in the auditorium among the audience (it may be necessary to have one reserved for him), goes on to the stage area and gets ready for the "preview." As Fire-Eater announces this (perhaps with much interference from Clown, who never utters a word throughout the play), the houselights begin to fade down, and, for the first time, we are using only the stage area — even so, Gepetto's presence among us, as one of us, preserves the relationship we have built.

I shall return to this precise moment shortly, but before doing so, we need to consider the attitude of the actors involved.

Later in this book, a chapter is devoted to *The Actor in Children's Theatre (see Chapter 8 pp 169-200)*, because there are many complex areas for the actor to consider, particularly during participation. Even at the simple stages we are considering in this opening of **Pinocchio**, of paramount importance for every actor is the quality of *total sincerity*. Everything said and done, even for Clown's comedy and Fire-Eater's flamboyance, must be wholly sincere and believable. The moment sincerity dies, believability dies with it, and the youngsters know the whole thing is a fraud and a cheat. If they believe that insincerity is the game we are playing, because the actors set-up that convention by their own behavior and attitude, they will adopt the same rules whenever participation arises, and, once that starts, the actors will find themselves struggling against the tide of hysteria and exhibitionism, each person vying to show he/she is cleverer at the game than others, either in the audience or in the cast itself. All of this can depend on these early moments in the auditorium.

Lack of concentration and absorption are the main factors that lead to lack of sincerity. Lack of confidence in simple improvisation can equally do so, as the actor then resorts to *ad libs*, which are usually attempts to collect cheap laughs and can often hide the fact that he does not know what else to say or do. Simple, short sessions of improvisation during rehearsals very quickly overcome the problem and many actors have been glad of this addition to their artistry. It is interesting how many actors in training go through the most extraordinary experiences in the name of improvisation and yet seldom seem to be helped with this type of practical application.

Once having achieved this absorption and sincerity, the fascination underlying even so simple an experience as the first entrance through the audience at the beginning of the play can whet — has whetted — many an actor's appetite for further and deeper experiences in children's theatre. As the actor's *awareness* grows when in the midst of the audience, so does the fascination increase. In fairness to other actors, I should mention also that there are some who after one such experience have wanted to retreat on to the stage and even, if possible, put a row of footlights between themselves and the audience, so unhappy have they been with this moment of total exposure. But, I know of very few who have still felt that way by the end of a whole performance.

After the short preview of the **Pinocchio** Harlequinade, the puppeteers and Clown take down the trestle-ladder erection, and then, with music, Mr. Fire-Eater and his troupe exit, possibly using the aisles through the audience, but not essentially having to do so. The intention of using the whole theatre has already been fully established. Indeed, except for Gepetto's first entrance, the stage itself has not yet been used at all in terms of exits and entrances, so that it may well be most appropriate now to have "the troupe" exit through an upstage exit, depending on the setting, of course, and, as they are going, so Mr. Gepetto, who, it will be remembered, has been sitting as one of us in the audience, now goes from us up on to the stage, waving good-bye to them. The music fades gradually, and Mr. Gepetto, so says the stage direction, "shares his thoughts with us". The nearer he can be to us the better—certainly, if staging will allow, outside of the proscenium arch so that we are all in the same room. Let us follow the text:

> Gepetto: Well, well, well, well. Upon my soul. Just think of it. Wasn't it wonderful? Simply beautiful. You know — I make puppets. Lots of them. Some of them for Mr. Fire-Eater. As a matter of fact I made those three — the ones you've just seen — for him. Hmmmmm, but that was some time ago. I have such a lot of fun making them. And yet, d'you know what I've always really wanted to do? I've always wanted to make a puppet that could walk without any strings at all! Yes, yes. Think of it. Me, a poor old man — what fun I'd have! Sometime you know I want it so much that I sit and wish very hard with my eyes tight shut like this *(he demonstrates)*. But it doesn't seem to work. I suppose the trouble is that I'm so little that I can't wish big enough. Eh? Could be that, you know. Oooooh! Oooooh! Wait a minute, though. Oooooh, I, — I don't want to trouble *you*, you know, but — but perhaps you'd like to help. Course nothing might happen — but then again something might — if we wish hard ALL TOGETHER. *(whispering)* Shall we try it? Shall we? Oh, thank you, thank you very much. Well, let's all close our eyes and wish, and wish, and wish, very, very hard. If only one of us so much as peeps out of the corner of one eye — then it mightn't work. So now let's try it. Close your eyes and wish — and wish — and wish — and wish — and wish..........

Of the twenty or more Gepettos I have worked with on this play, I cannot recall one who has not been thrilled and perhaps amazed by the moment of audience participation that can follow this speech. To be with over 500 children nearly each one of whom has his or her eyes tightly closed, silently and determinedly wishing is an extraordinary experience. Of course, it does not always work exactly like that, and some Gepettos have needed several performances to reach the fullness of the moment. Again so much depends on the total sincerity with which the speech is said, particularly the moment following the bracketed stage instruction — *whispering*. Questions during moments of direct address in audience participation are often hazardous. Indeed, I often recommend to actors that unless such questions are absolutely vital then it is wise to leave many of them out (advice I can give when working on my own plays), at least until they are absolutely confident of their own readiness to accept a very few, quiet and gentle answers. By the time Gepetto reaches the two questions: "Shall we try it? Shall we?" there can be such an air of "magic" throughout the whole theatre, that many youngsters merely nod their heads and do not at all vocalize their reply (a good reason for the houselights to be partially on so that Gepetto can see them all), or perhaps just a few very simple quiet sounds of agreement will reach Gepetto. He can take for granted there will be agreement.

The only thing he should not try at this moment is to get a *loud* vocal response. Vocal participation has been abused by actors who gauge participation of the vocal kind by "LOUDNESS". No doubt the reader is familiar with that type of moment in a play when someone asks the audience a question, gets a small response, asks for it again "louder," gets a reasonably horrible shout as response and then goes further with an invitation "to raise the roof." The result is a meaningless crescendo of hysterical noise. There may be some kind of theatre into which this type of experience fits, but I would reassure the many folk I know to be really worried about it, that it has nothing do to with genuine participatory theatre.

At the risk of seeming immodest I have always found this particular moment to exemplify an extraordinary area of the magic of theatre as a whole and of participatory children's theatre in particular, and I shall later quote other moments concerned with the same qualities.

Returning to Gepetto's leading into the "wishing". Often it is possible for Gepetto to vocally fade down and out his repetition of the words "and wish — and wish — and wish" so that there comes a moment of total silence in the theatre, with everybody sitting with eyes closed. The stage direction in the text then continues:

> *Slowly from the distance is heard "charmingly eerie music." The FAIRY comes from the audience to stand behind Gepetto. She is not a Christmas-tree Fairy. She is puckish, humorous, constantly busy, always either appearing or disappearing, constantly changing character, thus becoming all of the people who subsequently help Pinocchio out of his difficulties (e.g. Cricket, the Frog, the Bird and the Tight-rope Walker). For the first entrance she is "herself" on her dignity — but it is nice dignity, and there is a sort of "mystery" about her that makes us want to see her again. Gently she touches Gepetto. A gong or cymbal sound announces the fulfilment of the wish.*

There are a number of points concerning participation and the use of aisles to consider here.

The music fades-in during the wishing, and the moment of theatre experience is always that much fuller when the wishing is in total silence and the music faded in very, very slowly. The technical people in charge of sound and light are all part of this total theatre; they need to be, if at all possible, where they can hear everything and see all of the action clearly — remembering that both stage and auditorium are used for the action. The fading up and down of music and bringing in and out of light are things to be felt anew at every performance for their fullest impact. They cannot simply be "cued" by flashing lights. For example, if the sound technicians are given the words "— and wish, and wish, and wish, and wish....." as their cue for the "Fairy music," they will not know whether or not Gepetto is feeling his way to the total silence. Every performance will be different for him. Perhaps he "feels" the silence will not come and that he should continue with the words "and wish" in a whisper until the music takes over from him. Perhaps, as can happen, still with total sincerity, some or even all of the audience pick up the words "and wish," either in a whisper or softly vocalized. If this is so, then the fade-in of the music is affected in terms of volume as well as moment. If there is going to be some very full change of lighting with the moment, those in charge of lighting need also to be sensitively working with both Gepetto and the sound people. For example, the moment can sometimes be enriched by fading down all stagelights and the houselights (if they have been up during Gepetto's soliloquy) until the moment that the Fairy touches Gepetto with the gong or cymbal sound to "announce the fulfilment of the wish." And the Fairy herself needs to be working very sensitively with the wishing, the sound track and the lighting as she makes her entrance *through the auditorium!*

This is typical of the kind of adjustment necessary to make for this kind of theatre — entrances thought of as important in one theatre sense are seen to be equally important in a quite different sense. I can think of several actresses performing the Fairy who have, at first, been bemused that their first main entrance should be through the body of the hall instead of from the strongest upstage position on the stage itself. The audience is wishing the Fairy into being, however, so there is only one place she can come from — "from the very womb of the audience itself," as one Fairy described it. Even the fact that the majority of the audience is likely to have their eyes closed as part of the wishing, does not change the need to make the entrance from the body of the auditorium and it is fascinating how many actresses, who have performed the Fairy, have remarked on the depth of feeling of a bond with the audience resulting from this. Because of touring circumstances, some had occasion to make the entrance from a place on the stage at certain performances and have never found it to be either as comfortable or as honest.

When the Fairy arrives on the stage, she touches Gepetto, and the stage instruction says: "A gong or cymbal sound announces the fulfillment of the wish." In the early performances of this play, there was no such "announcement," with the result that some youngsters would, from time to time, close their eyes and continue wishing, (perhaps some still are!!!) Again the quality of the sound made is a matter of detailed rehearsal; it is not just a question of bashing a gong or cymbal to make a loud noise.

Here then, in contrast to processions, is the use of aisles for a single, significant entrance of one character.

Another major use of aisles in **Pinocchio** is that of *chases and journeys*.

My adaptation of the Collodi story of **Pinocchio** is very free, retaining many of the characters but avoiding the more nauseating sections of the story itself. Quite simply, Pinocchio himself makes many attempts to reach school from his home and, because of many different kinds of adventure and distraction, never seems to arrive there. One of these adventures includes a meeting with Mr. Fire-Eater and his puppets, and Pinocchio teaches the puppets how to walk and dance without the need for strings. When Mr. Fire-Eater discovers that Pinocchio was made by Gepetto, who made so many of his own puppets, he is delighted, and gives Pinocchio 5 gold pieces to take back to Gepetto. Many subsequent adventures surround these 5 gold pieces, which two rogues, Fox and Cat, are determined to steal, and they believe Pinocchio such an innocent that they will have no problem in doing so. But, they reckon without the Fairy in her many different guises.

The second attempt made by Fox and Cat, involves them in dressing-up as "Highwaymen" and attempting to obtain the 5 gold pieces by direct threat, and Pinocchio's last-moment escape from their trap is the first of a sequence of chases, all of which make full use of the stage and auditorium area — of that whole space where anything can happen — and also gradually involve more and more people and growing degrees of excitement.

In the play as a whole there are:
FIVE CHASES.
TEN JOURNEYS of varying types.
THREE PROCESSIONS.

Other sequences concern important points of participation or detail of staging.

The Chases

Inevitably chases generate a great deal of excitement with all audiences. But there is never any need for the excitement to get out of control or to border on any type of meaningless hysteria, provided the cast will wholly believe, give their trust to and so fully accept and follow the golden principle already mentioned: STAY IN CHARACTER WITH TOTAL SINCERITY!

If there is genuine pursuit, fully and genuinely motivated, then all excitement, all calling out of advice, all physical help will be geared to that end, and not just to take the opportunity to have a jolly romp and generally "muck-about." The lead comes from the actors. The youngsters very quickly sense the degree of sincerity and respond accordingly. They respond to sincerity *with* sincerity. They react to insincerity with "mucking-about." The whole basis of participation is that the youngsters want to help people they like, admire or enjoy and, if the opportunity is given, will give physical help or vocal help. These chases cater for both.

One problem is how the actor and the director approach such scenes during rehearsal when it is often impossible to give any full idea of the great mass of activity that will spread through the auditorium with the speed of a forest fire. After one performance even, those who have not experienced such theatre, before are able to make a tremendous leap forward in their understanding, and consequently, the way they handle the situation. After ten performances, they have probably encountered all the various happenings that can take place in a generalized way, but even then, they are going to be confronted by fresh and new details with every subsequent performance and must always by ready for the unexpected.

There are many details, however, that can be considered beforehand based on the factor of total sincerity and staying in character. Interestingly enough, I have found many casts worried about the "solemnity" of the idea of this sincerity. They say: "Surely the chases ought to be tremendous fun, particularly in this kind of fantasy." Of course they are fun. I would go so far as to say that collectively they comprise some of the most joyous experiences I have ever had in Children's Theatre. But the fun arises from the *characters in the situation,* not from trying to be funny. We are confronted with the simple difference between "solemnity" and taking the situation (and our role as actors within it) *seriously.* Let us consider some examples of the effect of characterization on these chases. The characters are built during rehearsal, with much imagination from the actors, as the author, often as not, gives so little direct guidance to detail of character. For instance, Fox and Cat are described simply as "two plausible rogues" — no more than that. In more than one company the actors have built up the factor of plausibility to include a great deal of clever cunning, but within the area of fantasy and a children's play, so they have not turned to the psychopathic or any other kind of twisted mentality in their character development. But in the chases their basic idea has enabled them to attempt all sorts of interesting devices to avoid their pursuers. Sometimes they have taken empty seats in different parts of the auditorium and helped to misguide their pursuers by sending them the wrong way. Sometimes they have suddenly become a tree or a bush, until the pursuers have passed them by, and then have run off in the opposite direction. Sometimes one has deliberately lead all the pursuers in one direction and on the point of being caught draw attention to the other character, who has then led the chase.

Much can depend on the general physical condition, age and even athleticism of the actors. One very agile Fox was able to climb up to one of the audience boxes at the side of the stage, and there have been several times when both Fox and Cat would leap from such a box to the apron stage. On the other hand, there have been several policemen who have been chosen for the part because by age and size and temperament they have been a kind of "father

17

figure". At the same time, they have been long past any lengthy or fast running, so, in some cases, they have remained on the edge of the stage guiding everyone else where to go. Some of the detectives have found themselves more concerned with finding their lost bloodhounds than they have with catching the robbers, and one bloodhound sat contentedly in the aisle being fed chocolate drops by members of the audience. Many are the possibilities of fun, but still within the overall intention of genuinely catching the thieves.

A few general points are so likely to arise that the cast should be well warned in advance. They must be ready, even while in full flight, for youngsters suddenly to appear in front of them in aisles, probably ready to offer advice. Their physical control must be such that there is no danger of collision, and they must be ready to take advice seriously and to act on it. Fox and Cat are very likely to be confronted physically in this way, and it is wise for them to accept a golden rule that once caught—whether by other actors or by members of the audience—they should give themselves up rather than either fight or struggle, though I know of many cases where Fox or Cat has simply slipped out of his/her jacket, leaving the clothing in the hands of the captors. Pinocchio will always receive the most support and help, often being hidden among legs and covered with a pile of wet mackintoshes. However, after a short while, he himself must move from such a position in order for the chase to go to other parts of the auditorium. This incident will apply mainly to that first scene, when he is himself escaping from the highwaymen, but he can use it as a ruse to ambush Fox and Cat in the other chases as well.

When Fox and Cat are first chasing Pinocchio, they will be in their highwaymen's costume, a full black coat, tricorn hat and a triangular handkerchief covering the lower half of the face. They should have highwaymen's pistols — one each — and are involved in asking members of the audience if anyone has seen Pinocchio. It is important that they do not suddenly stop close to a youngster and push their face close to the youngster's, as this can be a frightening experience, but, worse still, can result in nightmare experience. Far better to hold a position at the center of the aisle and talk to a group of youngsters rather than a single individual. And all involved in the chases need to keep a very careful watchout to avoid coming too close to very young children (say under 5 years old) for the reason given above. A few children will show off and make clever remarks, but such behavior invariably subsides, provided the company do not fall into the trap of thinking such children cute and drawing attention to them; it's best to ignore them and move to another part of the auditorium.

The pacing and timing of the length of each of the Fox and Cat chases is very important, and one real growth in a company can be that of a group sensitivity awareness of the need to end each chase. The final climax of all the chases is after the escape from the Courtroom. This does not mean necessarily it is the longest. Indeed if the previous one, that leading to the first capture and taking to court, has been extended and very full in its excitement then it can be wise to make this final chase very much shorter. There is then the moment of dialogue in the courtroom as follows:

JUDGE *(to Fox and Cat)*:	What have you two to say?
FOX:	I didn't steal it.
CAT:	I didn't steal it.
OTHERS:	Yes, you did.
FOX and CAT:	Prove it.
JUDGE:	That's right—prove it. We can't put them in prison unless someone saw them steal it. Did anyone see them?

Usually the immediate roar from the audience is so full that there is no need for the repeat of the question as contained in the script. Far better for the Judge to accept immediately and for the Policeman at once to march Fox and Cat off to prison, whereupon there will be immediate total order from the audience, satisfied that justice has been done and ready to see the story continue. The vocal roar has usually helped to "use up" the final energy generated within the excitement of the chase and, after Pinocchio has said good-bye to the detectives and the bloodhounds, comes the moment where he sits down and says "Phew! What a day. What an exciting day." I have known many Pinocchios who have, with the full exhalation of breath on the "Phew", brought a complete total calmness back to the entire audience.

The above suggestion—namely, that if the response to the Judge's question is full-blooded, then the repeat of the question should be dropped—brings up another important aspect of this kind of participatory children's theatre that has particular application to one moment in the sequence concerning Fox and Cat and their attemped robbery. They return from their direct Highwaymen attempt as themselves and persuade Pinocchio—despite warnings from Frog—to go with them to the Field of Miracles. But in this sequence it is possible, even probable, that the audience will advise Pinocchio not to go with them but to go to school (Imagine that—teachers are often amazed that such advice should be given by school children!). Now, Fox, Cat and Pinocchio must be ready for the possibility of this advice "to go to school" being taken up by large numbers of the audience at almost any moment from when they first mention The Field of Miracles to just before the moment that Pinocchio finally puts the gold pieces into the ground, ready to close his eyes and to repeat the magic spell. None of the three must anticipate or press the moment, but they, and the rest of the cast must be ready in case it arises. If a large number of the audience start calling out to Pinocchio to "go to school," then he must accept their advice, otherwise he destroys the bond he has made with them and makes wholly dishonest the very function of the participation. *This can mean all or part of the Field of Miracle scene being cut.* The decision may come from Pinocchio or from Fox and/or Cat. Once the decision is made, then Fox and Cat need to strike the gold pieces from Pinocchio's hand and run off with them. Pinocchio then cuts straight to calling for the Policeman for help—and the sequence is then able to continue exactly as written. The youngsters will not go on calling about going to school because their advice has been accepted. Of course, if only very few of the audience call out, and only in whispers, then it is perfectly logical for Pinocchio to be so absorbed with Fox and Cat that he does not hear or notice the advice. But once it is numerically and vocally strong, then it must be listened to and acted upon.

I recall one most unhappy production where, for some reason, the actors ignored this advice. The production was in the open stage, in a half circle aganst one long side of the hall. And the ludicrous moment arose when the whole audience of about 300 had Pinocchio, Fox and Cat pressed against the curtain covered sidewall and were baying their demands for Pinocchio to go to school, yet the three actors insisted on continuing with their dialogue, though now divorced altogether from any accompanying action, right through to the end of the scene. The youngsters did not listen to a word and the actors could barely hear each other. It was all totally pointless, very sad, and almost entirely undermined the actors' belief in this form of theatre. Fortunately, the performance took place in the morning and they had another in the afternoon at which they did adhere to the advice, cut the Field of Miracles scene and were amazed at the smoothness with which all else followed. Interestingly enough, they had another ten or so performances and were always ready to make the cut, but the need never again arose. Such can be the differences, performance by performance. It really is something of a truism to say that, in children's theatre, every audience is (or certainly can be) quite different from every other audience. Participatory theatre tends to reveal and give emphasis to these differences.

The final chase in the play is completely different from any of the above in that, though it takes place in the auditorium as well as on the stage, it in no way involves the active participation of the audience. This concerns the escape of Pinocchio and Candlewick from the circus, during the Tightrope Walker's circus turn. Perhaps, it is not inappropriate to speak of the turn itself and the setting within which it happens, as it is an example of the total simplicity which is a necessary and authentic part of this style of theatre. The circus people are all grouped in a half circle over the main part of the stage, linking round from one proscenium arch to the other, thus giving a feeling of completing the circle of a circus arena, the auditorium being the other part of the circle. Rostrum blocks of different shapes and sizes can help to make the grouping more interesting and exciting—and can be part of a permanent single setting **(See Section on Scenery on pp 201-231)**. In the space on the forestage or center stage, i.e. in the middle of "the circle," each of the circus turns performs, after being announced by the circus master. What turns there are depends on the size of cast and what they feel most able to master. There is some kind of general stage lighting during the announcement of each turn, then all of the lights go off so that the turn itself is focused within the circle of a single lime or travel spot. When it is her turn, into this light comes the Tightrope Walker (the Fairy in one of her many disguises). Caught by the spotlight, perhaps only head and shoulders, she "mimes" climbing the ladder to the high wire, a drum beat following each footstep up the ladder. She arrives at the top. There is silence while she prepares herself for crossing. Then a drumroll starts, and slowly and surely, followed by the spotlight, she starts her perilous journey across the imaginary tightrope. The spotlight holds her head and shoulders so that we are not concerned with her feet. In any case, if the experience is real for her, it will be real for us as well (sincerity again). In the shadows, we may just be aware of Pinocchio beginning stealthily to move. Suddenly he calls: "Run Candlewick, run." Both run. A second or two's hiatus. Then one of the circus turns calls: "Mr. Circus Master—the Donkeys!" At once, "all hell breaks loose." There is loud music. Lights flash on and off. The followspot moves rapidly from side to side. Everyone shouts. On the stage they run hither and thither in hopeless panic. The tightrope walker misdirects everybody. The circus master tries to take control. Nobody notices him. The action now begins to include the auditorium as well as the stage with people running up and down and across all available aisles. Soon there is no one on the stage, which is now in darkness (in practical terms this enables the "monster" containing Gepetto to be set up). The action continues in the auditorium with the only light being that of the followspot swirling around the general action and movement in the aisles. Now the shouts and calls begin to fade as everyone leaves the auditorium. Suddenly the loud, exciting music cuts out, replaced only by the sound of the sea, which might be made by Pinocchio himself as he is swimming down one of the aisles, or might be made on the main sound track. No one else is there—just Pinocchio, caught head and shoulders in the followspot, swimming down one of the aisles. If the theatre has any upstairs audience sections, then the gangway he swims along must be the one just in front of the stage, so

that all of the audience can see him. Gradually, faintly, light on stage picks up
the monster, as Pinocchio's feet reach "the sand bank" on which the monster
is stranded. Perhaps at this moment we see Gepetto's lantern as he sits inside
the monster, patiently waiting for whatever the future may hold.

It will be seen that this kind of chase is entirely different from those concerning Fox and Cat. The involvement of the audience is fully emotional,
spiritual, intellectual, but there is no room nor need for vocal and physical participation by them, *and they do not expect it.* Intuitively they know the appropriateness or otherwise of their capacity to help. I have never known an audience attempt to participate at this moment in the play as everything is so
fast and exciting. Yet, what has taken such a number of lines to describe is in
fact a matter of about 1 minute to 1¼ minutes only, from the moment that
Pinocchio calls "run, Candlewick" to the moment that he is alone, swimming
in the sea.

The whole of the above sequence can also be achieved in the open stage, in
a bare hall or gymnasium, with no lights at all. Music, however *is* essential to
help with the atmosphere.

Journeys

The journey is as integral to Children's Theatre as editing processes are to
film, and changes of light and/or scenery are to adult proscenium theatre.
Perhaps more important still, as integral as to children's own play and drama.
For example, we might have a story in which a group of people in a darkened
cellar are planning to kidnap an important man as he is travelling through a
forest. In film, there might be a slow fade out from the cellar and a slow fade
into the forest. There might be a slow dissolve from one to the next. There
might be a montage sequence of galloping hooves, horses' manes, the men on
horse back, etc., culminating in the forest itself, perhaps with stillness and the
gradual approach of the person who is to be kidnapped.

In adult proscenium theatre, the same development might be made with a
slow fade out of light in the cellar scene, perhaps bridged by music or other
sound to a fade in of the forest scene, possibly done only by subtle gobo
lighting effects or the use of gauzes or there might be a complete change of
scenery, moving from a frontcloth scene to a whole stage setting or vice versa.
In children's play at home, or drama in the school hall or classroom, the
youngsters are likely to leap on to imaginary horses and gallop the journey to
the forest, and the forest might well be in the same part of the room or hall as
that from which they have just galloped *but the change is complete for them,
because they have made the actual journey from one place to the other.*

In the open stage, Children's Theatre can follow the youngsters' own approach very closely. But also in the kind of theatre we have been concerned
with in this chapter, where we are using stage and auditorium together, there
can be many uses of the journey that contain a simplicity very similar to that
which is most familiar within the youngsters' own experiences. There are
many examples in this sequence from **Pinocchio**, some taking place only on the
stage, some mainly in the auditorium and some making use of both areas.
Some, at I shall try to point out, can be enriched by use of lighting, others are
best done with no change of either light or setting. So it is with the first in the
sequence, in which Fox, Cat and Pinocchio journey to the Field of Miracles,
with Frog (the Fairy) following closely, but keeping out of sight. This whole sequence can often be most excitingly achieved on a totally bare forestage area,
with light kept off any specific setting there may be in the background, and

without any need to come into the auditorium area, not even across the front aisle.

Either Fox or Cat can lead, according to the actual circumstances of each stage of the journey, the other when not leading always bringing up the rear, so that Pinocchio is always between the two and has no chance of suddenly running away. In one sense, the whole journey is a hoax invented by Fox and Cat to take him to the Field of Miracles, which is itself an exploitation of Pinocchio's innocence and vulnerability. So just as the Field of Miracles is itself a hoax (on arrival, Pinocchio says: "But it's a very ordinary looking field," to which Fox and Cat reply: "It has to be—otherwise everyone would know our secret"), so the journey to get there is built up in terms of verbal description and excitement of adventuring by Fox and Cat playing off each other, creating by their dialogue and actions the actual terrain that has to be covered and *is* being covered.

Decisions as to precisely what form the journey will take are made at rehearsals. If need be, the dialogue, started through improvisation, might eventually become so "fixed" that it can be scripted. On the whole, however, it has been found more interesting to leave it improvised so that allowance can be made for the many different audiences. For example, at some performances there may be a high proportion of very young children, in which case the journey may need to be both shortened and simplified. With an older and more sophisticated audience, the journey might be made more complex and longer. The actors eventually sense these factors intuitively and find it creatively exciting to have such opportunities.

Here is an example of such a journey, on a bare flat forestage area, without even the use of different levels of rostrum blocks:

First through this gate;

Now through this marshy field;

Now through this prickly hedge;

Now down this steep bank to the river;

Now across the river, using the stepping stones;

Now up these steep and difficult rocks;

Now along this narrow ledge;

Now jump down to the bank below;

Now across this wide brook, with one leap;

Now up the steep bank — and

"Here are are — the Field of Miracles."

In this particular adventurous journey, Cat was afraid of prickles, afraid of water, afraid of heights and, indeed, needed a great deal of sympathetic help from Pinocchio to achieve the journey at all. We — the audience — were excited by this adventure as well as having a great deal of honest amusement. The sincerity was again totally believable.

Throughout, the dialogue is improvised, Fox giving the lead with instructions on what needs to be done, Cat making many objections, Pinocchio trying hard and also aiding Cat. We must not pretend that improvising such an amount of dialogue is easy, but practice during rehearsal leads gradually to release and confidence. Whatever else is done, the aim is still to keep the believability and to avoid the "cheap" wisecrack just for the sake of a laugh or two. For example, one Cat said: "Oh, I wish I hadn't eaten three eggs for breakfast!" Cheap laugh—partial loss of belief. Later Cat said: "Oh Mr. Fox why do you bring us through these prickly hedges—you know it spoils my permanent wave." How cute! Another cheap laugh, especially from the grownups present. Further loss of belief. Later, when on high cliffs, Cat said: "Oh, Mr. Fox, I do wish I'd brought my parachute!" Cheap laugh, quickly capped by Fox saying: "You don't need a parachute, Cat. You're so full of wind you'll float anyway." More cheap laughs mainly from the grownups, but the youngsters were catching on to the cute phoney rules of the game by now, and belief ebbs away a little further. Then suddenly Mr. Fox said: "And here we are — the Field of Miracles!" A titter of uncertainty from the audience, quickly capped by Cat with the words: "Well, you could have Foxed me!" Uproarious laughter from all the adults. Not to be outdone, Fox replied with "What are you trying to do — make a puppet of me?" Now not only all the adults were laughing, but the three actors on stage as well! Some of the youngsters were laughing, too. Most were totally bewildered. All of the belief had died — for the sake of a few cheap and wholly unnecessary laughs. Incidentally, it is often such actors who complain that inprovisation within children's theatre never works — and by the same token nor, of course, does integrated participation.

If the dialogue is real and sincere, an enormous amount of genuine fun will exist, but the situation will remain wholly believable and far more so through the journey than trying to do clever things with whole or partial changes of set, which merely lead to the youngsters' wondering how the mechanics are being operated.

Yet, similar sequences of journey have been made using a very full set, with stairs and arches and bridges and various heights of rostra. While all these features, together with flats, etc., were part of a particular area of a permanent setting, by keeping light off of the flats it was possible to use all of the different areas with total conviction, including climbing mountains, crossing the edge of a waterfall and climbing down a cliff face. Whatever the physical circumstances, they can be adapted for the needs of the journey.

Soon after this, there are journeys concerning the Bird, which are different in kind from the journey to the Field of Miracles, and each Bird journey really contains its own simple logic. There is first, simply her entrance which needs to be through the auditorium, partly because of all the exciting things that have been happening on the stage area (the trial of Fox and Cat and the policeman returning to Pinocchio his five gold pieces), but also because there is going to be another Bird journey in the auditorium, and it is wise to establish the use of the area straight away. There is also the additional factor of the new costume now being worn by the Fairy in her new disguise. In all such circumstances of "newness," the more time that can be given the audience to get used to new physical changes before any dialogue that progesses the action, the more ready it will be for full absorption on that progression. Incidentally, the audience are sometimes no more aware of the factor of the Fairy's new disguises than is Pinocchio and this really does not matter at all, particularly because the end of the play clears up the mystery for Pinocchio himself for the first time, and possibly for many of the audience at the same time. Sometimes I am saddened by information given away in program credits, as for example: The Fairy, who also becomes Cricket, Frog, Bird and Tightrope Walker...perfectly correct professional credit for the actress doing all of the hard work, but either an unnecessary "puzzle" or else an entire "give away" for many of the youngsters in the audience. It always seems to me to be a little like printing the solution to a mystery novel as a foreword to the first chapter.

So the first Bird entrance is simply a journey through the auditorium to the stage area. There is a short explanation from the Bird about Gepetto being lost and then the dialogue and directions run as follows:

Audience Participation

PIN: Oh, dear. What can we do?

BIRD: Go and look for him, of course. We'll ask all the birds and the fish if they've seen him — and if they haven't we'll ask them to keep a very special look out and let us know if they find him. Now keep very near to me, Pinocchio, and then you'll be able to fly.

PIN: Fly?

BIRD: Yes, like me.

PIN: But how? How can I?

BIRD: Magic. Magic that works as long as you keep very close to me. Now — try it. Go on, try.

On the stage area, Pinocchio, keeping very close to the Bird, gradually finds that he can fly. Away they both go, through the audience, asking the birds and fish if they have seen Mr. Gepetto.

There are really two possible types of journey at this moment, one part in the auditorium, the other on the stage area only.

The gradual teaching of Pinocchio to fly, plus his early flying endeavors, keeping very near to Bird, can be a beautiful production moment using individual spotlights, silhouettes against a skycloth and combinations of both. Then the journey out into the auditorium. The fact that Bird has already suggested they should ask all the birds and fishes if they have seen Mr. Gepetto or know anything about him, will have already prepared the minds of the youngsters for the possibility of helping. It is important that neither Pinocchio nor Bird get involved in long discussions with individual youngsters; best to receive many suggestions and then move on. Again, the sincerity is deeply necessary as they remain absorbed and urgent in their inquiries, and on the whole, it is wiser for them to approach groups rather than individuals. If someone says "I think he's over there," then which ever character it is said to needs to fly "over there" to look, and not seeing Mr. Gepetto, can then go on with his/her questioning. At such moments, the actors need to be ready not to be caught off guard by some of the things that might be said. I recall, for example, one production in which Mr. Gepetto doubled parts by being one of the detectives and so directly before this scene with Pinocchio and Bird had been in the auditorium with his bloodhound trying to catch Fox and Cat. So when Bird asked if anyone had seen Mr. Gepetto, one very small youngster replied "Yes, I saw him go through that door with his dog."

If the intent is to produce the play in three acts, this flying scene leads in to the ending of Act 2, with Bird and Pinocchio thanking everyone for their help, then with music "They fly round and away over the stage area — and the music fades them out of sight."

Depending on the size of the audience, width of aisles and amount of foyer space, the ending can be changed, however, so that Bird can "work her magic" over the whole audience and they too become birds and fly away to seek Gepetto. Again I emphasize this must depend on the layout of aisles and the accessibility of exits, and, if Bird and Pinocchio intend doing this, they should *keep moving* and collecting more birds as they move. If they stop and invite many people out to a stationary position, there will be a sudden mob surge when they eventualy move and some people might get trampled. But with wide aisles and exits it should be possible to have nearly the whole audience fly away to the second interval. And the whole exit can be controlled by music.

The next two journeys are concerned with the Journey to the Land of the Boobies, and are again different in kind. At first, there is just the Coachman and Candlewick, the one in front of the other, waving his whip and calling "Gee-up there" to imaginary horses, as they gallop in a stylized way down the auditorium to front stage where takes place a dialogue with Pinocchio about going "to a much more exciting place than school." Then Pinocchio mimes getting into the coach next to Candlewick, and again with music they go right round the auditorium until they arrive at the foot of the stairs on one side of the stage. If the stylized movement of the three, sensitively keeping absolutely instep with each other, is held with great absorption, the youngsters totally accept the convention for this journey by coach, just as they accept the mimed delight of Pinocchio and Candlewick as they eat "chocolate and candy flowers and drink from lemonade fountains" and slowly, by physical and vocal change only — with no costume additions — become donkeys. Then, as donkeys, they are driven to the circus on yet another kind of journey, down the steps on one side of the stage, across the front of the auditorium and up the steps on the other side; the whole while, the coachman is improvising dialogue about their going to the circus, and finally calling for the Circus-Master as they go up the steps and back on to the stage area. So, there is no need for any change of setting for the Land of the Boobies or for the Circus. The characters have said where they are going and then journeyed to get there, and, as in Shakespeare's theatre, we wholly accept the new location because of the physical journey — and our imagination fills-in any detail we require for the new location, without the distraction of having to take in the detail of new scenery. (See section on Scenery, pp 201-231).

So, too, with Pinocchio's next journey through the auditorium after he and Candlewick escape from the circus, except this time the "monster" has already been set-up on the stage during the chaos of the escape itself. The convention that Pinocchio is swimming in the sea is wholly accepted by the audience. And with just a single suggestion from Pinocchio — "Wind and waves please help me" — many of the audience will vocally (and even with their hands and fingers) supply the wind and waves, and will cease making the sound the moment Pinocchio arrives at the foot of the steps and says that he can feel the "sand banks." Similarly with the next journey when Pinocchio rescues Gepetto and swims ashore with Gepetto clinging to him. Again the sound participation of the audience can supply a beautiful moment of theatre at the end of the rescue, where Pinocchio is so tired and out of breath that he says he'll only make the last few yards if the waves can help, and, with sound from the audience he nearly reaches the shore, only to start slipping back again; the waves again take him forward to the very edge of safety, but still he can't make it and is pulled back into the sea again, until one last big wave washes him ashore i.e. up the steps, to collapse on the stage area.

Candlewick's return as the donkey, is again a journey right down the length of the auditorium to the stage area, his "hee-hawing" donkey brays arresting the attention of everybody on the stage area.

The final two journeys both concern the Fairy. The first involves a repeating of the *wishing* at the beginning of the play, and can, of course, be done exactly as then with the whole audience closing eyes to wish and the Fairy journeying through the auditorium to the stage. But an interesting difference can, in fact, be made, whereby all those on the stage close their eyes and wish — and we in the audience this time wish with our eyes open so that we can see the arrival of the Fairy on the stage, and watch her as she goes through the group looking at each one in turn and finally touching Mr. Gepetto, with the same gong or cymbal sound fulfilling the wish for all those on the stage, so that they open their eyes. This experience can be an interesting contrast for us, letting us, as it were, "into the secret" of what happened at the very beginning of the play.

The last journey of the Fairy is, from our point of view, an entirely imaginary one, as we do not even see her leave the stage. She can achieve this very simply by quietly slipping away during all of the excitement and congratulations after Pinocchio has changed into "a real boy." And the author's stage direction and dialogue, then, rule as follows:

> *When the commotion and wonderings are over, they turn to look for the Fairy to thank her. But she has gone...*

GEP: And I did so want to thank her.

PIN: Listen!

> *From the distance comes the sound of the Fairy's music. And also in the distance the Fairy's voice, floating through space...*

Fairy: Good-bye, Mr. Gepetto. Good-bye, Pinocchio. And if ever you need me again you know how to call me...

Good-bye...good-bye...good-bye...

> *They all wave good-bye to the air, rather sadly...*

In production, if all the cast are turned upstage, and if all light has drained away except for the skycloth or cyclorama, so that everyone is in silhouette, and if all, as they wave, are watching the Fairy moving away into space, and, with total sensitivity, slowly turn as they look from one side of the stage to the other, then, for those of us in the audience, this entirely imaginary exit can be a most moving experience. Voice and music slowly fade away to an astonishing experience of total silence, and the spell is finally broken by the practical Mr. Fire-Eater!

FIRE-EATER: Come along, everyone. There's work to be done. Form up the procession — for all the world waits to see Fire-Eater's amazing stringless puppets.

And so the final procession...and the end of the play. Again, the whole of the above sequence can be achieved in the open stage, in a bare hall or gymnasium, with no lights at all. Music, however, *is* essential to help with the mood and atmosphere.

Processions

The first procession in the play, as mentioned earlier, is Fire-Eater's procession at the opening of the play. The next occurs early in Act III and is the Circus Procession, which can use every available person in order to fill the whole auditorium with exciting movement and color, the fun and antics of clowns and acrobats, the gaiety of music and the continuous improvised dialogue of the Circus Master, inviting everybody to "roll-up to see the finest circus ever."

(By now the reader must feel that this version of **Pinocchio** requires a cast of, well, if not actually hundreds, then at least dozens of people. In fact the play was originally written for a total cast of fourteen and I have personally directed it many times with a cast of twelve, and on two occasions with only ten. This means very careful doubling and even tripling of parts, usually to the enormous excitement and enrichment of the cast. Obviously the play does lend itself to much larger casts when and where people are available.)

The procession needs to be progressive to the stage area, so that it does not take too long, particularly as all turns that have been arranged have their opportunity in the circus itself.

The second procession is that of Mr. Fire-Eater's troupe, now returning to give the full performance of the show for which we had seen a short excerpt or preview at the very beginning of the play. Again, the procession needs to be through the auditorium, but needs not to be too extended or detailed now that the play is drawing towards its end.

The final procession, after the last good-bye to the Fairy, takes us through to the end of the play. There are many ways of handling it according to all kinds of circumstances, but it is important to bear in mind the environment of the playhouse itself. For example, the play was once performed in a large marquee within the wholly closed-in grounds of a castle. In this environment it was possible for the final procession to lead the whole audience out of the theatre and even around part of the castle grounds, because there was plenty of time and space for the excitement finally to die down before the youngsters set off home. This, however, would be very unwise in a theatre set on a main road with only a small foyer, as there is danger of the youngsters not having time to lose their high pitch of excitement and possibly running out into the traffic in the main road. In such a case, it is better for the procession, whether or not it goes round all or part of the auditorium, to finally go back on to the stage area and exit into the wings, leaving Pinocchio and Gepetto to call their fnal good-byes to the audience.

There is never any need for a formal curtain call at the end of a play of this kind, particularly as everyone has his/her chance to call their thank-yous and good-byes as part of or directly after the final procession.

The procession, the chase and the journey are all significant in Children's Theatre. But, there are many other forms of audience participation that can be excitingly integrated into such plays even in the conventional theatre with family audiences, large numbers and broad age groups.

The degree and depth of audience participation is always relevant to such factors as size and form of stage area, number in the audience and the breadth of age grouping, not to mention whether or not there are a large number of adults present as expected in a "family audience." A significant form of participation that, with young children (say up to the age of seven or eight, even sometimes with nine-year olds), is likely to happen whether or not we expect it or want it is that of *wholly* SPONTANEOUS PARTICIPATION, usually VERBAL.

Spontaneous Participation

We have probably all experienced the most primitive form of this type of spontaneous verbal participation at the movies, usually at a moment when the hero and/or heroine is in danger from someone or something approaching from behind them. "Look out behind you," call several voices from the audience (and not only young children either!) Some of the audience deplore this spontaneous reaction especially when it catches on and large numbers of others join in just for the sake of letting off steam. But, we must still face the fact that it can often be very real and sincere in its total spontaneity. However, in live theatre, I personally try to avoid this kind of *cliche* participation because of its association with other environments and circumstances. Nevertheless the actor can and should be ready for spontaneity at other moments, and author, director and the whole cast can combine to actually provide such opportunities as a constructive part of the play. One important reason for this concerns the concentration span of the audience, particularly that of very young children.

There are limits as to how long any age group — including adults — can sit absolutely still and quiet. It is for this reason that even in much adult theatre there are two intervals in a play and often in such intervals one will hear many people in the audience saying such things as "Oh, its good to stretch my legs," or "I don't think I could have lasted more than another few minutes without a break," etc. Indeed, I know of some theatre managers who deliberately put into their program such notes as "There will be two Intervals, Act 1 lasts approximately 55 minutes, Act 2 approximately 45 minutes and Act 3 approximately 30 minutes. The play will therefore end at approximately..." Some managers involved in this process have explained how much they have found this helps many members of the audience, particularly with an unfamiliar play, because it warns them of the length of period their concentration is expected to last, and, as one manager put it, "they can wind themselves up accordingly."

The concentration span is linked to a balance of using energy — a balance between moments of stillness and quietness and moments of physical and vocal activity. As adults we can consciously control the feelings arising within us when there is imbalance, so that we can force ourselves to remain still until that moment when "it's good to stretch the legs." Young children do not have the same conscious control so that when there is imbalance they instinctively move or turn or stretch; an activity we often describe as "restlessness." Parents often discover this factor of balance at children's birthday parties or other festivities. After a long period of vigorous activity, the youngsters suddenly become rather still and quiet; often it seems like a kind of lassitude. Anxious parents suddenly are worried that the "party is going dead" and hastily consult each other for new ideas as to new boisterous activities, almost as though the external sign of a successful party is one continuous frenetic activity after another. There is no need to worry, for instinct will restore the balance again in time and the youngsters themselves will show the need for renewed activity. Until they do, we might just as well let the quiet moments be of fullest benefit by not interfering.

Teachers in Primary schools who understand this balance of energy factor often realize that a few minutes of active drama, even in the middle of an academic lesson, can help to restore the balance and so bring back a fuller concentration on the academic pursuit. In these terms drama can play an important part in the everyday school life, other than certain periods of time devoted only to drama, and in the periods of drama they equally discover that there is no need for continuous vigorous activity, but that other quieter arts, like writing and painting, have a full balance of energy value even in the middle of the drama lesson. Indeed it is often through such discoveries that learning processes become more child-orientated, no matter the intention of the end products. Everybody benefits because we are working closer to the children's own natural rhythm.

Now, it would be and is impossible to state an exact time factor regarding this balance of energy in terms of Participatory Children's Theatre, though there have been certain kinds of such activity, with a controlled number and age group in certain physical conditions when I have felt very positive about the time, even in terms of minutes. For family theatre of the kind being discussed in this section I personally feel confident about warning actors to look on a period of about seven minutes as nearing the maximum of undivided concentration, often depending on the activity that is being observed and the nearness to that activity. And I do know for certain that properly controlled moments, as described above in terms of chases and processions, provide a very strong means toward the balance factor and therefore help to enrich other moments. For example, I know that the extraordinary magical quality that arises when Pinocchio is being taught to fly by Bird would not in fact be the same had the audience been sitting quietly through a long period of exposition directly beforehand, but as contrast to the full excitement of the Fox and Cat chases and trial scene, there is readiness for truly absorbed stillness as they watch Pinocchio learn to fly and as they view both Bird and Pinocchio set off on their flight.

I have not known any active participation, spontaneous or otherwise, during this part of the play. But earlier in the play there is another sequence of learning for Pinocchio — this time to stand up without falling over, to walk and finally to run — all without the normal puppet's need for the aid of strings. This sequence invariably brings all kinds of helpful and *totally spontaneous* suggestions and ideas for Pinocchio and Gepetto to consider and possibly use. The text for this section of the play says:

> *The dialogue and action for this episode can be built up during rehearsals (through improvisation). Gradually, Pinocchio masters first balancing on his own, then, step by step, walking, and then running.*
>
> *N.B. The whole sequence will be different in detail with each Gepetto and Pinocchio — it is impossible to script such a scene for the satisfaction of every pair. Pinocchio is about to master certain skills — and this is always of some genuine amusement to any watchers who have already mastered them. Sincere effort to learn by him, and to teach by Gepetto will bring in the humor, thus avoiding the necessity of trying to be funny.*

Invariably, at some moments of this sequence, there will be quite spontaneous suggestions from the audience. They do not have to be stimulated or sought after. Indeed, if such attempts are made, then the whole feeling can change and a new game starts, with everybody determined to "get in on the act." Once more, sincerity is broken and artificial gimmickery results. In a sense, Pinocchio has the least of the problem because he is so deeply involved in the learning process, whereas Gepetto is trying to do the teaching. If he is wise he will never so much as glance at the audience nor ask any such direct question as "What shall I do?" or "What do you think he should do?" An entirely absorbed, personal, reflective question is quite different, particularly if it is a low or quiet voice, e.g. "What on earth can I do now?" Some suggestions, equally quiet and sincere, may well come. If Gepetto accepts them and acts on them, the youngsters will be wholly satisfied. If Gepetto argues or asks for repetitions, then he is moving back into the area of potential shouting and heckling. Quite often in the sequence, Pinocchio finds himself trying to walk with stiff legs, with poor old Gepetto quite out of his depth as to what to do. The suggestions about "bending knees" come gently and sincerely — even the idea of "bend 'em and straighten 'em" has often come quite spontaneously, thus helping the development of the action. But at these moments, especially in family theatre, especially with a large audience, no direct attempt is made to involve a quite different and equally possible form of participation — *stimulated participation*. The reason for not doing so at such moments is simply because of the wide variety of ideas that the situation lends itself to. If all the different possibilities are being called out at one and the same time, then again we move towards that kind of hysterical shouting which has nothing to do with genuine participation, and which can lead to all kinds of unnecessary problems for the cast. Perhaps I should emphasize again that I have never known a Pinocchio and Gepetto who have not been amazed and delighted with their experiences in this scene, even those who have never before been involved in this type of theatre. Indeed, in this and the next scene I shall mention, the problem is usually one of having to remind them that the play must only run a certain length and this particular scene no more than a maximum of six minutes. The tendency is to become so intrigued by the work with the audience that the scene can go on for ten, even twelve minutes, with total absorption, sincerity and delight, and because the dialogue is improvised it can be difficult to stop.

Stimulated Participation

As its name applies, *stimulated participation* arises from the direct contact between actor and audience, in which a lead is given for the audience to follow and participate, *if they so wish*. One main example arises in **Pinocchio** at the opening of Act 2, and again concerns Gepetto and Pinocchio, who by now have made a very full bond with the audience.

At the end of Act 1, the two go to sleep, and, of course, if the curtains remain open or if they sleep on the apron stage, they remain in full view of the audience throughout the interval. Some youngsters may well come to see if they are asleep, and will leave them alone if they feel they really are. Should they be awakened, then they can ask simply to be left in peace, and go back to sleep again. Rather charmingly, some youngsters will leave them offerings during this interval, so that when they wake up they find all kinds of candy lying on the area around them. The question of whether or not the actors should remain asleep on stage in the interval is, of course, highlighted when there are performances in the Open Stage and it is virtually impossible for them to go off. On the picture frame stage the curtains can be drawn during the interval, so that Pinocchio and Gepetto can have a well deserved break. It is interesting that some Gepettos and Pinocchios, after trying both ways of approaching the scene, have expressed a preference for remaining asleep on stage with the curtains open because "of the strange feeling of extending the bond of trust with the youngsters" to quote one Pinocchio. By and large the youngsters do not attempt to come up onto the stage to visit them, but if there is any anxiety about this, then one can always have the friendly policeman on his night beat. And the risk of them attempting to come on the stage is minimized if the two can sleep as near to the front of the stage as possible. The sleeping itself is shared as a participation opportunity for any members of the audience who wish to take it. Here is Gepetto's final speech, which ends Act 1:

GEP: *(turning from Pinocchio whom he has just finished tucking in bed):*
He's asleep already. Just fancy that — my Pinocchio teaching all those clever puppets to work without strings. Isn't it wonderful? *(suddenly remembering)* Oh dear. Deary me — he hasn't washed, he hasn't cleaned his teeth and he hasn't said his prayers. Never mind. He can do them in the morning. *(he yawns)*Oooooooh — I'm a bit sleepy too. Think I'll turn in now. It's been an exciting day, what with wishes coming true and — and — no — ohhhh — it's not good. I can't keep awake any longer. *(to audience)* Why don't you go to sleep, too? I expect you're tired. Go on. All of you. I'll wake you in the morning. And if I don't the rooster will — he crows incredibly loudly round these parts. Go on then. Off to sleep with you. Goodnight.
He settles down and covers himself with a blanket — or goes back into his house and then sticks his head back through the door or through a window.
By the way, thank you for helping me wish like that. It did work, didn't it? Oh, sorry, Were you nearly asleep? All right, I won't talk any more. Goodnight.

On proscenium stages there is always a superb opportunity here for the use of music, a sunset, and a fade to a gentle night sky, perhaps with a single lantern or street lamp close to where Pinocchio and Gepetto are sleeping. During the music, three will be heard a lot of movement in the audience as many of the youngsters curl up in their chairs to join in the sleeping. And the house lights fade in. Now we are confronted by an interesting convention — for the actors remain asleep — but this is the audience's opportunity to go to the toilet, to enjoy ice cream and candy or whatever else comes naturally to them during an interval. Some may at first be a little puzzled as to whether it is all right to do all these things when they have just been invited to go to sleep and when the two actors still sleep on the stage. The convention is soon accepted, and can be helped by some such simple device as displaying signs in various parts of the theatre during the interval, saying such things as: PLEASE GO TO SLEEP AGAIN WHEN YOU RETURN TO YOUR SEATS. As soon as the signals are given for the end of the interval, and certainly as soon as the houselights begin to fade down, many will, in fact, curl up again and go to sleep, ready for the opening, waiting for the cockcrow and for Mr. Gepetto to wake them, which he duly does. And the dialogue at the opening of Act 2, very quickly takes us to a scene of *stimulated* participation. The opening of the Act runs as follows:

GEP: *(in a polite early morning whisper):* Good morning. Are you awake? Sorry to disturb you all. But you did ask me to wake you, didn't you. You know — I think it's going to be rather a nice day. Oh! Pinocchio! He ought to be getting up too. Wake up, Pinocchio. Wake up. Come on old son — shake a leg.

PIN: *(yawning):* Ahhhhhh. Who is it?

GEP: It's me — Pop. Come on — it's time to wake up and go to school.

PIN: Oooh, yes. School. Of course. I must hurry. *(Pinocchio is dressing during next section of dialogue).*

GEP: *(confidentially)* Pinocchio — there's something we forgot last night.

PIN: Was there? What was that, Pop?

GEP: Face, hands, teeth.

PIN: Face, hands, teeth! Face, hands, teeth? What about them?

GEP: We didn't wash them.

PIN: No, we didn't. Should we have done?

GEP: Oh yes. Always at night and again in the morning.

PIN: Why?

GEP: Why? Well, er — because it's best to have clean hands and face for meals, and very nice to have shining white teeth.

PIN: Oh. Then we'd better do them now, hadn't we?

GEP: Yes, I think so.

PIN: *(looking at audience)* All of us?

GEP: Ooh, yes. Everybody, that is, who's got hands and faces and teeth.

PIN: Oh, well, we'd better get on with it, hadn't we.

The remainder of this sequence should be built up in rehearsals. Pinocchio will lead the whole audience in washing and drying, cleaning their teeth, brushing hair, cleaning shoes, etc. (i.e. activities that can be done sitting down). After this, there is a simple breakfast to cook and eat — and all can join in.

N.B. No comic business should be worked out for this scene or else the audience is tactitly invited to watch — not to do. All that is required is for Pinocchio and Gepetto to genuinely and sincerely get on with their own ablutions, cooking, etc., with Gepetto having to teach Pinicchio a great deal — as he did in Act 1 with the balancing, walking and running. The newness of it all to Pinocchio will contain its own charm and amusement without having to force comedy. It is essential that no props are used for this sequence, otherwise the audience will not join in so readily. Pinocchio's aim should be to stimulate everyone to join in which can be done quite simply with a few words such as "Come on, everyone, lets start washing," avoiding questions such as "Would you like to clean your teeth?" and then to get on with it himself, remaining absorbed in his own ablutions, etc. In this way, the audience will "do" without necessarily copying Pinocchio move for move, who should make no attempt to demonstrate or instruct. Accuracy in mime is essential for Gepetto and Pinocchio but they should not worry the youngsters about this, and they should scrupulously avoid any kind of value judgement comments such as "Look at that little boy over there, isn't he doing it beautifully?" or, even worse, such comments as "I don't know what he thinks he's doing, but it certainly doesn't look like any cooking I've ever seen." Such comments destroy the bond with the youngsters, making some feel uncomfortable and embarrassed and leading others to showing-off or "being cute." The same sincerity applied to the end of Act 1 and the opening of this Act should remain throughout, both actors always totally in character with all their dialogue, which of course must be improvised, coming from sincerity of characterization. There should be no comic pantomime crosstalk about such things as "Don't forget behind your ears, lady," etc. Of course "ears" are a legitimate part of the scene, but must be integral to it and not an excuse for cheap laughs.

This scene can develop into six or seven minutes of stimulated participation, rebuilding the bond between the actors and audience after the interval.

Some Gepettos and Pinocchios, during the build up and preparation of this scene in rehearsal, have expressed a natural anxiety that one is perhaps being too serious with this kind of approach and thus losing opportunities for fun that is great entertainment. They can be concerned to the point of even wondering if the approach is "too precious." Without exception they have changed their mind in performance when they have seen what incredible fun exists intrinsically in the situation itself, because Pinocchio has never washed before, never experienced water or soap or a tooth brush or tooth paste coming out of a tube, nor all the various factors concerned with cooking and eating. He does not have to add any external clowning. Everything possible in the way of humor, fun and warmth exists within character and the situation. The other concern is whether the youngsters will in fact really see any of this if they are themselves busily participating. Again, the answer is that they miss nothing, because the rhythm of their own "doing" is so much faster and less detailed than the adult rhythm and they in fact have both the experience of participation and of viewing, the one following the other right through the whole scene.

This kind of stimulated participation can be extended farther, as will be seen in the examples that follow from other plays. In addition to quite *spontaneous* participation and *stimulated* participation, there is a third type, however, which is best called *directed* participation.

Directed Participation

As the name implies, directed participation is concerned with a direct statement regarding a particular need in the play, a statement made with total certainty that the audience will help, providing they know exactly the requirement. Sometimes a moment will arise in the play when the actor has a choice of trying stimulation or relying on the *directed*. Let us consider the moment we have already met in **Pinocchio** when Pinocchio has just rescued Gepetto from the monster and is swimming ashore with him. Pinocchio could say: "Oh, Pop, if only there were some wind and waves we'd soon reach the shore." This is stimulating an opportunity for the audience to participate, and invariably they will respond with the sound of wind and waves, and the sound may stimulate movement of arms and hands and fingers (movement and sounds often cross-fertilize in this manner, the one stimulating and thus enriching the other). But if the sound does not come, or if Pinocchio wants to be certain of an immediate reaction, he could use *directed* participation, in which case he would say: "Please everyone, help us with the wind and the waves," or, perhaps, "Everyone be the wind and the waves to help us reach the shore." The response will now be total and immediate. The important thing is that there should be a real need for the participation, not just a gratuitous throwing in of such moments in order to say that the play contains participation, which is what so often can happen when participation is forced on to a play rather than being an integral part of it from first writing and throughout production.

Actors without previous experience in audience participation are cautioned not to allow any personal disbelief that participation will occur to creep into the voice. If the actors communicate such disbelief or any anxiety, the audience will sense this and may react negatively.

A simple straightforward piece of *directed audience participation* requires no begging, no cajoling, no seducing. Identification, oneness, dependence on each other, and the participation comes simply and sincerely. Moments of *directed* participation build confidence in the audience. There is no doubt about what is expected of them, and they know the actors do not doubt that they will receive what they ask for. Further, they discover there is no comment, no value judgement, no being told to do it louder or softer or whatever. A mutual trust is born, which is going to help both actors and audience at moments of *stimulated participation*.

In **The Sleeping Beauty**, for example, three characters, as part of the story, decide they must collect everything from the Kingdom that could possibly prick the princess's finger. The audience are going to help with this, and the dialogue before the action stimulates in their minds the kind of help they will be able to give. vne of the characters says:

> The three of us are going to go all around the kingdom asking the people what sorts of things they think might prick the princess and we're going to write all of the things on a list, just so that we won't forget. Now each of us must go to a separate part of the kingdom. Quickly. Ask the people to tell you what sort of things you ought to collect. We meet here again as soon as possible.

The last line gives a degree of urgency to the situation, and the urgency should be carried through by all three in order that the participation sequence does not take too long. Each is responsible for one third of the audience, and should try to accept ideas in general from their section rather than asking individuals, which would hold up the action and possibly cause restlessness from those waiting or already spoken to. The three should avoid the risk of worrying or intimidating very young children, which might happen if they get too close physically or in any way seem to be "demanding" answers. On the other hand, overexcitement could occur if shouting by many voices is encouraged, so each should explore various ways of coping with this in order to obtain the most satisfactory results — keeping on the move and calling "I'll be with you in a moment" usually copes with the situation; also suggesting that we talk in whispers so the antagonist does not hear what is happening. As we have constantly considered, it is important to keep in character. All ideas should be accepted, however strange, as this encourages confidence that ideas are acceptable and thus will assist later participation. If "smart alecks" send-up the situation, simply ignore them and listen to the others.

Any one of the three actors involved can decide at any moment to end the participation if the audience seems to be getting overexcited. They need to feel very carefully the difference between genuine participation, no matter how excitable, and hysteria. All that is needed for ending the participation is for one of the three to return to a central point — perhaps center of the front of the stage or apron stage, or at the head of the center aisle, and to call loudly and clearly "Listen everybody." There will be an immediate pause and quietness from everyone, whereupon the other two immediately return and agree they have a very fine, comprehensive list of items. They quickly read through the lists, again without comment — certainly not of the kind that plays for cheap laughs. Now there is readiness for collecting the items, and perhaps other characters in the play will be asked to help with the collecting. All of the items are to be thrown into "a deep pit."

IMPROVISED SEQUENCE WITH AUDIENCE PARTICIPATION

The items to be collected, based on the lists already drawn up in the previous section, are, of course, all imaginary. But it is just possible that some youngsters may produce actual items (such as mother's jewelry). To avoid such complications, the actors can suggest that individuals or groups dig their own deep pit in the place where they are sitting into which they can put their own items. At the same time, a large pit is dug in a central area — again, perhaps at the head of the main aisle or at a central point just in front of the stage, so that many other imaginary items can be put into it. Volunteers from the audience (any number from eight to a dozen) can be invited to help with both the digging of the pit and the collecting of items. Care must be taken that this "selection" of volunteers be achieved smoothly and easily without letting any persons feel they are being rejected because there is something "wrong" with them, or any who are selected feeling it is because there is something very "special" about them. Often it is wisest to choose quickly from those who are closest to aisles and already very active. This is also a time when some of the older youngsters can be very helpful and enjoy the particular responsibility for looking after some of the smaller and younger ones. The whole episode must have urgency and truth all the time from the company members, doing everything they can to make the situation real and believable for the participants. All temptations to "ad-lib" comic lines (especially if there are adults in the audience) must be strictly controlled. When all the items are collected and in the pits, a central character announces the final item to be thrown in, and either just before this or at the same time tells the youngsters to throw in their final items: "Everybody throw in your last item, NOW." And with special music or electronic sounds, or even sounds made by the audience, the pits are filled in. A final *"There"* from the central character, or the cessation of sound/music will conclude the activity.

There are two important words in the previous paragraph: *"NOW"* and *"THERE."* With *directed* participation the need for help and the form of that help is stated clearly to the audience. For the smooth integration of the participation it is also useful to have a single "trigger" word for activity to start and another for its conclusion. Over and over again — almost to the point where one could perhaps venture to claim that it is "fool-proof" (almost—but don't let's be too certain of anything)—the use of the word "NOW" is all that is necessary for starting, and the use of the word "THERE" for ending.

Many authors, actors and directors feel the need for much more preparation than the simple use of the word "Now" and so use such instructions as: "When I count to three, then everybody do (or say or whatever)...Are you all ready? Then stand by. One — two — three — ..." Often this kind of preparation is deeply associated in youngsters' minds with the beginning of a race or the count down of a rocket-firing, and because of these unconscious associations they get themselves wound-up and ready for a "large" response. As has already been observed, size of reaction is never as important as sincerity, which will often be very quiet and controlled and thoughtful. Much, of course, depends on the faith of the actor or actress that it will work — and having that faith is, in turn, going to depend on the participation being an integrated and essential need, not just a gratuitous gimmick. Also, much will depend on the audience feeling from the outset that they are part of the play, including the factor regarding all of the theatre — auditorium and stage areas — being the "place" where the story is to happen. If we exclude the audience entirely, keeping the actors in their separate world on the stage, for, say, half an hour, and then spring suddenly onto the audience the need for their help, then of course we shall find even directed participation more difficult to achieve. A further factor regarding the point of the actor's trust in the audience response is centered round the actor's being absolutely ready for a "small" response, with ears and eyes ready to catch even the slightest murmur or sign of movement and then to use it to help everybody else. We must keep in mind the audience's need to feel confident. For many reasons that confidence may not be very strong to start with, even for so simple a reason as never having been allowed to participate before, let alone be invited to do so. If the actor keeps this in mind, then the following type of experience might happen: A character in a story needs, shall we say, help from birds, and has the line (directed participation):

"We need help from all the birds. Everybody, make the sounds and movements of birds — NOW." If even only one youngster makes the gentlest sound of a bird or the tiniest movement of a bird, then the actor makes use of it. Without even looking at the audience, and certainly not at the one or two youngsters involved, the actor goes on with deep concentration, enthusiasm and sincerity — possibly even in a strong whisper: "Yes, yes, I can hear a bird. And I can feel another is moving. That's it. More bird sounds and movements. Any kind of bird you like. Everybody make the sounds and movements of birds." Now the participation will grow considerably. The actor, as has been mentioned already, needs to avoid the use of all such words as "louder" — we are after quality of sound, not noise. But let us look again at the first sentence and see if further help can be given the audience at the very beginning of the moment of participation, the instruction that leads into it. If we develop the sentence from: "We need help from all the birds. Everybody make the sound and movements of birds — NOW" to something like: "The birds will help us. That's what we need. The sounds and movements of birds. Any kind of bird. Every kind of bird sound and bird movement. So, everybody, help us with the sounds and movements of birds. Everybody, make any kind of sound and movement of birds — NOW!" This is probably going to the opposite extreme in terms of preparation, but it is still more integrated than relying on the count-down method. By the extended statement we are making quite clear that the youngsters know what kind of help we need from them, and this is going to help the factor of confidence from their point of view. And, providing we are deeply in character and in the situation, rather than coming out of it to become a teacher-instructor fearfully making unnecessary and illogical demands of people we fear are not going to respond, then the whole situation contains a logic of need that brings forward a response on to which we can build further responses. But we must be just and fair about this. I have so often said to actors: "We have rehearsed for whatever number of weeks, and we still mutually agree that there are many things we have not mastered. Our rehearsal has happened in privacy, thus catering to our own innate fear of failure and slowly have mastered the requirements of the play. If it has taken all that time in special circumstances for us to achieve what we have achieved, what right have we to expect youngsters to give us a finished and polished moment of participation on one single instruction *that we may not have made fully clear to them,* in circumstances where they have as much right as we had in the early stages of rehearsal to feel afraid of failing, to worry that they might let down the character who has asked for their help? The remarkable truth is that they do not need the rehearsal time we needed in order to respond to us fully — but they do need an absolutely clear idea of what is expected of them — the words made clear, the idea made clear, and the moment for starting made clear." Seen in this manner, many actors have very quickly solved any problems they may have felt about participation, particularly the beginning moments of directed participation.

So, too, with the use of the word "There" for concluding such moments. Much again depends on the participation being integrated and containing a logical and specific need rather than being some kind of phoney gimmick. If, for example, in the above the only reason for the "sounds and movements of birds" is that someone has had a great idea about getting the audience to participate because that would be "kind of fun and cute" (yes, sadly, it does happen), then we must expect that the audience will quickly see through all inadequacy and insincerity of the purpose and if they do respond at all will do so with equal insincerity, just playing about for the sake of fun and games. But if, for example, those particular sounds and movements are one of the necessary ingredients for some kind of potion or mixture, then the response will be entirely different, and if the person collecting the ingredients takes them each in turn to some kind of mixing bowl, then the sound and movement will usually stop the moment putting them into the bowl has been achieved, but the completion of the moment will be helped by the use of the word "There" said firmly and strongly to reinforce the moment of completion.

The need for the "sounds and movements of birds" may be nothing to do with making a mixture, but a very particular moment in the story of a play. Let us say, for example, that a very special bird in a story is ill, or dying, or unconscious or desperately unhappy and in need of help. One character trying to help eventually says "We need the help of other birds." another says: "How do you mean? What kind of help?" And then comes the precise directed participation statement quoted above. The participation will then have a very specified purpose, and can indeed be developed in other interesting ways. For example, after a few moments, the main helper might say something like "Yes, its working, but I think we need a little more bird movements and less bird sounds" and a change will come. Or the person might say, "Yes, that's working, but the sounds need to be gentler. they need to have more of a magic feeling about them" and again there will come a change in the quality of sound. Completion can then follow the actual outcome of the help. The person says, "Look, look, it is working. He's beginning to recover. Just a little more. A little more. There. There. We've done it." And the two uses of the word "There" plus the definitive completion of the "We've done it" and the participants will stop both movement and sound because they know the job has been completed, and there is no need for anyone involved in starting or stopping the participation

EVEN TO LOOK AT THE AUDIENCE. Indeed, there are occasions when the depth of sincerity is maximized by NOT looking at the audience.

Suggestions made by the audience are often very inventive and contain a great deal of "childlike" humor. As actors, we must keep reminding ourselves of the essential differences between the childlike, which will be real and sincere, no matter how unexpected or unusual, and the "childish," which will be "cutely comic" and come mainly from the "smart alecks" (or from adults). If the latter are ignored, they will soon subside. A genuinely serious and sincere acceptance of the positive suggestions will encourage more of the same frame of mind, and of course there can be reactions of delight and surprise as these are reported. But, as we have met before, all of the actors must stay wholly in character, and must also avoid any kind of value judgement comments on the various suggestions. Certainly one must avoid at all costs any kind of "competitive set-up" for deciding which suggestions are best. In circumstances of this kind, it will become clear how helpful it is for the actors to seek moments of practice at improvisation during rehearsals so that an easy flow of dialogue comes readily to them within circumstances that can easily change at each performance. Some practice at improvisation helps to give full authority to every statement made, so that the viewer is unable to tell the difference between fully rehearsed scripted sections of the play and wholly improvised sections.

The confidence of the actor is paramount in Children's Theatre, together with an unsentimental feeling about youngsters, so that he is able to provide opportunities and enjoy the creative response. But he needs to know and feel the difference between a genuine response that is sincere and absorbed and one that is possibly just playing-up. It is unwise to develop a view that everything the youngsters do or say *must* be right — indeed, that is the zenith of sentimental folly, and youngsters know a sucker when they meet one. Just as adult audiences can differ performance by performance so too can and do audiences of children, and perhaps most of all in Children's Theatre for broad age groups (especially when including adults), rather large numbers and so on. Audience participation invariably highlights these differences, making each performance a fresh challenge, with new excitements and creative accomplishments. But we must all have experienced as actors the folly of blaming the audience when everything has not gone exactly right for us in adult theatre — perhaps we have not had the same number of laughs, the same tenseness of atmosphere, the same feeling of the audience hanging on every word, every moment of the play. As creative artists we have to wonder if *we* are the cause — if something was not quite right in our performance: had we become complacent because of previous successes? had concentration slipped? had control been less exact? and so on — the wise scrutiny of ourselves before blaming the audience. These same processes apply to Children's Theatre. But in the participation sections it is difficult to apply our thinking in the same way until we are able to accept the participation as integral to the play itself rather than as a different and separate addition. As so many actors have said: "I began thoroughly to enjoy and master the participation factors as soon as I felt the audience to be almost another character or group of characters within the play, rather then an instrusion that had to be put up with.

To return to the example of participation in **The Sleeping Beauty**. During the collecting and making of the lists of what might prick the Princess, the actors must listen acutely to the suggestions from the audience, which may well come in rather faint and diffident whispers, often the sign of deepest and sincerest involvement. The actor must also be ready not to be surprised by the ideas put forward, nor the words chosen with which to express those ideas.

Once we begin to feel this way about audience participation, then we can look at it constructively, seeing not only its function of fulfilling potential or actual need in the play, but also when we *do not need it* and therefore do not want it to happen. Two examples of this follow each other closely in **The Sleeping Beauty**. This story cannot exist in any form without the *inevitability* of the Princess pricking her finger. There must, therefore, be a sequence — possibly highly dramatic — when she goes to the attic or whatever room contains the spinning wheel, and shortly after arriving there accepts the offer to try working the spinning wheel herself. It is a sequence when *spontaneous participation is neither needed nor appropriate.* Personally I believe that because of a natural human compulsion to accept the inevitable, and possibly also because of a "hope" factor that, whatever happens all will come right in the end, the majority of youngsters accept entirely the inappropriateness of their intervention and therefore do not attempt to participate. Much may depend on how well they know the story.

It is just possible, however, that a few members of the audience may, probably in very hushed whispers, try to stop the Princess from going to the attic room. She should ignore them, should be so absorbed in her own intention that she does not even hear them, and above all, press through with the *rhythm of her action* without any pause or so much as even a glance towards the audience, let alone get involved in any kind of dialogue or discussion with them. A few moments later, when she is invited to try working the spinning wheel, because she has never seen one before, there again may be advice from some of the audience not to, and again she should not get involved in any dialogue about the matter. If there is strong insistence, however, from many voices that she should not touch the spinning wheel, she is still *able to touch it*, even by accident, so that the pricking of the finger is accomplished. Still she must not get involved in a dialogue with the audience. Indeed, if she stays fully in character within the situation, getting sleepier and sleepier, then the voices will subside because the youngsters know that the spell has taken so strong a hold upon her that she cannot hear them.

I emphasize the above points because they exemplify this factor of absorbed sincerity in character and situation, and also stress the point that we must not be sentimental about youngsters and permit them to control the whole situation whether or not their help is appropriate. This is, indeed, an example of when participation is of the heart, the mind and the spirit, but is neither vocal nor physical. The very fact that we have been "moved" means we are fully ready to help the moment our assistance is called for. We are almost straining at the leash so strong is our inner desire to help. So, in my own particular version there follows at once a sequence of participation that is *totally necessary* for the story and so is in the hands of a central character with whom we have all worked many times, and who involves us in a sequence of entirely *directed participation* in which we are all working at the same time on the same problems in roughly the same rhythm, under her guidance and control, *all of which is written into her dialogue,* which runs as follows:

> Have no fear. We still have time. Whatever plot is made against the Princess now, can only really start to happen when the hundred years are over. We still have time, but all of you must help me. *(She moves close to where a young man is lying asleep.)* Here lies the one person who would devote the whole of his life to the Princess. But many difficulties will stand in his way, so we must give him greater

strength and courage, greater wisdom and perseverance so that he shall indeed be a Prince among men. Help me to help him. Very quietly, make yourselves as small as you can. Curl up small. Now, very slowly, you are going to grow and grow and grow into the finest and tallest and strongest of oak trees — NOW! *(Sound comes and we grow with the sound until its climax and fulfilment.)*

A long growing cymbal roll is recommended for the sound. The character should remain strongly efficient and fully absorbed during the whole of this sequence which, incidentally, is directly related to the type of creative drama encouraged in the classroom with young children. The sequence and the actual working of the dialogue are important. The reason for repetition of some of the instructions is partly to make sure that *the whole audience hears everything*, and partly because very young children do not always register an instruction the first time it is given.

When we are all grown into oak trees the instructions continue:

And now, make the sound of the wind in the branches of the trees — NOW. . . and the wind gently bends the trees towards him and the wind carries the strength of the trees into him, into him, into him — trees, blow your strength into him, into himmmmmmmmmmmmm. *(And with the dying fall of her mmmmmmmmmm sound the wind dies. Should it not do so, then a single sharp sound on the cymbal will bring an end to the wind.)* Now, pick up all the acorn nuts lying on the ground at the roots of the trees. Pick up the acorns and put them in your lap. *(This means that they will all sit down if they have been standing as trees.)* Now, make a crown of acorns, a crown for the Prince to wear. *(And we all make crowns with our acorns. Do not expect detail of mime for this making! All the activities will be completed very quickly and there may be some gentle chatter during them).* Now — make a sword — make a sword for the Prince. You all have rods of steel. Beat them with a great hammer until you have made a long, strong blade. . . now, sharpen the blade with a stone. Rub it with the stone until it is really sharp. . . Now, we need a cloak for the Prince to wear. Sew and weave a cloak, sew and weave, sew and weave. . . *(As the cloak is completed, she continues:)*

Now, listen — listen. . .

And as we listen, there is music, and she raises up the young man in his sleep, and we see at once the new strength we have given him. She draws him towards the center and through the music she calls:

Bring for the Prince, the Crown of Wisdom.

(The crown of wisdom is brought and placed upon the Prince's head — it is a crown of acorns.) — Bring for the Prince, the Cloak of Perseverance. *(And two attendants bring the cloak and the Prince is robed in it.)* — Bring for the Prince, the Sword of Courage. *(And the sword of courage is brought and placed in the Prince's hand. And with the growing climax of the music she weaves a spell over the Prince saying as she does so:* Now a Prince. A Prince!

Because of our deep involvement in the transformation of the Prince, we feel a close affinity to him throughout the remainder of the story, including seeing how he makes use of the various qualities we have symbolically bestowed on him.

There is no need for the characters to worry as to whether, when she calls for the Crown, the Sword and the Cloak, any of the audience will run forward with the ones they have made. They accept entirely the symbolical area of help, including the fact they have *mimed* making *their* things and yet a *real* crown, cloak and sword are taken to the Prince. It is interesting to watch many of them joining in the ritual movements of placing the crown on his head and the sword in his hand — and the more richly ritualistic the approach is, the more likely they are to participate.

At the end of the above sequence, another useful approach to a moment of audience control during participation arises around the use of the word

"Listen." The word is used in the context of listening "for a sound" of some kind, *not* "listen to me" as might be said by a parent or teacher. If the word is said clearly, perhaps even with a sudden change of body angle followed by total stillness, it can prove an excellent method of control. The audience will stop talking and cease any physical activity they are involved in, in order not to miss whatever might be about to happen. The use of the word can be very valuable, for example, during the finding out from the audience what things might prick the Princess, and again during the activity of collecting and burying these things. Should keenness to help lead to voices getting stronger and stronger, then the single sharp-sounded word "Listen" from any character in that sequence will bring a sudden silence, into which someone can interject whatever words are necessary for the continuation of the action, which will now have fuller control from everyone.

In the above sequence, the dialogue has been carefully written by the author rather than leaving it open to improvisation. This is because the whole scene is part of *a ritual* containing its own atmosphere and gradual growth to a climax of the crowning. We shall meet later on many experiences where the youngsters are making something that is not part of a ritual growth and therefore can be done at a quite different rhythm, with the stimulator improvising language according to needs as they arise. In this sequence, the stimulator needs to feel the strength of the ritual throughout, and when the right level is found might well discover herself involved in an extraordinarily rich experience. Many people playing this particular character have been astonished by the experience as they build up from scratch, with an audience of four, five, maybe six hundred youngsters, a few minutes of *completely polished theatre*, as though it had been rehearsed for several hours. So, too, with many of the Princes I have worked with, who have remarked on the strange intensity of feeling that has emanated from the audience. "It is," one of them said, "quite impossible not to feel the totality of the transformation to the Prince. You feel you have been fully involved in what is meant by the 'magic' of theatre."

Let us consider a few examples from another play specially written for audience participation in conventional theatres with fixed seating and a large mixed audience, but again requiring simple physical arrangements of easy access from stage to auditorium so that the whole theatre can be the place in which everything happens. Like **Sleeping Beauty, Puss in Boots** is a very free and imaginative adaptation of the old fairy tale, with many developments dependant on the cat's magic and the assistance of the audience, starting with a somewhat different use of *directed* participation. The main difference is that it is not concerned with *immediate use* but with *preparation for future use*. It is almost a rehearsal of what is going to be necessary at a later stage of the story.

The boots worn by Puss are in fact magic boots, which enable her to be able to walk and talk, indeed, also to sing and dance. As soon as this is established, Puss uses musical instruments as part of the directed participation. She has a cymbal, a triangle, castanets, a drum and an old motor hooter and, starting with the cymbal, she says to us all: "Curl up as small as you can."

Let us look more closely at this instruction, which we have just met in the participation scene, in **Sleeping Beauty**, where a character starts her ritual sequence with us to help the Prince. When it happened on that occasion, the audience had already participated a great deal and so the character could rely totally on immediate cooperation and probably a great deal of confidence in the carrying out of her wishes. This time, the circumstances are very different, for this is the first moment of participation in **Puss in Boots**. The manner in which it is handled by Puss will set the tone for the rest of the play. While younger children will experience no problem in this request to "Curl up as small as you can," in a mixed age group audience, there is almost certain to be a lot of chatting and some laughter, both reflecting uncertainty as to what exactly is expected of them. Puss can assist us in achieving the moment by remaining still, quiet and serious with, perhaps, the repetition of the request or perhaps, by moving among the audience to encourage, with full seriousness, the activity. Additionally, Puss can instill a degree of urgency into the situation by suggesting that this kind of activity may be needed later on "to protect us from our enemies." And, of course, though necessary only as a last resort, the cymbal can be hit sharply to attract attention in order that Puss may impress on everyone the importance of trying out certain things for future use. Again there is the important point of staying in character, treating the audience as serious people, not as "kids" and maintaining urgency without becoming frenetic. Should the actors fall into the trap of treating this as a "game" which is not at all serious, then as the play develops and the participation becomes *progressively complicated*, the audience may ultimately become over-active, even hysterical, to a point where little, if anything, is of value. Despite all the above precautions, however, it is equally important for Puss to get on with the action as soon as possible, not waiting in the hope that *everyone* is going to curl up small and participate immediately. Many will wait until they see what kind of thing they are going to be asked to do. When they discover that there is nothing to be afraid of, that no individual is going to be picked on and watched by the rest of the audience, and that no one is going to criticize them or hold them up to ridicule, then confidence will grow and grow and with the confidence will come fuller participation and the probability that more people will become involved.

The idea of "curling up small" is always interesting with younger children, whether it be as part of Children's Theatre Participation or part of creative dramatics in the classroom. It places the participant in a position from which *growth* is possible — just as all nature's physical growth starts from some kind of embryo or seed. Once curled up small, the slightest movement is at once a movement outwards, and one is left a full area of development in the process of growing. Even to grow no more than returning to the position one was originally sitting in still involves a growth-movement area, which, depending on circumstances, can be further fulfilled by coming to a standing position. After we have curled up small, Puss continues:

> Now listen to the sound I am going to make. With the sound you will all grow into great big frightening monsters. . . listen. . . grow into monsters. . . NOW! *(Puss, using a cymbal roll, creates the sound for growing into monsters.)*

The cymbal is used here again as a stimulus. Puss should guage the intensity, volume and length of the cymbal roll according to the degree of audience response, and bring it up to a strong final climax sound for the completion of the growth. Again, since this is the first experience, there may be some reluctance, laughter or other manifestations of uncertainty. But the moment she reaches the climax of the cymbal roll, she needs to go straight on with the dialogue, coming out of the top of the sound, creating and maintaining atmosphere:

> And the monsters are all roaring at their enemies. . . roaring at them. *(And we all roar and roar and Puss ends it with a strong sound on the cymbal.) Differing audience by audience, the "roar" may be very strong and loud. Puss should judge the moment at which she ends it — without any attempt at all to encourage it to be stronger should it happen to be not as loud as she might expect — with a clear, sharp and loud sound on the cymbal. So we are using sound both to stimulate and accompany activity, and to control it. And as soon as she has made the "stop" signal, she again goes straight on with her next dialogue, perhaps feeling she can drop her own vocal volume, but not dropping by a fraction the intensity and the sincere urgency. Certainly not making any kind of value judgement comments. She says:*
>
> And all curl up very small again. . . as small as you can. . . *(She waits just a few moments for this to be done...)* This time we are all going to grow into enormous trees. . . great trees with huge branches to keep people out of somewhere. . . so, with the sound, grow and grow into trees. . . NOW! *(Again Puss makes the cymbal roll to climax sound guaging intensity, volume and length by the response from the youngsters, as this time they grow into "enormous trees with huge branches." And the wind sounds in the branches. . . and the branches swish at their enemies to keep them away. . .*

Because of the deliberate repetition of a new experience, the "curling-up small" will be easier for the whole audience to achieve, although there may still be some excitement and reaction to the unfamiliar experience, particularly from those who did not try the first time but now, seeing that there is nothing to be worried about, decide themselves to try it. And just as the physical experience is a repetition, so too is the procedure and the use of sound, thus helping to increase confidence through familiarity. And again, Puss establishes the climactic end to the activity by banging sharply on the cymbal. The sensitive use of the full potential of the cymbal for stimulation or control does demand a gread deal of practice, and care should be taken to obtain a good instrument. A cheap instrument makes not only an unpleasant sound, which is no encouragement for response, but can also damage the sensitive eardrums of very small children if they happen to be sitting close to where the sound is being made. For additional emphasis of "end" as in this kind of moment in participation, close the fingers onto the edge of the cymbal, thus removing any lingering sound. So Puss brings all the trees to stillness. Then she takes the hooter and says:

> Whenever the hooter sounds, everyone immediately settle back into your place, becoming absolutely still and absolutely quiet so that none of our enemies knows the secret of what we've been doing. Let's try it now. As soon as I hoot the hooter, everyone settle back into your place and be still and quiet. Now. *(Puss hoots the hooter and waits until all have settled back and are still and quiet.)*

Let us not be at all confused about the injunctions from Puss regarding the return to our place and the stillness and quietness. They are part of the *adventure,* and it is in the spirit of adventure, of the need for secrecy, for outwitting our enemies, that Puss is talking to us. It is important that she handles the lines in such a way that we feel fully that spirit of adventure and the logic of the requests made of us — all quite different from some poor harrassed actress (or teacher) trying to obtain a peaceful life.

The hooter has now been introduced as a very specific control and this instrument will *never be used for any other purpose.* The sharp bang on the cymbal has indicated "stop." The hooter takes us back to our seats.

And now, as the story continues, use is made of the other instruments — First the castanets. Puss says:

> Everybody. Absolutely still. Now, with the sound that I make, you will slowly discover every part of you is becoming stiff. *(Puss begins the sound)* Everything is starting to become stiff... Now. Stiffer and stiffer and stiffer... fingers and arms... and heads... and legs... and slowly becoming puppets... and all of the puppets are dancing and dancing and dancing... *(With a rhythm on the castanets, all the puppets dance. Then the sound stops — and the puppets stop.)* Now, let's try the hooter sound again. The hooter sound... Now. *(Puss hoots the hooter and everyone sits down again and is still and quiet. Then Puss uses the triangle.)* Everyone starting from where you are now — grow with the sound into icicles... really cold, sharp, pointed icicles. Grow with the sound — Now! *(And with the sound of the triangle, everyone grows into icicles. Then the sound stops and without any verbal warning, the hooter is hooted and everyone sits.)*

Perhaps it is too soon to "test" this reaction without any warning, in which case Puss needs to treat the moment with good humor, at the same time pointing out that when the real need comes for their secrecy later, she may well not have the chance to warn them so they must be ready all the time for it to happen. There must be no harsh criticism, but she must move quickly from her good humored approach to bringing back all the urgency. If she feels time allows and that the audience will enjoy the challenge of a second chance, she may well try repeating the icicles with the triangle. Then she picks up the drum and says:

> Everyone curl up very small again... as small as you can. Now, with the roll of the drums, you are all going to grow into tiny insects... small insects that can sting... but don't sting until I tell you to. Grow into insects — Now! *(She provides a drum roll for growing into small insects. Again the sound grows to a climax and then stops.)* And with each tap on the drum, insects send your stings up into the air, like arrows. *(She begins to tap the drum.)* Sting! Sting! Up into the air in all directions. Sting! Sting... sting... sting... *(The drum stops, the hooter is sounded, and all settle down again. Puss suddenly says:)* Listen!

The word "listen" is used in the context described earlier — an alerting of everyone, a stopping of all activity and at this moment there could well have been vocal assurances from many in the audience to Puss. In the long sequence of participation, there has been preparation and practice for participation that is to come later in the play, all of which is so integrated that it needs to flow with as little instruction and explanation as possible. In this sequence, the audience will move slowly from the early rather unabsorbed and perhaps worried beginnings to full cooperation and absorption. Puss can rely entirely on this, and indeed will find that, subject to her own sincere involvement, many audiences will attain total interest very quickly. Throughout, Puss has, in fact, had a companion (another character in the play) who establishes herself as "one of us," assuring Puss on our behalf, making the kind of enquiries we might ourselves like to make, and making clear the responsibility of our involvement in "the magic" and the need to be *guardians* of that magic, neither wasting it by using it at the wrong time, nor giving away the secret of it. Thus, we are no longer observers of the story; henceforth we are deeply involved.

Immediately following the rehearsal of the participation Puss has involved us in, there comes a direct test of its effectiveness when two rogues in the story attempt to capture Puss. At once Puss involves us in the participation with the drum. We become "stinging insects" who banish the rogues. The actors involved in the sequence are usually amazed at the atmosphere of totally silent suspense built-up with the audience as they grow into insects and then wait, motionless, for the signal to start their stinging. It is the kind of moment that can again make worlds of difference in peoples' minds as to what audience participation is about and the integrated place it can have in a play of this kind. After the "rehearsal" of the participation, this is its first genuine testing for the purpose of "assisting" a character in the play. It is, of course, so important that the rogues and Puss treat this with absolute seriousness. Puss must communicate the fullest urgency in her whispered request/instruction while also conveying trust that they will do it for her. The rogues should react forcibly and genuinely to the *stinging of insects* and should not view the audience in any way other than as insects. Coming as soon as it does after the practice at the participation, this incident establishes the reality of the subsequent "magic," which tricks and defeats the "enemies."

It is possible that there will be no need for the use of the hooter as the logic of the situation contains its own built-in control factor: the reason for becoming insects sending out their stings is to get rid of the rogues. Once they have gone, there is no further need for the activity and sounds, and they will die away with the rogues exit. The reappearance of Puss will confirm this. Because we have been at such pains to establish the use of the hooter, however, and because we may well need it on further occasions, it may in fact be wisest to practice its use now as reminder and completion, while settling back and being still and quiet. If Puss does use it, then she and her assistant must also repond to it, becoming still and quiet at the same time as we do. This is particularly important for Puss's assistant because of her total identification with us directly after practicing the participation sequence. This makes the difference between "adults using sounds to control children in the audience" and "characters using magic for the development of the story and the fulfilment of particular needs." If the assistant does not respond, then why should any of the rest of us?

There is a further development of the now fully established magic qualities of Puss's "boots," whereby there are moments when, without any help from the audience at all, she is able to exert certain kinds of control on other characters in the play, using the words "By my boots" and then adding her own sound and movement. But she also uses the magic of the boots and the phrase "By my boots" in *direct* association with our participation, this time not with the aid of the instruments but with a call to us for a "Magic Hum"; the Hum then becomes part of the spell affecting whomever it is concerned with. Thus, all of the participation that has been practiced is used during the act and works just as it has been arranged, but this additional opportunity supplies a new enrichment because of its unexpectedness and consequent greater area of spontaniety. But it goes even further than this, and actually involves the audience in the climax of the play. Puss's enemy eventually discovers the magic power of the "Boots" and creates a situation in which he is able to force Puss to give up the Boots so that he himself can wear them and thus increase his own powers. As she gives up the Boots, Puss says: "Trust the Boots; trust the Boots." Nothing else. No warning to us about not cooperating with the enemy, no line about the fact that the "Hum will not come for him because he is evil." There is entire trust that his plan will not work because we will not help him. He puts on the Boots. At once he commands all of us "to turn into birds and fly away." He tries several times. He adds the words Puss always uses: "By my Boots...," " but still the hum does not come, so he does not obtain the assistance he needs from the audience. This makes a most exciting moment of theatre, not without its first worries and fears for the cast who often simply cannot believe that an audience can be so much a part of a play that they can be entrusted with what after all could be the ruin of the climax. But, at the risk of over-stressing the point, all has depended on the absorption, sincerity and seriousness of the cast in its approach to the participation throughout the play, including this extraordinary factor of "magic."

Magic is the quality behind so many moments of participation that have been considered in this section. It is behind Gepetto's first wishing, when we help to "conjure up" the Fairy. It is an essential ingredient in the section where Pinocchio is taught "to fly." Again it is essential when he changes into "a real boy" towards the end of the play, and it gives an extraordinary atmosphere to the Fairy's last exit. It is indeed, without need for further specification, an integral part of all the plays that have been touched on in some detail.

What exactly is "It," this strange quality of "Magic?"

Perhaps it is both unwise and impossible to find a single definition. Certainly it is entirely different in kind from the wholly admirable work of the conjuror, the magician and the illusionist. Their magic is something that baffles the mind. Magic of the kind I am thinking of in Children's Theatre, with or without the active participation of the audience, has little to do with the mind, but is a thing of the heart and the feelings and the spirit. Indeed it is more a quality of existence that man seeks and finds when the mind is at its wit's end, when something larger than mind is necessary. Perhaps it is a synthesis of all man's different capabilities.

Or is this, as some actors have suggested (but usually *before* they have had the impact of direct experience), taking it all a little too seriously or getting a little "precious" about it? Obviously I do not think so or I should not have devoted so large a part of my life to precisely this form of theatre. But I am wholly sympathetic to the view, particularly when it is expressed by people who have not been involved, either as observers or participants. And I am naturally saddened (perhaps angry is a more potent description) by actors who too glibly dismiss the potential of this quality within theatre, when their only experience of it has been that of titilating around the edges of something they look on as "entertainment for the kids," for whom they so often think anything goes. Often they find it difficult to believe that theatre can be a genuinely "serious" experience for children, seeming to think that only hysterical giggling is the real hallmark of theatre for children. I am sad for such people, because as artists they are missing some of the finest possible theatre experiences open to them, and I am of course also saddened because there is little enough genuine theatre for children, and it will remain little until more actors are prepared to give their serious attention to the potential open to them.

I have mentioned above the audience participation that involves the use of a "hum." In many Children's Theatre plays, some of which I shall mention in subsequent chapters, I have made use of this particular moment of audience participation, and in one sense it touches the very core of this area of "magic," and this is used, though by no means always, in association with "wishing". Basically, to make a "humming" sound, one is making a breathing sound that comes from the very center of one's own being. The sound contains the fundamentals of deep personal sincerity and relaxation. Interestingly, one can always spot the few "pushing intellectuals" in an audience during such a moment, because their sound is strained, forced and hard and seems to be trying to burst through the forehead. One of the most beautiful sounds to be heard in the theatre is the participatory "hum" from an audience that has not been pushed with too much overexcitement and so is relaxed and utterly simple. Many musicians observing this have been interested in how quickly groups, even very large groups, find their own "group note," just as in other contexts they will find their own group timebeat, for example in moments when everybody is ask to "flick," with finger and thumb. Very young children may be confused by the word "hum" and so will say: "Hum-hum-hum-hum-hum-hum-hum" rather than go Hmmmmmmmm. They are very easily helped over this if the character asking for the sound simply adds the continuity of the mmmmmmmmmm sound the first time he requests a "Hmmmmmmmmmmmm-mmm." There will be no need to repeat the request in the same manner after the first experience.

This "working in depth from one's own center" is precisely what the quality of "magic" is deeply concerned with; hence the continuously reiterated point about concentration, absorption and total sincerity, always working from within character and situation, even in the most directed forms of audience participation, and of course it underlines the point about "quality" rather than "volume" of response always being the criteria for how participation is working. Many people associated with participatory children's theatre have used, without prompting from me, one particular word when describing the youngsters with whom they are involved — innocence. It is a word that perhaps most describes the fundamental difference between working with young children and working with older children about whom we can equally use the word "sophistication." Somewhere between the innocence of the young and the sophistication of the older there lies a kind of "no-man's land," as the youngsters themselves, in their own lives, are merging from one natural area of being to another, which is different but at the same time equally natural. To be driven out of "natural innocence" too soon, let alone by artificial pressure, is the root of precociousness. To move into the area of "natural sophistication" from a basis of precociouness is to develop a lack of sincerity which is very often at war with some inner instinct and can be as "misery-making" for the person directly involved as it is for those who have to suffer the results. Parallel with these two states of being, are two forms of theatre experience. For older and more sophisticated youngsters, there is conscious awareness of theatre as a creative activity, something made by the imagination and creativity of people. For the younger "innocents" there is no such conscious awareness of "theatre as an art form," so that, if there is full sincerity from the actors, the play itself can seem to be more real than the fact that one is sitting in a place watching a play being made. This full identification is what makes participation so easy and natural a factor in Children's Theatre for younger children. They want to help those they love through their journey in life. They want to help through active vocal and physical involvement, and we, be it as authors or actors or directors, allow for this as a perfectly logical and natural part of the play.

Some actors are interested in one particular view about "magic" and "wishing" that arises from this factor of "innocence" in younger children, namely its parallel with the whole concept of "prayer." When Man is "stuck" and knows not where to turn to fulfil whatever may be his immediate concern, he turns to a power that is larger and higher than himself, in some form of prayer. For those who are interested in following aspects of participation as far as this, the idea seems to be a very exact illumination of the process. Hence, of course, the intense sincerity and seriousness, and also the factor of not "wasting" the qualities involved.

These factors of "innocence" and "sophistication," both natural parts of the growth process of youngsters, highlight one of the greatest difficulties in Theatre for Children — the problem of age groups. The problem is one of the main reasons why I became interested in specialist children's theatre work where, among other details, I was concerned with finding out what was possible with very confined age groups, numbers in the audience and other factors of control. These matters are considered in detail in a later section. Here we have been looking at "Family Theatre," a form of utmost importance in the overall field, and a form which makes it incumbent on those of us involved in theatre itself to move from the narrower confines of specilization, whether or not we are actually able to solve the additional problems that inevitably arise. The first of these problems concerns age groupings. The second concerns the presence of adults in the audience.

AGE GROUPS

In my personal view, the only form of "live entertainment" that succeeds with the full breadth of family age groupings is the circus, mainly because of its wide variety of offerings. Even if there are some items that do not have full appeal for some members of the family, they will soon be involved with items they do like. Furthermore, the circus has an astonishing degree of *occasion*. At its best, it is total theatre. At its worst it is still brave. For children, there is invariably something awesome about the size, the glitter, the daring and the sheer pace. For teen-agers, there are many of the same qualities, added to which is a sense of wonder about many of the skills involved. But most important of all, it embraces both innocence and sophistication, and admirably caters for the bridge from one to the other.

There will be many who have been involved in Theatre for Children who will undoubtedly claim that they are able to, indeed for many years have been able to, provide theatre that is satisfactory in every way for all age groups. I do not in any way discount the obvious family pleasure of, say, the plays that I have written about in such detail in this section: **Pinocchio, Sleeping Beauty, and Puss in Boots.** Nevertheless, I know that the age group for which the plays are most suitable is the 5 to 11 year olds, and often participation reveals that the fullest experience is probably for the 6 to 9 year olds. The fact that other age groups also enjoy them is because of additional factors like "the family's being together," the "sense of occasion," the general excitement of "going to the theatre," the "anticipation," the "lights, the costumes, the music, the fun;" all important factors. The content, the storyline and the characters are basically "too young" (in the sense of unsophisticated) for the older young people. If the production and acting have total integrity, however, even this older group will find a great deal of charm in the plays and probably some excitement as well. And if they have much younger brothers and sisters in the audience, then they, like their parents, will find added enjoyment in the full participation of these younger ones, and will often, in fact, themselves join in as encouragement and as part of the general pleasure of the occasion. Certainly, from fourteen upwards this appears to be so. The people who can find most difficulty in coping with the circumstances are the 11 to 13 age group, who are caught in the stage between innocence and sophistication, thus feeling the content, etc., rather beneath them, and yet not fully sophisticated enough to join the more adult view.

The reverse situation with age groups can bring about many more problems — that is, when the play is written mainly for eleven and upwards but has large number of considerably younger children in the audience. My own adaptations of Dumas' **The Three Musketeers**, Stevenson's **Treasure Island** and Dickens' **Christmas Carol** were all experiments in forms of Family Theatre, both for performance in conventional proscenium theatres with fixed seating and for Theatre-in-the-Round. Each play contains a great deal of exciting dramatic action and, to this extent, has held the interest for at least part of the play right down to the age of 8. Most of **Christmas Carol** and **Treasure Island** would hold from 9 upwards, but **The Three Musketeers** is fairly heavy going for anyone under 10, except for the fights and other highly dramatic scenes. Certainly all three plays are wholly unsuitable for anyone under eight. They would be bored stiff for most of the time, and probably frightened out of their skins by some moments. Because the plays were written for the older groups, for those who have largely emerged from innocence into sophistication, there is no participation of the directed or stimulated kind, and basically it is unlikely that much will arise of the spontaneous kind, except from age groups for whom the plays were not written. This is not to suggest that there cannot be plays containing participation for the older age groups, but such participation belongs to a world of *conscious theatre* and is therefore quite different in kind from that which has been described in this section.

The predicament is whether we should call theatre that excludes all younger age groups "Family Theatre." I have never felt any compunction about advertising plays such as **Pinocchio, Sleeping Beauty,** and **Puss in Boots** as "A Play for all the Family," and I have had no experiences of parents complaining to managements that their teen-age youngsters felt the play to be too young for them. I have, however, always felt it most necessary to state very clearly an age group factor for the other plays, using nine as the lowest age for **Christmas Carol** and **Treasure Island,** and 10 as the youngest for **The Three Musketeers.** I have felt the need to stress this both on behalf of the younger children who may be dragged along to a boring evening, and also on behalf of the cast, who have the problem of coping with the demonstrations of boredom when they arise. In my experience, not all managements are very scrupulous about this, taking the line that parents ought to know better than to bring very young children to unsuitable plays. That may be fair enough provided the play is not advertised as "For the whole Family," but I know of many parents who have been most upset that they were not warned of the unsuitability of the plays for the under nines or tens.

In theatre that is open to the general public, it is very difficult to have full control over who does and does not attend. One worry I have always had is the presence of the *under fives* in such public performances. In my experience, for the majority of these very small children, performances are too long, often too noisy and overexcited and the whole occasion too awe-inspiring and confusing. Parents, however, have their own pride and pay scant regard to these points, being more concerned to say that their tiny children "understood" it all, making **that** the ultimate criteria of suitability for them. And if a play is advertised as "Family Entertainment" then all age groups will arrive, including, alas, babes-in-arms. It is interesting that a crying baby in a theatre will draw from even other parents a full objection to bringing "such young children" to the theatre. The dividing line, perhaps, has to be flexible. For Theatres that are attempting regular Children's Theatre performed for a local public, there are many opportunities to meet parents or in some way communicate with them and so gradually ease some of these problems. Theatre both for today and for tomorrow benefits from such an exchange of views and experiences.

But another problem regarding age groups for this kind of theatre centers round the in-schooltime matinee for school parties.

I have already pointed out how my own interest in Theatre for Children arose from many experiences dealing with large hordes of assorted age groups of youngsters attending matinees of plays wholly unsuitable to the majority of them. Once one is able to find material for particular age groups, then obviously the control factor that can be exercised by schools in their arrangements with theatres can lead to most constructive solutions, even to the detailed extent of stressing, for example, that **Pinocchio** is most suitable for ages 6 to 9, **Christmas Carol** most suitable for ages 10 to 12, **Treasure Island** most suitable for ages 11 to 13 and **The Three Musketeers** most suitable for 13 and above. Teachers are often suprised by a Theatre Company's ability to speak in such exact terms about specific age groups, and because of their own administrative problems may ask for some flexibility in the classes they send. These requests can usually be met, providing the age difference does not extend beyond a year or so in either direction. But then the real problem of the matinee of this kind is revealed as not simply one of age groupings and suitability of material, but the artificiality of the whole idea of filling a theatre with *only* youngsters, without benefit of homogeneous groups, causing possible age group problems, if one school has sent mainly the lower end of the age scale and another has sent the upper end, and so on.

So often, the "joy" of the theatre visit is eliminated from such occasions, and is replaced by an atmosphere that is still predominantly that of *school*, especially if attending teachers have anxieties about behaviour and discipline problems, anxieties that can often prove only too real. One has to ask oneself, in all honesty what has this got to do with a genuine experience of theatre? There are many expedient rationales, ranging from the opportunity for the youngsters to see a live performance of a text they have to study for purposes of examination, to theatres solving some parts of their box office financial problems by having a certain number of guaranteed full houses each season. There is also undoubtedly a great satisfaction and pleasure for very many of the young people attending such performances, as so many youngsters have put it to me personally: "It's beter than having to be in school, anyway." One *cri de coeur* of many theatre people, parents and teachers, in justification for such school matinees is that they will help to build audiences for the future. There is, in fact, no evidence of such a result.

Many interesting experiments are bing tried out regarding young people going to theatre, some of the most important involving teen-agers. Even with the school matinee, some theatres are giving to schools, not a single block of seats for the whole party, but various small allocations, leaving it to the school to run its own "box-office" on a basis of those allocations, so that the youngsters can go in their own friendship groupings, find themselves seated among people they do not know, and even make their own way to the theatre in time for the performance. This is one step nearer to a genuine experience of going to the theatre. It means a lot of hard work for teachers and theatre managements, but in terms of interesting youngsters in going to the theatre, a great deal more is achieved. Some theatres have gone even beyond this and have allocated seats in such a way that parents or friends outside of the school

can attend at the same time, so the audience is not only made up of young people from school, but includes others from the community. Perhaps we cannot
avoid the realities of some of the expedients mentioned above, but we can consider more adventurous and imaginative ways of approaching the solution to
such problems.

Specialist Children's Theatre work is concerned with some of these problems, in particular the breaking down of age groups and creating material for
each different group, including various forms of audience participation. It is
also concerned with moving away from the conventional theatre with fixed
seating. The plays previously considered in this section in terms of an approach to Participatory Children's Theatre have been largely concerned with
younger age groups within a Family Audience situation — what of older age
groups? Is it possible, starting from where we are, to bring in participation for
them? There is much to discover about this.

Pinocchio. *A proscenium stage production. The set up is permanent and never changes, despite the number of "scenes" and "locations." The set is basically a wide bridge with stairs down either side — Gepetto's house on one side, Fire-Eater's on the other. There is a cyclorama cloth backing with a simple ground row in front of it. In this photograph, Pinocchio is trapped by Fox and Cat (disguised as highwaymen). In a moment the Fairy, as Cricket, will call to Pinocchio to run, and he will jump off the 8'6" high bridge to the stage level (yes, actors have to be in superb condition for Children's Theater) and will run out into the audience and they will "hide and protect" him. Hence, the action of the play uses all the theatre — the auditorium as well as the stage. The curtain is never closed, even before the play, so the audience becomes familiar with the set to avoid its being a distraction. (Photo: Studio Edmark, Oxford)*

Pinocchio. *Fox and Cat take Pinocchio on a journey to the "Field of Miracles," and here they are climbing down a mountain after crossing a narrow ledge overhanging a ravine. (Cat is scared of heights!) Fox states exactly where the journey is taking them, and though the scene is improvised, it is done with the fully absorbed sincerity and polish of a rehearsed scripted scene. No gimmicks. No gags. No cheap laughs. In the permanent set-up, lighting could be used to isolate the action and minimize the setting detail. Equally, the journey can and does take place over much of the bare stage, and it could happen in the audience area as well. Anywhere as long as it is* real. (Photo: Studio Edmark, Oxford England)

Pinocchio. *An example of a production performed in broad daylight in a school hall during school hours. There is an audience of 250 - 5-11 year olds seated in a half-circle. The play uses a permanent setting of rostrum blocks in front of a backdrop curtain (right). This is the opening of the play when, after a joyful procession, Mr. Fire-Eater's puppet troupe begin to sell imaginary tickets to the audience for imaginary money. In the foreground, the manipulator in charge of the puppet, Columbine, has enlisted the participation of a youngster to hold the puppet strings while she sells tickets. In the background, the puppet Pantalone is being helped in the same manner. There is an aisle behind the audience for the actors' processions, chases and journeys. (Photo: Henry Grant)*

3

An Experiment In Teen-Age Participatory Theatre

Use of Proscenium Stage and Fixed Seating Auditorium

The approach to active participation with teen-agers needs to be one of sharing with them some of the creative excitement involved in the processes of theatre production and acting. As with all audiences of any age group, the teen-ager participates emotionally, intellectually and spiritually, but unlike young children, they are fully and consciously aware that they are in a theatre and that one of the basic rules is that one does not "interfere" with what is happening on the stage by attempting to participate vocally or physically. Apart from and beyond the rule itself, the majority of teen-agers are also in a stage of personal development where a perfectly natural type of self-consciousness and reserve inhibits any inclination to active participation. Their own peer group tends to reinforce the inhibition factor, and the presence of younger age groups not only adds a risk to their loss of dignity that is perfectly understandable, but also can make almost stubborn the refusal to be actively involved.

The importance of these factors is that, in general terms, it is most unwise for a company concerned with Theatre for Children or Young People to imagine that the directed, stimulated and spontaneous areas of audience participation that work so well up to the age of about 11 years, will work with teen-agers. They might well do so with a "selected" group of teen-agers who have already made a personal commitment to theatre, particularly if their theatre course includes basic practical work in movement and improvisation, though they are less likely to do so if that theatre course is largely academic and concerned with a book study of plays and texts. Those who have not made such a commitment are most unlikely to allow themselves to be caught off their guard so that, despite their own inclinations, they find that they are expected to participate. At one end of the scale of possible reaction they are likely to exhibit a stubborn refusal, and at the other end, particularly if they are pushed by autocratic domination, they are just as likely to defend their dignity by ridiculing the whole procedure, and their resulting participation is then often destructive rather than creative, the overall result being largely negative, with little value for any of the parties involved.

Our compassion must be with the young people in such circumstances. Authoritarianism may successfully dominate the academic world; it cannot and will not dominate the world of the arts, including the art of theatre. The youngster's point of view must be taken into account, and necessary adjustments must be made by the involved adult. The main adjustment concerns the fact that no matter how superior the adult may be in the intellectual sphere including knowledge and past experience he has no superiority in the emotional and spiritual sphere, which includes intuition, an area of human experience that defies hierarchy and gives emphasis to differences in which "right and wrong" are mere intellectual abstractions.

In physical activities, particularly when they are highly competitive, adults are able to acknowledge the superiority of youthful limbs. Thus, swimming champions can emerge among younger teens, and field athletic champions emerge among older teens. Other potential challengers for places in national and international sports teams are also spotted during the time of the teen-ager. The adult has no problem in acknowledging that the physical strength and agility of such an age is almost certain to be superior to that of the teacher, simply because of youthfulness and the physical condition of the person involved. Generally speaking, in the intellectual spheres of life, the adult always remains in the position of superiority, certainly during school-life, though the situation is often somewhat more flexible at Universities. Having lived longer, studied in more depth and achieved many qualifications, the superiority appears self-evident. While the arts follow similar procedures to the obviously academic disciplines, the same type of hierarchical superiority of adult over young persons always obtains. But as soon as we concede the possibility that the arts have their strongest basis in intuition rather than intellect, then we have to accept the possibility that even the teen-ager might be the equal, if not superior, to the adult in the practical arts. In fact, it should not be a case of "superiority" but one of differences. Fully academic arts courses sidetrack the problem, but in so doing tend to diminish intuition in favor of the intellectually known and mastered.

What we can be absolutely certain of in our approach to the teen-agers is that they have an insatiable curiosity about all creative processes and are always delighted when artists are prepared to share these processes with them, providing the sharing is at an adult level and is wholly free from any condescension or overt intention to "preach and teach." In these terms, they will even be prepared for direct involvement as part of the sharing process. They will live at risk in response to an invitation to be involved in the adventure and discovery of how a play is put together, yes even risking personal exposure through active participation.

We, the adults, have to be absolutely certain that we know the difference between genuine involvement in a "process of adventure and discovery" and a "process of instruction and academic know-how." The former is intuitively and emotionally rich and exciting, the latter is often intellectually dry and boring. The former is creatively swift and based on trust, the latter is often grindingly slow and based on precision. Intuition, swift creation and trust are all dependent on eliminating all fear of failure. I often count among my own personal blessings the fact that my early apprenticeship in theatre included being in several productions by Tyrone Guthrie, where one experienced the full emotional and spiritual richness of the theatre arts, with intellectual values being released by these basic human factors instead of being allowed to dominate them. Although at the time I had no awareness that I should eventually be so involved with Theatre for Young People, I was nevertheless absorbing precisely the approach that appears to "work" most adequately for both the committed and uncommitted.

The following outline of an experiment in participatory theatre with teen-agers is given in some detail in the hope that it might perhaps be of help to some groups interested in attempting or starting such an approach within the environment of a proscenium theatre with fixed seating or in the open stage. The basic intention was to interest young people in the creative excitement of theatre or, perhaps, the excitement of creative theatre. The method was to make the approach one of full participation and involvement by everybody in the audience, and because of the newness of the experiment at the time, the decision was made to confine the audience to a maximum of 400, preferably less, and certainly excluding the use of any part of the auditorium of a theatre except the main auditorium floor. Four professional actors were involved. The play chosen for the experiment was *Christopher Columbus*, a radio play by Louis MacNeice, published by Faber and Faber.

A radio play was chosen because its text would eliminate the need for scenery of any kind, yet lend itself to a creative and symphonic use of lighting and sound/music. I first came across and used the play as an experiment in open stage production at a time when there was little or no open stage theatre in England, and on many occasions *radio plays* proved the most exciting vehicles to use, as one of the main objections to the use of other plays was simply that they had been written for proscenium theatre. While it is true that the open stage is now fully accepted, nevertheless there are still many groups that have not ventured into the form, and I unhesitatingly recommend radio plays to them for their first attempts. *This* particular play was chosen because of the breadth of its canvas, the comparative familiarity of its theme, and the fact that it contained the possibility of several script-in-hand scenes that could involve the whole audience remaining seated, as well as several fully active scenes involving processions, etc., that would enable a number of "volunteers" to take part physically. There are also anything from a dozen to twenty parts of varying size for other script-in-hand scenes.

The preparation and provision of scripts was itself an interesting task. At first we provided people participating with individual roles a copy of the whole play, with markers carefully denoting each persons' particular scene. This proved unsatisfactory, as the inevitable tendency was for them to follow each scene in the text rather than watching the play and using the text only for their particular scene. All seemed to have a much richer over-all experience when we gave them only their own scene or scenes, typed, entered into manilla folders, with very clear red ink instructions regarding such matters as their moment of entry and the place of their scene in sequence. Providing rehearsal clarified these instructions, each person was then liberated from over-concern with irrelevant parts of the text and so could feel themselves more a part of the whole. For the crowd scenes, the scripted material was duplicated and the scenes bound, in sequence, in a manilla folder. At first, we provided every member of the audience with a copy (up to a maximum of 400 in the audience), but we soon found it was more satisfactory to ask pairs to share one script between them, as this gave each person an immediate contact with another, removing any feeling of isolation and providing a natural opportunity for various moments of discussion that arose during rehearsal; for example, discussing the types of characters they might be.

Under the guidance and production of one member of the company a few general introductory remarks need to be made before actual rehearsal starts. Different members of the company can rehearse different sections, thus giving the audience an experience of a variety of personalities approaching similar work. If there are many performances, the actors can take it in turn, if each is interested and has the skill. The members of the company need to be introduced to the audience, simply, briefly, professionally. The intention of the session needs to be explained, (much in the manner already described) as an experience of coming together to share the adventure of creating about an hour's theatre experience with everybody having the opportunity to take part. Then a word or two about the play and the author and a setting-up of the background circumstances of the action of the play which can be stated as exciting, human and dramatic facts, leading us straight into the rehearsal of the first main scene involving everybody. If scripts have not already been given out, they can be now.

Rehearsal thus begins with an opportunity for the whole audience to discuss the kind of people they are in the crowd, with encouragement to think beyond "attitudes" to considering a little of "personal characteristics" as well. We must not expect depth of character. We shall be surprised often by intuitive attack, particularly if the atmosphere is kept informal and uncritical, and yet professionally purposeful. Usually, inevitably, there will be the need to break down a natural kind of polite reserve in order to get the scene moving, and the opening itself often leads to that kind of good humor that makes the breakthrough, gives the right spirit of intention and enables fully productive serious endeavor to take over. It is always fascinating that the sooner this kind of humor comes into rehearsal the better. It draws away the inhibition and reserve and often brings-up some of the very points one needs to rehearse. After a joke, a single serious word, and full rehearsal begins to blossom, with everybody now working more seriously. If that opening is fully purposeful, it is remarkable how little rehearsal is then necessary for the scene as a whole.

There is need to look at and try out a few examples of two quite contrasting manners of using the scripted crowd — one where their reactions are individual and improvised according to their own feelings; the other where the author demands full choral utterance. The young people are generally fascinated by the differences, both in terms of the dramatic context and the acting potential, and it is this kind of experience in rehearsal that helps them feel something of the "adventure" of involvement in such crowd scenes.

After the crowd rehearsal scene, follows the need to cast and rehearse the individual scenes. Although many of these precede the crowd scenes when the play is run in sequence, it is still wise to leave individual rehearsals until this point, because by then there is a fully cooperative and constructive atmosphere built up with the whole audience, and the crowd rehearsals become a useful kind of "limbering-up" for those who become involved in the individual scenes, which take place on the stage itself.

Here is another immediate difference between participation in the plays for younger children and that for teen-agers who are working within the idea of *fully conscious theatre.* In plays such as **Pinocchio**, there would be no question of the youngsters using scripts for their participation, nor would any individuals be asked to come on to the proscenium stage area. With a play like *Christopher Columbus*, however, not only is the script-in-hand participation possible, but also volunteers from the audience are perfectly happy being involved on the proscenium stage. Indeed, some of them may have had considerable experience of this already, and be very talented. Who do we cast for these individual parts, and how do we approach the problem of selection?

When the audience is wholly homogeneous, that is all from a single school, then we can offer the school the opportunity of selecting, imploring the school to select by genuine interest rather than "school pride." Much of the object of the whole presentation is destroyed if some young people have to take part against their will and interest, simply because heads of Drama or English departments feel they will be a credit to the school. Even with audiences drawn from two schools, this scheme of preselection sometimes works quite adequately, particularly as the onus is always with the company to allow people to drop-out if they have had a change in mind, perhaps as a result of rehearsal in the crowd scenes. This seldom happens, but on the few occasions it does, at least the young people are saved the embarrassment of individual "exposure," and can still participate in the general crowd scenes.

Where preselection does not take place, then the company can take one of two alternatives — either to ask for fourteen (or whatever is the exact number) individuals to volunteer and then, having selected them, quickly to sort out who is to be cast for what part or, a slightly longer procedure, to give a quick thumbnail description of each character in turn and then ask for somec e to volunteer for each part as it arises. There are unlikely to be very large numbe .s of people volunteering for these parts and yet there will always be sufficie it. Company members involved in the selecting should trust good fortune and intuition, and so avoid risking the possibility of starting some bogus kind of instant audition. Once people are chosen, they should be fully and sincerely supported and protected from any kind of insensitive audience reaction, even when this takes the form of good humored banter which, interestingly enough, it often does.

The rehearsal of these individual parts highlights the advantages of using a radio play like MacNeice's *Christopher Columbus* where there are often many short scenes brilliantly juxtaposed and linked, with a single speech giving clear indications of characterization. The smooth flow of the author's scenes enables an equally smooth flow in production and therefore also in rehearsal. There is never any need to rehearse any one of the characters fully, the script itself giving them so much guidance. The main need is to make each person feel secure regarding his/her moment of entry and exit and the exact place to be for the scene.

To assist this section of rehearsals, the use of lighting is touched on for the first time. Prior to the arrival of the audience the company arranges for the simplest use of available lighting, trying to achieve no more than lighting four or five separate areas on the stage, perhaps with no more than one spotlight per area. As soon as participants see what area is lit for them and their particular scene, they are at once at ease as to where they are to be for their scene. Some may want to go over part of their dialogue, while many will prefer to leave it until the actual run. Although this is often a result of "nerves" because of the presence of the audience, it is remarkable how accurate are most of these self-assessments of personal needs.

The introduction of the use of lighting and moments of sound all help to sustain the interest of the audience during the rehearsals of the few individual parts. Because there is not the time nor the real possibility of these rehearsals having any kind of depth, everything must be done to build and preserve the confidence of the young participants, and the sheer pace of preparation usually helps this, the whole section taking no more than ten to fifteen minutes. The final section of rehearsals concern *processions* and more physically active parts of the play. All of these can be rehearsed by different individuals in the cast with volunteer groups from the audience, the number in each procession depending on the number of volunteers. Quite often, additional people will volunteer a few minutes after the rehearsal of the processions start. These are people who have held back through uncertainty as to what will be expected of them and as to whether the *uncritical framework* will still prevail. As soon as they see that it does, they are anxious to participate, and usually they can be incorporated.

From the moment rehearsal of the processions starts, it is wise to use music strongly, if possible to reduce the houselights to about half, and to make use of the spotlights on the stage area. All these factors will help the "release" of the participants so that they throw themselves whole heartedly into the scene from the outset. There will possibly be overexcitement and perhaps some "messing-about" in the first few minutes. This should be expected and create no alarm among the members of the company. Whoever is in over-all control can, if he or she feels it is necessary, suddenly cut out the music and bring lights back to full. This will bring an immediate cessation of all activity and provide a moment in which to say something to the effect that all is going extremely well, but now there is need for more concentration on making the scene *as real as possible for oneself,* and also making sure that one does not do nor say anything that can affect another person's concentration and activity. Emphasis can be given also to the effect that time is short and does not permit the opportunity to constantly repeat moments of rehearsal. In my own experience, providing such things are said with the fullest generosity of spirit, still within the framework of the initial idea of joining-in the adventure of swiftly creating some moments of theatre (all of which is quite different from a "teacher" simply trying to get "control") then the response of 99% of young people is immediately constructive. But the initial "explosion" must be expected and seen to be part of a necessary release. The use of lights and music (of course, remembering that the houselights must be brought in for the script-in-hand participation scenes involving the whole audience), the total simplicity of the whole approach, the fully rehearsed and polished work of the company members, and the intuitive trust in all other participants, invariably leads to a "performance" that is surprisingly polished. And because no more than about one quarter of the play has actually been seen in rehearsal, there is freshness and spontaneity of experience throughout, with many very moving moments of polished theatre.

Numbers of actors, teachers and others connected with theatre have been intrigued by this approach to participatory theatre for teen-agers. They have been particularly interested in the pace of rehearsal, the wholly uncritical and fully encouraging atmosphere, and full trust that "all will be well." And the young people themselves? Personally I have always refused to take part in, let alone instigate, any kind of *post mortem* discussion after an experience of theatre. Such a theatre experience is emotional and spiritual as well as of the mind, and to reduce it to mere intellectual quibbling at its worst, or at best, skating across the surface of facile curiosity, seems to me to diminish if not wholly denigrate some of the main functions of art. If I am "moved" by an experience of theatre, movies, concert performance or even a poetry reading, I do not wish to discuss with the performers, nor do I want them to cross-examine my reactions. I usually would prefer to be alone and quiet, at least for a little while. I have evidence enough to believe that many young people share this view and are glad to be released from the necessity to make "intelligent comments," so that, even with new experiments that can be glorified with the title "research" I adamantly refuse all forms of *post mortem*. I do not believe this has precluded me from obtaining information as to how young people feel about the kind of experience they have during this type of participatory theatre. The atmosphere of the occasion itself has usually made quite clear that there has been some kind of "experience," certainly commensurate with the limited amount of time and commitment asked of them. A few have let me know that they "think" the whole thing was "bullshit." A few have let me know that they "feel" the whole experience was "fantastic." The majority remain anonymously between these extremes. No amount of conscious analysizing through questionnaires, etc. are going to inform me of anything to do with the depth of individual experience nor, which is perhaps more important, is such "research" going to influence whether or not I personally continue such experiments or encourage others to do likewise. Intuitively one knows and should trust whether or not such experiments work and react accordingly, just as one discovers a great deal about one's approach from each attempt. For example, I know from direct experience, that as soon as the approach to rehearsal of such a program of participatory theatre with teen-agers slips from the intuitive-emotional to the wholly intellectual, then it tends to have all the boring qualities of the audio-visual aid approach to teaching, when the audio-visual aspect is used only as an intellectual re-enforcement rather than a stimulus to the feelings. I do not believe in theatre used as a new kind of audio-visual aid to teaching. I would not attempt the above program merely as an "illustration" of history or geography teaching concerned with Christopher Columbus. I will not do Shakespeare programs simply to help the English department to thrust past the edges of boredom of academic study of a great playwright in order to help examination successes. If Columbus proves successful for history study and Shakespeare programs add glory to examination successes, then they are fortuitous bonuses. I cannot accept the potential of a fortuitous bonus as a *raison d'etre* of a theatre experience and intuitively young people know precisely what is the basic intention, and react accordingly.

Many "art forms" are today stifled by a specialization that "turns-off" the uninitiated, leading them to feel that only certain "select" people can be involved. Activites that should belong to the majority thus become precious esoteric playthings of a proud and often not too easily approachable minority. The world of Children's Theatre has regrettably not escaped this fate, and people like me are as guilty as any for bringing about an air of "overspecialization." Of course, there must be certain degrees of specialization in almost every field in order for indepth experiments to be tried out and new discoveries constantly made. But once uncovered, such discoveries, or a large part of them, should become part of the general coinage, available for other, nonspecialist practioners to make use of and benefit from. Otherwise stagnation is inevitable.

The sadness of this vicious circle where Children's Theatre is concerned is that the victims are ultimately children and young people. If it were possible to discover how many children regularly see theatre, let alone theatre that has been thought out on their behalf, we should probably be amazed by the small proportion. Maybe it does not matter. Maybe a large diet of television and movies is sufficient for them. Maybe theatre must be reduced to an educational tool rather than an experience of wonder and joy and the opening of new experiences for heart and mind. I do not happen to believe in all those "maybes" as our only alternative. But if more children and young people are to see more theatre more regularly, including that particular kind of theatre that is the concern of this book, namely participatory theatre, then it will take the combined interests of many involved in theatre, either professionally or as a hobby, to begin to supply that need.

Many people who might be interested in participatory theatre have heard on the "grape-vine" that it is a highly specialized, rather "artsy-craftsy" activity that could not possibly take place in "their theatre," because they have a stage with a proscenium arch and fixed seating, and because the actors have not been "trained" in the "proper manner." Of course we must not be foolish and rush to an extreme which discountenances the idea that genuine thought must be behind participatory theatre. That is basically one of the troubles with a great deal of the trash already served up in the name of Children's Theatre, whether or not it contains any participation. An attitude of "anything goes with kids" is degrading not only for the youngsters but for the actors and for theatre as a whole. Money and taste have a great deal to do with the perpetuation of this kind of rubbishy theatre. Principals who pull in companies on an entirely commercial basis, taking the cheapest with total disregard not only of standard, but even of fundamental respect for children, bear as much responsibility as other potential "employers" of children's theatre who think that as long as their children are rolling around the aisles in hysterical and uncontrollable fits of laughter, then the play and performers that encourage this must be more successful than one in which the youngsters might spend minutes at a time in deep, silent absorption and thought. And possibly both are superceded by a company that can increase or reinforce the body of intellectual and academic knowledge, no matter how totally bored the youngsters might be.

If we are going to attempt participatory theatre, then there are many detailed approaches that need to be given a great deal of thought. The approaches that have been described in this section include the work of many groups of actors in several different countries who had *never* before been involved in participatory theatre. Once having become involved, however, having made their commitment, even on a temporary basis, they were all prepared to look *seriously* at what they had taken on, and to discover something of the specific disciplines that were necessary for a specific kind of work. It is hoped that other nonspecialist groups may find some similar help from this section of the book. And maybe they will find that subsequent sections offer a little help in addition.

MacNeice's *Christopher Columbus* was used for older secondary students as an exciting vehicle of *creative theatre*. For younger secondary students the same theme: that of Columbus, was used as an exciting vehicle of *creative drama* in its own right. The essential difference from the MacNeice was that there was no scripted *participation* and yet there was opportunity for involvement by quite large numbers of volunteers in an entirely *improvised manner.* The approach to both plays was towards the swift building or making of a play together, with company members taking not only "leading" roles in the sense of larger parts, but "guiding" roles in the sense that they were concerned with stimulating improvised participation and, at the same time, were ready to guide and control it within the over-all story intention of the play

This was a tremendous challenge to the improvisation capacity of the actors, particularly in the early stages of stimulation.

The improvised approach can still contain as many moments of a really full theatre experience as is possible with the more controlled area of the scripted and more rehearsed participation. Total absorption and sincerity — sensitivity between the actors so that they know fairly clearly what is in each other's mind — sensitivity to the youngsters, including an awareness of the difference of each group, so the actors do not try to impose the detail of one group on to another (always a temptation, especially when something has gone very well) — confidence in improvisation — readiness to encourage the less confident youngsters, and equal readiness to cope with the exhibitionists without squashing them — discipline and control so that we hold to the framework of the play which is essential since this is not a drama lesson but a form of theatre with an audience. These are some the things that must be mastered.

4

Approaches To Open Staging

T he extension and development of audience participation beyond the
examples quoted in the previous chapters are dependent on the use of some
form of open staging. The open stage is now so accepted that there is a generation of theatre goers and actors who are amazed to know that the basic idea
was ever in contention. Some, indeed, go so far as to express surprise that the
proscenium stage is still widely used and accepted. The main difficulty that
worries many people when first confronted with the idea of the open stage is
that it implies a form of theatre that must have the audience *all around* the acting area. This is not so. There are many alternatives in Children's Theatre as
in adult theatre. The governing factor is the appropriateness to each particular
play. Thus, in adult theatre, I personally feel the need for a very intimate circle
if I am producing a delicate play such as, for example, Jean Jacque Bernard's
Martine, but I should hope for a very large area for a program called "Great
Battles of History." and I should be glad, probably, to have a three-sided
stage for some of Shakespeare's plays. The style of play dictates its own shape
and requirements, if (as is seldom likely) one has total control over exactly
what shape and size of space one requires at any given time. So, too, Children's
Theatre dictates its appropriate style and shape, with *many possible variables.*
   The fundamental differences between open stage and proscenium theatre
is that of intimacy of contact between the actors and the audience. All forms of
proscenium theatre contain some kind of "gap" between actor and audience
even if, by such devices as a protruding forestage, some of the play takes place
outside of the actual proscenium arch. The essential difference is that the actors are in one room and the audience in another. Quite the opposite happens in
any shape or size of open stage theatre. The actors and audience share
together the same physical and psychological space, thus creating an entirely
different relationship of intimacy. Development from the proscenium to the
open stage need not be abrupt. It can be a gradual process, dependent on and

65

in keeping with the readiness of each group of actors. Even the use of aisles (already suggested) will begin to open up the possibilities, despite the fact those suggestions are based on fixed seating arrangements. But these simplest of possibilities begin to grow if we are fortunate enough to be in an auditorium with *flexible* seating, i.e. seats that are not screwed down to the floor, thus making it possible for us to arrange them according to our needs. For Children's Theatre, such flexibility immensely increases the potential for audience participation.

For theatre for any audience, this flexibility can help with further steps towards the discovery and use of the open stage without going to the extent of having the audience all around the acting area, and the extended use of aisles can also be particularly helpful for groups working on small and cramped stages, with very little wing space, especially in plays that contain many characters and possibly even some crowd scenes. Just *widening* one central aisle can solve many of these problems, as well as being the first step towards more open stage theatre, as the following two examples will illustrate.

One group was producing Shakespeare's *Midsummer Night's Dream* and using a large cast by having a number of fairy attendants to Titania and an equal number of "imps and sprites" in attendance on Oberon. They were working on a small and cramped stage in a quite large auditorium, with flexible seating. Titania's first entrance, accompanied by about twenty attendants, took the form of a dance, using Mendelssohn's music, and because at the time the stage was otherwise empty, it was possible for the movement to be comparatively full and free. Immediately after the dance was completed all the fairies settled into a still group and Oberon and his people arrived; but there was very little space for them to move in, and by the time they, too, were placed, the entire stage was literally crammed with people, shoulder to shoulder, and with Titania and Oberon downstage in front of them all. There followed an anxious hiatus, when we all feared that someone was "off," but all was well. It was simply that Puck was having considerable difficulty in getting through. There was then a passage of dialogue between Titania, Oberon and Puck, leading eventually to a general exit, which was again intended to take a dance form, using music. This, however, was quite impossible because of space. For what seemed an agony of minutes, there was a line-up of dancers on either side of the stage, all marking time to the music, waiting for space to get off.

Because the auditorium floor was flat and the seats were not fixed to the floor, consideration was consequently given to the idea of widening the center aisle, and also making a wide flight of steps connecting the stage and the floor. There was a central door at the back of the auditorium and, with the use of this, Titania and her attendants were now able to flood into the wide aisle, with ample space to dance, and then eventually to move up the steps to form their final still group, using part of the stage and one side of the steps. And Oberon and his people also had the whole wide space of the aisle for their movement entrance, before moving up to use another part of the stage and steps. Titania and Oberon's dialogue took place halfway up the steps, and was thus comparatively closer to a large section of the audience, and even "in the same room" with those not so close, and Puck was able to make his entrance with tremendous speed and excitement straight up the center of the auditorium. The final exit at the end of the scene included an exciting use of stage and auditorium with everyone having ample space to dance, and then to leave the acting area without any embarrassing line-up and waiting. As a result of these experiments, actual performance included the turning of the seats slightly in owards the aisle, which also included a rostrum block so that actors in the aile were raised on a higher level. This was also used in the Pyramus and Thisbe cene, when the Duke and some of his courtiers were able to become part of the ver-all audience to Bottom and the players. Again the aisle afforded excellent pportunities for courtly processions. *(See diagram I for seating arrangements or the* Dream.)

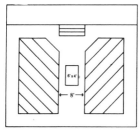

Diagram Number 1

A wider than usual center aisle (possible only with flexible seating) provides the "fairies and imps" in A Midsummer Night's Dream *space in which to move and dance before ascending the center steps to the stage area. A 6' x 4' rostrum block in the center of the aisle brings Titania and Oberon close to the audience for their dialog. This partial use of the aisle is helped by turning the seats a little toward the aisle.*

In case it should be felt that period plays, and Shakespeare in particular, end themselves most easily to the open stage, the second example concerns a nodern thriller. The production facilities included an inadequate stage and an uditorium with a flat floor, together with flexible seating possibilities. The pening of the play was very simple, with the potential for suspense, mystery nd excitement. Into a darkened room enters a man, *via* the window. Using his wn torch or flashlight, the man looks around the room, discovers a desk and tarts to go through the drawers. He hears a sound from offstage and quickly xits through the window. As he does so another man runs on from a doorway t the side of the stage. He sees the open window upstage, rushes to it and ires a revolver. There is a scream and the sound of a fall. The man rushes offtage and we hear many voices and footsteps. Eventually the body of the first nan is brought back into the room by two policemen and laid on the floor. Then lights are lit in the room.

When it was pointed out to them, the group was fascinated to realize how nuch of the scene had in fact happened offstage. Indeed, only the moment of he attempted burglary, the escape, the shooting, and then the return of the orpse had been shared at all with the audience and these moments were eparated by others of complete hiatus. So, as with *"The Dream"* described bove, we widened the central aisle in order to provide space for a street scene, nd we also adjusted fractionally the layout of the room on the stage: the main hange was to have an imaginary window center downstage, with a few steps o give easy access from auditorium level to stage level, creating opportunities or action which would include miming the forcing open of the window in order o climb into the room.

To help build up a street scene, we then developed in the widened aisle a equence of improvisations concerned with the mood and atmosphere of a larkened street at night, giving the cast an opportunity to discover and get he feeling of the open stage. Then, with careful selection from the many improvisations, we slowly built the new possibilities of the opening scene. The "villain," on his own, walks down the street, from the back of the auditorium. While appearing to be casual, there is something obviously suspicious about im, which is confirmed by his reactions the moment he hears the footsteps of, nd then sees, other people — first a "loving couple" strolling in the night;

then a couple of drunks lugubriously making their way home; then a policeman on his beat; then a sad, old, down-and-out tramp with nowhere to go, and so on. With each set of footsteps and arrival, the first man melts into the shadows until the person or persons have gone past. At last, certain he is alone, he goes to the downstage imaginary window, prises it open, climbs into the room, and, using his flashlight, starts to search. Now, as in the original version, he discovers the desk and goes through the drawers. Again he hears the footsteps offstage, but now he runs back to the window at the edge of the stage. As he climbs out and begins to run down the street (the aisle of the auditorium), so the second man enters from the door onstage, runs to the window, sees the retreating person, fires his revolver, and, in the middle of the auditorium, the man who has been shot stops, twists, turns and then falls. At once, the whole "street" becomes alive with people who have heard the shot and run in to find out what has happened; among those who return are the policeman whom we saw on his beat and another policeman. Together they disperse the rest of the people, and, under the supervision of the person who did the shooting, carry the body back into the house.

For actors and audience alike, the scene was electrifying because nearly every moment of the action had been shared. Practically none of it had happened offstage. Arising from this kind of experience, many people discover the uses and values of *Avenue Arena*.

AVENUE ARENA.

One of the values of avenue arena PLUS proscenium stage is that the first tentative steps can be taken into the use of the auditorium, with many scenes still taking place on the proscenium stage.

With a specific Children's Theatre production for secondary schools, something very similar to this process actually led into the eventual use of theatre in the round, while basically still maintaining the advantages of the avenue arena. The play was an adaptation of **Oliver Twist**. The stage was used only as Fagin's den, and the other end of the avenue (with an arrangement of rostrum blocks) was used as Mr. Brownlow's residence. This left the rest of the avenue space for street scenes, the trial scene, the scene at the bookstore, etc. Rostrum blocks, again, gave focus to these centrally used scenes, and the floor space around the blocks and from the blocks at the far end to Fagin's den on the stage lent themselves to the simple factor of "journey," an important factor in Children's Theatre. When the Artful Dodger first meets Oliver in the street, it is again in the auditorium. When Dodger persuades Oliver to go with him to Fagin's den, they have a simple journey around the floorspace blocks until they arrive at the stage end, already established as Fagin's den. In this manner, a simple flow and continuity of scenes is possible with each journey usually becoming a strong emotional part of the progression of the story itself through the use of music for mood and atmosphere. In this manner, 27 scenes followed one upon another with no break in the action, which could not have been possible on a proscenium stage with changes of setting and scenery. The actual venue of each scene in the open arena is made clear either because a character has said to another where it is he's going to, or else comments on it when he arrives.

Then a strange series of accidental discoveries took place in a short space of time. For several performances, some of the audience arrived after the play had started. Their means of access to the auditorium was through two side doors at the end opposite the stage, the same two doors that were being used by the actors for all entrances from the rear. Between the two doors was an expanse of wall space, roughly the width of the avenue itself. To accommodate the latecomers, a row of chairs was placed in front of this wall, with sufficient space behind them for the actors to cross from one side to the other; subsequently a second and third row of chairs were added, so that the action was now taking place in a *three-sided* avenue arena, with only a little discomfort for the actors, but surprising delight for these new members of the audience. At the time, most of these audiences were in five or six rows on either side of the avenue arena, and because there was no form of bleacher seating, there was natural concern about the viewing possibilties for the back two rows on each side. The decision to use a third side for audience meant that the back row from each side could now be moved to the end of the arena. Shortly afterwards, it was decided to experiment with moving "Fagin's den" from the stage itself to a build-up of rostrum blocks immediately in front of the stage, thus freeing the stage for accommodating even more of the audience. Now, there was audience on *all four sides* of the "avenue" and the original five or six rows were cut down to only three or four. We had, almost by accident, moved into "theatre in the round."

The actors were initially worried about having some of the audience always behind them, but we were interested to find that this never seemed of concern to the people in the audience. Our inquiries always met with the same kind of response. No one ever complained, but invariably someone would express their relief that they had sat on, say, side A as they were quite sure their position had many advantages over sides B, C or D. Immediately, another person would express similar pleasure that they had sat on, say, side C as they were certain this had many advantages over sides A, B, and D and so on. Meanwhile all of the actors felt a great artistic enjoyment through now being completely in the same physical and psychological space with the audience.

At a subsequent production of **Oliver Twist**, the same kind of seating plan was followed, and ultimately for a great deal of Secondary Children's Theatre work the ideal shape was found to be a rectangular area, usually 20 feet long by 15 feet wide, with the audience on all four sides, and gangways or aisles at each corner for exits and entrances.

The four diagrams on the next page clarify the possibilities:
    Diagram 2 - Avenue plus stage;
    Diagram 3 - Avenue, with stage for audience;
    Diagram 4 - Avenue across width of hall;
    Diagram 5 - Rectangular 20'x15'.

It will be noted from diagram 4, that where a hall or auditorium is square or nearly square, there can be a great advantage in setting-up the avenue parallel with the stage itself, thus enabling an excellent audience seating area in front of and on the stage. Where bleacher seating is available in narrow auditoriums, this arrangement can also be very useful. Where no more than 2 rows of seating on either long side, with the acting area in the center, six or seven rows can be built with bleachers at the end opposite the stage and three rows on floor level in front of the stage and three on the stage itself. Again one or two additional rows may be added on the stage if other bleachers are available.

Full Mixture of Picture Frame Staging and Arena

Many groups become interested in using both the proscenium stage — thus giving every opportunity to the designer for creating visually exciting

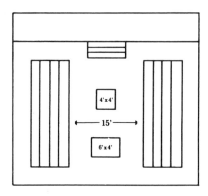

Diagram Number 2

In addition to the stage, the center aisle can be widened into a main acting area. This is avenue arena. Various arrangements of rostrum blocks can be used in the avenue: to raise the actors if needed, to provide places for them to sit, to journey over, around or between. The action is where the actors say it is. For example, "This is the forest of Arden."

Diagram Number 3

The avenue arena is a step towards theatre-in-the-round. By putting some of the audience on the stage, we go a step further. The audience now is on three sides.

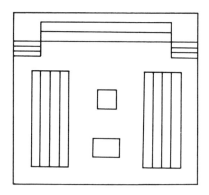

Diagram Number 4

The same system works well when the stage is on the long side of the hall rather than at the end. Part of the audience can sit on the stage. Others sit on the main floor level just in front of the stage with perhaps an aisle between the stage and the audience for use by the actors.

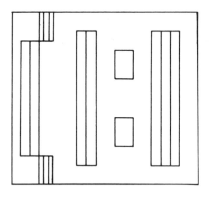

Diagram Number 5

This is the stage plus an extended area 20' x 15', rather like an Elizabethan stage. Both stage and extension can be used and the extension does not have to be the same height as the stage. It can be half the height or even at ground level, providing there are stairs of some kind for easy access. The audience sits on three sides of the acting area.

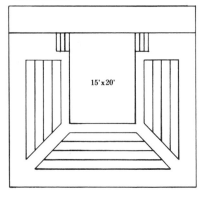

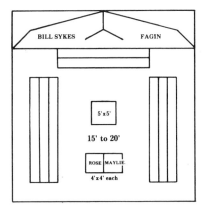

Diagram Number 6

In one production of **Oliver Twist,** *the stage itself was divided in half with separate lighting for each. One half was Bill Sykes' house, the other Fagin's. Both had detailed, realistic sets. At the far end of the avenue, Rose Maylie's house was on rostrum blocks with a little filigree trellis decoration. The central block represented many different locations — the bookshop, a hill, part of the courtroom, etc. The two "styles" of theatre were wholly acceptable and satisfied many different interests.*

Diagram Number 7

The half-arena, with backing curtains, rostrum blocks and aisles behind and through the audience. For actors whose previous experience has been only of the proscenium stage, this often is the best "first step" to take towards the Open Stage.

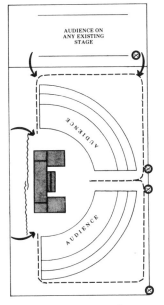

Diagram Number 8

The half-arena can be developed into a horseshoe shape.

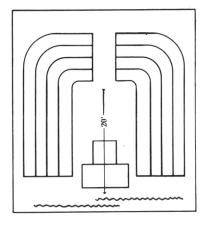

Diagram Number 9

The half-arena can also be flattened. The length and width of the hall, together with the needs of the play, are the deciding factors on final shape. The backing curtain is not essential, but is useful for entrances and exits and as a "tiring" house.

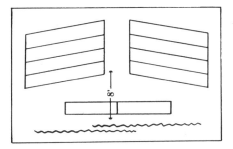

sets, and the avenue arena, thus giving the actors more space and, at least in some scenes, closer, more intimate contact with the audience. An excellent example of this again concerns a production of **Oliver Twist**, for which it was decided to use both stage and avenue arena, with the audience on bleachers five rows deep on either side. The stage was divided into two: one half was Fagin's den, the other half was Bill Syke's home. For these two "halves" of the stage, elaborate sets were designed and made, with all the full realism of a pro-scenium production. Each side could be lit quite independently of the other. At the farthest end of the auditorium opposite the stage, a combination of different levels of rostrum blocks was built for Rose Maylie's home and this included a very delicate use of "filigree" structures as setting. The rest of the floor space contained carefully thought-out uses of rostrum blocks *(See Diagram 6)*. This proved an excellent example of really genuine "compromise" in serving the different interests of set designers, actors and director.

Before leaving the basic idea of avenue arena to consider other forms of open staging, there are three particular problems that need to be mentioned:

1. Depending on the length of the hall, there is still the possibility in avenue arena of audience seated at the far end of the auditorium feeling rather cut-off from any long scenes on the stage area.
2. The actors need to be well aware of the extreme changes of "feeling" of the audience when they are moving from proscenium to open stage scenes and back again.
3. There is also a purely "box-office" problem that must always be foreseen. Obviously fewer seats can be set out if a large part of the auditorium is being used as the acting area. This can only be solved by very careful planning and budgeting, so that the price of seats and the number of performances are adjusted relatively.

HALF-ARENA

Possibly the most useful and least problematic form of open stage for groups new to the experience is that of the half-arena, which combines several immediate advantages:

1. For those having their first experience in open stage theatre it brings the actors immediately into the same room as the audience.
2. For actors who are diffident about being *surrounded* by the audience, it provides an area behind them where there is no audience.
3. For directors who wish to retain a certain amount of detail in the way of setting, it provides ample opportunity. It is therefore accommodating both to scenery and to total simplicity.
4. It is most useful for many kinds of children's theatre work and in particular it enables very close contact for audience participation.
5. Depending on the numbers in the audience, some form of bleacher seating can be used for the back rows.
6. The shape itself can be deepened into more of a horseshoe shape, or it can be flattened. *(See Diagrams 7 (half-arena), 8 (horseshoe), 9 (flattened).*

In a half-arena production, it is possible to use a backing curtain along with many rostrum blocks.

The backing curtain has many uses:

- it makes available three entrances to the acting area — one at either end and one through the center of the curtain;
- it covers a useful quick-change area;
- it means that the dressing room does not necessarily have to be im-

mediately behind the acting area;

- a light blue color gives the effect of a "sky-cloth," even in performances in daylight; this color also heightens the colors of the costumes (except, sadly, those which themselves are blue, a most important color in plays for younger children);
- for productions which might tour different school halls, the curtain covers-up the many pictures, trophies, rolls of honour, busts of famous people and so on, which often line the walls.

The development from the half-arena to playing fully in the round, an almost inevitable step once the half-arena has been experienced a few times, need not be a sudden and traumatic happening, but can take place gradually. One possible approach is to reduce the size of the backing curtain and the number of rostrum blocks in front of it. Eventually the playing area then becomes a deepened horseshoe shape, and the backing curtain really no more than a dressing room behind a very wide aisle. By these means one slowly moves to being very nearly in the round.

THEATRE IN THE ROUND

I doubt if there are any absolutes in theatre. There are fashions, personal interests, enthusiasms, joys and prejudices. I am prepared to postulate, however, that *some form of Open Stage Theatre is the most APPROPRIATE form of theatre for audiences of children and young people, especially if audience participation is involved.* This does not mean, as I have clearly demonstrated, that I am "against" proscenium or picture-frame theatre, particularly if it is the only form available, nor does it mean that, because I am so sure open stage is right, this implies always theatre in the round. On the contrary, as I have tried to suggest above, there are other shapes which may well be more appropriate to specific considerations. There is no doubt that for many actors and directors, as well as audiences, theatre in the round is a kind of ultimate in terms of intimacy of shared theatre exerience. But theatre in the round can itself be several different shapes, including the complete circle, the square, the rectangle and the oval. *(See Diagrams 10 (round), 11 (square), 12 (rectangle) and 13 (oval).* Whichever shape we choose, the advantage remains that whenever the audience fully surrounds the acting area, then everyone is placed closer to the action. For example, if there are 200 in the audience in the *half-arena* shape, then there are likely to be 6 or 7 rows of audience, depending on the size of the half circle. But if we complete the circle, then we halve the number of rows to 3 or at the most 4, all round the action. Thus:

Diagram 14: the half-arena shape with 7 rows of audience;
Diagram 15: the complete in the round with 4 rows of audience.

As I have mentioned before, it is possible that in the long run the nature of the play can govern the final decision as to what open stage shape one uses.

EXITS AND ENTRANCES

A question most frequently asked by actors during rehearsals of an open stage Children's Theatre play is: "When exactly is the moment, the point of my entrance? Is it when I come into the auditorium itself, or is it when I am at the outside far point of the aisle, or is it when I emerge from the aisle into the actual acting area?" Again it is not possible to make any rule of thumb generalization. However, in "Start From Where You Are, Chapter Two," the suggestion is made that even with fixed seating proscenium theatre, it is wise to think of the whole theatre, auditorium as well as the stage, as the acting

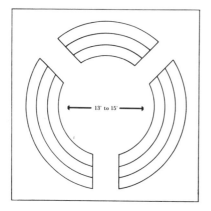

Diagram Number 10

In-the-round is literally a complete circle, which, according to the needs of the play, may have one, two, three or four aisles leading into the acting area. 13' to 15' is about the ideal size for primary youngsters. The actual dimensions depend upon the size of the audience. For 200, 15' is best. Whereas for only 80, 13' 6" or 13' would be better. For the use of the actors there are also aisles behind the audience.

Diagram Number 11

In-the-round does not mean the acting area must be a circle. A square is just as useful and may have aisles at each of the four corners, as well as behind the audience.

Diagram Number 12

The rectangular arena was found by Theatre Centre to be ideal for most Secondary School halls. An aisle at each corner and behind the audience facilitates entrances and exits to and from all parts of the hall. In the photos on pp. 166 this shape is seen, including the use of rostrum blocks.

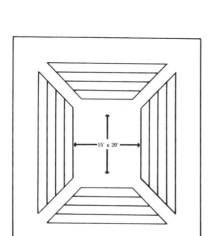

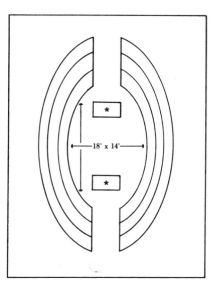

Diagram Number 13

The oval shape is also useful, particularly if there is much journeying in the play. Example, **On Trial.**

Diagram Number 14

In the full circle, the same audience will need only 3 or 4 rows, so that everyone in the audience is closer to the action.

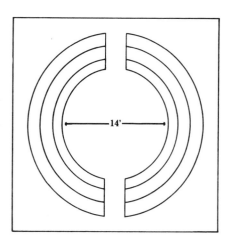

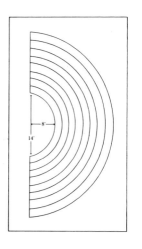

Diagram Number 15

In the half-arena or semi-circle, an audience of approximately 150 will need 7 or 8 rows.

area, particularly in plays for youngsters up to the age of about 11. This thought applies just as much to plays in the open stage, particularly if there is any kind of journey involving the space behind the audience. In these terms it is necessary for the actor to be fully in character from the moment he enters any door into the auditorium. In other words, we cannot look on the use of aisles as though they were the offstage wingspace of a picture-frame stage. There are some exceptions to this, but it is better to meet the exceptions individually from the firm basis of the thought: "If I'm visible to any part of the audience, then I need to be in character." This is even more true for exits, particularly for very young children, who watch the departing character until he is right out of sight and even then remain in thought and wonder about where he has gone, what he is doing and so on, depending on the nature of the story. This necessitates any other actors left on stage *suspending* the action until those seconds after the full exit are completed — a basically different feeling of timing from adult proscenium theatre, where more often than not the action goes straight on, hard on the heels of an exit. This point underlines the fact that the actor's preparation and rehearsal for Children's Theatre includes the need to suspend some of the techniques, attitudes, etc., that are used in adult theatre.

The basic practical problem of exits and entrances can be put as simply as "How do the actors get from the dressing room area to the stage area?" For a touring company, going from one school to another, possibly playing in a different environment every morning and afternoon, this can present some problems, which obviously diminish for more permanent theatres. Part of a touring company's limbering procedure needs to include the actors' meeting together to settle quite clearly all problems to do with entrances and exits and other uses that may be made of aisles. Let us look back at the diagrams of the various shapes that have already been considered, only this time to study the aisles as well as the basic playing area, and then to relate these aisles to actual exits and entrances in relation to where the dressing room might be.

As has already been considered, the adaptation of the use of the picture frame stage by incorporating aisles from the back of the auditorium for processions, etc., would appear to be comparatively easy. It is not always so, however, as so much depends on access from back stage to front of house. In a production of **Pinocchio** at one theatre, many entrances, including the very opening of the play, started from the back of the auditorium, and the only way to reach this area was to go out of the stagedoor and down a side street, in the open — in a very cold and snowy January!!! To their eternal glory, the actors did so willingly, wrapped-up in topcoats and blankets, and huddled under umbrellas. For the same play, at a civic theatre, where the theatre itself was two floors up from ground level, the actors had to go one floor down, cross underneath the auditorium and then climb back up another flight of stairs to the back of the auditorium — and on one occasion, one of the many doors they had to go through on the lower floor had been locked by a zealous janitor! This is the kind of problem that could well arise with the idea of Puck entering from the back of the auditorium (see p 66), or with the street scene opening to the house burglary (see p 67). Sometimes the problem is insuperable, and then the actors have to get from one end of the auditorium to the other by crossing behind one long side, using a space that must then be left between the audience and the wall. (*See diagram 12 on p. 74*).

This is one of the occasions when being in character is not only *not* necessary, but can be a positive distraction. Actors are often amazed that such a move can be fully accomplished in what might be called "neutral gear," and the young audience take no notice of them. Sometimes this procedure is helped (in terms of the actors' comfort) by covering their costume with a cloak or a rug, or even by leaving off and carrying some simple part of their costume, for example a hat. The timing of such a move behind the audience is of course all important, for to move swiftly through a very quiet scene can obviously be a distraction, as can the "over-doing" of trying to be secret and unnoticed. A simple quiet walk, with one's back slightly turned in the direction of the audience, usually suffices. Of course, if lighting is being used in the play, and the area behind the audience is in shadow, this helps tremendously, but the procedure can be accomplished equally well in daylight.

For work with younger children we need to think also of further uses of the aisles, particularly that of the journey, which is so integral a part of the youngsters' own play and therefore a great enrichment to theatre experience. The journey may be literally as simple as one character going to another's home to visit them. While there is no change of setting involved, there is full acceptance of the new place they are in, providing *they physically go there*, perhaps going down one aisle, around the space behind the audience, and back into the acting area via another aisle. At the other extreme, the journey may literally be the basis of the whole play, as for example in **On Trial**, when a large number of people from a community journey to find an herb which might prevent the growth of an epidemic. Each journey starts from inside the acting area, say, in an oval arena shape, goes round the aisle behind one half of the audience and back into the acting area. The next stage of the journey can then be behind the other half of the audience. There is total acceptance by the audience of the change in the geography of both the aisle areas and the main acting area, according to what the characters in the play state that change to be.

One other important aspect of the journey for younger children is "the chase" already considered in some detail for theatres with fixed seating and conventional stages. As in those circumstances, so, too in the open stage; all aisles can be utilized in chases. The sincerity of the actors is all important at such moments, as is a very strong sensitivity to natural delight and excitement going too far and becoming hysteria.

The position of the dressing room in relation to the acting area and entrances into that area is all important. One of the advantages of open staging, however, is the ease with which the acting area can be adjusted to suit various environmental circumstances. For example, in a production on tour of **The Mirrorman**, performed in an oval area, the selection of the acting area could almost always be placed exactly in order for one of the entrances to be directly opposite the dressing room, rather than up and down the length of the auditorium. Sometimes this meant the oval, in fact, went across the diagonal. The relationship of dressing room to acting area and entrances must also take into account the need for space behind at least one side of the audience, both if possible, particularly if journeys are involved.

Not all journeys have to use the aisles behind the audience, but can take place inside the acting area. For example, in **The Hat**, Peter is delivering a hat-box to Mr. Hump, the Man of Magic, who lives in the House on the Hill. Peter sets off on his journey with his *imaginary* dog, Fizz, who has already been clearly established for the audience. To have Peter go on his journey *behind* the audience would mean that Fizz would disappear from view altogether. So the journey takes place within the acting area, making use of simple rostrum blocks by going over and around them. Peter starts from one point and ends up at almost the same point on the floor, but is clearly now in a quite different place because he has journeyed there. *(See Diagram 16.)* He also improvises dialogue during the journey, thus enabling the audience to imagine exactly where he is at every stage.

Diagram Number 16

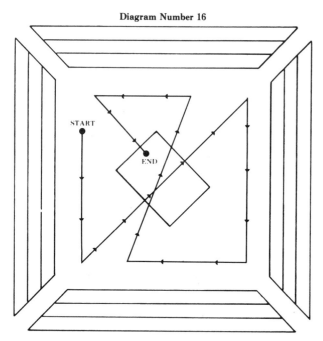

Many journeys can take place in the aisles and behind the audience. Sometimes, however, they are more appropriate when kept inside *the acting area, as for example, this journey in* **The Hat***. If the journey took place behind the audience, then Peter's "imaginary" dog Fizz, would disappear from sight. By staying within the area, the whole journey is shared by everyone. The central area is a 5' by 4' rostrum block, within an acting area that is 14' square with an aisle at each corner. Peter and Fizz journey from their home to Mr. Hump's house at the "top of the hill." The journey takes roughly a figure 8 shape and ends almost where it started (as in much of children's own play). Peter can improvise dialogue about each stage of the journey.*

SEATING THE AUDIENCE

Further mention of the problem of seating the audience will be made in the section on audience participation. Basically, however, for theatre in the open stage, it seems wisest to think of seating all ages up to about 11 years *on the floor* rather than on chairs or benches, and this is particularly important if, as has been explained, parts of the play include the use of aisles behind the audience. For secondary young people, such journeys are less likely to happen and therefore not only chairs but bleacher seating can be most valuable. There is also the important point of human dignity to be considered, as from about age 11 onwards, there is something about sitting on the floor that young people feel to be quite undignified. So, with the open stage we make our own physical arrangements of form and shape according to the needs of the play, adapting as far as possible the existing facilities of the environment to accommodate our needs.

Victoria Theatre, Stoke-On-Trent, England. **Sleeping Beauty, Puss in Boots** and **The Christmas Carol** *commissioned by Peter Cheeseman for Victoria Theatre). The theatre is a converted movie house, almost the ideal shape for some Children's Theatre. It seats approximately 400 on raised seating, with entrances at all four corners plus two central entrance areas, one down the steps (left) and one under the seating (right). The sound and lighting control panel is at top left. Although the three commissioned plays were originally written for this theatre in the round, they have been performed many times on proscenium stages. The only problem with this type of theatre is that the raised seating makes it impossible to use the aisles behind the audience as the actors would be out of sight.* (Photo: Ian Stone)

A rescue (by swimming) using the aisle between and behind the audience for a journey. The youngsters nearest the action lean away from it. But, without losing absorption or sincerity, the actor is ready to dodge outstretched limbs that may be in the way of his progress. The audience adds sounds of the wind and waves to help. Note: This production was in the half-arena with rostrum blocks permanently set in front of a backing curtain.

5

Audience Participation

Controlled Age Groups and Audience Size

Just as working in the open stage will add enrichment to Children's Theatre, particularly when some form of audience participation is involved, so too will the breaking down of age groups and the controlling of size of audience. The paradox arises that there need be *no minimum* size of audience, but we need always to consider a possible maximum. For professional Children's Theatre this at once creates economic problems, for, whereas the right size of audience in terms of quality of experience might be proven to be, say, 200, the break-even figure in terms of economics might be, say, 300. Something has to give, some compromise be made, and unless there are available subsidies or grants, invariably a rationale is found to justify inceases in size of audience. Until a more serious view is taken of the potential of Children's Theatre work, this situation is unlikely to change. Meanwhile, I believe it is necessary to consider the ideal, with the full knowledge that few of us will ever be able to carry out totally ideal approaches.

Are there such things as "an ideal size of audience" and "an ideal size of playing area for theatre in the round" (i.e. the audience surrounding the playing area, though not necessarily in a circle.)? At risk of being too pedantic, and bearing in mind the important factors of age group and kind of audience participation, I believe there are. The belief is based, not only on observation of thousands of performances, but also on *experience* as an actor in hundreds of performances. This latter is an important point when participation is used, for it is the actor who is responsible for both stimulating and controlling that participation, and no amount of theorizing or outside observation can equate with actual practical experience. Directors of participatory theatre who have not themselves been involved as actors often miss this factor. Administrators as well are often wholly unable to understand what difference a mere twenty or thirty in the audience can make. But teachers who are accustomed to a class size of, say 20 youngsters, very quickly feel the difference if that number goes up to, say 27 or 28. Double the twenty to forty, and the teacher feels confronted with an almost impossible situation. So, I would suggest the following:

For the age group 5 to 8 (or 9) years, seated on the floor around a circular playing area of diameter 12'6" to 14'6", the best audience size would be from 80 to 140, with the ideal about 110 around a playing area of diameter 13'6".

For the age group 10 (or 9) years up to 12 years, seated on the floor around a circular playing area of similar dimensions, the best size would be from 100 to 160, with the ideal about 130, around a playing area of diameter 14'.

When the numbers are at the lower end of the scale, then the diameter of the playing area needs also to be smaller; and when the numbers are at the higher end, then the diameter needs to be larger; in this way, the number of actual rows of audience seated on the floor remains more or less constant.

In both of the cases mentioned above, it is also important to note that I am thinking in terms of a *homogeneous* audience within a wholly *familiar environment.*

Generally speaking, experience suggests that there is only one place in which it is possible for *all* of these "ideal" circumstances to be met — that is in schools, during school hours, with the fullest cooperation of the school staff. Headteachers and Principals are invariably prepared to give sympathetic consideration to the specialized requirements of groups of actors who clearly and genuinely have a deep interest in children and what forms of theatre seem most appropriate to particular groups of them. This means that if a play is *written* for a particular age group to be *performed* in *very specific circumstances* to *carefully thought-out numbers,* there is a much greater chance of the acting team having all these rather exacting conditions met for them than when they are giving an advertised public performance in the youngsters' leisure time and so need to depend on parents' interest regarding age groups, etc. For parents it is obviously easier and more convenient for all of their children of whatever age group to attend together, and it is far more difficult to publicize or in other ways get over to them more exact requirements. In school during school time, there is also the important advantage of the homogeneous group, where, because the youngsters know each other, they work together easily without the concern caused by the presence of strangers who, at the very least, are something of a curiosity and thus a distraction. The same thought holds true of the school environment. Many theatre people quite naturally feel that it would be much more exciting an experience for the youngsters to get away from school into the new and exciting environment of a theatre, but for the younger of the two age groups mentioned above (the 5's to 8's) the journey to the theatre, especially if this involves coach or bus travel, is probably quite enough excitement in itself. For the older mentioned age group (9's to 12's) the new environment, about which they will feel a continuous curiosity, is likewise probably quite enough excitement in itself. For both groups, to be in an environment that is so wholly familiar that it forms no kind of distraction, it is much more possible to be wholly engrossed in the play itself, which is of benefit to performer and audience.

There is a further important factor concerning the *emotional* feeling of the environment. If a play is taking place during school hours, then the youngsters feel, consciously as well as unconsciously, a particular delight in the change from the routine of school subjects. If the performance takes place in the school itself, than the very building and all associated with it include an unconscious feeling of control. This accepted feeling of the environment can be of tremendous help, with aspects of participation, for both the performers and the audience. Often, when in a different building, during their own leisure time, some groups of youngsters feel that included in the proceedings is the opportunity for them to test and try out quite different relationships with adults. This may well be, indeed is, a natural part of the growing-up process, but it can make many very detailed problems for actors who are stimulating and controlling audience participation.

With my production of many of my own plays, I have always made quite clear to the actors that there are certain parts of the participation that *may not* work in the following conditions:

1. When the audience is not homogeneous: e.g. a school of not very large numbers inviting two or three other small schools to join them at their performance.

2. When the performance is not in a familiar school environment, but, for example, in a local parish hall. This circumstance is often mixed with point 1 above, particularly in rural areas, where there may be many small schools in a radius of, say, fifteen miles. None of the schools is large enough to have its own hall. Common to them all is a Secondary School with an excellent hall or gymnasium or a typical Parish Church Hall. Thus, the only way the youngsters from these many villages can experience a performance at all is for them to join together in one of the larger hall facilities. Of course, they must have the opportunity, but the actors should be made aware of the need for certain possible modifications within the participation sections of the play as it is certain that the "whole feeling" and "attitudes and responses" will be quite naturally different.

3. When a group of preschoolers aged 3 and/or 4 are added to a 5 to 9 age group. This is often done for the kindest of motives, but is seldom successful. It creates problems for the cast, for the audience for which the play is intended, and most of all for the preschoolers themselves.

4. At the other end of the scale, when the first and/or second years of a secondary school are added to a 9 to 11 age group.

5. When a disproportionate number of adults attends a performance that takes place in school during school hours. The adults may be students from a local teachers' training establishment or they may be parents, administrators, etc. A good safeguard is to work on the basis that, excluding the actual teachers responsible for the youngsters in attendance, there should be only a proportion of 1 to 20 additional adults. It is a sad truism that the majority of adults simply do not know how to behave at a participatory children's theatre play. They tend to "laugh at" or "find cute" the sincere and genuine participation of the youngsters. This adult reaction leads to bewilderment and either subsequent "showing-off" or withdrawal. It helps if it is possible to talk to the adults before the performance, when the majority becomes admirably sensitive.

6. When the Principal or Head Teacher puts in the wrong age group for the wrong play. This often arises when the administrator mistakenly believes that the criteria of age group choice is a largely intellectual factor based on I.Q., etc., and believes that the intellectual standards of his particular children are way above the "average." But the intuitive and emotional factors of the play are given just as much credence as intellectual considerations, and the wrong age group can make a tremendous difference, especially when, as I shall explain, the entire basic style of participation is wholly different for the two age groups.

7. When the administrator insists on putting in a much larger audience than that which "works" best. The actors must of course be reasonable about this. If the maximum is, say, 200, then the administrator may actually be confronted with the problem of excluding 19 or 20 children, or perhaps one class. This creates its own sadnesses. But that is quite different from deliberately raising the number to, say, 250 or even 280. Regretably, I know of many instances where this has happened even to 300 and the actors have risen to the occasion and "made" things work. On their next visit they are then confronted with an administrator who says "But last year you said the play wouldn't work with more than 200 and I gave you 300 and it was superb! So this year I'm giving you 375!!!"

8. When the administrator puts the young audience on chairs instead of sitting them on the floor. The whole question of sitting on chairs or floor has been thought through, experimented with and observed over a long period of time, and there is ample evidence that for *the sake of the youngsters themselves* sitting on the floor is far the most comfortable position, enabling any amount of "unconscious" small alterations in body position without disturbing their neighbours or the performers, and very specially allowing physical participation with greater ease than when on chairs, and with a greater feeling of group unity. For very young ones, the additional problem of using chairs is that young legs do not reach the floor and mostly swing freely to some kind of inner rhythm, with an outer clatter against chair legs, leading to all kinds of shushing and martialling from teachers. I have never known any teachers who have seen Children's Theatre performances with these age groups of 5 to 8 and 9 to 12 seated on the floor and seated on chairs, who have not finally agreed that the floor space is much the best.

The problem of theatre experiences for rural areas is perennial and world wide, and probably as applicable to the adult as to the child population. The problem will remain while theatre depends on its box-office takings for survival, and one of the strongest arguments in favor of various kinds of subsidy for theatres is that of enabling them to visit "theatreless areas." I believe one answer to this problem could rest with University drama and theatre departments. Many of these can easily obtain transport for touring and they do not have to pay actors' salaries. They would enrich the experience of their students by involving them in a community service. There are two many University Theatre Departments that seem quite divorced from even their own University Community let alone that on a broader basis. Actors, producers and writers would all be involved in an experience that cannot but enrich their own individual and personal work and talents. In addition to any specific work for children and young people, such student groups would have the opportunity of performing adult theatre, as well. Their audiences would be small, the physical environment possibly primitive, calling for simplicity and imagination, but they would have the very particular advantage of many more performances, thus supplying an opportunity to master one of their greatest problems — that of sustaining. Both theatre itself as well as its future adherents cannot but benefit from such an arrangement.

ADVANTAGES TO "SPLITTING" THE AGE GROUP

Groups that are most successful with Children's Theatre work are usually those who are prepared to take a little time and trouble to study and understand *children*. And let it be noted — Children! Not Education! Indeed, one of the saddest mushroom growths in Children's Theatre has arisen from a belief that if the work of Children's Theatre Companies is closely allied to current educational content then the powers in charge of finance — administrators, etc. — will value and pay for the work. This may be so. It may also be a desperate necessity for some groups confronted with harsh economic considerations. But let us be honest and say so, and meanwhile look at other terms of reference. I do not believe that Children's Theatre should be a kind of audio-visual aid for studying history or geography or English literature or political or religious problems. It can indeed do all of these things. But this type of audio-visual aid is usually much better done through forms of classroom creativity, including creative dramatics or child drama. The theatre experience can indeed be a stimulus, but it can be so without overtly setting out to *educate*. I believe theatre is concerned with opening the doors and windows of the heart, mind and spirit; I do not believe it is concerned with bending the mind.

The fundamental experience of theatre should be one of intuitive understanding through emotinal involvement, not of intellectual comprehension through novel ways of imparting facts. This underlying attitude to Children's Theatre was put exceptionally well by George Eliot:

"I believe aesthetic education to be the highest of all forms of education, because it deals with Man in his greatest complexity; but when it ceases to be purely aesthetic — *when the picture changes to a diagram* — then I believe it to be the most offensive of education."

The picture changes to a diagram the moment we are overtly and consciously placing a heavy emphasis on facts and comprehension. This does not mean that we should consciously avoid all the rich heritage of Man's experience, his adventures and discoveries, his quest for new worlds of experience, his finest and worst moments in his attempts to understand his own nature and the nature of the universe and the relationship of one to another; nor does one consciously avoid sharing Man's creative interpretations, records and communication of these experiences. All this is the very stuff of drama as well as of life. But if certain of these experiences are already being "studied" in school, then perhaps we should consider theatre as an opportunity for new and quite different experiences. With younger children there should be no necessity of constantly adapting and readapting those stories which for years adults have decided shall be the youngsters' favorites. Likewise with secondary young people, there should be no need for the theatre experience to be dominated by the literature syllabus, possibly even more narrowly linked to examinations. Why, then, has Theatre Centre, London, presented so many Shakespeare programs in English Secondary schools? Simply because Shakespeare, in my view, is probably the most exciting playwright ever, and youngsters should share part of that excitement as an alternative to "studying texts." But no attempt was ever made to find out which plays were being studied. No "explanations" were given nor was any attempt made to do potted versions of whole plays. There were many experiments of building exciting crowd scenes between the professional actors and volunteers from the audience. Basically everything humanly possible was done to make sure that "the picture did not change to a diagram," even sometimes asking teachers to support us by not mentioning the name Shakespeare in relation to the program until after the performance.

Now, let us look in more detail at the possibilities open to us by simply

Audience Participation

dividing the 5 to 11/12 age span into two separate groups, relating our decision to a concern for children rather than for education. Many clues exist for us through observation or study of children's own play and particularly their creative dramatic play. It is important for the reader to be aware of loosely rather than precisely defined stages of development. Observing and thinking about children within the general idea of Children's Theatre should be a joyous and fascinating experience, not a burdensome millstone that takes away the fun and enjoyment. So, very generally speaking, up to the age of about 8 or 9, children's experience in this field is largely one of unconscious drama beginning to be fully conscious, but not yet involving any conscious concept of theatre as such. After about 8 or 9, drama becomes much more fully conscious and includes an awareness of deliberately setting-out to create things in a certain manner — the early beginnings of conscious theatre, which become more established by the top end of our second group, i.e. at about 11 or 12 years of age. For both age ranges, but in slightly different manners, intuition and emotion dominate. For the younger age group, symbolism is dominant in importance, whereas with the older group, the intellect (processes of rationale and thought) begins to take over from symbolism to a larger extent.

The current, seemingly international, problem regarding the place of "The Fairy Tale" can help us to understand the factor of symbolism and its importance when related to intuition and intellect. The Fairy Tale, using "characters" symbolically, goes straight to the heart of a "story" or theme without intellectual considerations. Let us consider a basic fairy tale story:

"The Prince sets-off on a journey to rescue the Princess who is being held prisoner by the Wicked Baron. On his journey, the Prince has to overcome, first, the three evil dwarfs. Having done so, he continues his journey until he is confronted by the Wicked Witch. Having overcome this awesome creature, he continues his journey, only to be confronted by the two-headed dragon. And, having overcome this terrifying monster, the Prince, weak, faint and tired, at last reaches the Princess in the tower of the Wicked Baron's Castle, and frees her. His return journey with her may well include further dangers. The one certain, possibly final danger will be a confrontation with the Wicked Baron himself. The Prince succeeds in overcoming the Baron, and brings the Princess to safety."

At a symbolic level, the story contains the whole of Man's struggle with the forces of Evil, as he goes on his journey through life. And just as the essence of the problems are symbolic, so too are his means of overcoming them. The characters, the problems, the solutions, because of this symbolic essence, are what has become generally known as "fantasy." Bedevilled with the forces of Evil the Prince will need also the forces of "Good," often a character who's goodness is spiritual or ethereal or, as so often quite simply put in "The Fairy Tale," *magical.* This person creates some kind of "balance" of good and evil: maybe through a special potion to be used only at particular moments of danger; maybe through a precise number of "wishes" again at certain moments, and not to be wasted because of the limitations on the number of them; maybe by providing the ability to call on certain kinds of people or creatures to provide help at particular moments. A degree of "free choice" is often part of the responsibility that goes with this help. Unfortunately ultra-puritanism over the last century and a half, and taking varied forms, has destroyed this balance of good and evil in the parabolic construction of stories by introducing odious and insincere moralizing. Perhaps we should be wondering whether the sophisticated intellectualizing of the second part of the twentieth century might be doing rather the same thing.

The outcome of the Fairy Tale is as often as not The Happy Ending,

86

possibly even including the marriage of the Prince and the Princess and, equally often, the banishing, possibly through destruction, of the Wicked Baron. The overcoming of this particular source of evil thus restores the *balance* of good and evil. The Happy Ending means that we conclude with a feeling — maybe a *new* feeling, maybe a *renewed* feeling, but at any rate a *feeling* of hope, a hope that now, perhaps more unconsciously than consciously, transfers itself to becoming part of our own personal journey and struggle through life. At its simplest level, this is what is meant by the arts transcending life. To argue that it is not realistic and therefore providing a falsified view of life is quite absurd. The arts rise above life not merely repeat it, and much of the transcending lies within the realm of the symbolic. For young children it lies almost wholly in the realm of the symbolic. As one gets older one tries to depend more on self-help than on the supernatural. This means the adult must now have some of the balancing answers, so we invent a character who can do this. At one level this can overtly be a super-man, at another level, the Hero, and as Hero our continued link with "Hope." For all of us — and particularly for that 9 to 11/12 group, our hero still needs the Happy Ending, and again the fact that "life is not like that" is entirely beside the point. The function of theatre is to arrest the moment of time and change from *what life is like* to what it *might be* like, thus balancing potential despair with renewed hope.

Thus, with younger children — our 5 to 8/9 age group, we are concerned with symbolism, intuition and feeling. As the group gets older, more sophisticated, more able to "think" things through, so the fundamental use of the symbol changes. The story of the Prince and Princess might thus retain its same skeletal shape but change in its details:

"A young scientist believes that on a distant planet is a special mineral that will make considerable difference to life on earth. Together with certain male and female colleagues he sets off on the journey to the distant planet. On the way, his spaceship is suddenly involved with a shower of meterorites and nearly destroyed. Overcoming this obstacle, his journey continues until they are attacked by a spaceship from another planet. They overcome this, but are immediately enveloped by new gravitational forces that drag them toward the infamous but uncharted planet X, where he and his colleagues are taken prisoner by the mad scientist Ignoble, who escaped with secrets from our own planet centuries ago. By use of a "quaint device," our young scientist is able to reverse both time and his enemies' gravitational pull which enables his spaceship to escape and so to reach the distant planet and find the special mineral...and so on, with equally exciting obstacles on the return journey through to, be it noted, the happy and successful conclusion, whether or not a Lady equivalent of the "Princess" is involved."

The basic outline of the story is the same. The symbols change their detail, and, to an extent at any rate, Man is himself more master of his own fate. The enemy involved, Ignoble, takes the place of the "Wicked Baron." He may also be concerned with finding the special mineral. The conflict of the forces of Good and Evil are still with us, but their solution, their balancing, will depend more on the "reasoning" of the protagonists themselves. There is still a *hero*, a *villain* and a happy ending. The Fairy Tale is not so much distorted as "updated" to allow for the addition of intellect to intuition.

An analysis of many adult plays would lead us through similar structures concerning the hero or heroine, and their journey of short or long duration, in order to achieve a "particular." This goal is often concerned with the balance of good and evil or positive and negative, but will probably include a deepening of the intellectual and psychological factors. So we move from action to *action and reaction*. Hence to logical development, hence to psychological development or fuller human motivation.

The factor of "conscious and unconscious awareness of theatre," together with the element of symbol in story, has an effect, then, on the *content* of the plays we are able to offer as soon as we split the very wide age group of 5 to 11/12 into two. As explained in the chapter on *Family Audience,* start from where you are; there can be a simplicity and truthful charm of a play for the whole age range that will hold the generous sympathetic interest of the upper ages of the group, but as soon as they are on their own, there can be additional deepening of areas of experience that would be too sophisticated for the lower age range.

Within the conscious-unconscious theatre factor there is also a considerable potential effect on the possible range of audience participation. Because of the unconscious theatre factor, the lower ages are best involved in *general* audience participation, with everybody working at one and the same time from their place in the audience. No one should be asked to come individually or in small groups onto the acting area. If they do so, then their involvement at once changes to one of *pretending to be actors acting a play* just as it does in their own creative dramatics if they are confronted by an audience. Their concentration changes from a concern with what they are doing — working with total absorption and sincerity — to "what do the people who are watching think of what I am doing." With such divided concentration the basic absorption is undermined, resulting in insincerity that ranges from manifestations of shyness and embarrassment to blatant showing-off and exhibitionism. We see this clearly in their own "play." If we learn from it, then we do not arrange for any participation that involves a few of them coming onto the stage. They remain as a whole audience, and their help is given through vocal and/or physical participation as a group, remaining in their seats in the audience.

With the older group we can go beyond this. Indeed, we possibly must. The full audience involvement can still work, though its content will need to be more *sophisticated* than that for the younger group or a mixture of the two groups as in the Family Theatre circumstance. Because there is a more conscious awareness that "we are creating a play, making a piece of theatre," there is also the opportunity for inviting volunteers from the audience to join the actors, leaving their places in the audience, and coming on to the playing area. It must be emphasized, however, that this possibility with the 9 to 11/12 age group applies only to the *open stage.* To go up onto the proscenium or picture-frame stage would take them into yet another dimension of development in the growth towards conscious theatre, and, because they are not yet ready for this extension, they in their turn will start to "play at being actors acting a play" — with it's accompanying break in absorption and concentration leading either to shyness and embarrassment or to showing-off and exhibitionism.

Let us consider the two stories already mentioned and see at once the possibilities arising from the split age group. In the story for the younger group, the Prince goes on his journey to rescue the Princess. With this age group there can be all manner of ways in which the audience as a group help the Prince, particularly on such factors as "the magic". But there should be no question of a small group of the audience joining the Prince on his actual journey. On the other hand, with the older ones, the young scientist setting off in search of the special mineral on another planet, the scientist may well need and ask for a group of volunteers from the audience to go with him on the journey. This need not exclude some general audience participation as well, but such participation would need to be far more "realistic" than the kind of "magic" that would be so appropriate to the younger story. With the older ones, the whole audience might be involved in certain aspects of "making" part of the spaceship or certain factors in it. They might be involved in making supplies and provisions, even to the extent of quite complicated laboratory work with test tubes and heating instruments, complex dials and split-second timing. All of these would not only be wholly appropariate for this age group when on its own, but would be too sophisticated for the younger ones either on their own *or* as part of an audience embracing the full age range 5 to 11/12. The younger ones would probably be wholly out of their depth if asked to go on the journey itself, just as the older ones would likely be more self-conscious if they have a number of very young ones watching them. The intuitive assessment of and reaction to peer group situations is fascinatingly keen even at this age.

The *journey* and the audience's relationship to it contains something of the kernel of the difference in style of participation for these two separate age groups. With the younger group, a character or characters are helped on their journey through the directed, stimualted or spontaneous participation of the audience, sitting where they are and all working together. With the older group, although some similar possibilities might exist, there is the broad additional possibility of some (maybe all if numbers are very small) of the audience actually themselves going on the journey as well.

Let us consider, specific examples of each, in a play for the younger group, **The Bell,** and **On Trial,** for the older group. In **The Bell,** the main character, Tom, together with a companion is required as part of the story to go on a long journey. No one from the audience goes on the journey but the whole audience helps with many aspects of the journey. Indeed, but for their help, Tom and his friend would not even be able to start on let alone successfully complete their mission. As part of the preparation for the journey, Tom has been told of the need to make a special mixture, and the ingredients for that mixture — all carefully specified to Tom in a book of instructions — will be supplied by the audience in a sequence of *directed participation.* Thus, as we have met before, the audience through its help becomes more fully identified with Tom's needs and so with the story itself, as well as having a sequence of rich and integrated simple experiences of drama. And so when collecting the ingredients for the mixture, Tom improvises dialogue as necessary.

Actors in Children's Theatre must feel very at home with "improvised dialogue." In nearly all participation sequences this need arises and must not be left to chance. The problem for the actor is that during rehearsal he is without an audience, but at the right stage of rehearsal an audience should be provided for him by using other members of the cast. It must be made very clear to this "audience" that they can only help in rehearsal by genuine and sincere participation, which is as near as we adults can get to the "childlike," and not by playing about on the surface of experience (pretending to be children) and thus being merely "childish." The difference between the genuine "childlike" and the "childish" is worth spending a lot of time contemplating. Through participation of a genuine kind, the cast can help Tom to discover a simple, sincere and yet very full use of improvised dialogue, which must be absolutely sincere and only concerned with each moment of the story itself, i.e. the collecting of the ingredients. He must avoid all "gimmicks," all temptations to make "clever ad-lib remarks" that are invariably insincere and noticed as such by the youngsters. "Why don't you script it for me?" some actors ask. The answer, quite simply, is that each audience is different, so that their needs in terms of stimulation and the creation of mood and atmosphere will vary performance by performance. Some will be absorbed, bold and confident and an actor will find the need to say very little. Some will be diffident and shy, especially to start with, and will need ecouragement without in any way being led into the paths of overexcitment. On the other hand, some may start already in an overexcited state so that an actor may well feel the need to "calm" things down to a very quiet and yet detailed absorption. The breadth of an actor's experience grows in direct proprotion to the number of performances he is involved in, from what many actors have described as "a terrifying nightmare of uncertainty" to the most exciting actor-audience relationship.

In this particular play, **The Bell**, ingredients of the mixture, all involving audience participation, are as follows (with the sound or movement intention given in parenthesis):

1. The sound of hissing (small sound);
2. The noise of engines (large sound);
3. The flapping of wings (sound and small movement);
4. The marching of feet (sound through movement);
5. Smoke patterns in the sky (larger controlled movement);
6. A great explosion (large sound and movement);
7. The sound of insects (small sound — no movement).

Some detailed consideration has already been given to two important aspects of audience participation:

1) That there are three distinct kinds of participation — directed, stimulated and spontaneous;
2) That there are two control words that can be vital to the process of participation — "Now" as a way of beginning, and "There" as a way of completing.

In the example we are considering, there is unlikely to be any kind of "spontaneous" participation, but an actor is certainly confronted with fascinating opportunities concerning either "directed" or "stimulated" participation, and the whole "stimulation-control" area lies for him essentially in the use of "Now" and "There." Generally speaking, I should advise an actor to be securely ready with a format that will always work and yet one that he can withdraw from in all kinds of ways and degrees when he feels ready to do so.

With each ingredient, Tom reads from the Book of Instructions that was given him. He can read to himself, or he can read to his companion or without looking at the rest of us in the audience he can read in such a manner that he embraces all of us. However he does it, he is not admonishing us or playing any kind of teacher character who is instructing us. He is absorbed within character as Tom, needing help, personally astonished by the kind of help he is asking for, perhaps (as Tom) wondering a little doubtfully as to whether we shall be able to help (through he has no such doubt as "the actor being Tom.") This is all part of the sincerity of the situation.

So, looking at the book, he says: "The first thing we need is the sound of hissing." Because this is the first moment of participation, there may not be immediate response to this *stimulation* form of participation. In which case, as part of his own secure "format," he moves straight into the *directed* form and says: "Everybody make (or, we need) the sound of hissing - NOW." And he should feel totally secure that the hissing *will come*. It is planned as a deliberately simple beginning. The youngsters are not "caught out" with any complicated or difficult activity that could in any way worry them. The sound is a simple step beyond that of simply breathing. In other plays, where other sets of ingredients have been needed, a similar start has been suggested, but with different detail — the "sound of the wind," "the sound of bees," and so on. Now, the sound being there, whatever else Tom does, he must not, as from sheer relief that it has happened he may feel the need to do, make any kind of "value comment" on the participation. He needs to avoid any such remarks as "What wonderful hissing," "That's the best hissing I've ever heard," and even more does he need to avoid such as "Oh, dear, I suppose it's all right but I had hoped for better hissing than that," or, as we have met before, there must be no question of asking for such as "louder hissing." From within character and situation, he may well find himself saying to his companion, possibly with some astonished joy, "Listen! - there it is. There. The sound of hissing." At once he is into what the whole situation is about. He *needs* that sound as the first part of the mixture he has to make, and he must collect it quickly. In the story as he collects each ingredient, he puts it into a bowl for his companion to stir.

Before we go on to consider the factor of collecting, there is another point that is important in the original stimulating of sound, and all of the other different kinds of participation that are to follow with subsequent ingredients. It is this: Never, never, never must the actor *give a vocal lead* or *a physical demonstration of* what is required. If he does, although he may ensure the actual getting of the participation, what in fact will happen is an *external immitation of his inner experience*, which is quite different from the youngsters finding their own way of participating. This is one of the most important links that Participatory Theatre has with Drama in Education, perhaps sometimes helping teachers new to such work to see an approach that is genuinely creative rather than dependent on "imitation," and in the same way are helped by seeing directed, stimulated and spontaneous forms of participation. But it can be of interest to Children's Theatre actors to understand that just as Children's Theatre can help teachers in this manner, so is Children's Theatre participation helped by the work of teachers in the classroom.

So, the hissing comes, and the actor's task is to "collect it." How? Quite simply, he gathers the hissing in his arms, using wide sweeping gestures to gather it *collectively* from the audience, not from individuals, which would take too long and undoubtedly cause some to feel excluded. But he makes sure that his gathering does cover the whole audience area, starting from one point of the circle, perhaps by an aisle, and then gradually moving right around to the other side. Finally he puts the "gathered sound" into the bowl with the word strongly and emphatically vocalized — "There." And at once all of the sounds of hissing will die away, and there will be an interested anticipation of what is next required. So, the "Now" and the "There" gradually take on something of the form and value of a "ritual," which indeed is what this particular kind of audience participation is essentially about. The achievement of the first collecting adds confidence to collecting the remainder, backed by the urgency to collect *all* so that the journey can start. The format remains as a pattern, or a ritual:

— read what is required from the book;
— repeat it, unless there is an immediate reaction (sometimes there is not, simply because the requirement was not heard);
— use the "trigger" word NOW (unless the participation starts without it, which will often be so from about the third item);

— collect the "sounds and/or the movement" — and the actor needs the full feeling of the differences demanded of him in the collecting; for example, the difference between something as strong and heavy as "Marching feet" compared with the delicacy of "Smoke patterns in the sky";
— the completion of each item with the word "There" as the sound and/or movement goes into the bowl.

Item 6, "A great explosion," is an interesting experience for Tom, as he needs vocally to lead into *one single, big explosion NOW,* and then "catch" it all with one great sweep of both arms and put it straight into the bowl with an immediate "There." Unless it happens as instantly as this, he may have a chain reaction of explosions far more difficult to control. "Then," ask some actors, "if there is any such risk, why put in an explosion at all?" With the gradual growth of opportunity to participate with sound and movements, the youngsters gradually loosen up both in terms of confidence and effort. The explosion helps this to come to a natural completion and climax, and the declimax of the next and final ingredient, the "sound of insects," brings back a full calmness for the continuation of the story. The mixture has been made, and at various points during the story, there is need for Tom and his companion to sip the mixture in order to progress on their journey. We, the audience, have all helped by "contributing" to the making of the mixture, now we help at the moment of "sipping" as well. Tom reads this from the same Book of Instructions:...First drink some of the mixture and listen to the Hum...As the bowl is raised for the sipping, the actor says very quietly, "Everybody hum -now." And the "hum" will come immediately and will fade away as soon as the sipping is completed. From then onwards, everytime anybody sips the mixture the hum will come. If it does not, then the actor simply says, "Everybody — the hum, now."

So, with the younger age group, all of the youngsters become helpful participants with *preparation* for the journey that will be made only by characters in the play. At various points in the journey, the audience all help again, but none of them is asked to actually "come out" and be in the journey itself.

In contrast, let us look at the preparation for a journey in a play written for the 9 to 11/12 age group, **On Trial**, and let us keep in mind that we are with an age group for whom drama is a fully conscious activity with the beginnings of a very clear awareness of the idea of "theatre." This journey requires approximately 20 people, four of whom are the main company of actors each needing four volunteers. A dramatic exposition of the situation takes up the first 15 minutes of the story, including the fact that the journey will be long and dangerous and will be headed by "The Major" who is in charge of the outpost community that needs urgently to send out an expedition. The Major addresses the whole community — that is all of us in the audience — explaining the situation to us, and ending with the words, "We need volunteers - *Now.*" From the moment he says the word "Now" the participation begins, and, for those who volunteer and are picked, it continues until just five or six minutes from the end of the play. All told, there is something like thirty minutes of continuous involvement. So let us consider how much of the "success" of the continuous participation depends on the very careful foundations made by the company of four people in the first few minutes after the word "Now."

From the outset, they should be prepared in their minds for two polarized possible reactions to the invitation for volunteers. The unlikeliest extreme is that there will be no volunteers at all, or a strong apparent reluctance. This tends only to happen with very small audiences in remote areas, and if the audience is as small as, say, twenty to thirty, then the simplest solution is for everybody to go on the journey, which they will probably want to do with a little further stimulation from the four, all of them repeating the urgency of the situation and the need for help. At the other extreme, especially with larger audiences (and the maximum for this play is 200) can be a sudden burst of general excitement, with possibly every hand up, urgently hoping to be picked. This is a fascinating moment for the four actors, who must be in total control of the situation, *within character* and *within the situation of the play*, NOT by suddenly changing role and becoming teachers in charge of children. For each of the actors to take one section of the audience and to say something like, "Thank you people. I only need four or five so please stay where you are until I have picked you" (said from within character) is quite different from rather frenziedly clapping one's hands and saying, "Now boys and girls, please stay sitting down, with your hands up if you want to come. No, I'm not going to choose anyone who isn't sitting down..." This teacher-type approach at once changes the atmosphere and takes away from some of the spirit of the adventure, and it does not usually bring about any more control.

These two extremes happen, as I say, very rarely, but it is wise during rehearsal for the actors to discuss, rehearse and be ready for many very different types of experience. In this way they avoid trying to stereotype audiences into a single kind of acceptable behavior pattern, and become genuinely interested in that truism of Children's Theatre — *every audience* is different. The important point, which will hold for the whole of the rest of the play, is that of keeping in character with full sincerity and belief in the situation. The youngsters very quickly catch the "feel" of this underlying approach, which in turn helps their own absorption and seriousness of approach. As so many actors have said, "I could feel from the way they were looking at me that they were testing me, sensing just how real this was for me personally and you can almost feel the moment of their own decision to join you with the same attitude and approach." It is indeed a remarkable experience of relationships and it is from that point that one is able to kindle and rekindle imagination throughout the rest of the play. We, the actors, have rehearsed for a long time and they, the youngsters, *are not going to have any rehearsal at all*, but are going to pick up from us by *swift intuitive awareness*, dependent on the clarity of our sharing many facets of an exciting "theatre experience" — the changing moods, atmospheres, different physical activities, moments of spoken improvisation, and the strange sensitivity of total teamwork. And this is not cant. Nor is it based on any sentimental nonsense about "the dear kiddies being creative" and "we mustn't interfere with them!" — thoughts that cankered the healthy growth of creative dramatics in schools. It is based on a total belief in and an empirical proving of that belief — the fact that young people are genuinely creative, that they are not interested in wet, sloppy, sentimentalized approaches to control but are glad of purposeful, just and sensitive reasons for getting down to things, using the fullness of themselves, stretching experience, daring to fail without ever losing their spiritual courage, and looking only for a strong and purposeful lead from the adult world, be those adults teachers or, as in the making of a piece of theatre - actors. This, I believe, is what teaching is about, what the arts are for, and what is the basis of genuine audience participation in Children's Theatre.

But, let us continue to look at the picking of volunteers. Each actor is going to choose four or five people (later, when confidence grows, as it will over a number of performances, they may well want to choose 6 or 7 each) from the whole circle of audience around them *(see diagram, 13 pg. 75)*. Each of them needs to be ready to repeat the information already given by the Major about the needs of the journey. One character needs help with carrying provisions and with cooking. Another needs people to help plan and guide the expedition. A third needs a medical team, and the Major himself needs people to carry equipment and help protect the expedition. The repeating of this information helps to clarify for the audience the particular function of each character in the story. If all four actors are doing this at one and the same time, moving freely and easily in the acting area, then there is "less exposure" for those coming into the playing area. If it is done one person at a time, then it is more orderly, but the exposure factor can be worrying. If possible, it is good if each of the actors can take two or three youngsters from both sides of the audience area, rather than from just one small segment of the audience. The actors must be aware, however, of peer group potential. The 11/12 years-old may not be entirely happy either participating with or being watched by the 9 years-old and some of the nine-years old may be rather alarmed at being watched by the older groups. On the other hand if each of the actors have chosen, say, two of the younger ones and two of the older ones, then this may help to take away any worry or concern. Similarly, it sometimes is interesting to pick two people who are sitting next to each other and are possibly great friends. That friendship can be a tower of strength to them both, and to the play as a whole. The variations are legion, which is again why it is so helpful if many performances can be given rather than just one or two. Some of the decisions about age group choice, etc., can be discussed by the actors before each performance, and the actual physical area where different ages are sitting can be helped if one of the actors seats the audience (see the section on "Openings and Endings" or pp 105-133).

During the moments of choosing volunteers, it is important for the actors to appear *to select at random,* so that no youngster feels that any particular preference is being given. And having pointed at a youngster, it is important to wait until that particular youngster is moving and coming towards you. If necessary, one can add a descriptive phrase such as "the girl in the yellow dress," etc. If the actor does not clearly identify the person pointed at and then wait for them to come out, but moves swiftly on to another area for the next selection, it may well be that five or six others, the people sitting around the person chosen, will think they have been selected and move into the area so the actor discovers that instead of having four or five he has ten or fifteen It is unfortunate when this happens, because sending youngsters back can be an ignominious experience for them. (I am personally quite ruthless and insist that no one is to be sent back!)

As each person is selected, so they are invited to come and sit in the circle in order to be ready for a short discussion of the preparations for the journey. I have marked on the following diagram the places where the characters and the youngsters could be seated for this disucssion. The filled in circles represent the four actors and the crosses indicate the youngsters they are talking to. The youngsters have their backs to the audience which helps two important factors common to any small group discussion between actors and participants By having their backs to the audience nearest to them, the youngsters are less aware of the audience and so less likely to be self-conscious or to attempt to communicate with them. Second, the actors, too, are in strong positions for being heard by quite a large section of their side of the audience. If there are rostrum blocks in the acting area, then the actors should sit on them. By

94

themselves sitting on the block, the actors save the problem of the youngsters wanting to sit there, an experience we need to save them from as the higher position would in fact create diversions both for them and their friends in the audience. Also, if there is a gangway behind the blocks, the youngsters do not have any of their friends directly in front of them. Finally, again, by being raised up, the actors are in strong positions for being heard by quite large sections of the audience.

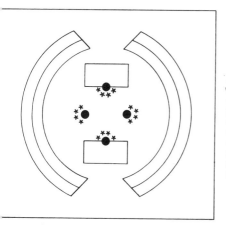

Diagram Number 17
Talking to volunteers in **On Trial.** *The four filled-in circles represent the actors. The two in the center of the acting area sit back to back with their group in front of them. The youngsters therefore have their backs to the audience closest to them and are not distracted. The other actors sit each on a block at either end of the acting area with their group close to them. The block and the actor "protect" the participants from too close a contact with the audience.*

The fact of being in a position to be heard becomes all important at this moment and will remain so for the rest of the participation in the play. It is most important that each actor does NOT shut himself off into a one to one relationship with his own group of participants by talking to them in the kind of intimate style that closes out everybody else. It is through the four actors — not through the participants — that communication with the rest of the audience is sustained. This is another reason why the actors need to practice a great deal of improvised dialogue, so that they can improvise with the confidence and panache of a scripted and rehearsed area of dialogue, taking full responsibility themselves for *progressing the action of the story.* This latter point is in fact the key to the whole, for it is progression of the action that is important, NOT a discussion or debate. The four actors are basically concerned with getting their team of participants *busily active* on preparations for the journey. This means that the actors need to give a few directions that swiftly and intuitively get the youngsters confidently busy, perhaps even involving other members of the audience, sitting where they are. Here are some examples:

One actor: We need as much food and water as we can possibly carry *(to two of them).* You two, take these water containers back to your own homes and fill them with water. *(By handing them two imaginary containers she at once establishes that all the "props" are going to be mimed. Then to the other two).* From your homes or from the stores, get as much bread and meat and vegetables as you can. Off you all go, and bring everything back here as soon as you've got it. The MAJOR *(to his team):* We're going to need guns and ammunition, and knives. So go to the supply depot over there *(and he might point to where a likely group of the audience is sitting or he might point to a blank area outside of the acting arena)* and get whatever you think we need and bring it back here. Try not to be too long as we don't have much time.

The other two actors will be doing something similar, getting the young people involved *in action and in doing* as soon as possible, accepting the role of leadership and carrying it out. As we have met before, this is a *directed* stage of participation, which works as well and correctly for small groups as we have seen it work for the whole audience working together.

The above approach is so different from the "debate or discussion" approach, where, for example, a character might say: "What food do you think we ought to take with us?" This single question raises so many factors. At an unconscious level, the group might well wonder why on earth this character is in charge and yet does not know what is wanted. At another, both conscious and unconscious level, the worry at once enters the youngster's mind — "Oh, this one knows that is wanted and is testing us to see if we are clever enough to know! I wonder what he/she has in mind! I wonder if I can guess correctly."

At once the reality of the story dies and we are back in a classroom-academic atmosphere instead of an adventurous intuitive moment of theatre making. But if action comes first, through the kind of suggested directed participation, then of course other things might follow. For example, when people return with their imaginary things, each actor fully absorbed, looking at or making lists, can check what has been brought in already and then, perhaps, say: "Fine, fine. Now, can any of you think of anything else we need that we've not already got?" And this may *stimulate* ideas, which are now more likely to flow readily and easily because the group has already been actively involved. Then, shortly, each of the groups is going to pack up its own supplies in haversacks, kitbags, boxes, whatever is appropriate, all of which the four actors can send members of their group to collect or, particularly if time is at a premium, simply hand out. Now, too, the actor-leaders can get their own group, or some of them, to help them put on their own haversacks and check that all details are right. This whole section, from the moment volunteers are asked for to the point at which all are ready to start the journey, should not last more than a maximum of 5 to 6 minutes, yet another reason why dragging fruitless "discussion" is wholly inappropriate. And this emphasizes *one of the major differences between Participatory Children's Theatre and Drama in Education.*

In my experience, most Children's Theatre performances, particularly when they take place during school hours, have to fit into some kind of detailed framework of time. For this reason, in a play like **On Trial** much thought has been given as to how long is necessary for each section of participation to take place, and the actors need carefully to stay within this time area or what is supposed to be a 50 to 55 minute play can soon run away to 80 or 90 minutes.

But there is much more to the problem than mere pedantry about timetable. In this kind of work we are concerned with *Partcipatory Theatre* and, in the final analysis, a *balance* between what might be called entirely *theatre experience* where the involvement of the audience is predominantly of the heart, the mind and the spirit, and *participatory opportunity* in action and in words for a limited number of the audience. The play itself contains that balance, but the balance can easily be upset by the actors either ignoring and thus diminishing the actual participational opportunities of the selected groups or, more problematical still, by going to the opposite extreme and extending the participants' involvement, as though it were a drama lesson with no one else involved, thus diminishing the fullness of the theatre experience for those not selected to participate. This can happen particularly with a group of youngsters who are having a lot of creative dramatics opportunity in school and therefore have the imagination and the confidence to extend and deepen the experiences offered them within the play itself. Actors very quickly sense this, and feel some frustration at having to "curb" developments. It is essential, however, they do so in this type of Children's Theatre in order to retain that right admixture for the whole. Some actors wonder whether there is a like frustration for the youngsters, and, of course, to an extent there is, but because at this age they are aware of theatre as a conscious activity, they are very quickly prepared to accept and follow the selective potential. This is also true of the concern, expressed by many theatre people, that it is unfair to extend an invitation to volunteers in the first place. "What about the disappointment for those not selected?" is the question often asked and, again, the answer lies within the youngsters themselves, who because of their awareness of making a theatre creation, wholly accept the convention that not all can take part. This is quite different from the feeling that would exist among younger ones if, in moments of whole audience participation, some were told they could not participate. This again, is one of the values of being able to split the broad 5 to 11/12 age range. If, as suggested above in terms of the selected groups going back into the audience to collect the various things they need for their journey, the nonselected people can be involved for a short while, then this is also helpful. There are plays in which, even for the older half of the age group, an attempt can be made to involve everybody on a journey.

The **On Trial** journeys, which use both the acting area and aisles behind the audience, require the fullest use of imagination by participants and audience alike. There are no properties, no lighting and only the simplest use of rostrum blocks at the head of each aisle in the acting area. Great variations of journey are possible. The script contains specific episodes involving the crossing of a swamp, and also a ravine by means of a simple "rope bridge," but there can also be rocks to climb, forests and deserts to go through, etc.

It is most important on all of the journeys, however, that the actors do not confuse the young participants by trying to be too specific about particular obstacles. We are back to the point of "changing the picture to a diagram," of changing intuitive experience to intellectual agony. If an actor calls out, "Rocks ahead!" then each person on the expedition finds his or her own moment for changing to rock climbing. Some may start before they are anywhere near the point at which they hear the words called, but this does not matter at all. Confusion and change of experience only comes if the actor calls out something like "Look out for *this rock*" and accompanies his words with a precise pointing out of the imaginary rock. This will lead everyone to having to remember the precise place, maybe even size and method of climbing that "particular rock" and so ruin the general potential of the experience, which should fundamentally be emotional and intuitive, not intellectual and concerned with "accuracy of mime," an art form which is not only way beyond the possibility of this age group but also wholly inappropriate to this kind of audience participation.

The same is true of other episodes such as "setting-up camp" that take place at breaks in the continuous journey, again with no properties whatsoever. Everything is mimed, but it is important for the actors to keep in mind that youngsters of this age do not pay attention to details of mime, nor should they be expected to do so. Rather, concentration and absorption should be the aim, with an emphasis on activity and a cheerful, purposeful mood. The whole sequence of such episodes as "setting-up camp" will happen much more quickly than the adult would normally do and thus expect from others and details of "the reality of time (e.g. cooking)" must not be a cause for concern. Very careful organization of activities in scenes of this kind should be well planned during rehearsals. Here again we can often see the mistaken conception that "improvisation" is a matter of leaving everything to chance rather than reaching out toward finish and full feeling of theatre. Of course the totally open-ended episode is valid as one form of improvisation, but it is not appropriate for this type of Children's Theatre participatory experience which depends on sound leadership, purposeful intention, and control from within the need of the situation and of the characters involved.

I have gone into some of these points in such detail in order to emphasize the potential open in Children's Theatre work the moment we are able to have some control over not only shape of playing area (namely using the open stage) but also over the number in the audience and a split in the age group, so that instead of having all of the 5 to 11/12 group together, we have the lower half the 5 to 8/9 for one type of approach and the 9 to 11/12 for another. The different approaches both arise from a detailed study of youngsters themselves helping us to see and understand what is appropriate to them at their own stage of development, rather than imposing on them all a single approach simply because it is one that is well known to us and has been the custom for many years. I must emphasize again that the approach is concerned with an *experience of theatre*. It is not a matter of making "modifications" to suit educational "thinking" or curriculum demands, nor is it using theatre as an audio-visual aid for teaching or bringing to life subject matters already being studied in the classroom.

I am personally worried that many fine actors, who would be so brilliant in Children's Theatre, are "put-off" by the feeling that this kind of theatre involves so many "special approaches" and is so "serious" that all of the creative fun is taken out of their acting. I therefore hasten to assure them that this simply is not so any more than it would be true to say that the disciplines demanded by cameras, etc., in television or film take away one's creative opportunity in acting. There are differences. There are new challenges to be met. There are adjustments that are necessary to make in comparison with performing on a proscenium stage in a "normal" three-act play. But, just as the majority of actors become fascinated with the new skills demanded of them by other media, so, too, can they find fascination with the particular approaches necessary to Children's Theatre.

e Hat (A). *The playing area is 14' square, with an aisle at each corner, clearly marked with a thick alk line. There is space behind the audience for the actors to journey. Because all the youngsters are 'ting on the floor, they can see the action of the play easily. The photograph is taken early on in the 1y, so most of the youngsters are sitting as they have been told to sit — with legs crossed. Soon ey will be able to relax through active participation (See B.) The teachers usually sit on chairs, ough a few do sit among their own class, on the floor. Sometimes the teachers sit too far away from e action and so do not hear as clearly as the youngsters. The cafeteria at the back (left) will soon art preparing lunches. The actors' concentration will overcome the sounds. The youngsters are used the noise.* (Photo: Ian Stone)

e Hat (B). *One of the four sections of the audience has a moment of physical/vocal participation, to lich they respond willingly. In quick succession, each of the other three sections will have a similar st moment, which will "break the ice" and also help them to relax from rigid formality. At the ck, a lady is beginning to cross the hall. There are many such comings and goings in school perfor- inces, but practice and full concentration help the actors to ignore the distrubances and the ungsters are hardly aware of it.* (Photo: Ian Stone)

A Journey. Boxes and rostrum blocks are important for all young children's play at home, for drama in school and for Children's Theatre with Audience Participation. This pile of blocks has stimulated the imagination of the youngsters so that they are starting upon an exciting adventure and journey. They have not yet fully developed the detail of their story, but action has started, and that will lead to decision making. (Photo: Ian Stone)

Even the smallest children are talked to with sincerity. There is no playing-down or talking-down to the "kiddies." The actor has crouched down to be at the physical level of the youngsters. His spine, however, is straight — the one way to make sure of not talking-down. (Photo: Donald Cooper)

For Children's Theatre, it is important to set a maximum audience size, but there need be no minimum. (Four is the smallest audience Theatre Centre visited!) Here, in the beginning of a play, two characters ae having a very real quarrel, as a result of which the youngsters will take sides. The story eventually includes a splended sword fight between two sides, with everybody involved. Note: The actors are fully absorbed in the scene. (No concession is made for children in genuine Children's Theatre. Consequently, most of the youngsters are concentrating on the argument.) Other actors are at the side and end of the hall, awaiting their cue. One visitor is in the far corner. (Photo: Ian Stone)

The pursuit of a highwayman around the back of the audience. The whole room becomes the stage area — a place where anything can happen. Some of the youngsters are moving out of the way, for this kind of chase cannot be "pretend" in the open stage. It is for real, with total sincerity. The youngsters' excitement finds an outlet in laughter. Note the half-mask of the pursuer (left). This half-mask allows for full use of facial expression while being wholly accepted as a symbolic basis of a new character.

The Storytellers. *The half-round or half-circle audience area enabling the actors to perform on one long side of the hall. At this time, Theatre Centre performed for the whole primary age group, 5-11. Subsequently, the age group was divided into two and eventually three, with a different play for each group. This enabled content to be deepened for the older ones, and appropriate areas of participation to be developed at each level. (As the two characters in the photograph are the Toyman and his reflection, they are identically dressed.)*

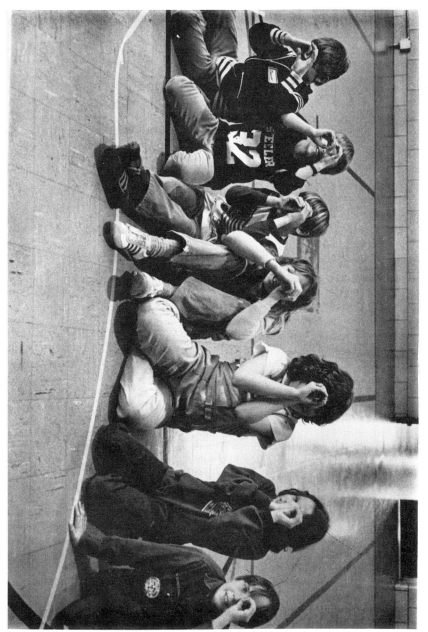

In secondary schools and in the upper grades of the primary school, for some participants feeling self-conscious of being watched by the audience can be a problem. If the audience is "busy," however, the worry is reduced. One way of accomplishing this is to ask the audience to become cameramen "filming" the crowd scene, as in **The Clown** *and* **The Angel of the Prisons.** *In this photograph, some of the audience are "taking photographs of the cameraman taking photographs of them!"* (Photo: D.R. Miller)

6

Openings, Endings and Content

The open stage, confined age grouping and limited size of audience all combine together to release entirely new approaches to how a play might open and/or end. This is not a question of better or worse than the accepted and well known openings possible on a picture frame stage with lighting and sets and a front curtain. It is simply a matter of being entirely *different* in its potential opportunities. Even the actual assembling of the audience can be affected by these opportunities — to the point where one or more of the actors helps to seat the audience, with the intention of "welcoming them." This can be especially helpful when performances take place in schools because, despite the many advantages already enumerated of the school as an environment for housing Children's Theatre, it can have the slight disadvantage of being associated with "formal assembly rituals," as there is a natural tendency for teachers in charge of assembling an audience for a play to approach it with the same kind of formality. The actor(s) must approach the matter quite different-ly. This is an opportunity for "making a bond" with the youngsters and to get "the feel" of them. Through this involvement the actor knows where different age groups are sitting, can pass this information on to the other actors and can take full responsibility for "special" arrangements. For example, if there is to be a class of 5 year old children, then the actor can make sure they sit in a group together, with the companionship of their own friends all round them, whereas, if the matter were left to the teachers, they are more likely to work on the basis of "the smallest should be in front," thus stringing out the five year olds right around the front of the whole acting area, a quite different and sometimes worrying experience at that age, especially if it is their first term in school as well as perhaps their first experience of "a play."

At the risk of offending large numbers of people, I have to say that for the kind of Participatory Theatre that is the subject of this book I do not see any place for the under 5's at all, and for preference would leave out the 5's as well.

Of course "they do so enjoy it," and of course "it seems unfair for them to miss the treat," and so on; nevertheless, as soon as they are present it is astonishing how many sensitive adjustments the actors need to make to ensure they are not upset or worried or maybe even frightened, none of which adjustments are usually necessary for the six years and upwards.

The opportunity for helping to seat the audience is also a great help to actors who may have had little or no experience of working or playing with children. Indeed they cannot have too many such opportunities. The actors' attitude is possibly the most important factor in participatory theatre. The worst fault of so much work with children as well as with "special entertainment" for children is that of *playing-down* to them, treating them as though they were a cross-breed between imbeciles, soft-toys and domestic pets. Of course, there is the opposite extreme of treating them as sophisticated "equals," usually thus begetting from them various forms of "cute exhibitionism." One would be amazed at the depth of contempt even quite small children feel about either mode of behavior from adults. One of the natural problems from a sensitive adult's point of view relates to the difference in size, and, in trying to compensate for this there is a natural tendency to *bend down* towards the smaller person(s) in front of one. Interestingly enough it is that *bending down* that actually leads to *playing down*. As soon as the spine bends at the waist, thus closing down the solar plexus, the kind of "twee" talk that is the outermost sign of playing-down seems to start. By making sure one keeps the spine straight and upright, the tendency is avoided. If one feels the need to come "down" to the child's level in terms of actual height and size, then this can be achieved by either crouching down or even going down on one knee, but still keeping the spine straight and upright. (By the way, if you do crouch or go down on one knee, don't be surprised if the youngster you are speaking to does the same thing!) Perhaps most important of all is our need to remember that small children are used to this difference in physical sizes. Indeed, as part of helping our own understanding of the child's point of view it is useful to spend a few minutes every day "crouching" or using whatever other physical adjustment will help us to experience their point of view, then we will see that it isn't only in relation to people that there is this difference. It applies to furniture, to basins, to the bath, to hedges and walls, to bushes and flowers, to all experiences of the physical world.

For actors in participatory children's theatre to understand some of these basic factors about children not only enriches their actual work, but gives them a fascinating foundation from which to work, enabling their own intuition to help them, often quite unexpectedly at various moments in a play. The ultimate value of this is part of the whole question of attitude, including the development of a quite genuine humility which enables the actor to consider his own functioning and the material within which he is functioning before blaming the audience if things do not go precisely as he would like them to go (or as they went at the last performance.) All theatre is healthier for this attitude. For Children's Theatre it is the fundamental ingredient, not based on sentimentalized gibberish about the sanctity of the "dear kiddiewinks," but on the knowledge that just as they are different from adults, so too the adults involved may need to make certain adjustments to the techniques, etc., that are no longer wholly appropriate. This is the basis of the idea that with the youngest age group plays (for the 5's to 9's), any character making an exit from the playing area in the open stage will be watched by the audience until right out of sight, out of the hall, not just the playing area, and that the youngsters will then continue to wonder for a few seconds where the person has gone to, what he or she is doing, etc. Meanwhile other actors left in the playing area need to suspend their continuity to allow for this. A similar kind of "suspension" often concerns the use of properties, costumes, etc.

In a play called **The Mirrorman,** two characters disguise themselves in front of the audience, helping each other with adjustment to hoods and cloaks. The situation at the time of doing this is one of urgency, and the actors' instinct suggests going on with the dialogue concerned with the reasons for the disguise. But in fact the youngsters are so intrigued by the actual costume work that they do not fully listen to the dialogue. Thus it is important for the actors to do only the dressing-up, with any improvised dialogue being sincerely concerned with helping each other. When the dressing is complete, and only then, do they continue with the scripted plot. A good basic rule for coping with this kind of situation is: *Never have more than one thing going on at a time.*

The same kind of adjustment is often important in terms of a character or characters in a play "discussing" some factor with the audience. In the same play, **The Mirrorman,** two characters are concerned that "the witch" has been there and done certain unpleasant magic things. They decide to "ask their friends in the audience" who are very anxious to help, indeed so anxious that they may even start telling them before they solicit the information. The inclination of the actor   particularly when concerned with a certain secrecy, is to move close to the front row of the section of audience nearest. This in effect, however, at once cuts him off from the rest of the people in his section. Thus he needs first to establish control by suggesting that "we all talk in whispers so the witch does not hear," and then finds a position that is best for him to be able to maintain contact with the whole of his audience segment. Having found that physical place on the floor, he needs to address more of his own words to the back of the group; if the back are in full contact with him, everyone between him and the back row will also be sharing whatever is being said. His listening concentration needs to be superb because the youngsters may well talk in whispers and the rest of his section of the audience may well not hear that whisper, so he repeats everything everybody says so the others can hear. In this way, it is perfectly possible for two parrallel discussions to be taking place at one and the same time, each of the two characters discussing with half of the audience and all without any loss of the urgency, of the atmosphere or of "control," without any coming out of character to enforce overt control. No one should pretend this is easy to achieve, but its probabilty of achievement is greater the moment the actors see and understand the quite different approach necessary from that used in adult theatre.

These adjustments may be necessary at certain moments within the play, but most of them for the 5 to 8/9 age group and not for the 9 to 11/12 age group. Again, the division into two different groups helps us with our basic approach, and this is most clearly reflected in the approach both the writer and the performers can make to the *opening* of a play, in the open stage, to a limited size audience. I do not believe there are any hard and fast golden rules, certainly no kind of "fail-safe" formulae and, indeed, a great deal of experiment lies ahead. The opening for the 5's to 8's often needs to be slow and gentle — slow in order for everyone to have a good look at everything, gentle so the youngsters are *eased into* the experience of the play and the story without one scrap of "playing-down" by the actors. The adjustment for the age group is made within the play itself and compensations do not have to be made by the actors. It is a question of the play and the playing, both of which are "slower" compared even with the rhythm of the next age group up, let alone of adults. The rhythm is adjusted to be closer to the rhythm of younger children, which is in itself "slower." From the point of view of "acting,"the factor of finding the right rhythm is one of the most exciting challenges of the artist's approach to Children's Theatre. It cannot be solved by slavish techniques of "slowing everything down," and yet there has to be a period of really conscious feeling-out of the rhythm. It is an emotional and spiritual, ultimately an "intuitive," mastery that is as difficult to pin down in practical terms as it is to find words on paper to describe it.

The director of the play is always of great importance in terms of this "rhythm" factor in Children's Theatre, simply because the actor is involved in an adjustment from what he/she is probably used to in adult theatre, as discovered in terms of such moments as exiting from the hall. So often, actors feel that "everything has dragged" and are amazed to hear that the slowness has not been in terms of the "pace" of their dialogue, but for some other reason like "indulgence in pauses." At other times they may need to be reminded that what felt to them like just the right pace was in fact far too fast, possibly because they were not using ends of words, and possibly because they were not listening to each other and thus going from indulgent pauses to "treading" on each other's dialogue. Often, this can only be seen and felt from the outside. When they do find the right rhythm for this younger group, they may need protection from adult observers who, possibly because they are used only to adult theatre, feel that the play was too slow and have not considered it from the youngsters' point of view.

Interesting points regarding this basically important factor of "rhythm" arise from the recent growth of what I call "Committee theatre," theatre in which the playwright is largely superseded by a team of actors exploring, discussing, inventing and selecting among themselves, largely through processes of improvisation. This is a fascinating and challenging process, and particularly valuable with "documentaries" when a vast amount of material needs full investigation through actual doing rather than merely discussing. Unless the team are really superb, however, in their mastery of improvisation then they are unlikely, with the best will in the world, to find the "rhythm" that will, by intuition or hard work, come readily to the individual writer. Similarly, if they dispose of the services of a director, then it is difficult to know in performance just how "things are going." Within my own experience, I am constantly surprised by the number of occasions when a performance has been "felt" as very good by the actors, but has been seen to be substandard by the outside eye of a director or producer who is not involved as an actor. The reverse is equally true. Many times actors have apologized for giving what felt to them to be an awful performance, where the outside observer has been able to see it as extremely good. Most of this is, of course, due to one form or another of "self-indulgence." If the number of different adjustments I am suggesting for Participatory Children's Theatre are valid, then the functions both of playwright and of director or producer are of paramount importance.

An interesting way of opening with the youngest group is to combine the welcoming and sitting of the youngsters with the actual action of the play. In this manner, the play has almost started before the youngsters enter the hall, and the seating is made easier because of the attraction of a character who is busy in the middle of the circle. Whether started this way or not, it is always advisable for the actor helping with the seating to do so from *inside* the circle, from which position it is possible to call the youngsters toward him and then point out what should be a very clearly marked line on the floor, inviting the youngsters to sit behind the line. This is a far more complex operation if the actor is *outside* the circle, as he tends to get behind the youngsters who don't know if they should look at him or at the floor. If adults are present as part of such an audience, they will probably prefer to sit on chairs, though it is surprising how many will sit on the floor among the children. When all the youngsters are settled, the adults on chairs should be invited to sit behind them, bringing their chairs close to the back of the final row — not settling against the outside walls of the hall, as they then "feel" like an audience to the participating audience as well as the play. Also, once the actors become fully sensitive to each different size of audience, their playing, including use of voice, should be delicately and exactly attuned to include everybody up to the back row. If they achieve this, then others sitting much farther away are really in no position to make such critical comments as "I couldn't hear the actors," or "I don't think they *projected* enough."

Despite the actors' doing everything they sensitively can in their consideration for these youngest audiences, there still may be one or two children who cry. It is important that the actors neither are distracted by this nor attempt to do anything about it personally. Certainly they must not unsettle the rest of their performance or start some kind of compensatory "playing-down" attitude. Usually it is possible for them to draw the attention of one of the adults to the upset child, then leave that adult to cope with the situation. It is unwise to assume at once that tears mean the child is "frightened" by the play or playing, because there are many other possible causes. In my experience, the main cause is the need to pee-pee, often because of excitement, and the awful problem of not knowing how to get away from where they are sitting in order to go to the toilet — another important reason for not stringing-out the smallest and youngest around the front row. They don't know the people behind them, and feel trapped. Of course, this does not mean the cast should *assume* the fault is not theirs, but there is usually an opportunity to check after the performance to find out if there was a specific reason. It is amazing the variety of reasons one does hear about, from "being a timid child" to "having only just moved to the area so everything is terribly new" and even including such reasons as "losing a handkerchief." Tears seldom happen with children 6 years upwards, particularly if they have had at least one term at school.

For both the younger and the older age groups, the aisles used by the actors for entrances and exits need to be very clearly marked on the floor with the marking going sufficiently away from the acting area to include the back row. Usually this can easily be done with masking tape, which can be removed after the performance. Then the actor or actors who help with the seating can have a quiet word of explanation to those flanking the masking tape, asking them to "protect" the space for them. Even the young ones enjoy this "responsibility" and it makes for a pleasanter atmosphere than leaving it to chance, only to find youngsters, because of their absorption in the play and their anxiety not to miss any of it, straying over the line and being yanked out by adult authority.

There are so many reasons why the approach to opening a play with the 5 to 8 age group be carefully considered. The trouble, thought, sensitivity and practice given to these factors by the group of actors is amply repaid in the resulting harmonious experience they have with each audience.

A whole new potential is opened up by having the 9 to 11/12 group separate, where so many approaches could be tried that would be wholly inap propriate if the younger ones were present as well. In one play, **The Island**, the opening is of machine gun fire, rifle shots and military commands — all from offstage. In another, **The Key**, there are shouts from offstage and one man comes in helping another in a partial state of collapse. In another, **The Deci sion**, the attempt can be made to start participation as the audience is assembling, and, in the very first speech of the play, a long description of the place and people of Xavia, the audience soon discover they are part of the play. They are the people of Xavia. So, as they assemble they can be quietly asked to "make" imaginary things — maybe carving wood, maybe moulding clay, weaving or making baskets. Many will be astonished by the request, for they are moving towards a conscious awareness of theatre and the possible beginn ings of self-consciousness in their own personal growth. Because of this, there are important peer group considerations and the older ones may feel unhappy about doing "this kid's stuff" if the younger ones (having possibly arrived first) are already involved and the younger ones may become bothered when they realize that the older ones are watching them. If the actor (the character in the play is called "Barsac") knows of these potential reactions, then he will quickly be able to sense how to handle the situation, knowing, too, that the fullness of his own absorption and sincerity are key factors, as must be the fullness of his compassion for the way *different audiences* will react. For exam ple, if there are many people in the audience who have been involved in par ticipatory theatre before — even perhaps only once, their reaction will be quite different from an audience that has had no such experience. If many members of the audience are involved in creative dramatic work in their own school lives, they too will react quite differently from an audience where few, perhaps none, have had such an experience. If Barsac is aware of such possible factors and their effects, then he will not "blame" youngsters who do not respond either as he would wish or hope for them to do or as another audience did at another time. So, with all audiences he might try this participatory opening. With some he may quickly and intuitively feel that for one reason or another it is best not to persist with it. With others he may feel quite differently, and even extend the experience for a minute or two before starting on the opening speech of the play. But even where it doesn't fully "work," there still is value in the attempt in terms of bond-building and helping the youngsters to feel free to chat with each other before the start of the play. They will also be less surprised when the moments of participation arise later on. I stress the above points in order to emphasize the necessity for "purpose and planned intention" in any and every form of close audience contact and all types of par ticipation. It is only when such activity is added gratuitously to a play, as a kind of gimmick in order to be in the fashion, that "things go wrong." But the reverse is possibly as true, when people take a play that has participation built into it as an integral part of the story and the action, and then decide to leave it out because they think participation "is old-fashioned," or because they have had one or two "unhappy experiences." To leave it out can be as unbalan cing to the play as to put some in that isn't meant to be there.

The differences in *type of participation* possible with the two different age groups has already been pointed out. Another important variant is the *timing* of such moments of participation and, again, it is helpful for us to think about children in their own creative play and from the point of view of the place of such activity within their school lives.

As a man of theatre, I fully symphathize with the view of those who feel

"Surely theatre should be a relief from all this business of school." I heartily
agree — a relief and let's hope an enrichment through experience that will not
necessarily happen at school. We must be tolerant, however, of the fact that
society has decreed that most children from 5 or 6 years old must spend about
hours a day, five days a week, 33 to 35 weeks of the year for 10 years or more
at school. That is fact. And to spend such an enormous segment of one's life in
such involvement means a very dominant effect on one, both consciously and
unconsciously. Nobody involved with any aspects of the lives of youngsters
can afford to ignore such a fact. Furthermore, I believe we should, in theatre,
be glad of the incredible range of understanding of children and creativity that
belongs to teachers who care about such work as an integral part of the
development of youngsters. This can be a vital two-way process. Without being exact in equations, I would basically suggest that half of my understanding of approaches to Participatory Children's Theatre comes from working
with children and young people in school. And half of my understanding of ap-
roaches to Creative Dramatics and other arts in school comes from experience and experiment in Participatory Theatre. The burden of the point I
am making is that in both cases I have managed constantly to keep "the
child" at the center of and as the fulcrum of both activities, rather than let my
personal interest in either "theatre" or "education" dominate. The child remains *whole.*

Human beings were not made to sit still for endless periods of time. One of
the values of drama in schools is found to be that by balancing moments of
physical activity with academic study, children and young people are in fact
helped in their concentration on the academic work — a quite different idea
from that of not taking any risk of losing their attention because you'll never
get them back. I have found this so very true of adults, as well, and, even at
such grave occasions as that of giving a keynote lecture for Universities, have
asked (usually to the surprise of my hosts) for a gramophone to be available.
Then, at roughly half hour intervals in the lecture I have involved the whole
audience in a minute or two of practical activity, whether or not they have
done any of that kind of thing before. Invariably I have then been able to point
out to them that it is now much easier for them to resume listening to me
because of the restoration of a perfectly natural "balance of energy." I have
not lost them or their attention. I have regained it. Incidentally, it also drains
any remnants of pompous formality.

This same factor of balance of energy is true for youngsters of both the age
groups we have been concerned with, but particularly true of the 5 to 8 age
group. Their concentration span when only sitting still, watching and listening, appears to be approximately 7 minutes. After that time come moments of
what is often called restlessness or lack of attention, but is probably no more
than the body instinctively (a kind of natural reflex action) seeking this
balance. If this observation is roughly true and if the basis of participation lying in a natural wish "to help" is also true, then in the construction of plays
with integral participation one of the aims of the author can be that of marry-
ing the two needs and making sure moments of logical participation arise at
"regular" intervals during the play. Such moments must really be integrated
into the story and not just put in to cope with restlessness. This is one of the
values of such moments as, for example, "drinking the mixture with the
lum" in **The Bell,** or the humming to go through the mirror in the **Mirrorman.**

There are, basically speaking, two kinds of individual reaction to this inner
need for "balancing energy." One is reflex and often both unconscious and

beyond personal control, the yawn (the body's gasp for oxygen), perhaps the one most common to adults and children. The other, the need to ease the stiffness of limbs and to change the weight of the body, etc. can be much more individually controlled. As adults listening to a lecture, we "find a moment," one that will not disturb the speaker or other listeners, to cross or uncross our legs, to lean forwards or backwards or from one side to the other, to fold or unfold our arms. Very often our happiest moment is when the speaker makes us laugh, and during our laughter we probably make an enormous number of movements before finally settling down into a new position. Young children (that 5 to 8 group) have many reflex reactions, which is one of the important reasons for letting them sit on the floor instead of on chairs. Quite naturally they are not able to exercise nearly as much in the way of conscious control, so again, regular moments of participation help them.

The older age group (the 9-11/12), however, has both more awareness and more potential for control, and, if as is possible, the nature of the play they are watching is one which grips their interest, then their concentration span when sitting still, watching and listening, will be much longer than with the younger group, and they do not need the same kind of "regular" moments of participation as the younger group. So the timing of their participation can be different. Again, there is no set formula, and it has been interesting to deliberately experiment with many different approaches for this age, but still keeping to the principle that the participation must be integral to the theme and story. It cannot just be gratuitously slotted in. So the actual nature of the content must be a governing factor.

CONTENT

I have tried to indicate the many advantages that accrue in terms of audience participation and opening of plays the moment one is able to divide the 5 to 11/12 age group into 5 to 8 and 9 to 11/12 groups. But, the principal advantage is possibly in terms of content, which in turn affects all the other factors including that of endings. The simplest explanation regarding the change of content is to say that quite naturally the older group can carry an intellectual content that is way beyond the potential of the younger group. This is, of course, quite true. What has surprised many people, however, including educationists involved with drama, is the extraordinary extent to which the older group can be stretched. Or is it really so extraordinary? Is it perhaps that in a totally controlled and highly systematically tested area of intellectual development it is possible that we underestimate the capacity of youngsters? Is it that we place too high a premium on intellectual knowledge as different from intuitive understanding? Indeed, do we perhaps not give sufficient credence to the latter? The factor of "intellect-intuition" is a vitally important one in terms of the theatre experience, especially for those of us who see theatre as an opportunity to extend "the horizons of experience" by "opening new doors and windows." Let us take the comments of two school administrators regarding this potential and a point of view relative to it.

Whenever I have written and directed new Children's Theatre plays, have always tried to give one or more free dress rehearsals in schools where have known from past experience that the administrator is interested in the kind of work being attempted. Such opportunities were very particularly important at such times as experimenting with the division of the age group 5 to 11/12 into two halves. I think it was quite natural for me to be concerned as to whether I was going too far in my developmental attempts with the separate age groups, particularly with the older group. After all, I was on a fairly secure basis with the younger age group simply because the plays for the over-all age had been weighted heavily in their favor, and at this stage little change was being made regarding content or production in terms of this age. The differences were, however, considerable in terms of the older group. One of the many questions I asked of the administrators was the simple and very basic question: "Do you think they understood the play?" Here are two very pertinent replies, which inevitably had an important effect on future experiments:

1) When I ask children to look at a picture or listen to a piece of music, the only question I do not ask them is "do they understand it?" I believe the same should hold true for the players and their plays.

2) If you mean do they "intellectually comprehend it?" then I must say that 10% of my children comprehended 100% of the play, and that 10% probably did not comprehend any of it. The remaining 80% would fall into varying degrees between these extremes. But if you are asking me how many *intuitively understood* the play, then I would say 100% understood 100%

I sincerely ask readers of this book to give a great deal of meditation to these two thoughts from brilliant education administrators. For me, in a nutshell, here lies the basic point of the arts in education — *intuitive understanding.* Here lies, as well, the core of Children's Theatre experience — *intuitive understanding.*

The vexed problem for many people involved in Children's Theatre is the realization that theatre can "help children *to think,*" mistaking the idea of "thinking" as synonymous with "feeling" and "intuiting." This idea is often behind the notion that Children's Theatre should be associated with problem solving, be the problems social or political. The situation is complex. Of course, there may be all kinds of problems to do with today's society and the changes in that society that children and young people should be encouraged to think about. But I personally believe it is both foolish and unjust to present, within the full emotional potential of theatre, any situation that creates a need for decision making in terms of current detailed social problems which we, as adults, have not been able to solve over generations. To do this seems to me to be "forcing the sins of the fathers." I do not personally feel that such proselytizing should be part of theatre, for any cause, political, religious or any other. This use of theatre is not so much associated with helping children to think as with quite straightforward and blatant brainwashing — the diagram, not the picture. Yet, the fascinating factor of theatre for this 9 to 11/12 age group is that it can include so much "stretching of experience," so many fascinating things to think about at the time and ponder about later and so many *pictures* to stimulate "wonder" rather than *diagrams* to solidify "knowledge."

At the end of the already mentioned play, **On Trial,** the audience is addressed for the first time by one of the central characters, when it is revealed that the whole story has been a flash-back over events during *his* trial for being responsible for the death of many of those who accompanied him on the journey. He says to us, the audience, "You, the jury, must decide. *You,* the jury." He goes and the play ends. When the character says that final line, that very moment is the *first* moment that it is suggested to the audience that the problem is one for them to wonder about. To have suggested, even hinted to them earlier that they would be confronted with such an end, would have been to distort the entire experience of the play and all of the circumstances surrounding it, changing it all from the intuitive to an intellectual experience changing the picture to a diagram. Personally I have never countenanced an group returning to the audience to discuss this decision. Let be. *Post-mortem* are not part of theatre experience if that experience is concerned with the pic ture rather than the diagram. Similarly, the need to "prepare" youngsters, o any one else for that matter, *before* they see a play can again change the pic ture to a diagram and in advance set-up the notion that for theatre the intellec is of more importance than feeling. Television and cinema will continue to wi their adherence for, among other reasons, their lack of need for such prepare tion.

Naturally there can ultimately be a great deal of value in discussing a sorts of factors surrounding the experience of a play, but the value depends o the *time lapse after the event.* Of course it is possible for intuitive an thoughtful decision making to be an integrated participatory factor in a pla for this older age group. Indeed, the very reason why the play, **The Decision** was so titled was because the audience, identified as members of the commun ty, are given the responsibility of deciding the future of their land — makin the decision as to whether their country should accept or reject many aspect of the advance of civilization. Their leader or ruler calls upon the community t make its decision. Do they really want to change their way of life? Will a change necessarily be for the better? The audience is invited to discuss th matter in small groups for a short while and then the vote is taken. The vot was always quite genuine, though I had assumed when writing the play tha every audience would vote for "change." I was soon to be proved wrong. A about the tenth performance the vote went the "other way," and did so fc several performances, necessitating the writing and rehearsing of an alter native ending to the play. As the play is written in verse, the actors did not fee as comfortable when improvising an alternative ending.

This play, **The Decision**, also involves an experiment in audience participa tion for this 9 to 11/12 age group. Quite deliberately there is *no participation a all* in the first 30 minutes of the play, except for the few moments durin assembly, as already described, of carving with Barsac. This certainly teste the play's capacity to hold the interest of the audience, and there are sufficien number of humorous sections which enable all forms of reflex necessities t move the body and change positions to happen without any kind of distu bance either to the actors or to other people in the audience. Then, after th decision is made, there is a ten minute sequence of very active participation i volving the whole of the audience (up to 200) all over the hall or gymnasiun Because of the long period of sitting, the four actors had to be very ready for possible "explosion" of physical release, the more so because the situation i the story calls for some urgency of effort. It was soon found that this type full audience participation was well worth trying with this age group, but great deal of company preparation was necessary for it to be a fully constru tive experience.

There were two basic necessities even in terms of booking performance One was to be absolutely certain that no more than 200 were in the audienc and the other that the age group should be the 9 to 11/12 group *only.* One ha to be very firm with people who say: "Really, what difference does one yea make? Our eight year olds are very intelligent!" — or similar pleas to bring i just another 30 or 40. This is where the actual quality of so much Children Theatre work can suffer because of economic considerations. With certai plays, some groups might solve some of their box office problems by overe ending what in fact they know to be the best maximum audience. With a play like **The Decision** such a risk cannot and should not be taken. When the work is subsidized it is often possible not only to play to exactly the right age-group but even to cut down numbers, thus ensuring better performances.

The problems of the participation itself perhaps center around the word "improvisation" and the attitude of so many that this means everything can be left to chance — "Free, flexible and open-ended!" We have met the problem before, but meet it even more acutely when four actors are each taking on the responsibility of one quarter of the audience, in fact, 50 youngsters each. The rule about staying in character applies here very strongly. Added to this, it is usually far wiser for each actor to *feel* in terms of "directing a crowd scene" rather than of being a teacher conducting a drama lesson. Many of these initial experiments in audience participation, however, were linked to the idea of helping teachers to see different approaches to the use of drama in the classroom.

At the start of the participation, one has to guard very carefully against creating an atmosphere of overexcitement either by pushing activities too fast or by overstressing the urgency of the situation. Yet, the very urgency is the backbone of the scene, without rush and panic. Most actors have found it wisest to start by gathering their group of fifty around them and outlining the over-all nature of their task. Because we are concerned with "doing" it is wisest not to start with discussion. To say, "What do we need to do?" merely sets off a thought in many youngsters' minds that this is going to be some kind of academic exercise and test, or perhaps the thought that this character really is a bit stupid if he or she really needs to ask questions like that. But to say, having outlined the whole project, "Right, everyone, the first thing we need to do is..." clarifies both the approach and the detail of action. They will accept the convention at once and it can be much wiser to have their first activity start where they are sitting rather than saying, "Go, fetch or do..." But this becomes fully valid when the actor is ready for it, or perhaps with a smaller group to handle or because the size of gymnasium lends itself. As we have met before, it is wise for the actors to avoid demonstrating activities and also to be ready for the speed with which each activity will be accomplished. There will not be the adult detailed concern for accurate mime, though actors are very quick to see within the first activity whether or not any drama is done by the group and therefore have some intuitive feeling for how deep the succeeding activities may turn out to be. As activities in this kind of participation develop to a wider use of the floor space, so each actor can go on with the very clear geographical factor that: "We're responsible for this area from here to here. So, work in pairs with a partner and go ahead with..." After a few performances the four actors can often time the start and completion of each activity to coincide for all groups, so that suddenly two hundred people are working all over the space, with a kind of intuitive group control. Always it is wise to keep in mind the phrase, "And when you've done that, then..." and go on to suggest the next activity. These words could be inserted before telling them to "go ahead." In this way we constantly feed a stream of intended activity. It is often only when something has been completed by the youngsters and they don't know what to go on to next that they "find something to do" which, as likely as not, will have nothing to do with the play.

Working in pairs helps build confidence for those who may feel a bit timid or self-conscious. Later, maybe, they can be invited to work in threes. Fours may not work, because they are quite likely to become two pairs, but it might be worth trying; similarly with fives, though we must be aware that fives will break into groups of 2 and 3. During each activity the actors can move freely among the various groups, telling them the next thing to get on with. So, each actor keeps a firm grip on the organization of the situation for his quarter of the audience. It is far wiser to really get on top of the organizational procedure in the first few performances, and then begin to assess the extent to which one can do more stimulation of the atmosphere of urgency and so on. Yet it needs to be done without killing the spirit of adventure and the kind of excitement that this opportunity for activity can so readily stimulate. We should not be concerned with control for control's sake, and we must accept as entirely human and quite inevitable that there will be a certain number in each group of fifty who will test their leader to see how far they can go. Again it is necessary for the actors to be firm about individual situations, but from within character. An actor can easily say, privately to the particular people it applies to: "I'll never cope with all this if you're going to muck about. We need everybody's full cooperation, so you three please go and get..." This is perfectly acceptable and real, but if the actor comes out of character and plays a new "teacher" role, then the atmosphere will totally change. So, with the activities broken down into sequence, all four groups of 50 will find that they do work closely in parallel.

Throughout the whole of such a sequence, the actors are far more involved in the supervision of activities than in actually doing them. Indeed it is probably best for the group of four to decide in advance NOT to be involved in any particular activity, both to avoid any demonstration-imitation and to be free to be fully aware of what is going on with their section of the audience. This does not mean that any one of them may not suddenly spot a possible moment of personal involvement that could in fact help in many different ways. For example, three boys were tending to "muck about" during one particular activity. In a flash an actor joined them, saying: "Hang on, I'll give you a hand." By no more than 15 seconds intense absorption on himself helping, he brought a whole new depth of concentration to the boys. He then said: "I've got to look after something else over here so you go on with this." Without a glance at them he left and they went on with the new depth of concentration he had stimulated. And very often the words: "Would you help me with..." or "Would you help us by doing..." also make for an atmosphere of cooperation. And the identifying word "We" is always important. "We need to get..." "We ought to fetch..." The identification is a bond-builder and we are making a piece of conscious theatre. Our reality and sincerity are all important.

There are disarming moments in this type of participation for this age group (and all age groups beyond) that the actors need to be ready for. For example, right in the middle of this great heave of activity one of the youngsters might well say to one of the actors: "Are you a real actress, miss?" or "Haven't I seen you on TV, miss?" If the actor knows such a moment might arise, then he/she can cope easily by quite simply saying: "No time to talk about that now. Here, we'd better help these people." The youngster will accept the reply. The situation only becomes awkward when an actor either tries to play games of logic: "There is no TV in Xavia," or gets involved in discussions based on whether or not he has been on TV.

For actors new to such work, there is one very conscious effort they must make in terms of their own group, let along the whole audience. They must learn to be aware of the pairs, the threes, the fives — whatever small group the youngsters are working in. If they are only aware of "the mass," then with so much activity going on it is very easy to arrive at a dispiriting conclusion that the whole thing is *chaos*. This simply is not so, except on the rarest occasions which, in my experience, are usually associated with such factors as non-homogeneous audiences, or buses arriving to take away half the audience, or when the cast has been over confident and has generated too much feeling of rush from one activity to another in order to create the urgency of the situation. But I emphasize that these experiences are rare. Usually what appears to be chaos is only so when one looks at the over-all rather than at detail. This is important for the actors to be fully aware of as soon as possible. They must by the same token be aware of the fact that very often adults who are present at such a sequence of participation do not know about looking at the detail and so think they are seeing chaos. It is good to find the opportunity of talking to such people afterwards. Once the factor is pointed out to them, they suddenly realize that it couldn't really have been chaos since all groups finished at roughly the same time.

FURTHER BREAKDOWN OF AGE GROUPS

Just as practical experiments with participation led to thoughts about the possibilities that might accrue from breaking the 5 to 11/12 age group in two, so did these experiments, together with the resulting effect on *Content*, lead to the realization that a further subdivision of the age groups would make possible even deeper approaches to content. The stretching experience with the older age group grew play by play until it became clear that content, although seeming to hold the interest of the 9 year olds, was really more suitable for the 10 to 11/12 age range. At the same time, the play being done for the 5 to 8 age group seemed possibly of least challenge to the 8 year olds. In fact it was clearly possible to have one play for the 5 to 7 years, another for the 8 to 9 years and another for the 10 to 11/12 years, with many differences in content and much opportunity for experiment with participation as well. The 5 to 7 group needed both the simplest forms of participation and the very simplest of story lines regarding content. Where participation was concerned, the 8 to 9 group were fully within the range of conscious drama, but not so toward conscious theatre, and the content factor could be deeper than for the youngest and yet not quite reach the possibilities that exist for the 10 to 11/12, who are really moving almost into a whole new area of work — that for secondary young people.

It is perhaps important for the reader to know and understand that all of these experiments, including the writing of the plays, were for Theatre Centre Ltd., London, England, a fully established professional children's theatre organization with many companies touring schools during school hours and with the closest possible links with teachers and educational administrators. I mention this because the circumstances were *very special*, enabling a great amount of experiment, even though the "commercial" or box office factors of the work had to stand through its own merits. There was no question of experiment for experiment's sake, with anything or everything goes. The plays and productions had to work on an incredibly high standard, established by the Theatre Centre itself. No one employing the Centre was prepared to accept any kind of falling away of standards simply in the name of experiment.

I fully appreciate that such detailed specialization of age groups and conditions is improbable for the majority of Children's Theatre groups, particularly commercial organizations. But I believe that, in terms of the future, the converse is possibly true — that there will be more support for Children's Theatre

117

from public and private funds when companies are able to demonstrate their readiness for, interest in and capability to do precisely the kind of specialization we are concerned with in this section.

One aspect of the approach to *Content* is this experiment of breaking down the 5 to 11/12 age group into *three* different audiences was to take a basic theme and approach it from three different angles, each appropriate to its own age group. Theatre Centre was actually able to spend several years performing in one school a day with a performance from 9:30 to 10:15 for the 5's to 7's, a different play on the theme from 10:45 to 11:35 for the 8's and 9's, and a third play from 1:30 to 2:30 for the 10's to 11/12's. The first of these trilogies was based on the theme: "The Clown Who Lost His Laugh." To emphasize the factor of the common theme, the plays were called: "Clown I," "Clown II" and "Clown III," though subsequently they were renamed: **Mr. Grump and the Clown, The Valley of Echoes,** and **The Clown.** Perhaps the easiest way of describing the *total distinction in approach to the theme* for the three separate age groups is to give the briefest outline of each story:

Clown I, for 5's to 7's: **Mr. Grump and the Clown.**

"Jenny and Claire ask the audience if they would like to hear a story, but before they begin, David and John join them and want to *do* a story rather than listen to one. With the help of costumes from a Magic Costume Box, each becomes a character involved in the story of the clown who lost his laugh, the amazing adventures in recovering it, and eventually bringing laughter and gaiety back to Grump Castle, which has been a miserable place ever since Mr. Grump lost his laugh."

Clown II, for 8's and 9's: **The Valley of Echoes.**

"To recover his laugh, the Clown is told he must journey to the Valley of Echoes and return the Echo King's magic glove. The journey, which contains an abundance of adventure and mystery, involves the Clown being chased through the Forest of Fear by the Shadow People, then a difficult climb over the Mountain of Memories, and a conflict with the Icicle Queen, who rules the Mountain. He is helped along his journey until he eventually reaches the very center of the Valley of Echoes, where he finds and returns the King's glove and so regains his laugh."

Clown III, for 10's to 11/12's: **The Clown.**

"In this quite serious study of the beginnings and routine hard work of a Clown's life, the major part of the play is concerned with a 'filmed' flashback, just before the Clown's retirement. As the story unfolds, we learn how the Clown started as a Circus roustabout with natural awkwardness and humor that caught the eye of the circus owner. After years of practice he developed a famous act with his friend, Jock, the Ringmaster, who is later killed as the circus is trying desperately to escape from a small country engaged in civil war. It is the death of his friend that causes the loss of the Clown's laugh. At the end of the play, we learn that although the Clown is about to retire because he is too old to carry on his athletic routines, he is to take Jock's place as the new Ringmaster of the Circus."

The themes are all quite different, geared as closely as possible to the age groups for which they are written. Interestingly, the middle age group, if split, could divide to the other two plays, the 8's joining **Mr. Grump and the Clown,** and the 9's joining **The Clown,** but neither of the two years would receive as full an experience as when staying together for **Valley of Echoes.** Certainly there could be no question of the 5's to 7's joining **The Clown** as almost every aspect of the story would be totally beyond them, and the 10's to 11/12's would find **Mr. Grump and the Clown** quite infantile. And again, while the 6's and certainly the 7's might well have a happy experience with **The Valley of Echoes**, it would certainly be quite unsuitable for the 5's.

But not only is *Content* affected by being able to "fine down" to these more specialized age groups. Inevitably, the potential for audience participation is considerably affected as well.

In **Mr. Grump and the Clown** full use is made of a Storyteller who has control over events and developments of the story and the place, need and type of audience participation. This, together with the use of a Magic Costume Box means that the whole story has total simplicity geared very carefully to the 5 to 7 age group and "control" of participation is even *practiced* with the use of a cymbal for different experiences involving "growing into" various things, creatures and people. Although all of this can work in the non-educational setting, there is clear intention to help teachers who see the play in school during school hours to have a first hand experience of one of the most important aspects of creative drama in the classroom, which is precisely this use of sound, developing as it does from the youngsters' own preschool discoveries of time-beat, rhythm and climax. Once more, from our own observation of "play" as such we can see so many ways of helping "a play" in terms of Children's Theatre.

An interesting problem arises here for the four actors. In the script they are named Claire, Jenny, David and John. But the simplicity of the opening, with Claire and Jenny simply talking about the idea of "having a story" and then David joining them to say that he would rather "do" a story than listen to one, often leads the group of four actors to want simply to "be themselves" at the opening, allowing room for character development as they become other people in the story. Of course, this is entirely possible, but it has its problems, because the most difficult person to enact on the stage is oneself. In one sense, being oneself is the very antithesis of *acting*, and I have, personally, when producing or directing plays of this kind advised the actors to find characteristics in even such a *straight* part that give them some creative essence to get their teeth into. For some actors this can often be a difficult concept to go along with, perhaps until some fortuitous accident helps reveal the difference more clearly. For example, an actor named Bob is cast as David but prefers to be himself and use his own name. To start with, this seems fine. Then one day he arrives at rehearsal rather tired and with a headache. As himself, i.e. as Bob, the tiredness and the headache can have a great effect on rehearsal. The person in the play, however, David, does not have this tiredness and headache, so it is much easier for Bob to overcome his predicament through the creative act of being David. I have even found this factor to be important in openings to Secondary programs when the actors have started the program with a "limbering session" in front of the audience, partly as a factor of bond-building. For many actors, limbering is a very private matter in their own personal lives, so it has been much easier for them to accept the idea of sharing this aspect by assuming a role slightly different from their own personalities in order to approach the limbering in front of an audience.

The person who is the storyteller in such plays also has fascinating problems to deal with, perhaps most especially for so young an age group. The difficulty lies in the fundamental difference between a storyteller and a narrator. As a writer of plays for Children's Theatre, I have always tried to avoid the use of a narrator simply because I have felt it to be taking the easy way out of dramatic problems that should be solved dramatically. So, outside of certain

Audience Participation

"linking moments" and even then looking for the possibility of narration being done in some exciting manner (e.g. over loudspeakers from the tape recorder, humorously, chorally, etc.), I have tried to avoid the ubiquitous narrator as such. The tendency, in my experience, is for narrators to be imparters of facts and, as such, to be often rather dryly academic and straightforwardly informative. The storyteller, possibly one of the oldest of all characters, is quite different from this, being concerned with the painting of action, with emotion and feeling. In a young children's play, particularly if there is even one doubt in our minds about whether the youngsters will comprehend, there can be a natural tendency to turn storytelling activities into explanations. This is an entirely different experience.

This point is very relevant to the training of teachers and others in charge of storytelling with children. So often, one hears such careful approaches to making each word clear with almost the pedantry of the already discussed problem of "playing down." Often one hears what should be exciting, adventurous, and filled with feeling and evocation of mood and atmosphere, trailing off the lips as a string of dry facts. There is no answer to the problem except practice, practice, practice. In Children's Theatre such practice can often be a really vigorous help as part of limbering before rehearsals. With a little thought and ingenuity, first the director and eventually each member of the cast soon find exercises to set each other that can electrify the whole approach to storytelling. Some examples I have found useful:
a) Describing one's own journey to rehearsal as
   — an exciting adventure story;
   — the funniest experience for weeks;
   — a grim, foreboding tragedy;
   — a horror film.
b) A similar approach to many other ordinary experiences in daily life —
   — the lunch break;
   — the family takes the dog for a walk;
   — deciding what to watch on television;
   — going to the cinema or theatre.
c) Reading (and if storytelling involves reading stories, then there cannot be too much practice at this)
   — a "diary of events" from a Newspaper;
   — advertised programs from Newspapers or TV guides;
   — the births, marriages and deaths columns from newspapers;
   — menus, or details from a cookery book manual;
   — travelogues and other travel brochures.
d) Reading from
   — newspaper and magazine reports of different kinds;
   — the syllabus of a course or workshop;
   — instructions for a "do-it-yourself" construction;
   — reading names, addresses and telephone numbers from a telephone or street directory.
Every group will think of many other approaches for themselves. For Children's Theatre casts, such an approach can often appear to be a "dreadful chore," but actors who have taken the trouble to involve themselves in such continuous practice, whether alone at home or as part of rehearsal, have always said what a difference it has made to any work they have had to do as a storyteller.

In my experience some actors do not spend nearly enough time *listening*

120

to some of our finest exponents of narration and storytelling or their ability to combine the two. For example, for many years I listened every Sunday evening to Alistair Cooke's "Letter from America." I never once did so as a conscious study of his techniques and yet I know deeply of the debt I owe for all that I learned from him intuitively. There are many such exponents of the art of narration and storytelling who, quite unconsciously, can help all of us.

Finally, might I suggest that no actor involved in such work can possibly do other than help his own development by reading aloud for a few minutes each evening from prose, verse or whatever to an entirely imaginary audience. NOT to bore oneself can be a most exciting first step towards not boring other people. 'Tis all a matter of practice, practice, practice and, in my personal view and experience, giving thought to the difference between the picture and the diagram.

In a play for the youngest of the age groups, much of the participation needs to be of the *directed* kind, as the youngsters are not wholly ready for the stimulated. This is so for **Mr. Grump and the Clown.** In **The Valley of Echoes** for the 8 to 9 age group, although there is naturally still much directed participation, there is more opportunity for stimulated moments, many of them initiated by the central character, the Clown who lost his laugh, and is helped to find it by his friends, "the audience." At the opening of the play, Clown talks directly to the audience collectively, not to individuals. He should pause briefly for answers to his questions about what might have happened to his laugh. It doesn't matter if, at first, we are slow to respond. This is an introduction to the whole play and his approach thus sets the tone for further participation. He should concentrate on character and his worried, anxious mood and avoid "talking down" at any time. The members of the audience are his friends and equals. Answers to his question at this point may vary from the "smart-aleck" type to genuine helpfulness. Clown should ignore the former without being unkind, and follow-up the latter. For instance, someone might say, "It's in your mouth," in which case he can accept the idea but explain that he's already looked there. In fact, he could produce a mirror and look again. Or, it might be suggested that his laugh is inside of him. Again, he can explain that it used to be, but simply isn't there anymore. The key is to establish his urgent practical need of help from anybody and everybody, which is built-up throughout his speech culminating in his asking the whole audience to try to make him laugh. It is expected that this will be through "pulling funny faces," but individuals should not be encouraged to move from their places into the acting area to do "tricks," since such offers are likely to cause showing-off and exhibitionism. Should there be any such offers, Clown should suggest that they all do funny things sitting *where they are* and that it will need a lot of people doing things or pulling funny faces to make him laugh. This is another example of starting with the "offer" of *stimulated* activity, but being ready to move into *directed* participation, should that feel more advisable. In this particular scene, as already indicated, there are many potential moments when quite *spontaneous* participation might arise. The clown's final words "Thank-you, thank-you" will cause the efforts to stop and reseat any who are up. Again, this is an example of participation that happens in order to help a character, not just for its own sake.

The mystery and adventure that develop in the story from this and other characters are also indications of growth areas when the 8's and 9's are having a play to themselves without the presence of five-year olds. Participation becomes more closely linked to characterization and more dependent on the actor staying in character fully and sincerely for the participation. One pertinent point regarding the stage of development of the youngsters in relation to consciousness of theatre was revealed in early performances of this play. Apart from the full audience participation, an attempt was made to have two separate groups of six youngsters come from their seats in the audience to help one particular stage of a journey. It was soon found, however, that quite unlike working with the 10's and 11's, the conscious awareness of "making theatre" was not yet strong enough to overcome the selfconsciousness and worry of being watched by so many of one's peers. As far as one could tell, even with groups who were experiencing a certain amount of creative drama in their own school work, this factor was still true. The particular kind of small group participation was abandoned, and the needs of the characters and the moment in the story so adjusted that the entire audience was once more participating, but in two parrallel groups. I mention this because it is the kind of discovery that can only be made when there is genuine opportunity to experiment. I do not believe we would have discovered this specific detail unless we had actually tried experiments with the 8 to 9 age group separated from the 5's to 7's and from the 10's to 11/12's.

Groups concerned with a genuinely serious approach to Children's Theatre may often find themselves making similar adjustments almost performance by performance if they are playing a piece for a lengthy period of time. Maybe at one performance they realize they have a predominance of younger ones or of older ones, and realize that a few simple adjustments will be helpful for each particular audience. Of course, this does not mean making changes after just one or two performances simply because something or other has NOT "worked" as the actors hoped it would work, for there may be many other reasons for this including that of the actors having not yet quite mastered the particular moments. This is another example of where the outside and objective eye of the director is of vital importance to the actors, for it is nearly always impossible for the actors themselves to really spot the nature of problems when their direct involvement makes them a part of, maybe even the cause of, those problems.

The Clown, the third play in the experimental trilogy and for the 10 to 11/12 age group on their own, provides a tremendous contrast from the other two plays in content, character and approach to audience participation. In terms of content and character the nature of the change is perhaps best expressed in the words of many actors involved in this and subsequent plays for the same age group: "It feels more like rehearsing a play for adults. Indeed, except for the participation, it might be straightforward adult theatre."

This, in itself, is an interesting view of Children's Theatre with very direct bearings on rehearsal procedure when a group is able to rehearse even two plays for different age groups, let alone three. Which play does one rehearse first? It is interesting how many groups feel that the youngest play is the simplest and therefore the easiest and quickest to rehearse, and so tend to take the view: "Well, let's get that one out of the way as soon as we can, then we can get down to the more difficult older play." In fact, the very reverse is often the case, particularly if the actors have not had much, if any, experience of participatory children's theatre. If they feel the older play is closer to adult theatre, then they do not feel they have so many adjustments to make from their own adult theatre experiences. The adjustments they do make arise from the participation, and if these are made with a generous amount of time given to really thinking through the problems involved, then they are helping themselves to get on to a wavelength that is sure to be of value when they reach the younger play. Perhaps the most important factor of help for them is that by the time they start on the younger play, they are more ready to see how many so-called "adjustments" have already been made in the writing, how many others will need to be in terms of production and direction and *how few, if any,* need to be made by them in terms of their own approach to *acting.*

This third version, still based on the theme "the Clown who lost his laugh," approaches it from almost a documentary point of view. The device of the "flashback," is used as the life of the Clown is "recreated" at the request of a reporter and photographer who, hearing of the Clown's pending retirement, decide to make a film of his career. The participation includes both small group and whole audience participation.

Small Group:
6 people become reporters and six photographers, under the guidance of the appropriate actors.
20 people join the four actors as circus turns.
Whole-audience:
A sequence for the film in which everyone is involved, under the guidance of the four actors, with the whole procedure of setting-up the circus, unloading trucks, feeding the animals, setting-up stands and booths, preparing refreshments and raising and staking-out the "big top."

The control and organization of this whole audience sequence of participation has many similarities to that already described in detail for the final scene in **The Decision.** Possibly the sequence in this circus scene is easier, as the cast is able to make fairly clear decisions of what they will and will not try in terms of the size of audience, space and so on. With an audience of 200, it is even possible to do the whole sequence without anyone moving from their places, if this seems the most advisable approach. It may well be so for the first few performances.

In the small group participation, the two groups of six are involved throughout the entire play, mainly "taking photographs" of any action that interests them, using as "mimed" cameras their fingers and hands to make a viewfinder. As part of their practice at doing this, the whole audience is involved in the same activity, sitting where they are in the audience, looking for long shots and close-ups and the imaginary use of a zoom lense.

This is again an example of the interchange of ideas between creative activity in school and shared ideas with Children's Theatre. A great problem for teachers and others involved in creative dramatics is that of bridging from drama as *doing,* where everybody works at one and the same time and there is no audience at all, to moments which include *sharing,* where there will be the first experience of having to cope with "an audience" watching one's activity. In work in school, I have found that one helpful bridge toward this development was to make sure that those watching were as busy as those doing, so that there was no question of anyone's sitting as cold, objective, critical audience. This was best achieved by dividing the class into halves, with each half preparing, for example, a journey — maybe cutting their way through a forest or climbing a mountain, or crossing a jungle swamp. Both groups would try out their activity at one and the same time so as to become secure in their attempts to explore the potential of their theme. Then one group would repeat its journey with the other group making "a film" of it, using their hands and fingers as camera viewfinders, even moving from one position to another. They should be sensitive about not getting in the way of anyone actually involved in the journey. Then the second group repeats its journey, with the other now making their film. In this way, there is a first experience of "being looked-at," but because the audience is equally busy, one is not affected in the same way in terms of self-consciousness and challenge to one's concentration.

In this third version of **The Clown**, the major part of the small grou par- ticipation concerns the 20 youngsters who are "turns" in the circus, including two circus processions and an exciting journey sequence. Much of this par- ticipation takes place in the middle of the play, rather than as in **The Decision** toward the end, thus preserving rather carefully the balance of *theatre ex- perience* (participation with mind, heart and spirit) with *drama experience* (vocal and physical participation). This is a very exacting and difficult balance to find. The future of Children's Theatre writing contains enormous openings for experiment in just how far participation can be taken without the *theatre* experience being wholly taken over by the *drama* experience.

In another play, **The Key**, also for the 10 to 11/12 age group, the attempt is made to involve the whole audience, originally up to 200, in a journey that lasts for most of the play. Here again is the cross-fertilization of interest both in Children's Theatre and in Drama in Education. In their own creative drama, youngsters utilize (or teachers can introduce the idea of) two quite different forms of journey. One of these is perhaps most suited to a large space such as a hall or gymnasium, the other most suitable to the classroom because of its utilization of furniture. Either of these can be done in a larger or smaller space, however. The first kind involves the participants actually *travelling*, physical- ly moving from point A to point B and so on. The latter involves the participants *remaining in one place*. The actual journey is in the mind and the imagination.

With the experience of **On Trial**, many people had expressed their concern that only a limited number were involved from the audience, thus disappoint- ting the majority. To an extent I shared the concern, though I remain convinc- ed that becuase this age group is consciously aware of "making theatre" that the majority accept "the rules of the game" and their disappointment is neither long lasting nor deep. I also harbored the hope that many would in fact experience the journey in follow-up work with their own classes, and this un- doubtedly proved true. The challenge, however, was not to be overlooked. It is possible to have the whole audience involved in some kind of journey, as well as in the already fully proven moments of whole audience participation where everyone is involved in actions and sounds, but sitting in their places? **The Key** is an attempt at precisely that, having the whole audience of 200 involved in a journey, but the kind of journey where, *for the most part*, they remain in one place, with the journey happening in the imagination. Naturally, the scale of such participation involves the need for a great deal of creative organization by the four actors, again working within character and situation, and this is helped by dividing the audience into family groups of four or five at the very beginning of the story. These family groups work together throughout the whole journey. For actors who are not very experienced with this kind of total audience invovlement, it is obviously wisest to start with audience of about 80 instead of 200. It is also wise for the central character, in charge of the over- all organization, to have some kind of control instrument, again to be used wholly within character and situation. The instrument can vary. One group us- ed a whistle, but the connections with football, the school playground, the police, etc., always left a slightly uncomfortable feeling of a whistle not being wholly appropriate for this type of adventure. Possibly the most exciting and appropriate instrument to use is "the human horn," though again there may well be communities where this instrument would be as inappropriate as the whistle in others. Whatever instrument is used, the actor needs a moment of practice of its use with the whole audience, and again in character, and perhaps with emphasis on the need for immediate reaction to it as it will also be used in moments of danger or crisis. There is another important point to consider concerning the control of the participation when it is taken as far as it is in **The Key**. In some respects, it applies perhaps to almost all participation. Always there are two problems confronting the actor:

1. Will it work? Will it really happen? and then when it does...
2. How do I control it? will it get out of hand?

In my experience, participatory Children's Theatre is at its very best when the dominant concern in the actor's mind is not whether or not it will work. This is particularly reflected in the earliest performances of a brand new play. But, it is in these circumstances that actors need to work by trust and intuition and by "sheer sweat of the brow." Of course they need to be thoroughly prepared regarding points of being in character, of sincerity, of not "whipping-up" and so on, but many of these points are factors of trust and find a basis in intuition. Meanwhile, a slight element of uncertainty about whether everything is going to actually happen often helps the actor to put in that extra bit of energy that can tend to tie away once there is familiarity and certainty. These can be some of the most positive memories to recall at later performances. Quite different from this is the association I have had with the revival of some of these plays, perhaps several years after they were first performed. The Key is a case in point. On its revival there was an over concern with "control." It was fully known from past experiences that the participation would in fact work. No one had any doubts about this. But memories reflected some of the most difficult moments that had arisen with, say overstimulated and overexcited groups, or perhaps even the concern of some teachers or other adults who, because of their inexperience at observing "so much happening at once" tended to think the over-all was chaos instead of seeing the details of absorbed interest. Thus the revival became over concerned with control and preparation of the actors for that control, instilling in their own imagination a dreadful potential threshold which they felt a conscious need to avert or to sidetrack. For some of those involved, this inevitably stifles some of the intuitive challenge by overpreparation with intellectual techniques, and in turn this can take away some of the joy of the youngsters' experiences, as they can soon discern people who are overworried about "discipline" and so are holding back on opportunity. I recall one performance about when I could only say afterwards: "It went as smoothly as clockwork and was as *dull* as clockwork." There was none of the risk of heart and intuition, only the solid certainty of techniques. At the risk of belaboring the point, this is another example of the 'picture changing to a diagram."

In my own view and experience, there is with regard to the ending of Children's Theatre plays only one golden rule whatever the division of age groupsings, but particularly with younger children. They must never be left in a state of hyperexcitement, which for the performance in school can create problems for teachers who then have to take over their classes and settle back into the ordinary school and class routine. For the performance out of school such a state of excitement can lead to the youngsters themselves being careless about leaving the building when going out into the main roads with accompanying traffic dangers. Beyond this there are so many possibilities.

With youngest children I have usually felt the need to "tie-up all the ends" so there are no doubts or uncertainties that will bother them by overlapping into their normal lives. Very often it has seemed both logical to the play as well as a "fun thing" in its own right to end with music and some kind of very simple dance, even recapping in dance form a kind of outline of the story itself and the theme. But with the older half of this 5 to 11/12 group, the overlap possibility does present itself, so that the story can often end with a question mark, or perhaps at the end of one sequence of action that naturally leads the thoughts into further developments. For example, the journey is completed — now what happens? Maybe a new community is to be built, etc. For many schools, this type of open-end gives a natural birth to follow-up work in the classroom.

THE USE OF MUSIC AND OTHER ARTS

The field of experiment with the use of other arts in Participatory Children's Theatre is immense, and I do not refer simply to the growing exploration of such use in Theatre in Education projects, which usually have the advantage of more than a "one-off" performance, but actually within the span of a single Children's Theatre play of, say, 45 minutes to an hour's duration. Time, as such, is certainly an important factor and, even within the plays mentioned below that incorporated other arts, very much more "successful results" would have been possible except that in all cases the circumstances of performance were within the very tight timetable of a schools' tour, which enabled very little, if any, extensions of time in order to try to deepen and enrich experience. The few opportunities that did make this possible were sufficient to lend credence to the notion that the potential is very wide.

Before considering detailed examples, it is again worthwhile to consider the nature of children and their own creative activity, and the place of specialization in school curricula. Basically, the situation is quite simply that all children are capable of doing all the arts up to a certain age. I would not like to define that age terminal point because so many artificial factors affect it, and because so much depends on the attitude and approach of teachers and parents during the "formative years." Thus, I believe it is possible to preserve a simple delight in all of the arts for most of school life, if the fundamental approach is devoid of "criticism, false standards and the idea of progression." In schools, such a philosophy may or may not exist in primary and elementary education, but invariably will stop with Secondary Education, by which time the whole syndrome of "You are no good at..." will have wholly superseded the personal feeling of "I do enjoy..." Mix the effects of this background with the whole puberty growth area, including self-consciousness, the deep necessity for the preservation of personal dignity and self-esteem in a competitive world that mercilessly thrashes attempts and process if the product does not come up to some other person's standard or ambition and it is small wonder that the majority of teen-agers will opt out of the Arts and leave them to those who for various reasons wish to pursue them in a specialist manner. So, taking a very rough age that is linked with school age grouping, one could say that certain general approaches with the arts might be tried safely up to the age of 11 years or within the framework of the Primary or the Elementary School. Can Children's Theatre at least up to this age link-in with other arts? That is a challenge which fascinated me personally.

Within the general nature of Children's Theatre work, there seemed quite certainly to be two lines of approach worth attempting and it was these two that were incorporated into a very few plays. One consisted of an approach to "child music," the other to the making of masks and headdresses. In some senses it is perhaps true to say that the least number of experiments that have been made within the field of children's creativity concern music. While music is possibly the most accepted art form in schools generally, it is usually associated with singing, or with musical appreciation or with learning to play a recognized instrument, e.g. the piano, the violin, etc. There are, of course, many educators who have been concerned with creativity linked to totally non-sophisticated instruments, including very primitive instruments made by children themselves, but their approach is by no means common in schools. Pre-school children discover for themselves many basic elements of music, such as time-beat, rhythm and climax. Music, for many different reasons, is an important basic element of creative drama in schools, with its earliest use linked closely to what children themselves discover and try-out with quite unsophisticated instruments. Thus, in drama, music is closely linked with the development of all forms of movement, with feeling through mood and atmosphere, with the development of speech and language use, and even with the experience of and mastery of story-making and other forms of logical thinking. It is both interesting and worrisome that in this penultimate decade of the twentieth century, the official expectation of or demand for *accountability* in the arts is leading to more and more rejection of intuitive potential in favor of intellectual certainty. This means throwing overboard many approaches to the arts, which can only be based on long term developments, in favor of approaches that are slick and instantaneous and can be glibly accounted for in terms that are recognizable to those who mistrust the notion of intuition but feel secure with the apparently obvious developments of the intellect. Inevitably all creative work suffers from such an approach. "Instant imagination" is never more than the reflection of and manipulation toward someone else's ideas. Sympathy, tolerance, understanding and sensitivity belong to the realm of feelings, the training of which can take just as long as the mastery of such skills as reading, writing and arithmetic, although particulars and specifics, as externals, can easily be imposed by *thinking about feeling* rather than actually experiencing through emotion. In terms of *accountability* these approaches are fully approved because they can be seen to demonstrate successful training in rational thinking. Perhaps we should be asking ourselves: "Do we really want any further training in *rational* thinking?" The world that we live in is very largely the produce of rational thinking. If we are happy with that world, then fine. If we have doubts about it, then perhaps we need to turn to those aspects of experience that are concerned with imagination — the dream, mystical experience, intuition and hypothesis. The arts have a large part to play in such experience. Perhaps it would be a pity to debase them entirely to fit in with current trends of dominance of intellectual training, merely in order to gain them a say in the structure of education. Again, the picture and the diagram. The most significant area of work that has been thrown overboard in drama has been the use and development of improvised movement and dance drama, with their accompanying use of sound and of music. This deprivation is justified on the grounds that, except for the very few who might turn to some form of movement or dance as a profession, there is no real development accountability for the use of movement, if we have made the goal of drama the development of rational thinking. So we must try to be very clear that the *goals* of drama go way beyond this one factor — indeed that this particular factor has only arisen since the need for rational justifications about the use of drama. It is difficult to get closer to the snake devouring its own tail or "the mouse within the wheel" than that specific example.

This book is not the place to go into the detailed values of the part movement can and should play in the broad intuitive, imaginative and sensitive development of young people. But it is necessary to reiterate that such a case can be made, very closely linked with creative approaches to the use of music for physical expression, and to paint, clay, mask-making, etc. for expression in other arts. *Expression* is a vital balance in a world that is more and more filled with *impression*. Pre-school children have no problems about making music, if we as adults can perceive the difference between *noise,* a derogatory term we tend to use for all and every form of banging, etc. and *sound.* Only school and erroneous moments of correction in the home cause the birth of the fear of failure.

We have already considered sound associated with so many moments of audience participation. Sometimes the participation itself has actually consisted of sound made by the participants, vocally or with hands or feet. Sometimes, sound has been used by the actors to stimulate and to control that participation. In two plays the attempt was made to extend the use of sound to involve dance and to provide the audience with the means of *making sounds with instruments,* thus involving music participation. The music participation is primarily stimulated and controlled by one character in the story, who himself has and uses a tray of different instruments, including a tambourine which he uses as an over-all control instrument. But the tray also includes a Glockenspiel or Xylophone, some kind of maracas for shaking and a simple stringed instrument for plucking. Very early on he uses these instruments to help build up some simple dance movement with the participation of the whole audience responding with different parts of the body to different sounds that are made. Then the sounds are used for creating mood and atmosphere rather than beat and rhythm for dancing, and another character is helped in the story through the use of special "magic" music. All of these simple experiences, which involve the whole audience in *response to sounds*, are also helpful pre-experience for when they, themselves, are going to make sound with less sophisticated instruments, but with similar purpose and intention concerning either movement or mood and atmosphere. The following types of "home made" simple instruments are recommended for handing out to the whole audience:

Various types of SHAKERS
Items that can be used for DRUMMING or TAPPING
A few DOUBLE STICKS
A few PLUCKERS

The SHAKERS can be of various types:

In tins or other simple containers (sealed, so the contents cannot fall out) are dried peas, pins, rice or a few pebbles. These can be held in one or both hands. Similar SHAKERS can be made from plastic eggcups scotchtaped together and from some kind of shell fastened in the same way.

The TAPPERS can also be of various types:

Two simple pieces of wood with either another piece or a cotton reel fastened to one side of each piece as a handle. Two pieces of doweling can be taped together.

The PLUCKERS are the most difficult to make, but can be achieved with thin wire across a home made box frame (cigar or other wooden boxes), or even with various strengths of rubber bands stretched over boxes in a similar manner. They are worth spending a lot of time and trouble on as they are the main means of getting some "longer" sounds, in contrast to the ease with which one can make instruments that create short, sharp, staccato sounds. Of course, each group's ingenuity or experience will lead to many other kinds of instruments to experiment with, keeping in mind the need for simplicity in playing and also no problem in holding and controlling the sound maker *when it is not actually needed* as part of the story.

An example of this latter problem arose in early experiments with the use of the very charming and magical sound that could be made with very small bells. Accordingly sufficient bracelets were made with a few such bells hanging from each. All or the majority of the audience was to wear one, even if they also had another instrument. Of course, once these bracelets were placed on the wrist, even the slightest movement of the hand or the arm set the bells a-ringing. It was soon discovered that, even with an audience totally absorbed in the story going on in front of them, there was one continuous stream of very small unconscious movements, mostly of the hands and the fingers. Imagine the sound of from six to eight hundred bells as a continuous background to the actors' voices. One of the actors, from a moment of sheer inspiration, which one is often driven to by desperation, suggested that the "magic was leaking away," so asked everyone to hold the bracelet very hard with the other hand until the sound was really needed. This rescued the first performance and was incorporated into the next two or three. But the length of time at certain sections of the play where the sound was not needed was too long to impose so stringent a restriction on the youngsters. So the bells were banished.

For the play, **Balloon Faces**, instruments are all set out on a gaily decorated two, three or four level trolley, which can be easily wheeled into and around the acting area while the instruments are handed out by two of the characters. As they hand them out, the characters invite the youngsters to "explore" all the different sounds the instrument can make. This gives everyone something positive to do, and also drains away much of the excitement that is naturally generated. It also makes easier the whole challenge of using the instruments in very particular ways required by later stages of the story. It cannot be emphasized too strongly that before any handing out of the instruments, the controlling actor needs to have practiced response to his own control instrument. This can be done with warmth, humor and urgency, and needs to contain something of a challenge to each individual as well as bring some feeling of personal satisfaction when it is achieved. For example, the actor can say: "See if it is possible, the moment you hear this sound, *(makes strong sound on tambourine)* to become absolutely still, as still as a statue! Let's try it!" He invites everybody to be busy, and then tries out the sound. Maybe he says: "Yes, that's coming fine. Let's try it again. This time, whatever position you are in, the moment you hear the sound, freeze in that position. Oh, and if you happen to be chatting at the same time — oh-oh this is difficult — see if you can cut yourself off right in the middle of a word. Let's try again." And again, they practice. Maybe even a third practice is necessary, followed by a repetition of the fact that at any time he needs us all, the sound will come. As has already been mentioned in another section of the book, this is a much more personally exciting manner of being confronted with self-control than the disciplinary idea of "When you hear this sound, you will be quiet, sit-up, face front and listen to me!"

Once all the instruments are given out and everyone has had a little time to explore the potential of the instrument, the actor can stimulate many different sound experiences as a type of pre-experience of moments that will arise in the story, but without mentioning those moments or in any way trying to make a formal rehearsal session. The mastery achieved by general pre-experience will lead to simple intuitive awareness of particular needs when they arise. For example, the actor might try out the different *groups of instruments* playing on their own — SHAKERS, TAPPERS AND PLUCKERS; then, perhaps, simple time-beat, possibly for him to march about to; then perhaps, adding atmosphere, a different beat for him to "creep away" to; then a sound "so quiet that not even you yourself are sure you can hear it." This is an electryfying moment of total control. Then, he moves from these to "ghostly sounds," as though in a haunted forest; then perhaps adding very quiet ghostly vocal sounds as well as the instruments. Each group, and especially each actor soon finds, depending, of course, on how many performances lie ahead, what seems most appropriate to different audiences, affected by size and age and other circumstances. The above description applies mainly to a play for the 5 to 7 years old.

There are similar procedures, pre-experience and uses of the instruments for the 8 to 9 year olds whose mastery and control will be that much quicker than with the younger group. So, too, probably their inventiveness.

While I personally believe this experiment in Music Participation is most fascinating, with an enormous potential for future experiments, it would be grossly unfair to minimize the colossal organizational factor involved. Just the making and maintenance of so many instruments is a major task. They cannot be shoddily made, not only because of the aesthetic factor, but also because shoddy articles soon break. To have even one break during performance can lead to tremendous hold-ups as it is only fair to the youngster involved either to replace or repair the instrument at once. For this reason, the factor of maintenance is also burdensome, as every instrument needs to be checked after each performance to anticipate pending breakage. It is also burdensome to have to wipe over many of them with a damp cloth because of their use by many excited, but rather grubby and sweaty fingers. In actual performance, the giving out and collecting of the instruments is a most exacting task for the two actors involved, who must stay in character and need a phenomenal patience to cope with the excited joys and hopes of so many youngsters, not to mention possibly trying to answer dozens of pertinent questions at the same time as keeping the flow of giving out the instruments.

Finally, for many groups there is once again that most horrendous of all participation problems — TIME. I have mentioned this factor so often in these pages about audience participation, but must do so again here, particularly for groups that on the one hand may be very confined by time but also may be anxious to take every opportunity to experiment in some depth. These rigors of organization plus time apply equally to many potential developments of participation with Art Materials.

In a play for the 8's to 9's, **Magical Faces**, and in two plays for the 10 to 11/12 ages, **The Island** and **Adventure Faces** there is integrated mask-making. For this the audience is asked to be in groups of four. In each group three people create a mask on the face of the fourth person using raffia, gummed paper and tissue paper on a pre-cut blank square sheet of sugar or construction paper about 12 inches square. The pre-cuts were worked out in a series of experiments on uncut paper and eventually evolved to a sequence of slits and holes as in Diagram 18. A hole on each side is used for a piece of raffia which will be used to tie on the mask. One sequence of slits is used for a nose insert and another two for eyeholes. A third is used for creating a mouth with or without teeth. The remaining holes and slits can be used for raffia (including beard and hair) or for pressing through pieces of tissue paper which, together with the colored gummed paper can also be used for various forms of decoration. The intention is to achieve the complete mask *within approximately five minutes.* Even twenty minutes would not necessarily be long enough for all groups to fulfil their aspirations for the mask they want. On the other hand, sheer pressure of time helps everyone to get on with the task, trusting intuition rather than depending on intellectual exactness. This is made possible by the fact that no criticism is made of any of the work, and none pointed out as being good, better or best.

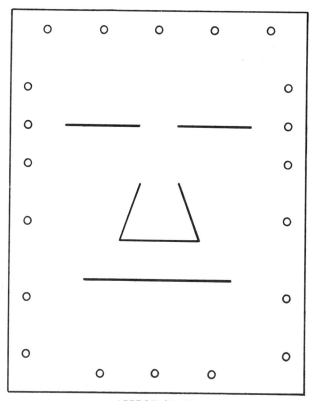

APPROX. 8"x11"
Diagram Number 18

Construction of Paper Mask Base
The eye slits and mouth slit can be enlarged and developed with scissors or simple "tearing." The nose is cut as a flap, but, if wished, can be torn off at bridge. The three holes to either side of the eyes are used, with raffia, for tying on the mask, according to fitting. All other holes are for "decoration" — example, using raffia as "hair" or "beard" or tissue paper for the same effect. The slots below the mouth can be used in the same manner. Gummed color strips are supplied for additional decoration.

131

Audience Participation

The mask participation in the play for the 8's and 9's is comparatively simple as everyone is free, within their groups of four, to make any kind of mask they wish with the materials available; there is also in the situation of the play itself no exposure of those wearing the masks. Indeed, until the climax they are deliberately hidden by their peers and only at the last moment revealed from their place in the audience.

The task for the 10's to 11/12's is both more complex in the making and the use. In one, the masks are made for a "Carnival of the Seasons," which forms the mainstay of the climax and ending of this play, and involves the audience itself dividing into four groups so that each group has a particular season as its main focus of activity. For this purpose the colors of the mask materials are carefully sorted to suit both season and the type of masks to be made, which in turn are linked to particular sounds and approaches to the ritual of the Carnival.

Season:	Element:	Colors:	Masks:
Summer	*Fire*	*Reds and purples*	*Devils and witches*
Autumn	*Water*	*Russet, green, brown*	*Monsters and Sea creatures*
Winter	*Air*	*Whites, blues and greys*	*Sprites, spirits, etc.*
Spring	*Earth*	*Greens, yellows*	*Trolls and earthly creatures*

The sound accompanying the movement of the mask-wearers can be made by appropriate instruments or through song and humming, and the theme for each section of the Carnival is the transition from one season to the next. The hope and intention is to build a definite form of ritual, but this, again, depends on availability of sufficient time. The danger is that the whole sequence of participation can be overstructured, thus taking away some of the intuitive pleasure in favor of precision and order, or else of leaving it all too free, in which case it may lack satisfying form and purpose. More than in any other play for this older age group this experience reveals the more fully conscious awareness of *theatre* that exists among the young people. The self-consciousness factor needs time and fuller rehearsal in order to be fully overcome. The unconscious and intuitive leanings towards mastery of a fascinating problem also needs more time for rehearsal. The fullest use of an approach to ritual with as many as 200 youngsters needs a great deal of organization. But, again, for groups that are fortunate enough not to be beset by the heavier time pressures, there is a great deal of experimental work that needs to be done with participation that involves some use of art work.

Groups attempting participation with mask making need also to be ready with the problem of litter at the end of the play. It is interesting that if not too much material for the mask making is given to each group of four, and if there is continuous encouragement from the actors for them to use *every scrap of the material* they have been given, then in fact there need be very little litter left at the end of the play. All the same it is wise to have a few broad brooms, a dustpan and some garbage bags available for an immediate swift clear-up after the audience has left.

The people wearing the masks can be invited to keep these and perhaps find them useful for some kind of continuity of aspects of the story at another time. In this way, the seed can be sown of possible follow-up work.

CURTAIN CALLS

Although there is no golden rule for ending plays for these age groups, except for that of not ending on any kind of peak of over-excitement, many groups of actors question the problem of a curtain call after the completion of the play. There are many who prefer to forego a curtain call in all types of theatre, including adult theatre, and I certainly share that thought with some kinds of theatre from the age of Secondary young people and upwards. With the youngest children, however, certainly with the 5's to 9's, whether they be in one audience or separate for different plays, it is important again to consider the viewpoint of the youngsters. No matter how gradually and slowly a play reaches its ending, there is still the moment when the characters are, as it were, suddenly snatched out of our lives and are gone, without even a single, final, special glance that might have been given if one knew for certain one would never see them again. Without being the least bit sentimental about it, there is something very stark about this sudden "disappearance," which can so easily be solved by the actors returning for the very simplest of curtain calls. This has nothing to do with the formal bowing to applause that happens in adult theatre. Indeed, it is as well for the actors to be ready for the fact that there well may not be clapping unless adults are present, in which case they will lead such. What we are really concerned about is an opportunity simply to say "good-bye" and "thanks for helping." So by walking in line, very simply around the acting area, with a little thought as to who should logically lead and who end the line, and as they go round, simply waving and calling "good-bye and thank you." It is remarkable how many actors have discovered that, within even only a few such experiences, they can catch the eye of almost every single member of the audience during this simple journey. If the attitude is one of "Gosh, I'd like to shake hands with every one of you," then the spirit of the event is soon caught hold of, and all else follows from there. It is wise not to attempt actually to shake hands with any single person for, once it's done with one, it is difficult to justify not doing it with all. The walk around for this curtain call should be with the heart toward the center of the circle, the natural way the majority of people go round a circle, including youngsters in their own drama or dance movement anywhere. Moving in the opposite direction is associated with "evil" and "witchcraft" and so on. This is an intriguing point for those concerned with producing or directing a play which contains actual witch characters, or any evil character. The "widdershins" movement is unconsciously recognized by the audience.

7

Audience Participation
in Secondary Schools

The main experience the majority of teen-agers have of live theatre is probably the school play which, in one form or another, will be familiar to most readers of these pages. For the most part, the occasion takes the form of a play in *one to three acts performed on a conventional proscenium stage* in the school hall or theatre. Seating can vary in sophistication from fixed and raised to a flat floor with chairs in straight lines.

Most of Theatre Centre's experiments in Children's Theatre for Secondary age groups were of necessity linked with English Departments in schools, both before and after the advent of Drama Departments as such. It might be worth tabulating some of the basic intentions of such Children's Theatre work over the thirty years from 1945 to 1975, for while the majority of these intentions may no longer be valid in some communities, it is more than possible they could be in others — indeed as valid today as they were a generation or more ago. The attempt is made to keep the tabulation within the historical perspective so that the gradually evolving intentions can be seen. Of course there are definite overlappings of such intentions:

1. To take an experience of live theatre to young people in theatreless areas. It is difficult to define a "theatreless area." In certain concentrated urban areas, five miles of built-up main roads, etc., could make a theatre possibly even more inaccessible than thirty or forty miles of rural roads. In vast areas of the United States 300 to 400 miles might well be looked on as an adequate comparison with 30 or 40 miles in England. There is no one simple yardstick.

2. To present theatre in the *open stage* so that no place was deprived of a performance on the grounds that it did not have conventional theatre facilities, including blackout and lighting.

3. To adapt and present in the open stage "books" that were well kown to teachers and possibly known to the young people. The choice, however,

was not to be confined to the "classics" or to any examination text. Consequently, such texts were adapted as *Oliver Twist* by Charles Dickens, *Grinling Gibbons and the Plague of London* by Austin Clare, *Silas Marner* by George Eliot, *Midwinter* by John Buchan, etc.

4. To write new plays for audiences of young people, possibly based on the lives of famous people, possibly adapting material already written by others, either in play or novel form, but without consideration of either examination texts or precise studies in school history or literature departments. To present these plays in some form of open stage.

5. To experiment with and to develop forms of audience participation through *rehearsed crowd scenes*. Part of the objective was to help young people to have an experience of the adventure of putting together a crowd scene. It was also hoped that teachers interested in drama, as well as the school play, would find the method of approach of interest and help.

6. To find open stage approaches to the production of some Shakespeare scenes, including crowd scenes with *rehearsed audience participation*, which would help young people (and possibly teachers) to experience Shakespeare as a vital and exciting dramatist rather than a literary figure. No attempt was made to link choice of scenes to any examination syllabus or specific requests from school English Departments, nor was any attempt made to present forms of "potted Shakespeare" or potpourri versions of entire plays.

7. To incorporate in open stage productions with rehearsed audience participation the experience of the actors' craft (through both demonstration and personal involvement), hoping to help teachers with their own growing development of drama as education and also to expand young peoples' view of the actor and theatre in society.

8. To find, within open stage theatre, approaches that incorporate media, including film and other visuals in conjunction with sound, tape, etc., all linked to both Shakespeare and original texts.

This final point regarding imaginative use of media is probably the closest guide to not only the type of theatre that would most interest teen-agers, but also a full new range of adult theatre for the future. The few experiments made by Theatre Centre in this field were short lived, for only one in ten schools visited had blackout facilities in any room large enough for a performance to take place. Economic factors thus became a major stumbling block. The hardware for a program that uses 16mm sound film together with 2 slide projectors synchronized to a stereophonic sound track, plus even a modest array of dimmers and spotlights, is costly in both capital and maintenance, making it necessary to have audiences of about 200. Smaller studio spaces that would blackout would hold audiences of only 60 or 70, sufficient for the program but not the economy. The project was discontinued, but not before there was ample confirmation that the interests of many young people today will be more fully served when live theatre and various media amalgamate. The exploration of potential participation in such theatre opens some of the most exciting challenges for experiment in the future.

Of the other points tabulated above, 5, 6 and 7 are most pertinent to this book because of their basic concern with participation. Some deeply held personal convictions compel me to mention, however, some considerations arising from points 1 to 4. In an earlier section I have already said what a liberating feature it is for theatre to be thought of as "a space where anything can happen" rather than a building with raised seating and a stage at one end of a large room. Once so freed, there is no community, anywhere, that cannot have experience of live theatre, because there is no dependence on such a theatre building. Many different spaces are valid. Indeed, there is opportunity for all kinds of inventiveness to be brought to the problem of how to utilize such spaces excitingly, yet economically, even on a basis of touring such communities. But who is to contemplate the rigors and ardors of touring? There are professional actors who are prepared to do so, though fewer and fewer seem really to be interested in the idea. In terms of professional theatre, however, the economic factors are prohibitive, especially for companies that work with Equity salaries and touring allowances. One of the main limitations for such groups is that they must always be small in numbers, because of this factor of salaries. Who, then, could do such work? My personal view is that the main responsibility could and should be taken on by theatre departments of universities and possibly on a much smaller scale by senior students in theatre or drama departments in secondary schools. Much could also be undertaken by theatre and drama schools concerned with professional training.

This is a matter of a "philosophy of theatre." Often actors say with great personal hurt that most communities are too lazy, indifferent or uninterested to make the journey to the theatre. What perpetuates this myth? Where interest lies predominantly in a literary study of theatre and aping of Broadway or West End major productions (together with many small scale student productions attracting largely a student audience), there is often a resulting insularity that divorces theatre from the community. If we continue a form of theatre training that is based on our conscious or unconscious belief that we have some kind of right to expect the public to wish to attend our largely self-indulgent rituals, we must face the fact that the majority are going to be perfectly happy to stay at home and watch television, with opportunities, incidentally, of seeing some of the finest actors in some of the very plays that are likely to be put on locally. Large scale competitive festivals in already established cultural centers tend to exacerbate rather than ease the problem, as they are almost overtly insular in both intention and practice.

In many educational institutions, very sharp and stringent specialization adds to the problem. On the one hand we hear that drama and theatre are the most unifying of all the arts, but on the other we see, in practice, a separatism that rivals, even outstrips, professional theatre, TV and Film Union Regulations. In these latter there may be sound economic reasons for such sharp division. But I personally see no validity for them in centers of training. The contribution of any actor in theatre is enriched if his training includes nonspecialized exposure to technical aspects of theatre. Specialists in the technicals are enriched by being exposed to certain aspects of the training of actors or directors or writers. *All* are enriched by the opportunity of considering that theatre is not a private indulgence supported by the public in addition to grants of either public or private funds. Theatre should be philosophically (not politically, often the last desperate thrust of those with a social conscience) involved with the community in a very broad sense. This can include a servicing of nonlocal communities through the kind of touring mentioned above, especially in "theatreless areas" — however we define that term for our own geographical area.

I believe there would be no lack of interest from student bodies in a comprehensive project that planned to take theatre to theatreless communities.

The range of interest would include architectural and seating problems, ways of erecting portable lighting and media equipment, property and costume departments, music by live groups as well as prerecorded. Playwrights could be involved, as well. The whole range of disciplines that constitute the theatre experience would be the business of everybody involved, with a few specialists of each discipline providing the ultimate finesse. A philosophy of theatre based on community interests would give the impetus for solving many practical problems, the majority of which would be financially much less arduous than those that confront professional theatres. Even the hospitality of the community would save costs of accommodation and some aspects of transport. Any kind of theatre degree or other qualification could include such work, without detriment to academic standards, and those who for one of many different reasons ultimately use their qualification for teaching of one kind or another, rather than for a career in theatre, will in fact be that much more equipped to contribute to society's needs.

Within the orbit of such projects could indeed be Children's Theatre work for every type of school and age group, including the Secondary schools. Because of independence from proven and accepted approaches in order to ensure economic survival, new experiments could constantly be attempted; so, too, could such factors as having a cast larger than four for primary performances and six for secondary. The constant need to limit the size of audience could be by-passed. The *maximum* might still be pertinent, but the *minimum* could be tailored to actual need without box office considerations. Any students with an ultimate specific interest in teaching would also be able to try out some form of follow-up work, perhaps even on a long term basis.

Unrealistic, altruistic and idealistic as all these ideas may be, the fact remains that however much universities may have as their fundamental aim the enrichment and enlightenment of each individual student according to personal interest, this philosophy cannot hold true for theatre, which is not just a question of the actors and directors having the opportunity to bring life to a play, but all of that in relation to the audience and ultimately the community.

SHARING THEATRE WITH TEEN-AGE AUDIENCES

One of the factors mentioned earlier about the difference between Proscenium Theatre and Open Stage Theatre was that of not having to play the game of *pretend*, with the actors pretending they are involved in "real life" and the audience pretending that they are peeping at real life through "a fourth wall." In the Open Stage, to repeat Tyrone Guthrie's words, the actors cry aloud "We have come to play a play," and the audience says, "Let us go and see the actors play a play." The audience can be and is still often "transported" despite this entirely open acceptance of the fact that a play is being played.

For teen-age youngsters theatre is a fully conscious affair. As with adults, their participation is of the heart, the mind and the spirit, but unlike younger children, they know or intuit the "rules of the game," which do not include active vocal or physical participation. Therefore there is no *spontaneous* participation of the kind which can be built-on with the younger plays, already considered in detail.

Does this therefore mean that audience participation is both undesirable and impossible with teen-agers? Are there kinds of participation which, though quite different from that with younger children, might still be valid for the sophistication of this older age group? I personally believe there are, and see such participation taking place in two main forms:

1. Taking part in the *creative adventure of making theatre,* perhaps most easily through involvement in either the production of a crowd scene or as witness to others so involved;

2. Sharing in different aspects of the creativity that underlies the actor's art, and again that sharing can include actual personal involvement.

Let us first consider the latter of these two main forms of Participation. In the next chapter I suggest in some detail what has been found the necessary minimum in the way of limbering for an actor in Children's Theatre, particularly if his work happens to include touring and thus many different kinds of physical environment. In early productions for teen-age groups in the open stage but without any form of audience participaton, it was interesting how many questions were asked of the cast privately after performances. Only the very smallest proportion of these questions were about the play, its content and characters; the kind of academic questions fostered by members of staff. The great majority of the inquiries were concerned with a genuine interest in (no matter how cheekily presented) the actual lives of the actors: where they came from, how did they become actors, what did being an actor involve, what was training about, how did one get into theatre and even what do they do for a living? From various comments made by the young people, it was also fairly clear that they seemed to lump together *all* actors, and envisage them and their lives as epitomized in the glossier theatrical or film magazines — late to bed and late to rise, with an easy life of buying and playing long-playing records until time for the show in the evening, followed by the restaurant or nightclub and the next late night prior to breakfast in bed. There were also many sexual innuendos, all accepted by the actors as a natural aspect of misinformation, muddled information or no information at all.

From this there developed a very simple sharing of some of the actors' limbering, together with a commentary on exactly what the life of a touring actor is like (and at the time, the mid 1960's, it was anything but comfortable). It was an organic and natural development from this point to an actual involvement of the audience so that they could share some simple experiences for themselves. In many schools, where a serious approach to drama was just being started, teachers commented on how it had helped their work for the young people to see professional actors involved in some of the exercises they themselves were fostering, not to mention actually joining in with the actors in their experiences. To do even a few minutes of such sharing at the very opening of a program (sometimes the actors were discovered actually involved in simple exercises during the assembling of the audience) is a great bond-builder with young people. Certainly this had tremendous advantages in programs that involve any subsequent audience participation, particularly as the exercises that were shared usually involved simple approaches to concentration and some loosening-up of a physical kind.

For actors attempting such an approach, it is most important that the attitude should be seriously and sincerely professional. Any playing down, which for this older age group is usually patronizing, is very quickly spotted, with a result that the actors are likely to be "played-up." The actor should *expect* early reactions of laughter and, when one thinks of it, for the uninitiated, there is something very amusing about what actors attempt when limbering. But there should be no playing up by the actors to that laughter, just as there should be no signs of hurt or of aggression. All that is necessary is to get on with doing the job thoroughly and honestly. Any commentary accompanying the limbering should include the fact that normally this is an extremely private and personal effort, which now is only being done in public in order to share some aspects of the life of an actor. With this approach, young people are quick to control their reactions and, though an underlying humor will remain, it will not be vindictive and will eventually come from a full generosity of spirit and admiration for the actors' willingness to share aspects of their own private artistic lives.

Should the extension of the exercises be made to offer an opportunity for the audience to participate in a few simple aspects of the limbering, then two other points are also important. First, as far as humanly possible, the actors should *not demonstrate* for the audience to copy. Clarity of narration is all that is fundamentally necessary. Secondly, it should not be expected that more than about 25% to 40% of the audience will become *genuinely involved*, even though a much higher percentage will *appear* to go through the motions. If the actors do not expect a higher proportion then they are not disappointed and so do not make value judgements on a circumstance that has many more ramifications than they are ever likely to have time to uncover. These can range from self-consciousness to a deeply ingrained belief that all things of theatre and the arts belong to one section of mankind just as all sections of the sciences belong to another, and never the twain shall meet. Whatever our personal view of the rights or wrongs of such a development of education, the fact *is precisely that for many people,* and we must hang on to an entirely compassionate view of the results in terms of human attitudes and behavior. Basically there is seldom any form of maliciousness behind the reactions of even the least interested. There is the inevitable and very usual bonus of touching on the inherent but as yet unborn interest of a few who need this simple catalyst to open a new window or door for them. Most of us at some time in life experience circumstances that lead us to say something like: "I never realized before that there was so much behind..." Theatre as the principle exponent of communication should have much to offer in terms of revelation about itself, its purpose, function and procedures.

This, however, is an historical perspective, which, nevertheless, need not be dismissed as "merely history" — the theatre's interest in young people more than matched educationalists' interst in the potential of theatre. A good example of this factor concerned the approach of Theatre Centre to many different programs of Shakespeare in tours of English Secondary Schools. As has already been mentioned, the approach was that of interesting young people in the essentially *dramatic* quality of Shakespeare's plays, not in trying to be some kind of visual-aid for teachers confronted with the problem of having to cover a certain amount of Shakespeare material because of the demands of examination systems. No doubt there is much truth in the fact that early experiences govern many of our subsequent future actions. In this resepct, it is perhaps of interest and relevance for me to mention that I was personally the victim of the most boring Grammar School approach to Shakespeare. I learned "by heart" endless and meaningless soliloquies. I listened to theories. I looked up interminable glossaries. I pondered the facts of annotation and wondered why we always skipped over such luscious italicized phrases as *"He stabs him," "A battle rages,"* and so on. Into the bleakness of this systematic destruction of the works of a great playwright came, for a few short months, a remarkable English Teacher who was a wholly uninhibited exhibtionist and, on reflection, a frustrated actor, as well. I recall vividly the few experiences I had of him suffering for only a few minutes the awfulness of reading through a

Shakespeare play, round the class, one at a time. Suddenly, with a kind of Divine fury, he would tell us not to bother, and would himself take over, acting all the parts, shouting and ranting, waving his arms, almost, so memory recalls, frothing at the mouth. I do not recall what the plays were. I do recall a feeling that there was more to them than I could take off the printed page in preparation for examination questions.

The long playing records, TV productions and films of so many of the plays, performed by the finest Shakespearean actors, must so ease the burden for any teacher confronted with the task of teaching Shakespeare. But there was and, I believe, still is value in experience of live performance of some scenes, particularly opportunities for personal involvement.

So to the other of the two main forms of Secondary Participation: *The creative adventure of making theatre.*

Many different approaches evolved over a long period of time, but one of the earliest was concerned with an attempt to approach the essence of aspects of certain plays through *intuitive experience* rather than *intellectual comprehension.* The obvious artistic means of such an approach was through dance drama and improvisation. The work was in the open stage, using a three-sided acting area of 20' x 15', backing, wherever possible, an existing stage, which was used as a "tiring house" or dressing room. (See **diagram below**). Performance was in daylight and, although full costume was used in later scenes, the opening or introduction, including the limbering, was in modern dress, with the whole cast in white tops and black trousers or long skirts, a kind of sophisticated "practice" dress, impeccable in design and professionalism of presentation (i.e. no tattiness of any kind).

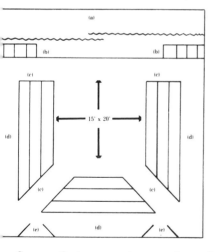

Diagram Number 19

Three-Sided Open Stage Seating
Arrangements for Shakespeare Scenes

(a.) The stage, with curtains closed, used as dressing room.
(b.) Steps down either side of stage to acting area.
(c.) Entrances to acting area.
(d.) Aisles behind the audience for access to entrances.
(e.) Doors at back of auditorium. These are usually connected to the dressing room by a corridor on one or both sides.
The main acting area is 20' x 15'. Rostrum blocks are used within the area according to the requirements of particular scenes.

Scenes that were subsequently to be presented included extracts from three of the following five plays: *Richard III, Macbeth, Romeo and Juliet, The Merry Wives of Windsor* and *Henry IV.* In the case of the latter two plays, the scenes chosen concerned Sir John Falstaff.

Without narration or explanation, the program opened with three dance dramas, interspersed with improvisation based on the plays above, taking some kind of thematic essence rather than precise detail. So: for *Richard III,* the dance drama was based on Richard's nightmare before battle; for *Macbeth,*

141

the dance drama was based on Macbeth's conscience after the final of his many murders; for *Romeo and Juliet,* the dance drama was based on the family feud between the Montagues and Capulets; for the Falstaff plays, the dance drama was based on "Falstaff and Women." All three dance dramas followed each other in hard succession, separated by a brief improvisation based on some aspect of the preceding dance drama. All were performed to the same piece of music, "Let there be Drums" by Sandy Nelson, which at that time was Top of the Charts and therefore a favorite for the majority of the young people viewing the program. This link into the young peoples' own world was electrifying, yet was done without either gimmick or condescension. The pertinent point is simply that having intuited the decision that dance drama could be an interesting approach to Shakespeare with this age group, a further decision had to be made regarding what music should be used for the dance dramas. Music that would be of interest to youngsters was quite natural and wholly adequate from the actors' point of view, but brought an entirely new and contemporary area of experience to the youngsters. It is important to emphasize that though these dance dramas were based essentially on "improvised movement," not on any one school of movement, they were nevertheless fully choreographed and polished to the highest performance standards.*

THE REHEARSED CROWD SCENE

The type of dance drama described above, together with links to the actors' own limbering, was one approach to the introduction of Shakespeare. Another approach, embracing also the experience of creative production (of other authors as well as Shakespeare) was *the rehearsed crowd scene.* Such scenes were sometimes integrated into the program as a whole, but more often constituted one whole half of a two-act program. With rare exceptions, the crowd scene was in the second half, thus enabling the actors to use part of the interval between acts to discuss with or otherwise prepare some aspects of the scene with the participants, although rehearsal itself was usually in front of the whole audience, in order to share with everyone the approaches to building such a scene.

Fundamentally, the approach to audience participation with teen-agers must be based on an understanding of *their awareness of fully conscious theatre.* Even the use of improvisation as the core of their participation must include an understanding of that awareness, thus making the difference between "vague ad-libbing" and genuine attempts to achieve, as far as time, preparation and experience will allow, an experience of getting deeply into the skin of the part portrayed and into the situation, with a full intuitive attempt at absorbed sincerity of involvement. When and if improvisation is used as a kind of shoddy short cut to product, it becomes possibly the most abused of potential art forms. Improvisation can be an art form in its own right, but to be such requires release and control, sensitivity to the group by each individual within the group, and a reliance on intuitive truth rather than intellectual slickness. Many of these qualities can still be expected and utilized in even the swiftest production of a rehearsed crowd scene.

As with the plays for younger children, audience participation for Secondary Schools must take into account the *age group* of the young people, which might include the broad span of 12 to 17 years. While all are fully aware of making a piece of theatre, the range of self-consciousness can vary con-

---

* *The choreographer was Margaret Faulkes Jendyk, co-founder of Theatre Centre, currently Associate Professor of Drama at the University of Alberta.*

siderably, with much depending on what experience they have had with their own creative drama. In the case of the older half of the group, much depends on whether or not they have developed a personal interest in theatre and acting. The following variables can be anticipated with almost any audience of, say, 200 of the full age range 12 — 17, based on an approach where the actors ask for volunteers and choose them with the kind of approach already described on pp 93-94:

a) the youngest, being the least self-conscious, are likely to be *the most eager* to volunteer;

b) older ones *will* volunteer, particularly if the company's approach is that of the fully sophisticated idea of actually *creating* a piece of theatre;

c) the younger ones will invariably be worried about *being watched* by the older non-participants, because the hierarchy of school suggests to them that whatever they do must be inferior to the older ones. In performances in schools at the beginning of the school year, this can be a very particular problem for those who have just moved up from primary or elementary school and are traditionally looked upon with a certain derision and scorn as "the new kids";

d) the older ones will invariably be worried about being asked *to participate with* the younger ones (particularly the first years), although they cope more easily than the younger ones with the idea of being watched by the non-participants;

e) however much the sexes mix in normal school or private life, expect them at once to separate. It is both unwise and unfair to embarrass them by trying to insist that they mix, if they are unhappy about it;

f) whoever in the company is responsible for the over-all rehearsal of the crowd scene needs to be ready to make a perfectly simple human-cum-artistic appeal to the generosity of spirit of those watching to give some consideration to the feeling of the participants. This is by no means always necessary and when it is it can be done without any need to change roles to that of teacher concerned with discipline. A quiet word about how difficult it is to be involved suddenly in an audience situation, and how hard it is to hold one's concentration in such circumstances unless there is a sensitive concentration from the viewers, is usually quite sufficient to lead to full human consideration and cooperation. If the director of the crowd scene conducts all of the proceedings as a theatre or film director rather than as an instructor or teacher, then the atmosphere will be conducive to better results.

Whatever else is our concern for experiments with audience participation with this age group, we must never lose sight of the fact that their stage of development includes the full dignity of young men and women and must be respected. In my view, the preservation of that dignity is more important than achieving successful participation by robbing them of it through reliance on adult authoritarianism. If we are really concerned with such experiments, then the onus is with us to find any and every way we can to preserve the *intuitive* relish of the experience at the same time as helping them to get as deeply into the scene as is possible in the available time.

One solution is, as with the primary or elementary ages, to split the age groups, and to have a different play for the 12's to 14's from that for the 15's and upwards.

These factors were taken into account in the approach to production of scenes from Shakespeare, which formed the main core of participation crowd

scene experiments by Theatre Centre's touring companies. While scenes of one
kind or another were presented from 17 different plays over a number of years
crowd scenes were produced from eight: *Romeo and Juliet, Henry IV Part 1
Henry V, A Midsummer Night's Dream, Julius Caesar, Hamlet, Macbeth* and
The Tempest. Although it is important to group or categorize these scenes, i
is also important to bear in mind that no such sequence actually arose in prac
tice. The crowd scenes mentioned above really fall into four groups of two
each group containing a particular intention:

1. Ceremony and processions: *Midsummer Night's Dream* and *Hamlet*
   The end of the *"Dream"* and of *Hamlet* both provide opportunities for
   simple processional and ceremonial forms of participation, and these
   scenes were used both independently and as the climax to a play about
   the Globe Theatre — **Speak the Speech I Pray You...** — in which
   Shakespeare and his own company are joined temporarily by an
   "Observer" from our own time in order to see how the Elizabethan ac
   tors approached their work.
2. Fight Sequences: *Romeo and Juliet* and *Macbeth.*
3. Spoken participation by a whole audience of 200: *Julius Caesar* and
   Henry V.
4. Small Group Improvisations: *Henry IV, Part 1* and *The Tempest.*

1. CEREMONY AND PROCESSIONS

The end of *A Midsummer Night's Dream* provides a simple *processiona*
opportunity for the assembly of the Duke's Court to watch the performance o
Pyramus and Thisbe, together with reactions to the play mainly led by
scripted lines from Theseus and Hippolyta. The organization of the scene i
comparatively simple, as is the arrangement of helping the whole audience fee
that they are part of an occasion in a role different from themselves if they
wish.

The second of the *Ceremonial and Processional* scenes was the final scene
of *Hamlet,* potentially one of Shakespeare's most exciting crowd scenes. Its
fascination lies in the gathering together of a group of people for one seemingly
ly innocent purpose, which suddenly and abruptly changes, until its ending in
grim tragedy. To accomplish this with 6 actors, 40 participants, a rehearsal
period of about 25-30 minutes and a running time of the scene itself of approx
imately another 25 minutes — all in broad daylight in the average school hall
or gymnasium during school hours — has over and over again been one of the
most exciting experiences of theatre. But to attempt to describe it is to fall in
to precisely the trap one is anxious to avoid regarding George Eliot's *pictur*
and the diagram. I often feel that a full understanding of what is meant by
that distinction can arise from an experience of producing or directing a crowd
scene with a group of teen-agers.

When crowd scenes are built with mathematical precision, with the actor
little more than ciphers in the hands of the director or producer and their con
cerns with the exact nature of groupings, etc., then we move into the realm o
the diagram, of the fulfilment of an intellectual idea. In the end, each person
has to depend, for almost every move and gesture, on a sequence of demonstra
tion, copy, repetition and so on, until there is a kind of perfection of a skeleton
— *sans* heart, life, inspiration, intuition...in short *sans* spontaneity!

With due respect to many hardworking and very well-intentioned pro
ducers of the school play, I knew from experience the agony of mathematical

boredom that so many young people had suffered — hours of watching what they should do, where to move, how to hold head and hands, infinite boredom of trying to say "rhubarb, rhubarb" or "numbers" or "the alphabet" or irrelevant "quotations" from other texts, and to say them with different types of "feeling" and in different "volumes" and alternating "rhythms" and all this in some kind of juxtaposition to the central action of the play, likely as not action that is or should be the cause, the very *raison d'etre* of their own particular existence. This sounds far more critical than it is intended to be. I am aware that the situation is very different in many places for many young people today in their own productions, but the point is still worth making in terms of Theatre for Young People which includes audience participation. It is perfectly natural for those attempting to direct or produce such a scene to feel the need for it to "go right" and therefore possibly to fall into the trap of the *diagram* instead of trusting their own intuitive feeling for the *picture*. Inevitably our own background, training and experience are important factors. I am therefore always grateful that in my own most formative teen-age experiences, my background should have included taking part in many different crowd scenes produced by Tyrone Guthrie. Long before I even heard of the idea of the difference between "the picture and the diagram," I was having numerous experiences of "the picture" through working with him. I was absorbing intuition in his own ideas, inspiration in his stimulus of those of us in the crowd, and his trust in our intuition once that stimulus had brought real life into us all. He taught me, unconsciously, that one can only control what is released. All other control is sterile intellectualism.

The full creative enjoyment of a rehearsed crowd scene in Children's Theatre begins from the moment one is concerned with exciting the imagination of young people and then trusting what comes from their imagination. Obviously this means from the outset that one needs to eliminate or come to terms with the factor of the word *crowd*. The problem for inexperienced young people is that of realizing that a crowd is in fact a large number of *highly individual human beings* gathered together. Sometimes they may well feel, think and act at one and the same time, occasionally even in unison, but they are still individual people. Whether a crowd scene involves 20 people or 200, fundamentally this idea makes for an approach that embodies the essential difference between the "picture" and the "diagram."

So, with the *Hamlet* crowd scene, one can describe sequence and procedure, detailed moments of the scene that need a minute or two of rehearsal. One can give warnings of factors of *control* that may or may not arise, and even suggest, from experience, many precise moments that become focal points of not only the scene but also detail in rehearsal. Yes, one can *describe* all of these things, and end up doing no more than very exactly drawing a *diagram*. The *picture* can still be wholly obscure. There is no way of detailing through the printed word all the factors that make up the picture rather than the diagram. How does one describe tone of voice...balance of joyful fun with serious intention...use of the controlling cymbal for a moment of silence that is immediately followed by fullblooded and gripping atmosphere...encouragement, stimulation and removal of fear of failure by creating an atmosphere that is so filled with intuitive risk...sheer joy of giving oneself to rather than resisting moments of total discipline...being sensitive to one's peers, yes even at a moment when to be doing so, let alone to be seen doing so, might mean losing face in terms of the social mask temporarily set-up...exposing and sharing one's innermost private feelings of creative joy, yes, even to the point of possi-

ble ridicule...sharing with the actors the finesse of sensitive teamwork, a
moving slowly together toward an inexorable pitch of artistry...making
minute adjustments to the requirements of each different audience...believing
totally, passionately, sincerely and intuitively that *this impossible thing wi*
work? How does one put any of this down on paper so that it helps to make th
picture and not merely outline the diagram? Not only do I not have the words
I fear they do not exist. We are talking about an attitude of mind and spiri
and emotion that is either felt or not felt. We are talking about a philosoph
that, if believed, needs constant practice in an uncritical framework to bring i
to full life.

Curiously enough, the logical way of rehearsing this *Hamlet* crowd scen
is to start with the ending, with the corpses of Claudius, Gertrude, Hamlet an
Laertes, each sprawled or lying precisely in the final tableau of death. Th
director or producer is then able to give a brief but graphic description of th
events leading up to this mass slaughter in such a way that even members o
the audience who are wholly unfamiliar with the story of *Hamlet* will have a
understanding of at least its outline. When the play is in the Open Stage (
would not advise attempting the crowd scene as audience participation on th
proscenium stage) the lead into the need for participants is wholly logical, link
ing with the Elizabethan Theatre where there was no curtain to shut off the ac
tors or lighting to fade to darkness, so that it was necessary, as well as ex
citing theatre, to "take up the bodies" and, with pomp and ceremony, musi
and cannonfire, take them from the stage. Most young people are fascinate
with the idea that Shakespeare's own company needed to call upon the ser
vices of "hired actors" as extras to his own permanent group in order to carr
out such a scene. It is now a matter of deciding how many people are necessar
for carrying each of the corpses, obviously depending on the size and weight o
each individual. Experience suggests no less than eight people for each body
possibly ten for Claudius, working with an equal number on either side. That i
at least 32 people form the outset. Depending on the size of the acting com
pany and style of production, additional people may be necessary for mor
ceremonial duties, such as dagger or sword bearers, or carrying the tray o
goblets and wine used in an earlier part of the scene.

Because the task for which they are needed is so clear to them, young peo
ple are able to volunteer with a certain degree of security, rather than wonder
ing what it is they're going to be asked to do, as so often happens in scene
where the logic is to start at the beginning rather than at the end. The im
mediate sequence regarding the selection of volunteers has already bee
touched on in detail on pp 93 to 94, but there is the additional point here tha
the director needs to sense whether or not to mix the sexes of the pall-bearer
or whether to have only boys carrying the male corpses and only girls carryin
the female corpse. This factor is not as trivial as it may sound, because we ar
again confronted with preserving the dignity of the young people in a scen
which, for all its early "fun," is ultimately going to involve fully absorbe
solemnity, sustained for quite a long period of time, in terms of quite intimat
physical contact with the adult actors in the cast. If a young lad is going to b
embarrassed by, for example, finding that his task is that of supporting Ger
trude with his hand or hands under her buttocks, then it may be a much mor
comfortable experience for him to be helping one of the men. Usually it i
wisest, having decided how many people are necessary — say, 32 — to have al
come out at the same time and sit on the floor in the acting area and then in
vite them to go to whichever corpse interests them most. Consquently it i

asy to see those who have a particular interest and lack of other concerns, and
hose who very definitely do not want to be anywhere or with anyone except
he person they choose. Then there are usually sufficient numbers who really
lo not mind one way or the other and they can be finally distributed to get the
balance of numbers per body correct. The rightful concern in the back of the
lirector's mind regarding sexes and so on need not be made conscious to the
young people at all. It is sufficient that the actors themselves are sensitive to
t.

Now, the warning that has been made about almost every piece of au-
lience participation in these pages — time! Once again, time is of the essence.
The reason here is two-fold. Firstly, the intention of the whole scene being
rehearsed in front of the audience is to enable them to share in the *process* of
creating a scene in a brief period of time in order to arrive at the product within
he same session. At most, the session should last no more than an hour, and
he scene itself when run straight through lasts about 25 to 27 minutes; so at
maximum there is about half an hour in which to rehearse everything
necessary. Secondly, again a point which has been touched on before, the
pressure of time opens the way both for the actors and the participants to find
a trust in their intuition rather than the precision of intellectual certainty. So,
n terms of time, from the moment the young volunteers have been selected to
he point where they are ready for the first serious run of the funeral proces-
ion they are working towards should be no more than about 10 minutes, dur-
ng which time the following sequence seems to work best for them:

a. With the corpses "spread about on the floor," the young people first
need to discover with every possible kind of help, advice and cooperation from the actors and from the director keeping an eye on all four
groups, just how they can manage to lift the body to shoulder height.
Expect an enormous amount of laughter and fun at this stage. This is
healthy and relaxing. It also helps the actor and the participants to
make a bond and to overcome any shyness or diffidence about the close
physical proximity. The "watching" audience also has a chance to chat
together and to come to terms with and settle peer reactions with participants.

b. Repeat the same procedure, but with the four corpses starting from exactly the positions they are in when they die. This could mean a different experience for the young people, depending on the production.
For example, Claudius and Gertrude may die on the same throne area,
and possibly Hamlet quite close to them, so the pall bearers now have
the task of reaching their particular body before going through with
the lifting. The "fun" side will naturally die away a little by now and
the growing seriousness can be helped by the attitude of each corpse to
his or her group, and by that of the director to the rest of the audience.

c. This second attempt should also include now trying out the very
solemn, stately, slow funeral march step, with bodies held steadily at
shoulder height being carried feet first. It is often at this time that the
discovery is made of the need for one or two more people per corpse,
and new volunteers can soon be absorbed into the teams because they
will have seen what is happening and there will be a very precise function for them at this stage. Through these stages, as well as subsequent
rehearsal, I recommend that the director use a cymbal as a full control
instrument; but he or she can now also use it to give experience of the
timebeat of whatever funeral march music is to be used in the scene itself.

d. Now the corpses again return to their final group so that the par
ticipants can run the whole funeral exit, with music added to help the
atmosphere, but without taking the whole scene through to its final
climax (the fullness of the total theatre experience is thus left open)
Before this final run of the procession, the director can explain to the
participants that in a moment they will be trying out their entrance
which will be in pairs to the throne to be greeted by the King and Queen
after which Osric, another company member, as a sort of Master of
Ceremonies, will indicate one side or the other of the throne for them to
go to. The director can then quickly suggest some go to one side, some
to the other, so that they have the experience of coming from a specific
place to their particular corpse, and then continue as rehearsed. With
the director giving the cue-line "take up the bodies," and the music
fading in, the whole processional exit is tried out, with Laertes going
first, then the Queen, then the King, and finally Hamlet, and, if there is
the strength in the group, perhaps Hamlet being hoisted high to the
full extent of stretched arms. They all go through the exit opening, (see
**diagram for one suggested arrangement of seating, rostra, exits and
entrances below**) and then each group has practice at lowering the body
they have been carrying, all done, in about 7 to 8 minutes. Throughout
this final run, the director has the opportunity now of
bringing absolutely full seriousness, solemnity and dignity to the occa
sion, and this might include the need for a gentle but firm appeal to the
watchers to help the concentration of the participants by their own con
centration and sensitivity.

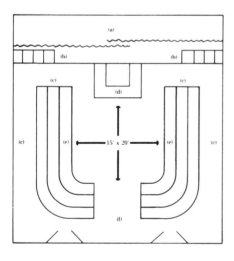

Diagram Number 20

Seating and Rostrum Arrangements
For the *Hamlet* Crowd Scene

(a.) *The stage, with the curtains closed
used as a dressing room.*

(b.) *Steps down either side of the stage to
acting area.*

(c.) *Entrances to acting area from dressing
room, including aisles behind the audi
ence.*

(d.) *Rostrum blocks "throne" on which
Claudius and Gertrude die.*

(e.) *Front row of audience left empty so
there is no danger for any audience
members during the Hamlet/Laertes
fight sequence.*

(f.) *Wide central aisle for entrance and exit
processions, and as much space as
possible behind audience for assembly
of participants at beginning and end of
the scene.*

The acting area remains 20' x 15'.

So the first part of the rehearsal is complete, and because it is the ending
of the scene there is a kind of logic about what follows. Quite simply, who are
these people and what are they doing there in the first place? The director can
fill in quickly and excitingly some more of the background to the play and,
because of television plus so much general knowledge, he or she might even be
surprised at how many in the audience know of or have seen or might even

have been to the Castle or Palace of Elsinore in Denmark. To compare the time of the play with our own time can help as well. Leisure activities were very different and quite often took place at the Palace at the invitation of the throne. On this occasion, two of the finest fencers in the land are going to entertain for the evening with a display of their fine fencing art. The King has already placed his bets, and no doubt many others would be making their own wagers as well. Possibly a highlight of the year would be such an evening. Now, all the participants must decide *who they are* as they arrive at the Palace in pairs or small groups. Some may wish to be courtiers and perhaps rather grand, but many other kinds of people would be there — soldiers back from the war or about to set off for war, others who are permanently stationed at the Palace, members of the household staff — domestic, kitchen, gardeners and groundsmen; — then people from the community: craftsmen, taverners, shopkeepers, etc. And they can be of all different ages and temperaments...and so on, opening up opportunity by an imaginative stimulus of available possibilities. The suggestion can be made to the non-participant "watchers" as well, that maybe they would like to talk to the person sitting next to them about different people they might be on this occasion. Everyone is given two or three minutes to talk about the people they would like to be and the active participants get into pairs or threes for their first entrance.

When these arrangements are settled, the director can paint-in a little more of the situation and the scene, as well as share some of the fascination of the theatre creation itself, of the making of mood and atmosphere, of the truth that arises from each person creating their own truth within themselves, including speaking whatever words they feel right for them in the situation at certain moments of "crowd reaction," and of the astonishing nature of the discipline of group acting at certain moments of the scene. The director's painting of the background needs to give significance to the fact that nobody, *but nobody*, has an inkling of an idea of the great tragedy that is about to overwhelm Elsinore and the whole of Denmark. Nobody. Only Claudius and Laertes know that anything untoward is going to happen and, even for them, the scope of that happening, ghastly as their intentions are, is but a fragment of the whole tragedy. Depending on whether any earlier scenes from the play have been performed in Part I, the director may then need to sketch-in quickly and dramatically just enough of the background for everyone to be aware of the situation.

The director's outline, which I personally feel needs to be improvised, but which is, of course, always a matter of individual preference, needs to *paint* the picture with all the full-blooded drama that the situation is concerned with. I do not believe it matters at all whether the youngsters can *remember* all the names or *comprehend* all the details. What *is* important is that they have an *intuitive understanding* of the background so that their own imagination is stimulated and they have certain points of confident anchorage in the over-all shape of the scene they are to be involved in now. Ritual is an important part of scenes of this nature. Despite the delight of the occasion or perhaps because of it, there is the ritual of the arrival of the guests, who, in their pairs or small groups, proceed to the throne, under the general guidance and control of Osric and/or the director (who might well be Horatio and will certainly need to be in a company of only 6 actors), and are greeted by the King and Queen, perhaps even with moments of improvised dialogue, depending on the confidence of the youngsters and the sensitivity of the two actors. There can be the ritual of the arrival of the sword and dagger bearers, and the bearers of the wine and goblets. Then there is the ritual of the saluting at the start of the fight itself. All such rituals contain the full intrigue of the theatre experience and have the potential for captivating the interest of young people when participating in such a scene. At the head of the procession, Osric, without fuss, indicates to the participants which side of the throne to go to group themselves. As they have already been warned, this might be different from the position they were given before the final run through of the processional exit. The young people will not be worried by this nor do they need to be fussed about precisely where they should stand, as intuitively they find natural groupings for themselves as they arrive.

By now, there are really only two things necessary to rehearse, both concerned with helping the young people to feel confidence in their contribution to the creation of the scene as a whole, and in particular to its two very contrasting atmospheres. First, a little of the early fight between Hamlet and Laertes needs to be run through so that all can see that this has nothing to do with "heavy slashing" at its start, but with two brilliant swordsmen almost demonstrating the finer arts of swordsmanship, which many among the viewers would recognize and respond to either vocally or perhaps with applause. One or two such moments can be pointed out and tried out. The second rehearsal needed is that extraordinary moment of theatre, bringing about a total change to the style of fighting and to the whole atmosphere leading to the inevitable climax and tragedy — the moment when Laertes suddenly rushes at Hamlet with "Have at thee, now," and draws blood with the envenomed point of his sword. With the right timing of the moment in rehearsal, the action brings a reaction of absolutely spontaneous shock from all involved, especially if they are not familiar with the play. It is the attempt at recreating this moment that becomes one of the essentially graphic roots of the whole notion of the crowd scene and the mutual endeavor to create theatre. Once the full change in the over-all atmosphere is caught, then the rehearsal can end. Now it is all a matter of trust. A minute or two of break and relaxation and refinding one's starting position and then the whole scene can be run. If time allows, part of the Osric scene with Hamlet and Horatio can prove a good lead-in, otherwise, starting from Horatio to Hamlet: "You will lose this wager, my lord," right through to the end of the play, with the final funeral procession and exit. Of course, I am assuming that the company scenes have been *thoroughly rehearsed and polished,* including the two very contrasting stages of the fight, the delicate sword play before the Laertes lunge and the incensed fight to the death after this moment.

Depending on the size of the acting area being used and the style of the fight, very detailed safety measures should be taken to make sure that no one in the audience is in danger from the sword fight. Working within the space shown in the diagram, I have always kept the front row clear during performance. And because Hamlet's final killing of Claudius entails running him through on top of the rostrum block, Osric should make quite sure that no one, when grouping round the throne, actually goes behind the throne where the King will be seated. It is wise allays to rehearse the fight in the exact dimensions of the acting area, with some watching each of the front rows for even the slightest sign of either Hamlet's or Laertes' sword crossing the audience area.

One of the great advantages of the *Hamlet* crowd scene over others from Shakespeare is the built-in discipline of its ritual and ceremony. Yet it is the very basic idea of purposeful ritual that can so often help the preparation and actual rehearsal of nearly all such crowd scenes, whether or not there is actual ritual or ceremony built-in to the scene itself, as a kind of attitude of mind about the preparation. I can recall very few performances of this scene, out of well over a hundred, which have not been intensely moving. And I cannot recall any actors who have not been astonished at what can be built so quickly with a group of young people. A truly rewarding experience.

2. FIGHT SEQUENCES

From the final scene of *Hamlet* to the opening street scene of *Romeo and Juliet* is quite a leap. Yet, there is again a fight between two central characters, Benvolio and Tybalt. This time it is a lusty sword fight from start to finish. But among the street fighters of the Montague and Capulet households, there are aspects that border on ritual, from the "biting of thumbs" which leads into the fighting, through the entrance of the Prince and his final threat to both households: "If ever you disturb our streets again,/Your lives shall pay for forfeit of the peace," and thence to the clearing of the street, including the quite unceremonious removal of the dead and the injured. There is a kind of ritual each step of the way, guiding the moments of necessary rehearsal.

Similar ritualistic approaches exist with the final scenes of *Macbeth*, with the movement of Malcolm's army as Birnam Wood coming to Dunsinane, the battle between Macbeth's forces and those of Malcolm, and again the fight between two main characters, Macbeth and Macduff, leading to Macbeth's death and the ceremonial ending of Malcolm being greeted as the new King of Scotland. Again, at the end of battle, there is a kind of ritualistic clearing of the battlefield as the wounded and the dead of each army are helped away by survivors.

In many senses both of these scenes extend beyond that of *Hamlet* because in *Hamlet* only the actors are involved in actual fighting, the participants being observers of the fight. In *Romeo and Juliet* and in *Macbeth*, the participants are themselves involved in fighting. Yet the whole organization of rehearsal can follow a very similar plan to that of the *Hamlet* scene described in such detail above. There is the selecting of volunteers, the painting of a picture of the circumstances of the scene or scenes involved, something about the main protagonists and their relationship, some moments for the young people to talk about their own characters, and a clear delineation of the geography of the scene in terms of exits, entrances and cue lines.

The major difference is that of the young people having time to rehearse their own fight scene and, of course, they do not have actual swords or clubs or other weapons. They accept this completely, both in terms of the obvious need of safety, and also in terms of the fact that they can really get into the "guts" of the fight if they are not worried about possible injuries.

Because in both *Romeo & Juliet* and *Macbeth* crowd scenes, the central one is an actual fight with weapons by two of the actors, the audience gets the full flavor of what sort of fight can actually take place. Indeed it can be wise for the protagonists to enact part of their fight with weapons so that the young people can see the type of weapons used and the style of fighting possible with them. This can perhaps include the essential difference between the Benvolio-Tybalt fight with very light fast moving swords, and the Macbeth-Macduff fight with heavy broad swords. Either weapon demands a different style of combat.

One reason for becoming involved in audience participation crowd scenes that involved fighting of any kind was again through the link with young people themselves, together with an interest in the development of creative dramatic work in secondary schools. Many teachers had expressed alarm at the number of fights (without harm or hurt) that so often broke out as part of improvised dramatic activity. This is governed by all kinds of reasons that really have no place in this particular book, except to say that fighting is a perfectly natural part of the development of such work, and is of course also influenced by the amount of violence observed constantly on film and television. There is, however, clear need to find ways of using the energy and emotion behind the aggressive instinct in a constructive manner that does not destroy the fundamental interest of the young people themselves, but gives to both them and their teachers a feeling of purposefulness and even mastery of certain skills, not least of which are those of concentration, imagination, recall and sensitivity to other people, all of which are possible as soon as the fight situation is accepted instead of rejected, and time given to build-up a detailed fight.

The number of participants in the kind of fight scenes mentioned above must depend on space, the readiness of those directing the scene, and thought for the confidence of the young people. The latter point really involves one in not thinking of so low a minimum number, perhaps because of control, as to leave the young people feeling over-exposed to "an audience." The old hackneyed phrases of "being lost in a crowd," of "safety in numbers," have very real application to this type of scene. In these terms I should prefer to think of about 20 people as a minimum for either scene. In *Macbeth* this provides two armies of 10 per side. In *Romeo and Juliet* this provides two lots of opponents in each of the four quarters of the acting space, plus one keeper of the peace per four, who can get into the center of the four and so swing his (imaginary) club in order to spread the fighters apart. These numbers are probably a minimum for the "confident comfort" of the participants, and certainly should not be too many for the director or producer of the scene to feel fully in control.

It is wise at the very outset for the director to sit the participants down in the acting area and then talk to all, including the nonparticipating audience, about the basic ideas of building a fight in theatre. Seen on stage, screen or television, sword fights that are well done appear to be entirely spontaneous, which is far from the truth, as the fight has to be slowly and methodically built-up, one movement at a time, and gone over again and again until wholly committed to the memory of the body as well as the mind. It is wise to mention, for example, how much rehearsal time has been spent on the Benvolio-Tybalt scene, or the Macbeth-Macduff scene, depending on which crowd scene is being attempted, then to introduce the idea that the participants, in pairs, are going to have x amount of time to build up a fight of y numbers of movements. Let us say that the fight is going to contain 10 movements, each movement consisting of the moment of attack by one and the parry by the other. The participants share the acting area available to them and take careful note of where each is and where his or her partner is. That is *their* space and only theirs. No one else will encroach on their space, just as they must make sure they do not encroach on anyone else's. A moment or two is necessary to consider the length and weight of the weapon they are using, and any other details that aid their concentration, without becoming over-intellectual about the "miming" involved, then a few minutes to work out and run over the first five blows of the fight, during which no one is wounded or killed. When it is guaged that sufficient time has been given, and the director can go around checking how each pair is getting on, then these first five movements can be tried out to the sound of the cymbal, each sound being the moment of the clash of the steel of the swords. When the fight is first being worked out, it is wise to encourage the use of slow motion, with intentions very carefully stated by each person: e.g. "I am going to aim to cut your ankle" to which the other replies, "I am going to swing down my sword to a point between yours and my ankle in order to parry the blow." The director, using cymbal, keeps to the slow-motion for the first run of the five movements, everybody working at the same time. After a moment to check that all has gone as planned, the same five are repeated, with cymbal, only this time a little quicker. Again, after checking, the sequence with cymbal is run again at the proper speed of the fight with the participants holding still in "position 5." Now, they have time to work out the next five blows, starting from number 5 in order to complete the ten, and by number 10, one of the pair is killed or wounded. They decide for themselves. Again a few minutes is given to work out this second half of the fight, and then movements six to ten are tried out three times, starting in slow motion and then building to the proper pace. The first five movements are quickly recalled and the whole fight of ten movements tried straight through.

The cymbal helps to give control and form to the build up of the fight and, when the scene itself is done, might still be useful, even if there is backing music for the scene when run through. After the fight is settled, a few moments need to be spent on how the stage is to be cleared, who is dead and needs to be carried or dragged off (there will be nothing of the funeral pomp and circumstance of the *Hamlet* scene in either *Macbeth* or *Romeo and Juliet*), who is wounded and will they manage to get off on their own or do they need help; if so, by whom and in what way? Once decisions are made, the action needs to be tried and reiteration made of the discipline behind recreating the scene exactly as it has been worked on rather than deciding on new things to do, or, even more difficult for others to contend with, spontaneously making changes during the actual running of the scene.

Again, I must say how difficult it is to convey on paper more than the mere external organization of the workings of the scene, but to the rehearsal of it must be brought the continuous spark of stimulating life and encouragement. Even the discipline that is required needs to be conveyed as an artisitic and creative challenge rather than a dreary chore. The young people themselves are quick to spot the total difference between a kind of "teachery" concern for tidiness and order, and a genuinely inspiring invitation to really get into the "guts" of the scene, with total trust given to them to find what is constructively exciting rather than merely taking the opportunity to "mess about." At the same time, the director can handle the situation with total firmness. Indeed, I always say to people directing such a scene for the first time: "Forget you are in a school with a group of young people helping. Look on the occasion as a genuine opportunity for creating a scene with a great crowd of people maybe in the middle of a desert, surrounded by 200 extras. You would not tolerate messing about from the extras in such circumstances and you would deal with the situation professionally. Then approach this kind of audience participation crowd scene in exactly the same manner — professionally." This approach can indeed be an important part of the youngster's experience.

3. SPOKEN PARTICIPATION BY WHOLE AUDIENCE

Perhaps the most difficult experiment in audience participation crowd scenes with this teen-age group is attempting to involve the entire audience of 200. Certainly it is daring. Certainly at times it can be very exciting. At others it can be foolhardy. Perhaps most important of all, at times it might be very unfair to the young people themselves, particularly with performances in school, during school time, when the custom of authority and obedience may impose a demand about which some might feel very unhappy. In the other scenes mentioned above, there is opportunity for *volunteers* to take part. In *Hamlet*, a further invitation is extended to those who have not volunteered to attempt participation during the final scene by some form of role playing, *if they so wish*. The matter is then entirely in their own hands, and I know of many people who have for but a few seconds tried just this in the *Hamlet* scene. For whatever reason that is personal to them, they may not have been able to sustain it and have been able to slip back into being just observer. Perhaps a little later, they have tried again. Who knows? But the situation is quite different from an audience where volunteers are not asked for, and even worse, where there is a kind of bland acceptance by the actors that everyone *is* going to take part whether they want to or not. Nothing can really be more unfair than that.

Ultimately it is a matter of the mode of presentation by the company. They need, through their director, to reverse roles with the audience — to say that they themselves would like help to discover whether it is possible for a whole audience in a theatre to take active part in a crowd scene. They *ask* for the help of the audience. To ask is quite different than to *expect*, and certainly it is wholly different from an acceptance of some kind of undeniable right to that help, mostly based on the authoritarianism of the adult to demand what he needs and to expect unquestioning obedience. Better not to attempt such a scene at all than to do so from such a standpoint.

The funeral oration sequence from *Julius Caesar* — "Enter Brutus, Cassius and a throng of citizens," followed after Brutus's oration by "Enter Antony and others with Caesar's body" — is a superb participation scene with up to a maximum of 200 young people. We must make clear, however, that what we mean by CROWD is an assembly of individuals. In many ways this scene highlights this factor because of the brilliant manipulation of the citizens' view by Brutus and Antony. This is not a "mob" change. It happens gradually, first with a few individuals, then more and more. It contains totally the cliche about the forest fire. Young people are fascinated by this idea and more so if they experience it directly through their own *detailed listening* to what Antony is saying, rather than through detailed rehearsal of crowd reaction.

The approach to putting the scene together is not dissimilar to suggestions made for other crowd scenes. But in the *"Caesar"* scene there is greater need for flexibility of space, including some kind of built dais on which Caesar's body can be placed for all to see and around which people can gather closer and closer at Antony's behest.

Time needs to be given for the director or one of the cast to give some of the background to the story and the people involved. The more dramatically rather than academically this can be done the more stimulating it is to the imagination of the participants. We meet again the point that intuitive feeling for the situation is more important than intellectual knowledge and analysis.

It will be possible to allude to contemporary affairs and how the media and partisan interests use them to shape the point of view of "the man in the street," who becomes enmeshed without knowing the full detail of what it is that involves him.

There needs to be time for the audience, under the guidance of actors in the company, to break into groups in order to talk about the kinds of people they might be in the scene. The size of these groups would depend on the number of actors available to help, but there should not be less than four groups under the leadership of each of the four citizens to whom Shakespeare gives specific interjections. In an audience of 200, these groups would still be very large — 50 per group.

It often helps if the actors themselves can think through with some simple clarity a few details of the citizen they are portraying and then talk about this freely and easily with the young people. But they need to avoid clever psychological analysis of character, as this only confuses the youngsters and makes many feel the task is beyond them. On the other hand, young people of this age group are well able to go beyond mere "occupational diseases," such as being a shopkeeper or "just an ordinary sort of person." As soon as possible, it is useful for each large group to break into smaller groups, perhaps of three, four or five. They may well fall into their own friendship grouping. Now, they can sort out further details with greater privacy than in the large group. At this point some may even decide they want to stay in pairs or threes or whatever for the scene itself. Ten minutes given to this opportunity to think about the people they are being and why they happen to be at or near the Forum at all on this day will enormously help the scene as a whole and will charge it with feeling of "real people" making up this great crowd.

The director needs 12 to 15 minutes to draw the scene together, to make clear such factors as the geography of the area, including entrances, exits, etc. It is wise to keep in mind what was said earlier about professionalism of approach and to have the cymbal as an easy "control" instrument. There is never need for quiet for the sake of quiet, but only for the sake of progressing the development of the scene, and that cannot be done without the self-control of each individual. Keep in mind that the young have an infinite curiosity about the creation of theatre and the workings of actors and directors.

Possibly half a dozen salient moments of the scene need to be picked for rehearsal, in order that the over-all shape of the scene can be glimpsed by all. At these moments, fullness can be given to the idea of *listening to the words spoken* as the main guide to one's reactions. And there are the "four main citizens" to help give a lead, just as in every crowd in our real life situations there are those who give a lead and those who follow or reject.

The director and the actors should also be ready for the fact that one of the problems for the young people, especially if they have not experienced much drama, is vocally letting go, especially in the early stages when they are quite naturally concerned about and shy of peer reaction to anything they might say. This can often be helped by experiencing together, under the leadership of the director, a *radio fade-in* of everybody talking together at one and the same time, starting from a whisper and gradually coming to full voice and gradually, with a radio fade-out returning to silence. If this is attempted, then the young people are helped if they are given something very specific to talk about, so there is no danger of anyone's feeling a reliance on "rhubarb-rhubarb." Perhaps the theme of their talking might actually be the first growing rumor that Caesar has been murdered. It might be taken in contemporary terms of a rumor that "The Prime Minister or the President or the Pope or some other famous national or international figure has been assassinated." It should be expected that the first time through will be difficult to sustain and may break into various manifestations of humor. Fine! Use it. Let it come right out. Everyone enjoy it. Then — suddenly the director: "Right, now let's try it once more. You all know the problem we're involved in. It's one of hanging grimly onto our concentration and allowing nothing to distract it. But let's face one very strong fact. Many, perhaps the majority of us, are going to find that concentration and sustain it. Some of us may not be able to do so, for all kinds of understandable reasons. However, we all have one personal responsibility; if we are not ourselves deeply in the scene we still owe it to everyone who *is* to make absolutely certain that we do nothing and say nothing that could disturb their concentration. Right, stand by to try it again. Now — just to help our concentration, everyone close your eyes and listen — listen to your own heartbeat or to your own breathing. " Allow some seconds for this and you can feel calmness, seriousness, come back to the whole group — so: "Start the whispering *now.*"

The practice of the *fade-out* can have great relevance to the ending of the scene as this is likely to involve all 200, under their leaders, leaving the Forum with full-voiced fury to take their revenge on the assassins. Probably they cannot leave the actual hall or gymnasium, so, to finish up at the farthest end and then use their gradual radio-fade-out can dramatically solve the problem for them. And the scene ends with Antony's final words, in the ensuing silence:

"Now let it work. Mischief, thou art afoot,

Take thou what course thou wilt." Pause and exit.

By this time, a calm will have returned to the young people, so that the crowd scene does not end with everyone in a state of over-excitement.

In *Henry V*, much the same kind of approach as to *Julius Caesar* can be used to develop a crowd scene around the incident at the Gates of Harfleur, though the scene itself has not perhaps quite the same impact.

4. SMALL GROUP IMPROVISATIONS

Possibly more than in any other type of audience participation for teenagers, the attempt to provide improvisational opportunities for small groups acting independently of each other is the most difficult from the point of view of the young people themselves. Each small group, perhaps numbering only four or five, feels so *exposed*, so aware of the non-participants when the focus of action settles on them, even if only for a short while. Nevertheless, the approach can have value, and, as I shall go into later, there are safeguards that can be taken to help the situation.

Comedy is the most difficult form of audience participation to attempt because most young people do not have sufficient experience to cope with audience reaction, particularly laughter, and so will, as Hamlet says:....."themselves laugh to set upon some barren quantity of spectators to laugh too." In the young peoples' own improvisation in the classroom, there is in fact a great deal of humor, wit and boisterous fun, but the classroom situation has not the same audience problems as in participatory crowd scenes.

Henry IV, Part 1 (Act IV, Scene 2), provides an excellent basis for small group improvisation and for controlled comedy. Falstaff, it will be recalled, has been charged with the task of raising an army through the King's Press. He sees in this an excellent way of making a little on the side by allowing himself to be bribed by many families and individuals. Having thus lost all the fit men, he has to take whom he can and eventually finishes up with an army of "scarecrows" etc. This is the ragged group Prince Hal finally inspects.

The crowd scene based on the incident can be built up through the following stages:

a) The acting area is rectangular, 20' x 15', with an aisle at each of the four corners, and the audience seated either on 3 or 4 sides, as we have seen before (**see diagrams 12 and 19 on pages 74 and 141**).

b) The acting team initially selects 20 to 24 volunteers. After hearing a general outline of the scene, these then split into groups of 4 or 5 per group, making up at least 4 but no more than 6 family groups. Despite *family* intention, no attempt should be made to coerce the participants into mixing the sexes, unless they are clearly comfortable doing so, which usually depends on how much drama they have done together in class. If they represent more than one class, then they probably will not have so worked together.

c) While most of the actors disperse to various quiet corners of the hall to talk to the family groups (see "e" below), Falstaff explains the background of the scene to the rest of the audience. He then asks for new volunteers to make up his army of wretched scarecrows. Possibly 12 to 16 are selected and then given a few moments to discuss with a friend what kind of "outlandish and unlikely character" they will be. Falstaff then drills them, including lining them up in two or three lines, as eventually they will be for the inspection by Prince Hal.

d) Falstaff then selects a final volunteer to be in charge of his "drum," as an NCO accompanying the King's Press on its search for recruits. (The actor playing Falstaff may intuitively feel that it is wiser to have two people in charge of the drum; one person on his own can feel rather isolated and overexposed.)

e) Meanwhile, the actors have explained to the family groups that it was the custom of the time for the King to "press" young men into the army quite unexpectedly. The majority would not wish to go, and each family has to think about, discuss and, if time permits, even quietly try out a short improvisation concerning their reasons for not allowing any of their family to be "pressed." A few suggestions are made by the actors — e.g. that there is only one young man in the family and the farm will die if he is taken away; perhaps one of the family is suspected of having the plague; maybe the only eligible person happened to break his leg the other day, etc. Just sufficient and varied enough suggestions to stimulate the inventiveness of each family. The seed is also sown that the "Press" may not be above accepting a bribe!

f) The above selecting, organizing, describing and rehearsing will take approximately 15 to 20 minutes, at the end of which time all will be ready to run the scene. Each family now has its own rostrum block within the acting area, and the participants are asked to go to their own block where they remain throughout the scene, bringing to life their own improvisation as they hear the drum moving towards their particular "house." When all the houses have been visited, the families leave the area. Falstaff counts his ill-gotten gains (perhaps gives a tip to his drummer to keep him quiet) and then orders his scarecrow army to fall in. He marches them about the area, until hailed by Prince Hal for the inspection. There follows *scripted* dialogue between Falstaff and the

Prince about the army, and a great deal of humor arises from the fact of *no dialogue being improvised* between either them or between Hal and the army. The whole scene can be played on exchanged looks between them during the inspection that intersperses the scripted lines. Not improvising at this time is part of the discipline of the scene. The scene ends with Falstaff marching his troop away.

As so often mentioned before, *time* is the great problem with this kind of scene, although, in this particular instance, because of the improvisational nature of the individual family episodes, the 30 minutes allotted to the scene might as likely be too long as too short, depending on the experience and confidence of the young people. I have known groups who have done so much improvisation that each family scene has been a superb example of easy and confident speech flow and sustained characterization, and in these cases it has often been difficult for Falstaff to get the scenes completed. At the other extreme I have known groups who, despite their enthusiasm to participate, have been so overwhelmed with shyness once surrounded by the audience, they have found it most difficult to sustain the scene, and Falstaff has had to carry it almost entirely alone. In such cases, an experienced Falstaff will be able to try many ways of stimulating responses, but will also have to know when and how to end the "agony" if any group is clearly unhappy. It is interesting how often Falstaff has realized that one of the difficulties for some of the young people is that of being confronted by he himself — "a real live actor" — and so has given the onus of responsibility for some episodes to his drummer to see if the peer contact will help the situation. If it does, then Falstaff withdraws even farther, until he senses that the episode should be rounded off. The majority of groups, however, fall between these two extremes, needing some stimulation to "get going," and then sensitive interplay with Falstaff.

This scene is a positive example of the need for the actor to be extremely experienced in serious improvisation as differentiated from slick and clever ad-libbing, otherwise the very character of Falstaff lends itself to the worst temptations to get "cheap laughs." Throughout the crowd scene he is also called upon to make many swift, intuitive decisions in order to help the young participants. He must never dismiss any group as hopeless, particularly by comparison with other groups. He, more than most, will discover the full truth of the fact that every group is different, without necessarily being better or worse than other groups. He must always be ready to try, by his own skillful questioning (like a good interviewer) to stimulate responses that go beyond mere "yes and no" answers, and yet he must always be ready to round off an episode either because of time or because he senses that a group is beginning to reach its maximum capacity for sustaining. And, of course, the scenes he will round off quickest are those where a few exhibitionists are just showing-off.

The safeguards that should be considered by any group of actors attempting such a scene are as follows:

i)   The audience must be homogeneous. Again this is the value of the theatre *going to* the audience. I have never known the scene work as well as it might when two or more schools have joined up together.

ii)   Although the scene can and will work with an audience of up to 200, it helps to have fewer, say a maximum of 120. Certainly the scene should not be comtemplated with more than 200.

iii)   A confined age-group will help the participants. The problem already mentioned of having a full range of 12 to 17 is exacerbated when small group improvisations are involved. If the scene is confined to say the 12 to 14 or the 15 to 17 age group, this will help considerably.

iv) The actors should check carefully with the teachers how much improvisation has been experienced by the young people. For a scene of this kind, it can be wise for the company to forewarn the school of the nature of the scene as there may well be a drama group in the school who would most like to have the experience and who, if they know in advance, will become the main core of volunteers for the crowd scene.

v) All of the actors should be experienced in improvisation at a very serious level, and should have constantly extended practice at improvisation during rehearsal. (See the next chapter for further thoughts about this as part of The Actor in Children's Theatre.)

vi) The actors should also be helped to understand a great deal about stimulating young people in drama.

vii) All volunteer participants should be selected at one and the same time for the family groups, and invited to sit in the acting area. Only after all have been selected and assembled should they be asked to divide into family groups, and the choice of grouping should be left entirely to them. In this manner the young people will tend to join with others they know, which will be helpful to their improvisation. When selecting people, if an actor notices two sitting together with their hands up, it could be wise to take both and disregard the general idea of trying to pick from many different sections of the audience. Friendship pairs, as with friendship groups, can be very helpful to this type of scene.

viii) When talking to the family groups about the *organization* of the scene, (as opposed to stimulating ideas for content) the actors should give a clear picture of what will happen, without too much fussy detail, which the young people may fear they might forget. They need mainly to know the "geography" of the acting area and which block each family will be using. They also need to know about beginnings and endings that concern them. Then, during the moments of stimulating ideas, each actor needs to remain with a group until he/she feels that ideas are flowing with confidence. At this point it is possible to withdraw. Even then the actor must not go too far away in case his advice is sought, and he must also keep the group aware of how much time is left for preparation. While busy with these preparations, most groups will momentarily forget that soon they will be surrounded by an audience of their peers. Suddenly, just before the run of the whole crowd scene, the realization will hit. Many will be "stricken by stage fright." The actors should be ready for this and neither ignore it nor attempt to dismiss it lightly. Indeed it is often best to identify with the feeling and have a moment of trying to help. For example, the actor might say, "I know how you feel. No matter how many times I perform I always feel the same. I find that I get over it by the depth of my concentration and I do a few seconds of a concentration exercise to help me. Try it with me now. Close your eyes. Now listen fully to your own heart beat or to your own natural breathing. Listen. Listen. (Allow, say, 15 to 20 seconds of this.) There. Open your eyes. If you can hang on to that depth of concentration, you'll find the audience won't worry you nearly as much."

ix) The actor in charge of the over-all organization and direction of the crowd scene (usually Falstaff) can also spend a few moments talking to

159

the audience of non-participants about how much they, through their own concentration, can help the participants, for whom such an immediate and spontaneous experience can contain many difficulties. This point has been made before but is worth repeating. The genuine and willing use of this kind of sympathetic understanding and compassion from young people gives them the opportunity to use resources that perhaps we do not often enough call upon them to exercise.

x) Very occasionally a group may ask one of the actors to be part of their family. Sometimes the actors may feel that joining in can in fact be very helpful and so even volunteer to do so. Swift, intuitive assessments must be made of such situations by each individual actor with each separate experience. If they do take part, then they must find a very delicate balance between being a valuable stimulus and taking over entirely. They might find, unless very careful about it, that they are pushed into a dominant role by the youngsters out of deference to their adult and professional status. The skillful actor will know to what degree he should accept or reject this role.

xi) The over-all shape of such a scene contains neither the "ritual clarity" of the *Hamlet* crowd scene, nor the obvious need for built-in control as in the *Macbeth* and *Romeo and Juliet* fight scenes, nor the organizational needs as in the scenes involving all 200, as in *Julius Caesar* or *Henry V*. Nevertheless, the scene from *Henry IV, Part 1*, even though used as a basis for improvisation, must contain the same professional purposefulness of approach and not be allowed to become a loose classroom drama exercise. The aim should be to make the final product involve as much experience of the finish and polish of the other more structured scenes.

xii) Please! No post-mortems as to which of the young peoples' improvisations was best!

The Tempest provides a similar opportunity for group improvisations within a crowd scene, but the problems for the participants are not as acute because each group is led by one of the actors, the scene is more structured and often all groups are working simultaneously and so do not have the same exposure as in the *Henry IV* scenes. The scene from *The Tempest* is the very opening scene of the play, the tempest itself. It involves four groups of participants with 5 or 6 people per group, as:

— courtiers who are passengers;
— members of the crew;
— part of Ariel's creation of the storm, symbolizing through movement many different aspects of the storm;
— a "technical crew," working with a member of the company on sound effects for the storm, e.g. a thunder-sheet, drums, cymbals, etc.

The progressive build up of the scene in rehearsal is very similar to those already described.

I make no apology for the above emphasis on crowd scenes from Shakespeare's plays because all of the scenes were chosen for their theatre value, not for academic reasons. Shakespeare is temporarily out of fashion (old fashioned?), particularly with Children's Theatre Companies. I believe this rejection to be a passing phase, which probably reflects how boring so many people found Shakespeare at school, where academic study of his plays is the epitome of the diagram rather than the picture school of thought. No doubt it is also because so many of his plays are now on film, video and records, often with the finest artists and the greatest directors. We must be thankful for these developments as there is no doubt they are tremendously exciting for young people to see and/or hear, and are produced with an expertise and flourish that are way beyond the means of the majority concerned with live theatre. We should keep in mind, however, that these other media do not provide two experiences that live theatre can:

1. actual involvement and participation;
2. the "communion" experience of many people — actors and audience together — sharing in creative communication. This sharing is a basic human need that live theatre helps to fulfil in a truly unique manner.

NON-SHAKESPEARE CROWD SCENES

Many other crowd scenes were attempted by Theatre Centre, one of which is important because it fulfilled a very particular function — the bridge from Primary to Secondary Children's Theatre, one of the great problems for all educationists. In most societies, the break between the two forms of education is very abrupt. One day the youngster is "top of the heap," a senior member of a primary school, often with accompanying responsibilities, and certainly with the dignity that hierarchy bestows on seniority. A matter of mere weeks later, the youngster is at the bottom of the heap, derisively known as "a new kid," confronted by a very different physical environment as well as new methods of teaching, change of teacher attitudes, etc., and bereft of all hierarchical dignity. Teachers of drama in Secondary schools, if they are aware of this situation, are able to ease some of the problems involved by keeping their early secondary work similar to that of the final year of the primary school. The youngster gains confidence from such continuity.

Children's Theatre actors often have an advantage over teachers because they may well meet all or nearly all age groups, which can be quite different from the experience of many teachers who spend much of their teaching life concentrating on only one, or at most a few, age groups. Children's Theatre can learn from the above example of the Secondary teacher by helping to bridge the gap from one kind of schooling to another, particularly as the same gap is associated with the full change in the experience of young people from unconscious drama, through conscious drama to fully conscious theatre, as discussed in earlier chapters.

A play called **The Angel of the Prisons** was one attempt to bridge the gap between elementary and secondary audience participation. One direct link was through the *journey*, in part a parallel with the journey in such plays as **On Trial** and **The Clown**. A further link was a group improvisation crowd scene, much as those described above for the Shakespeare scenes.

The format of **The Angel of the Prisons** is cinematic, including the fact that one of the main characters is a film director, who is constantly using a camera view-finder. This becomes a built-in possibility for helping the factor of concentration both for the participants and for those watching. In the manner already mentioned for **The Clown** the whole audience is invited to use fingers and hands as camera view-finders. The main subject matter of the play concerns Elizabeth Fry, who did so much to change prison conditions in 19th century England (and much of the rest of the world). One scene concerns the journey of manacled prisoners from Newgate Prison to the dock-side to embark for Australia, and it is this scene that the audience is invited to film. The camera view-finders give the audience something positive to do, so that they are no longer cold, passive, inactive, possibly critical viewers, and, because they are not such, the participants are less worried by them, even though they are in fact being looked at in considerably more detail. Indeed, it is often interesting to note that several participants may suddenly start using parts of themselves — maybe the hands, the feet, the face — in a more detailed manner, due to awareness that "close-ups" are being taken by the many cameras all around them.

For this particular play, the young people are invited to volunteer to participate directly before the intermission, thus giving the company a chance to talk to them about the kind of "tough, ugly prisoners" they are going to be in the scenes to follow in Act 2. They are told that the prisoners fight amongst themselves a great deal, are often drunk and have no means of keeping either themselves or their clothing clean. The youngsters are then invited to disarrange their clothing, and to use sticks of make-up for dirtying-up themselves, if they so wish. The photograph on page 166 shows a group who did so wish, and there is no doubt at all that this changing of external appearance helped their concentration in the two crowd scenes that followed. The initial amused reaction of the audience was perfectly natural, but soon died down, and had very little effect on the participants, who felt "protected" by the make-up. Meanwhile, for many of them, the factor of the journey itself was a natural link with their drama experiences (including Children's Theatre participation) in the Primary school. The first of the participation scenes is in Newgate prison, with the procession scene following later. However, in terms of rehearsal, of overcoming first audience reaction, including the general use of the cameras, the procession scene is rehearsed immediately after the intermission. Nearly always this first part of rehearsal brings the release of self-consciousness from everyone through laughter. This should be expected and accepted. Then the whole situation, including the factor of concentration, is made more serious for everybody. The use of strong music with the procession helps. It may not be necessary to rehearse the whole of the procession — just sufficient for everyone to "break the ice," and to be clear about such simple geographical factors as where and when they enter and exit, factors usually helped by having at least one of the actors involved in the scene with them. Interestingly enough, as is so often the case with rehearsal of these crowd scenes, the main scene of involvement in Newgate prison hardly needs any rehearsal at all — often perhaps no more than the opening of the scene, providing concentration and confidence are achieved in the journey rehearsal.

A play like **Angel of the Prisons**, although originally written for performance by a group of professional actors involving part of their audience in the participation, can as easily be performed by any drama group with a large cast. In such a case, the crowd scenes can be as fully rehearsed as the rest of the play.

There are many other audience participation crowd scenes that can "echo" the classroom drama of the late primary school, while developing a more sophisticated level of rehearsal and presentation for Secondary young people. The detail of organization and build-up of rehearsal will vary according to the exact age-group, numbers in the audience and experience of the actors, but the theme or content can fundamentally be the same.

The following themes and crowd scenes are mentioned only in so far as they may contain new factors of shape or approach from those already described. Otherwise they can all be built-up through similar procedures of "sharing the excitement of creating a crowd scene."

From **The Survivors**. A Mining Disaster, involving three groups of participants:
— the survivors, at the coal face, on a ledge, watching the rising flood waters;
— the rescuers, slowly digging a tunnel in order to try to rescue them;
— those at the pit-head, some in charge of the rescue operation, others the families of those trapped below.

Each of the three groups is led by an actor, and over the half-hour length scene, the interesting device of "frozen and suspended action" can be used, with music linking one scene to the next. Thus there can be a scene at the coal face, and, as this ends, the group becomes still, and music bridges to the pit-head, where the group there "comes alive." Again, as this scene ends, the actors involved become still, and music bridges to a scene with the rescuers. The freezing can be entirely logical because all the groups are involved with *waiting*, with the need to rest, with long periods of total stillness and silence while they strain to catch any sound. The effect can be very cinematic, and the actors are fully in charge of the rounding-off of each scene and the opening of the next.

This kind of scene can clearly be enriched by the use of a few isolated spotlights, each with its own dimmer. If the audience is in more than two rows, then it is essential to have some kind of bleacher seating, because the action for the rescuers and at the coal face nearly always happens on the floor or on low rostrum blocks.

From **Discovery and Survival**. Within a four-sided, open-stage space, perhaps square in shape (15' x 15' to a maximum of 20' x 20'), the participation attempts to involve the *whole audience sitting where they are.*

The crowd scene is concerned with the sinking of an ocean liner by a German U-boat in the middle of the Atlantic Ocean during the Second World War. The four sections of the audience, each under the lead and general guidance of one of the actors — with a fifth in charge of directing the whole scene — are involved as follows:

Sections 1 and 2, on opposite sides of the arena, are passengers on the liner, plus some hotel crew staff — waiters, chefs, entertainers, etc.
Section 3, at one end of the arena, are the Captain, Officers and crew of the liner.
Section 4, at the opposite end of the arena, are the Captain and crew of the U-Boat.

No section ever leaves its audience area, although once the liner has been torpedoed there is a great deal of small movement *within* the passenger areas. The "freeze-music-bridge link" from scene to scene, is again used, as described above, with the actors fully in charge of and fully rehearsed in the beginnings and endings of each scene. Apart from the build-up to and the excitement of the actual torpedoing, the scene can also develop various rescue operations, depending on the time available and the capacity of the audience to sustain the scene. Again, much will depend on their previous experience of drama. Like the Mining Disaster scene, much can be made of suspense and tension.

From **The Struggle** (a free and modern adaptation of John Bunyan's *Pilgrim's Progress*). Act II of this play is devoted to a crowd scene in which many small groups of participants devise and set up their own "stalls" in the "City of Vanity Fair," in order to tempt the hero to his own doom and destruction. The actors stimulate the individual group improvisations in much the manner described for the Falstaff crowd scene in *Henry IV, Part 1.* Again the

163

"freeze" technique is used as the main character moves from "temptation to temptation." Because all groups are involved simultaneously, even though only one group is "unfrozen" at a time, the exposure for the young people is less hard for them to cope with than in the Falstaff scenes. The final part of this crowd scene involves the whole audience in a trial, with opposing factions being led in group reaction by the actors.

Even a cursory glance at the foregoing chapters should suggest to the reader that the most important individual in **participatory** theatre is the actor. Oh, yes, the writer, the director, administrators, officials and many others are all important. But still the most important of all is the actor.

/ In concluding this chapter, I should re-emphasize that the above crowd scenes are all concerned with a balance of the *process of drama* (the preparation and rehearsal) and the *product of theatre* (the final performance of the scene, with rehearsed actors playing the main parts). The *process* is speedy because it is largely intuitive and emotional, but nevertheless it has as much validity as the longer intellectual processes of in-depth classroom study. The differences are important. Both are valid. One approach should not be rejected because it is different from the other.

This is one of the essential contrasts between Participatory Theatre and some forms of theatre in education, where often the performance product is less important than the detailed intellectual concern with the *content*. The argument that "theatre should help people to think" has superceded the fact that the theatre experience will lead people to *feel* deeply, as a result of which they genuinely think for themselves. *Theatre experience* thus has its parallel values with *intellectual inquiry*, particularly when, without overt intention, it opens doors and windows to emotional and spiritual experiences.

All of the above crowd scenes could indeed be used to *stimulate* inquiry: the Falstaff scene could lead to a study of conscription and drafting; the *Hamlet* scene to an investigation of the place of monarchy; the mining disaster to a study of all kinds of industrial-sociological problems; the Elizabeth Fry scenes to an examination of prison reform and capital punishment, and so on. But the educational importance of these factors in no way invalidates the importance of the practical experience of theatre itself as an act of creation, whatever the content. None of these scenes was planned, written or produced with any overt intention beyond that of the theatre experience. The content is, in many respects, irrelevant, as the basic aim is to involve participants and audience in an experience of *theatre*. This is different from, not necessarily better nor worse than, those types of experience that are deeply concerned with content, either because of overt educational intention or because of superficial, or even in-depth, study of social problems, Again, both are valid. However, in my view, there is today less concern or regard for the experience of theatre in its own right, even as fundamental stimulation, and far more concern for the intellectual inquiry within and about the content. Observation suggests some reasons for this:

1. The economics of theatre *in schools during school time* have led those who hold the purse strings, and consequently those who wish the purse to be opened, to take a strong view that time and money must only be given to clearly demonstrable overt educational intent. That intention from the official educational authority's point of view is invariably the narrow one of intellectual rather than emotional and intuitive experience, and tends to exclude or minimize the *intrinsic value* of theatre as such.
2. Many people involved in the planning and running of such work have not

themselves had sufficient in-depth experience of *theatre* itself, certainly not as an exciting and dynamic creative entity. Bored with the plethora of commercial drivel, dismayed by an elitist approach to culture, and disillusioned with all forms of heritage, from the fairy story to the classic, they are anxious to relate theatre to the realities of today's world and its problems.

3. Distressed by society as a whole, they see the theatre as a tool for reform and use it as such in a direct intellectual manner, with insidious emotional overtones, in an effort to "educate" others to their way of thinking, even though they would claim that that thinking is objective and for the general good.

   I can only say again that theatre is, in my view, for opening the heart, the mind and the spirit — not for bending the mind in a particular direction.

The Angel of the Prisons. *Participants as rough prisoners in the Newgate Prison scenes. Volunteers were selected just prior to the intermission so that during the break they could disarrange their clothing and use a few sticks of make-up to "dirty" themselves. Elizabeth Fry, the famous prison reformer, sits with them. This is not an actual scene from the play, but was posed at the request of the school after the performance was over. It reflects some of the absorption and sincerity the young people bring to this form of participation, and there is no doubt that the make-up helped this factor in this particular play.* (Photo: Fox Photos Ltd.)

The Struggle. *Adam is accused by three masked and cloaked symbolic characters in this modern, free adaptation of Bunyan's* Pilgrim's Progress. *Note that the audience at the far end has five or six rows, without bleacher seating, so that the back row is forced to stand; that the playing area is 20' x 15' with a rostrum block at the entrance to each aisle — these are helpful for raising the costumed figures; that the two teachers sitting at the head of the aisle have placed themselves there after seating the youngsters — the aisle affords them good viewing, but often impedes the entrance of actors.*

Angel of the Prisons. *Starting to rehearse the participants in the procession from Newgate Prison to the docks to embark for Australia. At this starting point of rehearsal — mainly to show the geography of the stage — there is little absorption from participants or audience. Soon, however, growing confidence of the participants brings about concentration by all. The audience will be invited to "film" the scene, using their hands and fingers as camera viewfinders, which will help them to be busy and so diminish the self-consciousness of the participants. Note the closeness of the audience and the interesting arrangement of rostrum blocks used as a permanent setting in this production. (The blocks are of decreasing sizes so that they can be placed inside one another for transportation. The largest is 4'6" x 4' x 15", the second largest is 4'3" x 3'9" x 13" and the smaller is 4' x 3'6" x 11".)*

167

Discovery and Survival. *Absorption varies with each group of volunteer participants. In the center of this action, three youngsters are clearly absorbed, and two not nearly as deeply. The audience in the background, however, are quite absorbed. Note the actress on the left stimulating the participants from within character. She remains a little behind the pace of their work so that there is no danger of her "demonstrating" or being copied. She also makes sure she does not fuss them about detail of mime. Intuitive experience is much more important then intellectual accuracy.* (Photo: Ian Stone)

Preparation for Participation. *A serious discussion about a scene with one of the actors. There is no nonsense about "playing at being actors acting a play." The full impact of genuine theatre creation governs the attitude of the actor and so totally engages the interest of the young people.* (Photo: Ian Stone)

8

The Actor In Children's Theatre

Every year shows an increase in the number of people who become involved in Children's Theatre activities of one kind or another (and perhaps I should remind the reader of the narrow limitations covered by this book, as stated in the introduction).

The actors who become involved vary in background, training and experience, from those at the top of their own adult professional careers, to every kind of nonprofessional until we reach the other end of the spectrum where secondary school students perform for pupils in elementary schools. Behind much of this work lies dedication, enthusiasm and a genuine desire to share a love of theatre with younger people in the community, particularly with those who would have no theatre experiences of any kind except for such efforts. Others become involved for largely educational or recreational reasons; some even for almost entirely commercial reasons.

Whatever the reason, whoever the people, one truth is paramount: what is offered and the way in which it is offered must be of the finest quality arising from the highest forms of artistic integrity. Nothing else will do. Anything less is a sham and a fraud and is seen by the young people themselves for the inferior work that it is. The young people may not be able to articulate their disappointment or disgust, but they feel it nevertheless. Exploitation of this innocent guilelessness ultimately has the most unhappy affect on people's attitude to theatre in later life — they simply stay away from it.

Stanislavsky was asked once: "How do you act for children?" He replied: "The same as for adults, only *better*." This simple statement should be engraved in the heart of every actor of whatever age or experience who attempts to perform in Children's Theatre with audience participation. Whatever the training and experience of an actor, the truth remains that there will be many moments in Participatory Children's Theatre where there are new things for him to consider, as I hope has already been indicated in the chapters on Audience Participation. For many the first basic adjustment that has to be made is that of *attitude*. If, for whatever reason, the attitude is one of "anything goes for kids," then the work is almost doomed before going into rehearsal. If the attitude is one of "how can we make this an unforgettable experience for the children or young people — despite the paucity of our resources," then the work will be based on very exacting but rewarding foundations. Thus, the actors will go to all lengths to reach the highest standards, even if it means retraining or new forms of training.

What are the qualities necessary for acting in Children's Theatre, particularly with forms of audience participation?

— a deep and indestructible concentration and absorption bringing, among other qualities, a full and total believability in the characters being portrayed and the story involving them;
— an acute and astute awareness of every moment of every performance;
— a capacity for flexibility and adaptability, partly based on genuine forms of improvisation as opposed to facile and clever ad-libbing;
— a full vocal and physical control, based on genuine release rather than moments of hysterical "letting-go";
— a versatility of characterization, without dependence on make-up, props or costume, or of lighting and scenery;
— a rich capacity for inventiveness and use of imagination, yet highly disciplined and responsive to direction;
— a detailed sensitivity to other actors leading to an interest in and experience of genuine team or ensemble work;
— a capacity to sustain, or at least to be aware of the problems involved in sustaining, if involved in many performances of a play;
— a full-hearted readiness to discover and adjust on a performance to performance basis;
— a strong trust in personal intuition, particularly with audience participation.

Of course, most of these factors are equally desirable in adult theatre, many relevant to the proscenium stage. There are, however, many fine proscenium actors who feel very unhappy in the open stage, and many equally fine actors in both proscenium and open stage who have had no experience of improvisation, and possibly no particular interest in it. There are some who feel almost naked without make-up and costume. I would find it presumptuous to criticize actors for the above, but I could not cast them in Children's Theatre with Audience Participation in the Open Stage unless they were prepared to attempt to master these factors as part of rehearsal and preparation. In truth, most are willing to try, and perhaps regret not having had some of the experiences before. Children's Theatre is often enriched by their involvement because of the excellence of their acting and their depth of other theatre experience. I do not personally believe that all Children's Theatre actors should be under a certain age and/or radical thinkers about theatre. Indeed I believe that theatre loses much when there is no form of hierarchy of experience. It is an art in which one learns more every day, not just in training, and many young actors must owe so much to their more experienced seniors, not necessarily through overt teaching arrangements, but simply through the spin-off from working together over a period of time. The reverse of this is also true when the older, more experienced actor learns from the younger. This can be particularly helpful when an established company decides on a new venture, such as Children's Theatre with audience participation, and then deliberately engages two young actors who have had prior experience of such work. In these circumstances, the experienced younger members can help with every process in production, especially that of attitude and belief. If otherwise established actors have never seen, let alone acted in, such theatre, they often have a perfectly understandable cynicism about the whole idea, which may have its roots in stories they have heard on the grapevine about poor examples of such work. However, if they *have* to be involved in such work, the majority are totally willing to change their attitude, providing the director of the play they are involved in really does know his/her stuff about such productions, and does not share the cynicism. Directing in several different countries on such a first exposure for the majority of the company, I count among some of my most exciting experiences of Children's Theatre. Helping to change attitudes and preparing for genuine audience participation is an arduous but rewarding task, with its fullest satisfaction coming immediately after the first performance when the actors are amazed and delighted that everything (or nearly everything!) worked, and *they* had done it. Immediately, the last vestiges of doubt and cynicism are erased, and efforts are doubled to ensure the sustaining and increase of success. Part of the joy of working with such professional actors is that their performances are often of the highest quality from the outset. Only the participation requirements are a basic problem for them.

With new professional actors or with students, the reverse may well be true. They are quickly or already convinced of the participation and probably experienced in improvisation. Their problem, then, becomes that of wrestling with such factors as charactization, and, above all, that of sustaining over a long period of time.

I said in my preface that I believe it to be bordering on impertinence for one director to tell another how to set about directing a play. So it is with a little trepidation that I address this chapter on "The Actor in Children's Theatre" mainly to directors, in the hope that those with less experience in Participatory Children's Theatre will find some helpful approaches to such productions, particularly to preparation during rehearsal. Furthermore, I hope the ideas might help both kinds of actor mentioned above.

There are three main approaches I would recommend with, of course, many detailed points within each. Much of this book already contains many such details, and some of these may well bear the repetition given to them in this chapter.

The main approaches are concerned with:
1. The initial setting or blocking of the play.
2. Limbering-up during rehearsal and before each performance.
3. Using improvisation as an approach to audience participation.

1. THE INITIAL BLOCKING OR SETTING OF THE PLAY

I become more and more convinced, with adult as well as children's theatre, specially if it is in the open stage, that the initial blocking needs to be *swift*. This entails outlining the general shape, being specific about the use of entrances and exits, and perhaps some salient moves. The major task then is to encourage the actors to trust their own intuition and to follow through any impulses they have to move, without waiting for instructions.

With a 45 to 50 minute play (or one act of a three act play) I would aim at this first swift setting taking about three hours, certainly no more than five. Then run the whole straight through. The director, during this run, can, if need be, quietly remind actors of what they did before, should they forget.

Remarkably enough they seldom do forget when working from this basis of swift intuitive discovery and development.

I need to digress here.

I am constantly surprised by the number of actors who have to pause to write down every move when a play is being set. Even actors who deplore most other theatrical traditions fall back on this most traditional and quite meaningless feature of rehearsal, both its origins and purpose obscured by the mists of antiquity, and yet perpetuated in most forms of training and production. In fact, part of the origin is associated with the times when there were elaborate sets which were not actually seen until dress rehearsal. All kinds of chairs mnd boxes were used to represent furniture, and chalk lines used to mark out the demarcations of the set as a whole, including the position of doorways, etc. Add to this the pressures of weekly repertory when 3-Act plays were being produced in four or five half days, and many scenes run through no more than once, and the actor needed every possible aid to his memory. Without such problems the needs are different, and the implication of writing down moves at a first setting is that they are the *final moves* rather than an early exploration. One of the advantages of the swift procedure suggested here is that there is no time to write down anything, and the actual intuitive flow sustains a living vitality instead of risking an early sterility. Of course, there may be need at certain moments for actors to jot down a note or two, but usually these can be made when off-stage, between scenes or at other breaks. It is interesting that in open stage work the majority of actors feel far less need to write down moves because so much of the movement and grouping is based on logical human relationships rather than the artificiality often necessary on the picture-frame stage. (The same goes for prompting; seldom have I known an actor to either need or expect a prompt in open stage theatre.)

The major advantages of this swift blocking are:

a) it encourages the actors full use of intuition as well as of mind. Often the swift intuitive "risk" releases and reveals all sorts of factors that reason either never reaches or else takes many hours of searching for;

b) it caters for the actors' need for end product, and thus helps to restore and sustain the patience necessary for the whole rehearsal period;

c) it helps all of the actors to feel the general shape and wholeness of the play before dissecting it and mastering one section at a time;

d) it enables the actors to feel the fullness of their own character and relationships with other characters;

e) it enables the director, particularly if he/she is working with some of the cast for the first time, to sense the manner of approach to creation of each individual;

f) it reveals to the director, designer, wardrobe, even stage crew, the "workability" of the setting, particularly with simple permanent sets of rostrum blocks that might be used in the open stage;

g) it reveals to the director many three-dimensional aspects of moves, relationships, etc., which are not so easily worked out on paper or in his/her mind;

h) it can help the playwright, director and actors to feel the wholeness of a new and untried play, and reveals any weaknesses that may exist but cannot be found out until there is a three-dimensional experience (sitting in a circle reading the play never reveals as much);

i) it makes very clear, in children's theatre with audience participation, just how genuinely integrated that participation is, and reveals any possible artificiality;

j) it includes for everybody involved an intuitive awareness of the *rhythm* of the play as a whole;

k) it helps with such simple factors as timing each scene or act.

2. LIMBERING-UP BEFORE REHEARSALS AND PERFORMANCES

For the majority of actors in Western Theatre the idea of limbering-up before every performance is comparatively new, and its range of use varies from a few conscientious individuals with an intelligent plan of intentions, and ensemble groups that work closely together, to those at the other extreme who look on the whole notion as precious nonsense. Somewhere in the middle of these extremes are those who feel the need to limber, and are convinced that it must be valuable, but simply do not know what to do. Many of the latter group pick up the externals of what they observe others doing, but seldom are really aware of the effect either on themselves or on others. In my personal view, all limbering should be basically functional and practical, concerned with self, the rest of the cast and with the environment in which one is performing, including the audience within that environment.

In theatre, the actor is confronted with the only art in which *the performer and the instrument are one and the same.* The musician has an instrument, the painter has palette, brushes and paper, the sculptor has stone and tools, the potter has clay and glazes. If the piano is out of tune, an expert tunes it. Paint, clay, etc. can all be renewed and tools sharpened. The actor has his own body, voice, senses and so on. If they need sharpening the responsibility is his, and he is not going to be able to purchase a new voice or a new body. The greatest pianist in the world will give only a poor performance on a piano that is out of tune. Much the same can be said for the majority of actors, some of whom will say after a poor performance: "It's my fault. I was lazy in my preparation before the performance. I must learn to discipline myself." I must learn to discipline myself! The wisdom behind these words underlines both problem and solution. The discipline is *personal.* A major problem for many actors is that their training takes place with a class or group. Unless the teacher of the class gradually makes clear to each student on an individual basis precisely what movement and voice work are for and are achieving, and how to continue with it on one's own, then as soon as training is over and the class or group no longer exists, the majority of actors feel alone and out on a limb. In rehearsal, a director can usually see very quickly an actor who has been trained to know his own instrument and how to keep it in tune. In my experience, there are sadly very few. It is part of the shyness and natural dignity of the majority of actors that they will not say so, and because individuals have different backgrounds and attitudes it can be very difficult in rehearsal for the director to instigate any particular form of limbering without creating dichotomies, even offence, both of which will lead to defensiveness and self-consciousness.

One solution to the problem is to base rehearsal limbering, at least to start with, on the down to earth, practical functional necessity for limbering *before performance,* which in terms of children's theatre includes the following basic reasons:

— the factor of audience participation;

— if performances take place in a school or different schools, the mastery of each new environment;

— if performances take place during school hours (e.g. between 9:00 a.m. and

3:00 p.m.) then the human instrument, against all natural reluctance must be helped to achieve peak condition for such unnatural hours;

— if performances are in the open stage and in broad daylight, then all possible "cover-ups" for the actor cease to exist. He must overcome every problem;

— the tradition (no matter how appalling it is) in adult theatre that there is always one performance that does not matter as much as the others — e.g. a mid-week matinee with only a few in the audience — cannot exist in children's theatre. Every performance must be the finest. It may be the first and/or the last the children and young people will ever see.

Just these basic reasons are usually sufficient to alert any group of actors to the necessity of limbering before performance. If these reasons are spoken of at the first rehearsal, then they provide a basis for limbering in rehearsal, with everybody having the same object in common. Indeed, the situation might be looked on as rehearsing the limbering as well as the play.

So let us consider first of all limbering for performance, and then look at the extension to other forms that are valuable in rehearsal, but impossible in terms of time before performance.

When we introduced a Shakespeare program into our secondary work at Theatre Centre, we overcame the actor's reluctance and reserve by incorporating a limbering session as part of the opening of a play, and in a subsequent program invited the youngsters to join us in some of the exercises.

The full purpose of the limbering-up before performance really falls under four headings: *Concentration; Physical; Vocal; Sensitivity.*

A. *Concentration.*

No form of theatre reaches a point worthy of sharing with an audience without the very fullest concentration from the actor in performance. However true this is, and I believe fully in its truth, there always seems to be need for even deeper concentration in the open stage, and particularly in children's theatre that involves audience participation.

There are three definite factors in this concentration, each concerned with a depth of awareness. Firstly there is the full awareness of the self, linked to relaxation and to breathing; secondly there is the need for a full awareness of the environment in which one is performing, and that means — as explained in detail earlier — an awareness of the whole auditorium, not just the acting area surrounded by the audience. This awareness is fascinating, for it is surprising how many factors can affect performance just through spatial relations. Shall we say that we are performing in a 15' circle or a rectangle 20' x 15'. We may perform in 100 different halls without the *size of those playing areas ever changing.* But the over-all size of the hall *does* change. Sometimes the hall will be so vast that the acting area seems the size of a postage stamp on an enormous envelope. At the other extreme, the hall may be so small that one is worried as to whether the full audience can be accommodated along with the acting area. Indeed, on some such occasions, there is need to make slight reductions of the size of the acting area, which itself calls for even greater concern with limbering. Some halls will have a very low ceiling, others very high. Some will have few windows and all rather small; others may have the whole of one wall a complete window with a hot sun streaming through it. There are many, many different physical environments, demanding the actors' total awareness.

The third factor concerning concentration is the need for an awareness of the environment *outside* of the main auditorium and acting area. This is particularly necessary where *sound* is concerned. Traditionally our theatres are places of total silence, shut off from sounds outside of the building and with all sounds inside so controlled that the silence can be total during performance. This cannot be so in the school environment. On the other hand, the youngsters who live and work every day in the environment have come to terms with this "sound world," and if actors are forewarned and prepared to notch up their concentration, then they too can reach the point of mastery where the sound no longer distracts them. During rehearsals, as part of concentration exercises, the actors can be subjected to the wide variety of sounds they are likely to come up against: people preparing or clearing away meals; classes reciting French verbs or mathematical tables; the music lesson in the background, either vocal or instrumental; the constant passage of individual or group footsteps; the school bell or tannoy announcements; a teacher's voice from another classroom; the more insidious sounds of the secretary's typewriter, the telephone and the hushed telephone conversation; the light or heavy thud of various kinds of ball in the school gymnasium. These are the sounds *within the immediate environment.* To these must be added further sounds in the *larger environment* of the playground and the surrounding neighborhood: vehicles coming and going in the playground; the delivery of oil or school dinners; maintenance of the outside fabric of the building ("Sorry about the hammering, but I've waited six months for that drain pipe to be fixed!"); local traffic and, if a main road is close by, then heavier traffic as well; in some areas, there are underground or overhead trains, not to mention the occasional dramatic shrieks of fire engines, police cars or ambulances; and few areas are wholly free from sounds of airplanes; in some areas, the most deafening sound of all can literally be *a sudden few seconds of total silence. The youngsters are used to all this.*

By limbering, by being fully aware, the actor can find a point of concentration where he is not bothered by these factors, and this very blending with the environment is of itself an important part of his offering in performance. Of course, there are extraordinary moments that are quite impossible to prepare the actor for. For example, the teacher who wanders into the arena in the middle of an exciting moment of the play — and always such incidents seem to happen *at* exciting moments of the play — to ask "How many of you visitors want coffee and how many want tea?" or: "Would you mind moving your van, please, the school dinner people want to deliver!" Hilarious moments in retrospect, but very challenging at the time.

B. *Physical.*

Whether on tour or in a permanent theatre, if performances are given during school hours, then as likely as not they can take place as early as nine in the morning. Even if it is an hour or an hour and a half later, it makes little difference. The fact remains that the morning hours do not seem to have been fitted by Creation for the function of creating, and the majority of actors would confess to not being at their best at such hours — *unless by deliberate act of will they do something about it.* This usually entails physical limbering, at the very least some form of natural stretching and relaxation. There is no need for the kind of physical exercising that is more fitted to the playing field. It is extraordinary, however, how many actors appear to feel such a need, with most wearing themselves out for the rest of the day, rather than helping the body to be part of a relaxed and fully tuned instrument, totally within the control of its owner.

In my experience, there are very few accidents causing physical hurt to actors that cannot be traced back to a lack of limbering. Twisted ankles, strained muscles, slipped discs, stiff necks, bruises; all of them, with very rare exceptions, are connected with a failure to make certain that the body is both fully flexible and under full control. For this reason alone, physical limbering is valuable.

In open stage theatre, where the whole environment is used, the limbering must be extended to include an exploration of and mastery of that environment, especially every time one moves into a new environment, which for those touring could be twice a day. The surface of one floor might be like glass, of another like a hard sticky substance; some floors are wooden and splintery, others may have the occasional tripping place. Jumping on or off rostrum blocks needs to be checked carefully to make sure they do not slide, and entrances and exits need to be fully examined because they can change in length simply because of a different shaped hall. The aisle around the back of the audience area, if it is to be used in the performance, must also be checked carefully not only because of changes of distance, but also for unexpected hazards like fire extinguishers, window handles, radiators and so on. Always one must beware of any form of curtain hanging close to such aisles. In my mind's eye I see the face of one actor, distorted with agony, as he ran along an aisle the whole length of which was covered by a beautiful red curtain. Behind the curtain, at elbow height, was a narrow shelf for a fire extinguisher, and he broke a small bone in his forearm with the collision. With graciousness be brushed aside all sympathy, cursing himself for assuming that the curtain covered a bare wall, instead of actually "limbering" the aisle. All of this discovery and mastery of the environment needs to be done while wearing the footwear that is part of one's costume. How many actors have fallen on their backs because they have limbered in their own outdoor rubber soled shoes, and then made a swift entrance in the leather soled shoes that are part of costume. Cloaks and any other flying garment need also to be used as part of this limbering; again, so many fine and dramatic entrances and exits have turned into "the best laugh of the show" as the actor finds himself suspended on the knob of a radiator or the handle of a door, the hem or lining of a cloak seemingly inextricably wound round the offending furniture. It is so sad to experience such a moment, which a little thoughtful limbering will obviate. Doors to dressing-rooms or passages on the outside of the auditorium are also potential hazards; swing doors that slam back into the face of the actor following; doors that open only inwards when one expects them to open outwards; doors that have something impeding them from opening fully, creating an enormous crash if one thrusts too strongly; doors that have strong springs on them and swing back shut with an even greater crash; lightly hung doors with well oiled hinges that cause them to go on swinging backwards and forwards for several seconds; doors that have not been oiled in years, and scream their agony as someone tries to open them silently so as not to disturb a scene in progress; doors that open into a large storage closet instead of the passage one is expecting; doors one assumes are open but are in fact under lock and key. On one occasion, even a door that set off a burglar alarm when an attempt was made to open it, an attempt which was unfortunately not made until halfway through the first scene of the play, and such alarms may be easy to set-off, but almost impossible, so it seems, to stop.

One needs to remember to limber certain properties as well, especially in association with doors and entrances. Whatever may be said by architects to the contrary, for actors it is *not* true that all doors are of a standard height, and I can bring forward many actors to bear witness to this — such as the one who lost the top of his pike-staff, the lady who left hat and wig behind her, the golden goblets struck from the tray and smashed on the ground, the man whose top hat was knocked off in a play the whole story of which was that the hat *couldn't* come off, the umbrella attached to a cart, snapped off on entrance, the bruised forehead of more than one very tall actor. So many incidents, all perhaps amusing to relate, each of them a moment of embarrassment at the time, and, without exception, every one of them happening for lack of a few seconds limbering. Perhaps most important of all, any kind of fight — swords, fists, wrestling, whatever — needs to be limbered, not only with the right shoes, but with the acting area marked out exactly and with all rostrum blocks in place. It is not just a question of "going through the motions" or checking over the audience, but of running the fight with the full vigor of performance. Unless this is done, then danger extends beyond the actors to the possibility of hurting someone in the audience as well.

Doors and their problems perhaps serve as an easy link to the next area of limbering — vocal. There can be many problems of hearing cues from the main acting area when inside a dressing room with the door fully closed, or even in a passage or a nearby room, if there is a door between. Such cues need to be limbered carefully, and it is wise not to assume anything! I can recall several occasions when actors were quite certain that space relations plus good acoustics meant for certain they would have no problem of hearing cues, only to find that for some reason or another this was not so in performance. The matter should never be left to chance. Unhappily, by some quirk of fate, it seems always to be actors with the least facility at improvisation who find themselves standing on stage waiting for someone to enter, who is simply not doing so because he/she has not heard the cue. The ensuing hiatus invariably spoils some moment of the play, and can lead to a lot of bad feeling between actors. These problems can again be solved if they are part of limbering.

C. *Vocal.*

In many ways, this is the most important aspect of all, but of course it is not going to be fully valuable *without the physical limbering* preceding it. Personally, I find it the most difficult area to help actors with because I know of the harm that untrained "Teachers" can do in this field, and because I am particularly anxious not to interfere with background training each actor may have had. Nevertheless, the fact remains that many have *not* had vocal training or perhaps have undergone the wrong type of training. Yet *all* need a vocal limber before performance.

Few Open Stage Children's Theatre performances are likely to take place in purpose-built open stage theatres with benefit of acoustic expertise backing the original construction of the building. Many school gymnasia are notorious for their poor acoustics, unless they have been built as theatres, in which case they often have raised and fixed seating, making them impossible to use for open stage theatre. At the other extreme, school gymnasia are often constructed without any concern for acoustics, and those multi-purpose, mixed gymnasiums or performance areas, often have the worst acoustic problems.

The actor's straightforward task is to become aware of and then master the problems involved. It is never easy. Only the most conceited of actors fail to see the problems they are up against. One difficulty is that there is no consistency, even under one roof in one space. There are halls where, if the actor stands in one part of the acting area he feels as though he is in the center of a gigantic bell, and yet when he moves several feet away to another spot, he suddenly feels he is muffled in cotton-wool. There are areas that appear to need a very strong voice, and others that appear to need very little voice, and in many cases the reverse of what appears to be true is in fact the case! This is where actors need to help each other, thus leading into the next area of limbering, *sensitivity*. There are spaces which seem to reject the first sound of each word, others that reject the final sound.

I do not believe there is any single generalized answer to the problem, and I certainly see no point in the type of limbering where actors wander aimlessly about, vaguely "counting" or making "singing sounds" that are like the laments of limbo, alternating this with the screechings of constipated sea gulls and a few guttural machine gun rolls! Yes, I would understand, if only the actors seemed to be the slightest bit aware of what they are doing and why, why here and now in relation to the problem of this particular hall at this particular minute. It is when there is no relevance or thought or listening; just a kind of sonambulant wandering through a world of accident habits, the mind probably on something quite different, that I cease to understand.

Artistically, to be aware of the problem, and then to reach out towards its mastery, is one of the most exciting and exacting of tasks. To ignore or underrate the problem results in underselling one's own performance, and eventually such things as hoarseness, lost voice, loss of hope and subsequent despair.

At Theatre Centre, we tried to overcome some of the problems by, during rehearsal, offering the actors some help from an expert who is sensitively aware of what is involved, and yet equally concerned not to interfere with the background knowledge of those who have been trained. Below, Perri Way writes of some of the exercises she suggests to the actors. Unfortunately the time given to her in rehearsal was limited, but the value of her contribution for the majority of the actors was unquestionable.

VOCAL LIMBER.

Why this need to include a vocal limber? The chief reason is that we cannot know ourselves vocally, because our mind is divided. How can we concentrate on what our voice is doing when our mind is already fully occupied with what that voice is saying? How can we remedy this? Only by doing one thing at a time.

We have two machines under our control: the thought machine which looks after our ideas, and the voice machine which is responsible for our communication. Both machines are directed by the brain, but the brain can only consciously manage one machine at any one moment. The work of the other must be done subconsciously. It is obvious which one it has to be. The conscious mind is the creative mind, and while we use our voice it is kept working at full pressure forming our thoughts, using our words and arranging our sentences. Therefore our voice machine must be left to the mercy, especially during performance, of the subconscious. To it is relegated the way we breathe, resonate and the whole process of speaking. The subsconscious mind is the habit forming mind. It cannot possibly create, but it can faithfully reproduce.

During limber we are using our conscious mind to establish the vocal essentials in the way physically intended, so that they become unconscious habits handed over to the subconscious to respond freely to our needs during creative performance. We need to develop the habit of a rich, full and colorful voice by releasing the natural tones that lie dormant in every human instrument.

Although all of the following exercises are based on sound medical and psychological knowledge, no technical details are given, otherwise the intellect would take over and academic concerns would become dominant. Where simple explanations occur, they are few in number and relevant because *you cannot master that of which you are unaware.*

Relaxation.

Relaxation is the first essential accomplishment for all actors, because:
(a) It allows physical and emotional functions to work with maximum efficiency.
(b) It eliminates all blockages of artistic intuition.
No vocal work should be attempted *ever* without being preceded, during limbering, by conscious relaxation. Simply because, factually, most sizeable tensions concentrate around "The Center of Speech," i.e. the throat muscles, around the larynx, the jaw above, the shoulders below. These are the areas being the first to tighten, and the last to be released. Thus, tensions from all body regions fly straight to the most sensitive vocal throat area. Obviously then, if a full vocal limber is carried out during total restriction of the vocal region, voice — the actor's instrument — is soon impaired, limited and unreliable.

Exercise 1.

i.   Lie supine on your own floor space. Arms by sides, palms down.
ii. Close eyes now and throughout.
iii. Check that teeth are not clenched; if so, drop jaw to natural easy position.
iv. Squeeze eyes — tight, tight, tighter — LET GO. Repeat iv. Now feel eyes sinking heavily into the head, under closed lids.
v.   Be aware of how heavy the head feels, like a concrete sphere; feel it sinking through the floor.
vi. Make hands into fists. Clench fists hard, harder, harder; bite nails into palms, feeling tension throughout the arms — LET GO. Repeat vi. Now arms by sides as (i), palms down.
vii. Using middle and fourth finger of each hand, "walk" hand towards feet without raising shoulders from the floor. Walk as far, and a little farther, than comfortable, feeling the stretch of the lowering shoulder girdle. Now, palms flat on floor again, let them slide back to normal position by your sides.
viii. Curl toes under; harder, harder, harder — feel tensions through length of legs. LET GO. Now Repeat viii.
ix. Feel the weight of your legs, heavy in lead diving boots. Be aware of the backs of the heels pulling your heavy legs through floor.
x.   Allow the dead weight of the whole body to sink and sag. Sigh, with enjoyment, sink and sag.
xi. *Now you are coming out of your relaxation.* Don't move; just register this suggestion:

From there you alone will be aware of which physical area and limb needs to move first; allow it to judge the proportion of movement. Now follow through with ease and continuity using every part of the torso. Copy the effortless movements of a cat reawakening — stretching each section in comfort, but fully. Arch the spine gently, swaying the tail with rhythm from side to side. When standing up once more, reach up to touch the ceiling with finger tips, stretch higher, higher, imagine you are trying to separate your chest from your abdomen. LET GO.

Audience Participation

If there is limited time for limbering, as between performances or if touring schools, here is an equally valuable relaxation exercise of much shorter time duration, requiring only seconds for each section.

Exercise 2.

Seated with closed eyes and spine and head comfortably erect, body relaxed, not collapsed.

i.   place palms, finger-tips touching, on your middle.
ii. Be aware of the gentle movement happening beneath the fingertips. Realize, of course, it is your breathing rhythm.
iii. *In your mind* say OUT as you feel exhalation under fingers.
iv. Say IN as the breath is replaced. Be sure not to make your breathing fit in with IN-OUT. You follow the rhythm's lead, OUT-IN. Then Repeat (iii and iv) several times. Open your eyes.

This is the only simple way of emptying the ever active mind — shedding tensions and retrieving one's own individual rhythm.

BREATHING.

Breath is the power that makes life possible. Breath is the power making speech possible. The lungs are never empty and never still, whether we are vigorously active or unconscious. So we don't even have to remember to breathe to stay alive. Strange that the easiest job in the world should be done so badly. Nature is in charge of the process and can be trusted to carry out the procedure as intended, if allowed. Additionally, the body and lungs are only too ready to cooperate by extending extra capabilities to actors when, and if, taught along the natural lines of breathing as an involuntary action. Unfortunately, actors have "techniques" thrust upon them while in training, and sadly blame themselves when these gimmicks of techniques prove so unworkable during their early work in theatre.

Never make a *thing* of breathing. Wasting valuable limbering time trying to achieve some technique alien to the anatomical design of the human being can only result in panic and frustration plus cramp in the chest muscles. Because Breath is not only the Motive power of Speech, but also the Driving Force, actors need to bear in mind and use this fact: *The ACTIVE breath is the exhaled one. The PASSIVE breath the inhalation to fill the vacuum.* Therefore breath should pass OUT and IN, *not* In and Out, thus automatically supplying an actor with strength in the outgoing breath, motivated by a driving force resulting in power and timbre vocally.

Voice is as strong or as weak as the Breath it rides upon. Base your breathing on *Comfort, Capacity* and *Control.*

Only one *breathing exercise* is required because it is one that, in its utter simplicity, contains all the attributes every actor seeks (and is unable to find in pseudo voice production): powerful sound, stronger diaphramatic control, natural easy breath control, plus the bonus of re-energizing oneself in the process.

Exercise 3.

i.   Standing position. (Head being in normal erect position. Look ahead at eye level throughout.)
ii. Inhale, a slow full breath. Form lips into whistle shape. Expel the breath forcefully in strong even puffs.
iii. With lips remaining in whistle shape, draw in next full breath, strongly and evenly, like a straight solid rod.

iv. Lips still remaining in same whistle position, expel the air forcefully, yet very *evenly* like a similar straight, inflexible rod.

When expelling the breath as in (ii) by even forceful puffs of air, the important factor is that the cheeks must not be used as in normal puffing out. Transfer instead the identical process of forceful expulsion to the diaphragm area, and feel it react.

RESONANCE.

Without resonance, no member of the acting profession could achieve work, however dedicated to the art. Resonance means the amplification of sound; to re-sound with full vibration, rather like the effect given by the use of the *right* pedal of a piano. The actual sound produced by the vocal cords when one speaks is so unbelieveably small (no more than the volume made by a taut rubber band plucked by the finger), but nature has supplied us with numerous areas at five different levels of the body, to enable that small vocal sound to be directed and amplified in these enclosed, vibrating *resonators.*

Actors performing in the round *must*, through total use of the resonators, including those situated in their back, vocalize every subtle emotion in its fullness. The audience, whether seated behind or facing an actor in performance, should equally receive every minute facet portrayed.

Voice goes anatomically where you think it. In the following, and all other exercise plus vocal communication, apply this principle. Think (visually if it helps) any sound emitted, beginning from your diaphragm and travelling UP, towards the mask of the face, and OUT.

Exercise 4.

i.   Standing, extend the arms fully at *shoulder level.* Cup hands together.
ii. With the full strength of one complete breath used as a "HM" sound, aim this sound with the impetous of something solid into your cupped hands. Now, repeat (ii) once more.

Nasal Resonance is totally necessary for all members of the acting profession. So get accustomed to using it alongside with all other vocal usage daily. The need for limbering and using the Nasal areas has always been agreed upon unanimously by hundreds of fine actors during working sessions with them. Yet never have any achieved Nasal Resonance, though assurity had been given of total mastery of such during their previous years of training. What they thought was use of Nasal Resonance was always NASALITY. I feel it necessary to state this, otherwise readers of this section may also be innocently unaware of the need for an exercise to re-awaken the nasal-sinus areas.

Exercise 5.

i.   Wrinkle nose fully (like pressing tip against a window pane).
ii. Keeping nose to the *full* wrinkle position, place tongue tip against back of your two center front teeth (upper jaw).
iii. Use the next full breath on the 'HM" sound while forcibly "pushing" teeth out with tongue tip. Aim the powerful sound, like a solid object, into the cupped hands as before (exercise 4).

All resonators, frontal and in the back, must be responding *totally* to the voice. The spine also must be limbered, being the only resonator running the full length of the body.

Audience Participation

Exercise 6.
To limber and give ultimate amplification of sound in all body areas.
i. Choose a lyric, tune, theme — anything to use for the exercise.
ii. Staying in one area (on the spot where you are), hum your snatch of music and, while doing so, use the body, limbs, head. Do not co-ordinate freedom of body with rhythm. Just fling, kick, sway, bend — be abandoned.
iii. Continue humming, now distorting the speed of chosen music to unrecognizable rapidity. Let your body activity also be uncontrolled in speed and selectivity. Faster, faster, fling head towards knees, shake head violently from side to side, aim limbs freely in any direction. Quicker, quicker, until you are seemingly worn out, but still fling, bend, swing body sideways, round, backwards.
iv. Now STOP.

The implicit expression of Man's thought, belief and emotion is available only through his wonderful gift of expression through speech. Vocal release is natural, being the birthright of Mankind, only needing to be reawakened. Because a released voice is real, it turns an actor into an artist, for everything is achieved to form the balanced whole. Wider variety of sound levels, modulation, ultra-flexibility of inflexion, etc., soon become part of the actor, so that each character portrayed is worn as a skin, not a cloak.

Exercise Preparations:
First find one's own voice level. Simply *sigh* a long deep audible sigh. It must be expressing "How nice," not "Oh, dear." Use the "AAAAH" sound (the first sound after birth and last sound before death). Be aware of the vocal level of the final "AAAAH" concluding the sigh. Repeat again, to remind oneself, and erase uncertainty. That final sound of the "AAAAH" is yours exclusively. *And you have found your Center.*

Speech is intended to be alive and free, because it is the one vital element by which the human voice transcends all other mediums of expression. Speech is closely linked with the human mind and emotions, both seeking to reveal themselves.

Light creates color. The light of the imagination puts color into speech.

Exercise 7.
Using prismatic colors, thus adding other missing values to a human being.
i. Vocalize softly the colors of the rainbow, in order: RED, ORANGE, YELLOW, GREEN, BLUE, INDIGO, VIOLET. Before using a color vocally, visualize it in the mind.
ii. Take the colors in turn again, audibly — SLOWLY — feeling, seeing privately all the depth of favorite color(s) and vocalizing accordingly. Equally so, vocalize fully the dislike of the color(s) and the full impact of your private reasons.

Exercise 7A.
Sigh — with content and ease.
Vocalize BLACK and its meaning to you.
Vocalize WHITE and its meaning to you.

Exercise 7B.
Now, choosing your favorite color, indulge in saying it warmly and with affection. Savor every happy connection you have with an object or garment, etc. of

that color. Vocalize fully your feelings as you remember anything of joy linked with it being *your* color. No one knows your reasons or thoughts, so don't hold back.

Whispering.
As a prepration for performance vocally, whispering should never be omitted from any limbering session. So complete in itself is this exercise that the audible result is instant and unbelievable.
A *real whisper* has everything that voice has, chiefly full power, with the sound cut off. To actors, this exercise is invaluable, but only if a real whisper is used, so check first that your version *is* a whisper, not a mouthing of words.

Exercise Preparation:
Check whisper so: Standing, head normally erect (not bowed) breathe with full force of breath to de-ice an imaginary window in front of your face. Breathe a fresh breath often. You need to for the fullness each attempt at melting your "frozen window" requires. Now that you realize extra-effort had to be given breath-wise, apply the same effort in the exercise.

Exercise 8.
i.   Choose any Nursery Rhyme. Quietly check it over in your mind.
ii.   Vocalize it, in your natural voice, to yourself, but do so slowly enough to listen to the over-all vocal sound.
iii. Keeping that window pane there, represented now by fully extended arms at shoulder level, hands cupped, WHISPER SLOWLY your chosen Nursery Rhyme as you aim the strength of each un-voiced word forward into cupped hands. Take the rhyme slowly, and renew the breath *very very often if necessary* and it always is.
iv.   Sigh. And again.
v.   Now vocalize, in your normal tone, slowly enough for you to register results, the same rhyme, to yourself.

LIMBERING OF HALL.
Because acoustically no two halls visited by a company of actors is the same, each actor *must* discover, during limber, to what degree and in which direction vocal adjustment is necessary for him/her personally. BUT factually no one ever hears his own voice as it sounds to others, the simple reason being that we are listening to ourselves vocally from the inside, and hearing our vocal sounds from the Bone Conduction. Everyone else hears us from the outside, after our sounds have left us and are affected by Air Conduction, thus riding on sound waves. There is only one natural and sure way of hearing oneself, and thus limbering the hall.

Exercise 9.
i.   Each actor select and go to a separate corner of the hall. Only ever use the four corners. Face towards center of hall.
ii.   Cup one hand behind each ear, thus holding the outer ear and lobe to "face front." Rest thumb of cupped hands on relevant cheek.
iii. Retaining this hand-ear position throughout, vocalize anything — e.g. months, rhymes, days-of-the-week, etc. — using the same strength, volume and timbre of your average voice during performance.
iv.   While carrying out (iii) do so while walking unhurriedly from your corner towards the acting area, vocalizing continually.

v. On arrival at performance area, continue to use your voice, hands still cup- ped round ears, as you walk around and across area. Then, while vocally in the middle of some chosen flow of words, continuing in exactly the same voice since (iii), drop the hands from around the ears and carry on speak- ing until your begun flow of words reaches conclusion.

vi. Hear, after dropping the hands, how unbelieveably different your voice sounds to you from the way you were convinced it sounded.

Note: While some actors have found hardly any vocal power, after renewal of cupped hands and being sure until then of their strength and clarity of voice, others have heard a booming hard distortion in themselves, instead of the sensitive emotional voice heard as theirs when speaking.

From this exercise, each actor knows in which direction a slight or large adjustment is required, in any particular hall during performance in order to enhance his artistry and especially the company performance as whole. This *wholeness* is part of individual and group sensitivity.

D. *Sensitivity.*

One of the greatest experiences of theatre, either as actor or audience, is that of genuine *ensemble work*. At its finest it is a kind of spiritual union — "Communion" as one actor suggested. Unfortunately, such ensemble work is believed to depend on single units of like-minded people working together over a long space of time, and there are many examples of the truth of this. But I do not believe that this type of work need at all depend on the *total* like- mindedness of people, or on the length of time of being together, and have had many happy experiences of quite disparate people working over a short but very concentrated period who have reached a similar goal. Of course, they have been like-minded to the extent of there being no antagonistic or destruc- tive person within the group, but not necessarily in any kind of detail beyond that. This is again a matter of attitude, and can be deeply tied-up with intui- tion — trust in one's own, and belief in other people's intuition.

Sensitivity work in limbering before performance is a renewal and con- solidation of the artistic bond between actors, just as sensitivity work in rehearsal is part of building the original bond. The creation of such a bond can be far more meaningful for working together than any personally based scheme of friendship. Indeed, I have known as many groups who enjoy each other as people who work poorly as a team, as groups who have no particular personal affections, but act together superbly because they have worked hard to achieve such a situation. It *is* work, serious work, which as likely as not may start with the superficial but, with perserverance, will grow more meaningful every day.

Possibly every director has his own approach to such work. Mine has been, and is, an infinite variety of exercises fundamentally based on *mirror exer- cises*, working with and without alternate leaders, in different characters, with different feelings and with and without music. And all the time the slow development towards being able to hold each other's eye with steady simplici- ty in pair work, as well as to feel a full sensitivity in larger groups.

This book is not intended as a manual of theatre exercises, so I shall detail only a few. But I will assert that, in the long run, the confidence in *personal in- tuition* and the development of a *group intuition* is more possible through these means than any others I have come across. The bond of sensitivity that is subsequently created is what brings a very particular quality to open stage theatre, and a particular dynamic to audience participation.

Sensitivity Exercises. (with the director in charge).
Sequence 1.
In pairs, face each other. Raise arms straight in front, parallel with ground, so
that middle fingers touch.

NOTE: In all pair "mirror work," physical relationship should be found in
this manner. Thus each person has his/her own space to work in, to
work outwards from or to retreat within. Fear of invasion of one's
own space is thus always avoided. One also has a maximum space
within which to move without losing contact with one's partner,
which would be the case if, for example, the pairs moved 2 or 3
times that distance away from each other.

Lower arms to sides. Try to hold each other's eye quite simply, without staring
each other out. When feeling "ready," both begin to move as reflections of
each other, using only arms to begin with. At the start, movement will be slow,
insecure, ultra-cautious, almost an inch at a time, dominated by intellectual
worry about not keeping exactly together. Expect this. It is almost inevitable
for any two people working together in this way for the first time. However, as
"the feeling of togetherness" begins to come, encourage again and again that
risks should be taken, that the movement can flow more easily and that more
of the body can be used. Do not continue for too long. All pairs freeze on a
signal (e.g. hand-clap or finger flick). Add imagination, e.g. A new statue appears in a park in the shape made by the two of you. The artist had something
definite in mind. What might it have been? Decide for yourself, then discuss
with your partner.

Sequence 2.
In pairs, but with different partner. Call selves A and B. Find relationship
with arms outstretched as described above. Lower arms. Hold each other's
eye, comfortably. No strain. Now A, using just arms to start with, from the
shoulder, move as you wish. B, you are A's reflection, keeping the same pattern of movement. Encourage flow and *trust*. As B is now following A's lead,
the harmony together is much easier. After 15 to 30 seconds, without stopping
and starting again, B takes over leading. A follows. Change again to A leading.
Then again to B. Perhaps once more each. Then for a few moments, nobody
leads. Again the freeze on signal, and adding imagination (e.g. a still photo of
two people in an exciting adventure story). Pairs discuss.

Sequence 3.
New pairs. A and B again. Find relationship as before. Lower arms. Hold eyes.
When *music fades in,* A move as you wish. B follows. Change leader every 20
to 30 seconds. Constantly encourage trust for flow to grow with not only arms
but whole body. Freeze when music stops. Again add imagination. Discuss
with partner. NOTE: Music should be very slow. e.g. *Claire de Lune* (Debussy).
Meditation (Massagnet).

Sequence 4.
New pairs. *NOT* A and B this time. Find relationship as before. Arms down.
Hold eyes. When music comes, start moving together, aiming as soon as possible at a full free flow and trust, using more and more of the body. On the call of
the word "CHANGE," each pair separates and, still holding their pattern of
movement, each person finds another partner and continues working with
him/her — until the word "CHANGE" repeats the pattern, and so on. Ac-

cording to numbers, perhaps continuing with several changes until the end of
the music. If this is too long for all to sustain, then freeze as music fades out.
Again add imagination, and discuss. Use very slow music. Often it helps to
keep using the same piece of music so that it becomes familiar to everyone in
growing detail.

Sequence 5.
Repeat (4) above (even perhaps starting from the end of music freeze position),
but this time with fast, syncopated music that will bring even more release.

From a matter of ten minutes or so per day over a period of several days,
this type of sensitivity exercise will bring about some or all of the following
results (certainly the beginning of all of them):
— As trust grows, the mind with its fear of failure and of going wrong will
   slowly be superseded by an intuitive trust that all will be well (and that
   the world will not fall apart if unity is lost for a few moments).
— By following others as the reflection, each person discovers new and
   different ways of moving.
— Eye to eye contact becomes secure, and will add so much to the security of relationships in the play.
— The experienced and the inexperienced, the clever and the not so clever,
   etc. begin to find the harmony of what they have in common, leading to
   sensitive team work based on mutual respect.
— Imagination and the body are linked and constantly toned up.
— In the quick changes of partner, with the music, intuition and trust are
   developed even farther, because of lack of time to seek intellectual safety.
All this can grow from just these few simple exercises over a few days with
a brief expenditure of time per day. Yet this need be only a starting point. The
potential developments from these simple beginnings are legion, limited only
by time and the inventiveness of the director, or whoever is in charge of the
limbering sessions. Here are some examples:
— In pairs as A and B. A leads, then B. Then A takes over, moving with
   great power and strength. Then B, with a gradual change to feebleness
   and weakness. Then A again, with gathering determination. Then B.
   again, slowly growing to triumph and stillness. Add imagination and
   discuss.
— In pairs. Any of the above sequences (without music) but now with
   each pair finding its *own completion and ending* rather than freezing on
   the signal.
— In pairs, again A and B. A slowly changes whole self, including face, into a Clown. B follows. Sound added for clown dance. B then slowly
   changes whole self into a witch or wizard. A follows. Both add own
   sounds and develop a dance. The above can lead to infinite variety according to chosen character.
So far, all of these sensitivity exercises have been suggested *only for pairs.*
Once trust and freedom have grown, however, all can be developed in a similar
manner through 3's, 5's and so on, with growing numbers until the whole
group is working together. Yes, even up to 24 and, once in my experience twice
that number. Fours can be difficult because of the natural tendency to become
2 pairs. This can be overcome by having the group of four work in a diamond
shape, not facing inwards, but all facing in one direction, towards A. On a

signal the whole shape turns so that all now face toward B, who's back is now turned. Then to C and to D. Slow motion skiing is useful for this, again to slow music.

Once the numbers are larger than pairs, there is no possibility of holding eye to eye contact. Each person needs to keep his/her eyes, at about chest level, on a point at the center of the triangle made by threes and the center of the circle made by all groups larger than 3. Each person can again in turn lead. The others should try not to look at the leader but at the center point, which helps them to be constantly aware of the whole group rather than just the person who is leading. These sensitivity exercises contain a superb admixture of creative "fun," joy of release and triumph of simple mastery. A word of warning. Nearly all groups find them a chore and are reluctant to start on them. Once started, however, the positive values already mentioned soon take over and create interest. Like the grooming of one's personal appearance, the constant and regular grooming of the actors' sensitivity ultimately pays dividends in terms of mutual trust, personal trust in intuition and a growing feeling for genuine ensemble work. But I must emphasise again and again that the exercises have their main value in growth of intuition and fearless trust. Sadly, the approach has often been allowed, even encouraged, to become one of harsh, almost mathematical exactness, bringing an attitude of intellectual challenge, personal fear of failure and group intolerance.

Now, if these four areas of limbering, concentration, physical, vocal and sensitivity, are valid as a basis for *pre-performance*, we must face the fact that they are not going to be achieved if one waits until the first performance to start on them. They must be started on in rehearsal, because they give to all a common denominator related to the necessities of performance. Intellectual blockages will arise if in rehearsal they appear to be done for their own sake. Furthermore, it must be remembered that one of the goals of the practice of limbering in rehearsal is for the cast to be able to achieve *in minutes* before performance what will have taken considerably longer during or before rehearsals. To find as much as half an hour for limbering before performance is an excellent and possible goal for permanent base theatre groups. For people on tour, particularly with a change of venue at mid-day, to find only ten minutes available is a greater reality. But even those few minutes can be of inestimable value if, through diligent and concerned practice, each person knows precisely what they are about and why. *The conscious effort of rehearsal-limbering leads to the subconscious HABIT of performance-limbering.*

Once a group of actors have reached a level of confidence regarding different aspects of the limbering process, then we can move to the third of the suggested approaches:

3. USING IMPROVISATION AS AN APPROACH TO AUDIENCE PARTICIPATION

To be able to improvise dialogue, fully in character, with the finish and polish of scripted and rehearsed dialogue, must be the goal of any actor involved in any form of audience participation for any age group in any playing area. Only an arrogant fool will suggest that this is easy or can be achieved without a great deal of practice at improvisation.

There are three main avenues open:

i   improvisation directly related to the play, but not necessarily to the participation;

ii   improvisation directly related to the participation;

iii improvisation related to the actors individually and as a group, but perhaps only loosely related (or even not at all related) to the play.

The above sequence in no way implies an order that should be followed. To be most useful, improvisation is often a "thing of the moment and the need," unplanned, spontaneous. Yet again the difference between intuition and intellect, between George Eliot's picture and diagram.

Improvisation can often be most useful for the plays for younger children because, although the story line and the language may be simple, the fantasy content often needs translating into a reality closer to our own in order that we can fully grasp the truth and sincerity of character and situation. A good example of this concerns "the collecting of ingredients for a mixture or a potion," as arises in several plays (e.g. **The Bell** see pp 90-92). To fully discover the urgency of the situation and to make it more real for himself, Tom might well be helped by an improvisation in which he is collecting clothing and blankets for people who have just lost all of their possessions in a flood or fire. In **On Trial** (pp 92-96), to catch the reality and the urgency of the need to make a long journey to collect herbs that might help stave off an epidemic is helped if the actors improvise the scene (not in the scripted play) when someone is suddenly taken ill with an unkown disease. And many aspects of the journey itself can be made more real through improvisation.

In many different ways, the journey is a real link between all three of the above approaches to improvisation, because it involves *movement*, and, as soon as the body is fully involved, imagination is stimulated and words flow more easily. There is no doubt that one of the most useful improvisational approaches is through the use of improvised movement and dance. I emphasize again, *improvised* movement and dance, both individually and in groups, and including the swift intuitive development of *dance dramas* symbolically related to the theme of the play under rehearsal.

Often this approach can be even more important than that of spoken improvisation. It is through improvised movement that we can reach out towards a full, total and uninhibited *release*: the release of the body, of feeling, of the voice, of the imagination, of words, of sensitivity and of characterization. Release of every part of the actor's instrument. On the whole, in my experience, few actors in training meet this factor of improvised movement, as nearly all of their movement work is based on one or another school of movement, and thus involved in mastery of a technique and a vocabulary of movement. This is often concerned with the teaching of "control." Control of what? The reply is usually "Control of the body, the emotions, etc., etc." *But without release there is nothing* to *control.* In fact, what is called "teaching control" becomes really a matter of imparting technical ways of showing outward results of control, despite there being no actual release leading to *genuine* control.

Improvised movement and dance dramas, with many different kinds of music, help the process of release, and that very release contains the seeds of its own intuitive means of control, linked to an unconscious awareness of the logic contained within the music. Many people fear this form of release, fear that it might become self-indulgent, fear that to release feelings through the use of music will lead to dependence on the music. So movement veers towards a mixture of technical steps and something akin to a physical education drill. Often the P.E. factor is so dominant, with its clutter of bar-bells, bicycles, medicine balls, etc., that a visitor could be forgiven for imagining that he is seeing advanced preparation for the next Olympic Games rather than a basic training for acting, which should be fundamentally concerned with relaxation rather than strain.

Of course, a period of rehearsal is not going to provide enough time for a director to develop a full use of improvised movement and dance drama, but something can be accomplished, and it will benefit each actor and the group as a group.

Examples:

a) For relaxation and overcoming inhibitions and self-consciousness. Being silly people in outlandish situations (e.g. novices decorating a house.) Cartoons with highly exagerated characters in fmrce situations (possibly even derived from well known cartoons, but with an original story). Send-ups or spoofs of TV commercials, aiming at very exact precision with the music, which, for all the above needs to contain a very strong and obvious beat.

b) For much the same purposes as (a) above, various kinds of *Nightmare*. These can be wholly original, and then linked with such themes as *Richard III's* nightmare before battle, Macbeth's conscience, the world of Hamlet's Father's Ghost, etc. Again the music can contain a strong beat, or else can be that with a powerfully evocative mood and atmosphere.

c) "Growth" of one kind or another, best achieved from starting in a curled-up position so that growth is of the whole self rather than turning on externals. A good theme for growth is Creation itself, the evolution of Man, starting from amoeba, growing to under sea creatures, which reach land and become monsters, sprout wings and become birds, land as birds and become apes, and then eventually Man. Within any part of this process the Journey can again be very important. All growth — the seed to the tree, the egg to the bird, the spark to fire, the single cloud to the tempest, — all contain valuable intuitive and symbolic processes that enrich the actor's work. Again use emotional music.

d) Symbolic essence and conflict. Associated, posibly, with (c) above. *A* grows from a seed; then *B* grows and overcomes *A*. *A* finds renewed strength and finally overcomes *B* - the essence of all conflict in drama. It is open to every kind of interpretation from the battle of mythical gods to the battle of the elements, to the battle between red and white blood cells in the body.

e) Sustaining atmosphere. With eerie music or sound, lasting 4 or 5 minutes, sustaining the atmosphere of a haunted house, the enemy in the jungle, escaping from a prison camp, defusing a bomb, mine etc. Sometimes with dialogue, sometimes in total silence.

f) Form. Rituals of many different kinds, complete with beginning, middle and end, within the confines of a single piece of music. Rituals can be supplicatory, celebrations, giving thanks, various rites and ceremonials — traditional, real or entirely made-up. They might well include processions, chanting and group or individual improvised dialogue.

I am not suggesting specific pieces of music for any of these (part of the interest is to find and be inspired by one's own ideas). But I have suggested a heading for each group of ideas in order to reiterate the purposefulness of intention. Dance dramas can become woefully pointless and indulgent. Definite purpose prevents this from happening and gives greater opportunity for using such work for specific benefits in rehearsal, even if actual links with the play are largely symbolic. Such movement work can often be linked to an aspect of enriching individual skill at spoken improvisation by following the dance drama with a repeat of the music while each person, sitting privately and alone, narrates in words the sequence of the dance drama. Words can be whispered or said very quietly, perhaps into an imaginary microphone, but they must come from the lips rather than stay in the mind. This approach has led some people into fascinating experiences of improvising poetry to music. But even for people who do not wish to go so far, speaking to music, particularly after the direct release of the movement experiences, brings a flow of richer language, helping to overcome what is often the bane of so much spoken improvisation — the paucity of words — often justified in the name of realism.

Pair exercises in spoken improvisation are very valuable, expecially when the pairs are taking diametrically opposed points of view on whatever topic they are talking about, and then, on the given signal, change points of view, with equal conviction, sincerity and clarity. The same kind of exercise, but using different accents or dialects, or else becoming very broad characters, even caricatures, are also useful, particularly for practice at sustaining a role.

The following would seem to be the minimal values that will arise from a few minutes spent daily on various form of improvisation (following a limbering-up, not instead of):

- tests concentration and seriousness, both basic to audience participation;
- helps speech flow;
- adds to sensitivity and intuitive trust;
- deepens characterization;
- brings greater reality and truth to situation;
- helps relationships, both between characters within the play, and between the actors as people and artists;
- aids spontaneity of scripted dialogue;
- makes needful moves away from script during audience participation more easy to master;
- helps talking to youngsters from within character;
- enables actors to cope with all contingencies with calm and assurance, without coming out of character or situation;
- helps to clarify in Secondary work (e.g. Shakespeare) obscurities of situation, character, relationships and language. (Try the Falstaff speech from *Henry IV, Part 1* several times in your own words, and then using the text);
- leads to fullest sensitivity in mastering space of every kind;
- helps to avoid all temptations to play down to children and young people.

Playing-down and Characterization.
Of the many statements I could quote from actors, perhaps the most telling of all arose from an actor's first performance with an audience of youngsters.
Actor: I discovered a phenomenal truth today that has never really occurred to me before. Children are people! They may be small people, but that's what they are through and through — people.
Setting aside the charming naivete of the statement, the truth of the basic observation is often the difference between genuine acting for children and that worst of all approaches mentioned over and over again in these pages — *playing down to the kiddies.*

Playing down often has the laudable intention of wanting to be friends and of trying to illustrate that intention through manner and tone of voice, rather like the way many of us conduct affairs with a strange and rather frightening dog! But even dogs will sometimes curl a lip and look back at you as though to say, "Don't you patronize me!" Children will not say it, but many feel it intensely, and it can have precisely the opposite effect from that of winning friendship.

There are two aspects of the problem: one is concerned with acting and charactization, the other with direct approaches to the youngsters through audience participation. In fact, more often than not, they are one and the same problem, but actors new to children's theatre that contains audience participation, tend to think of them as separate to start with.

When actors are arranging the details of an interview and audition, they often ask the question: "What sort of thing do you want me to do for the audition? I've never done children's theatre plays." Generally they are surprised to hear the reply: "Do anything that shows your work in its best possible light. Do what you would do at an audition for the West End or Broadway." Their concern is only partially appeased, as they then feel there must be a "special way of playing" whatever pieces they have chosen, in order that we can see whether they have the ability to adjust to an audience of youngsters. I believe that there are many actors who do not even consider the idea of working in children's theatre for this very reason, and many are quite amazed when they see a performance to discover the full-blooded, non-compromising, non-patronizing approach that is both necessary and right.

If a play has been especially written for an audience of children or young people, then, providing the author has studied and worked with children, the adjustment is made *in the writing*, not in the approach of the actors. Any compensation added by the actor is almost certain to lead to playing-down. The actor needs to be deeply and imaginatively involved in the part. This depth of absorption is what brings that main essence of *sincerity* to Children's Theatre work, and the lack of sincerity is immediately spotted by youngsters. thus swiftly destroying their own interest and enjoyment. Fundamentally, playing-down is a factor of insincerity. It is not making a bond of friendship, it is merely illustrating that one wants to. It is the same as holding the hand to the ear or over the eyes which has nothing to do with genuine listening or looking — it is merely illustrating the point. Stop demonstrating what you are doing — "simply do it" is the need.

Once actors realize the truth of this, they are amazed at the potential acting opportunities in Children's Theatre plays. I go so far as to believe that an imaginative actor can probably find more opportunities for exciting and imaginative approaches to characterization in Children's Theatre than in most other kinds of theatre, because so often the author depends on precisely that quality in the actors. For this reason, I am nearly always astonished at the final product of *a new play* because of the dimensions brought to it by the actors. An interesting parallel can be found, in a sense, in Shakespeare's small parts, where so much is left to the actors' imagination. For example, take Balthasar, servant to Portia. The part appears to be "straight," and no doubt it can be as much "Portia's page" as "Portia's servant." It can be approached as "the old family retainer" or as a "decadent Lord," or a "young lad," and so on. It would be much more difficult to "play around" with Bassanio, Antonio, Lorenzo or Gratiano in a similar manner, because these have been written in more detail and, to an extent, depend less on the broader imaginative approach of the actor. So it is with a great deal of acting in Children's Theatre. Of course, there are large numbers of parts that are very precisely written, ones that can-not be "played around with" in any indiscriminate manner, but equally there are many that lend themselves to great invention by the actor. The task for the actor is to avoid the *cliche*. What so often goes wrong in Children's Theatre characterization, as another aspect of playing-down, is the feeling that the *cliche* is in fact an important and positive approach. It is not, and never will be.

Let us consider what is often almost the bane of theatre for young children: the King, the Queen and the Princess and/or Prince. I must have made use of one or more of this quartet in about eight plays. Any one of them could be "played straight," — could, in fact, fall back on some *"cliched"* thought. I hope and believe that there are indications that each in fact is dif-ferent from all the others, but I know that I fully depend on that third dimen-sion brought by the actor to be fully free from *cliche*. The actor brings his own imaginative zest to bear on the character, and, with some actors who have re-mained with a company for some while, it is fascinating to see their own discovery of the infinite variety of character that is possible. The differences are not as obvious as those in plays for secondary age groups, particularly when those plays are adaptations or draw in scenes from other plays. Thus an actor could play King Louis in **The Three Musketeers**, King Charles in **Grinl-ing Gibbons and the Plague of London,** and King Claudius is an extract from *Hamlet* in **Speak the Speech I Pray You**, and find no difficulty in seeking dif-ferences in characterization, because of the greater breadth and subtlety of the parts as written. That breadth and subtlety is unlikely to be written into "Kings" in plays for 5 to 8 year olds, but bold differences can still exist in the playing of them. (It is of course necessary to be careful not to go to the op-posite extreme — *overplaying* can be as insincere as *cliche!)*

So, there is need for true and genuine characterization, held with great ab-sorption throughout the play, including audience participation. Problems of playing-down are solved when participation remains from within character.

If participation is genuinely integrated within a play, then its existence depends on the needs of the characters in the story and there is usually very little problem about either stimulating or controlling participation, providing it comes from the characters and not from a group of people who suddenly stop being the real people in the story and become a kind of parent-teacher substitute asking the youngsters to do this, that or the other. Out of character, the more the chances are that the actors might doubt the participa-tion will "work," so the more they tend to beg, whine, cajole, and so again are back at the playing-down for winning friendship. Also, when out of character it is very difficult to be in genuine contact with the *quality* of participation, because there is no reality to this basis for obtaining it. When it comes, it is likely to be insincere, and the actor, lacking the reality because of not being in-side character, is likely to look for and demand *quantity* instead of *quality*. Thus the audience is urged to make "more noise," to be "louder," to "bring the roof down" and all kinds of other insincere gimmicks that may well belong to the foolball field, but have no place in genuine participatory theatre. When sincerely *in* character, this overexcitement, this toppling over from genuine participation to mere hysteria, seldom happens, and the actor finds it easy to eradicate such demands as "louder," "noisier," etc.

Many of these points have been written about in detail in previous chapters. They are mentioned now as part of the actors' approach to characterization and the director's work with that process.

Interestingly enough, as mentioned before, nature provides a helpful guide regarding playing-down. If ever an actor finds himself bending at the waist, he can be almost certain that "playing-down" could creep in. To keep the spine stright can be a tremendous safeguard, and if one wants to go down to a lower level because the youngsters are sitting on the floor, then this can be fully achieved by bending the knees, but still keeping the spine straight. There are other signs and safeguards, like the words one speaks to youngsters — words like: "kiddies" or "little ones" and so on. Also value judgements have affects on youngsters, particularly when they have nothing to do with the play itself, but are usually a spurious attempt to encourage, phrases like: "that was very good" or "that's the best I've ever heard that done," or "I'm sure such nice little boys and girls can do better than that," etc. This is wholly irrelevant, quite unnecessary and invariably arising from playing down, which, in its turn, will have its basis in losing character, or with lack of absorption, or with insincerity.

Characterization and Children's Fears.

One genuine concern for many actors and directors is that of frightening children, and fear of this often accounts for *deliberate* playing-down and intended minimizing of character, even making a serious character funny so that nobody is frightened of him/her.

The "witch" is a character that often deeply concerns actors, as for example in the already mentioned play **The Mirrorman** (pp 107-109).

The witch has been used as a symbol of evil in plays for hundreds of years. But the stereotyping of the witch in performance was probably most influenced by Disney's film "Snow White." One problem for actors attempting this stereotype in theatre is that, perhaps because of the concentration on externals, they seem invariably to arrive at a parody of their own caricature. On the other hand, many who are determined to move away from the stereotype, often for the most laudable reason of not wanting to frighten children, tend to end up with a kind of comical buffoon at one end of the scale or a charming and gentle person with a nasty psychological kink at the other end. Both lack truth and sincerity and merely bewilder the youngsters. Yes, it is most important that we give a great deal of thought to the whole question of not frightening children, but if in order to achieve that end we have to destroy the integrity of the play because of such a character as "a witch," then far best not to do the play at all. In **The Mirrorman**, as probably in many plays with this "symbolically evil character," the actor finds the solution to the problem of characterization as soon she places her full concern on what the witch is trying to achieve rather than on physical appearance. In every scene, she has only one object — to the point of obsession: that of stealing the Mirrorman's "Book of Instructions." She goes to any length to achieve this, including using magical powers to put spells on people. I have never known an actress to have any difficulty with this part when she has approached it from this point of view. She soon discovers that anyone with such an obsession has eyes that are incredibly alive and alert. That people who make spells have a free, full controlled use of their arms and fingers. She also knows the energy-conserving value of stillness. Vocally they get on with the main job in hand, sharp and to the point, but ever ready to move from one approach to another if that will help fulfil their objective. So they find they do not need cackling voices and twisted, gnarled limbs, nor hooked noses and green complexions, puffs of smoke or weird sound tracks. (Many of these external factors were invented as part of the answer to the communication problem in very large proscenium theatres.)

193

However, having got rid of all these stereotyped externals that are in themselves frightening, we still discover that the factor of fear exists in the play, fear of the "power of evil," fear of the relentless determination of that power, fear that despite our own inner assurances that all will be well in the end, still perhaps it might not be! This is a quite sufficient exciting and dramatic or theatre experience for 5 to 8 year olds, providing all does come well in the end, and as long as the forces of good balance those of evil throughout the story. To ensure this, there is participation by the audience whereby, through the intense and determined sincerity of our "wishing," we ourselves are able on several occasions to thwart the witch in the nick of time.

Adults who are used to the conventional, stereotyped witch, find the character that is created from the above approach rather tame, and tend to say things like: "I didn't think your witch performance was very fierce, what was the matter? Were you afraid you might frighten our children? Well, you needn't worry about that, our children don't scare easily, especially with all the muck they see on television." Fortunately the integrity of the actor, backed by some study of youngsters, can soon overcome such spurious and facile observations. On the other hand, I mention this particular experience in order to suggest the one potential for creating a certain kind of fear that the very intimacy of open stage theatre has partly in common with television and film — the sudden *close-up* of the human face. It is the close-up that can go deep and reappear during sleep, causing dreams and nightmares. Actors in intimate open stage theatre need to keep this in mind. Yes, even the "goodies," because if they suddenly rush at children and crouch down with their faces very near, this will have the same effect as the close-up. For this reason, when directing a play such as **The Mirrorman,** I will go to enormous lengths to make sure that the witch or any other character never inflicts that close-up experience on any of the youngsters, and will make certain the actors concerned understand exactly why. Thus adjustments are made not only to performance but to direction as well. Maybe the psychologists are right when they say that the majority of us need the occasional experience of the horror movie. I personally do not see anything in the whole potential of theatre for youngsters that gives me the right to risk even one of them having an unpleasant nightmare simply because I am not prepared to compromise and adjust my creative imagination, an adjustment that can be made without interfering in any way with the integrity of the play or the characters.

So, if the witch runs to the *center* of the playing area, more or less equidistant from all of the youngsters, and then turns through 360 degrees while speaking, she is unlikely to create immediate fear or nightmares.

Almost as a general rule it is wise for all of the actors to avoid very swift movement towards any single group, or suddenly stopping too near a group. Without being pedantic, in such circumstances it is best to stop a full metre or yard away from the audience one is approaching and then turn to speak to the *larger segment* of the circle, with one's back to the smaller segment that one is closest to. (See diagrams: next page.) This is worth keeping in mind for any section of a play concerned with direct address to the audience. Talking to the nearest segment is always talking to the smallest number, and talking with one's back or side to the smallest segment means always talking to the largest number.

As I have tried to show, these adjustments may be necessary at certain moments within the play, but most of such moments occur with the 5 to 8 age group, not with the 9 to 11/12. Again we see that the division into two different

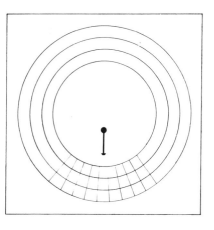

Diagram Number 21

Direct address. If the actor talks directly to the section of the audience closest to where he is standing, he tends to include only a small number and may seem to be excluding the majority.

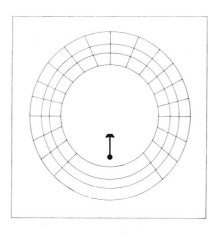

Diagram Number 22

If he turns his back to the small section closest to him, however, then he is able easily to talk to the majority and because of their physical nearness to him, the small section behind him does not feel excluded.

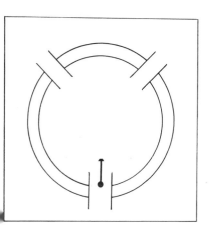

Diagram Number 23

If he has a great deal to say, then it is wisest for him to be in the opening of one of the aisles into the acting area, from where with just the slightest movement of his head, he can easily include everyone. Indeed, in a "long story" he could easily use each aisle in turn.

audiences helps us with our basic approach, and this is most clearly reflected in the approach the writer and the actors make to the opening of the play, in the open-stage, to a limited size audience.

Often in circumstances such as those considered above, we need carefully to reconsider whether we have the right age-group for the play, if the audiences are consistently very young, or whether we have the right play for the age-group. Sometimes one has in fact made a production for one age group and suddenly found a much younger one present. For example, **The Mirrorman** is normally for an age group of five upwards, but sometimes schools will bring in, as a treat,(!) a group of threes and fours, many of whom will be totally bemused by the whole proceedings, and some of whom may well be frightened. In such cases, however, it is much wiser for the cast to hold on to their performance with total integrity, but reduce volume, intensity and pace. And, as has been mentioned before, with such an audience it is essential to make sure that all the youngest children are grouped together in a block, with a teacher amongst them, rather than spread around the front row simply because they are the smallest. In a block, each youngster is close to people he knows, and thus finds security. If there is any warning that a group of such very young ones are attending, then it is helpful if all of the cast (in costume, but perhaps without final detail like hats etc.) help with the seating, so that the first "shock" of meeting is taken care of in circumstances different from the play itself.

There are other factors that should concern us regarding fear. *Sound* is an important one, in particular the sound of feet, of hard leather soles or heels on hollow rostrum blocks. The use of such instruments as a cymbal must also be sensitively considered. Indiscriminate "bangs," particularly if too close to some of the youngsters, can be quite frightening. The tone of the cymbal is important. Matters of economy often lead to groups buying cheap instruments, and a cheap cymbal will not only make a harsh and ugly sound, but can actually damage an eardrum.

Perhaps most important of all is the fact that an unnecessarily loud, screeching human voice can be a great instrument of fear. This is where vocal limbering is of such practical importance. Vocal sounds that are satisfactory in one hall might in another take on ugly and fearful characteristics, and one can often cause children in the audience to cover their ears to get away from the pain of the sound. But none of these factors, even with the smallest children, involves a need to play-down or to come out of character.

Children are people. When actors and everybody else associated with theatre respect the dignity of them as people, we achieve the most necessary, fundamental attitude for Children's Theatre. The remarkable but unmistakeable fact is that as soon as the actors' attitude is right in this form of theatre, he/she is at once *released* to a rich fullness of creative delight. The mind is freed from unnecessary problems of overcoming phantoms that exist only when the attitude is wrong. All good acting contains this underlying spark of delight, which is intuitively, unconsciously and spiritually shared by the audience. This ultimately brings about what I call, without sentimentality, "the warm hug of rememberance" just before going to sleep — recall of an important experience, of "that was the best thing of all the week." Such experiences are surely part of the very *raison d'etre* of the arts, particularly of theatre and of music. They are rare experiences for all of us, and perhaps most rare for children and young people, for whom considerably fewer experiences are available than for adults. I can never decry the many and variable intentions people have in supplying theatre, including the most overt of educational intentions, as long as these are not an ultimate replacement of this particular form of intuitive, emotional and spiritual experience. There are so many ways, including theatre, of pursuing intellectual enquiries, of gaining knowledge and information. There are so few ways in which human beings can gain the kind of insight that transcends the everyday, commonplace problem-solving, so that they soar to the very pinnacle of human capacity. The genuine experience of theatre, through the art of the actor, is one such way.

Before performance. *A typical school hall, photographed from the stage, which is used as a dressing room, with the curtains closed. Steps on either side of the stage give access to aisles at this end of the acting area; aisles at the far end provide further access, and there are aisles behind the audience on each side. The acting area is 20'x15' wide. There are three rows of seats on either side and six at the far end. Bleacher seating would solve the problem of visibility, already partly solved by having the front rows on benches that are a little lower than the chairs behind them. Members of the company are arranging rostrum blocks, which are canvassed and painted grey, and can be wiped with a wet cloth before each performance. Shortly, the company will use the area for limbering-up:* Concentration, *as there will be many distracting sounds within and outside the school;* Physical, *by examining doorways, aisles, etc., as well as body warm-up;* Vocal, *as the acoustics in this type of hall can be very difficult.* (Photo: Ian Stone)

The closeness of the audience in Open Stage Theatre demands the actors' total concentration, absorption and sincerity. Further, costumes, hats, etc., must be made with the greatest care as every false detail is clearly visible (e.g. safety pins). Most costumes need ironing before every performance. (Photo: Ian Stone:)

An extract from **The Three Musketeers.** *The same hall as in previous pictures with the play now in action. The audience size is about 150. Some audience members in the back rows have to stand, because of difficulty in seeing without bleacher seating. The sword fight has been carefully arranged in the center area for the safety of the audience. (The fight must be run through prior to each performance.) The rostrum blocks have rubber studs at all four corners so that they will not slip on the polished parquet floor. In the far right corner, an actress in the play is seated on a rostrum block that is several inches lower than the chairs, so that the audience behind can see easily. Note the teacher standing in the aisle behind the audience — why? To see better? To help with any "disciplinary" problems that might arise? Soon he will have to move, because the aisle is for the use of the actors. Note other visiting teachers (at back center) quite apart from the main audience. (Photo: Ian Stone)*

9

(Parts of) The "Magic" of Theatre

Many people, at all levels of theatre, find their greatest creative interest and enjoyment in the technical aspects — scenery, lighting, costume, properties, sound etc. — and Children's Theatre, no less than any other, caters for such interests. The paramount demands are on *taste, economy, imagination* and *selectivity*.

As we have met time and time again in these pages, the attitude of "anything goes for the kids" is not only erroneous but sounds the death-knell to any theatre associated with it. There are theatres with sufficient funds and resources to be almost carelessly elaborate in their design and making of sets, costumes and props. I count myself fortunate never to have been in such a position, because it has imposed on me the necessity to think economically and thus selectively, and to discover the vast difference between *detailed artistic selectivity* and merely doing things on the cheap. The challenge is positive. The solution lies, as in every aspect of Children's Theatre considered in this book, in considering what is appropriate for children and young people, and the necessities of the play as a whole, rather than on the strictly visual. It is a truism that "good plays will survive poor staging, but bad plays can never be rescued by elaborate staging."

What I call the *trap of sentimentality* needs to be considered within the context of the technical aspects of children's theatre. There was a time when the change of scenery from one act to another was almost awe inspiring. The climax of such wonders was often the "transformation scene," in which the scenery changed in front of our very eyes. Such changes naturally took place on the picture frame stage, and often the finest moment was the first moment, when the houselights went down and the curtains opened (or rose) to reveal the first setting. Even today, in adult theatre, the moment often brings spontaneous applause from the audience. The moment was, and is, part of the *Magic of Theatre*. As such, it will always have its adherents, with perhaps a very special place in musicals, both extravagant and modest, and including the most fascinating uses of revolve stages and media of one kind or another. This type of "magic" of the theatre is one part of its transcending capacity, often exciting, irresistible and breath-taking. At best, the experience is aesthetic, affecting, touching and memorable. Large, elaborate and expensive theatres will always have this capacity to "transport us" with a sense of wonder and delight. Let us cling to it, love it and nourish it, especially if it happens to be the kind of theatre we personally most enjoy. *But*, do not let us be over nostalgic about it, and so fall into the *trap of sentimentality*. Other factors have arisen during the last fifty years: film of many different kinds, with constant developments in the technical realm; television in the majority of homes; open stage theatre without a picture frame and therefore without the need for pictures *to* frame; and active physical and vocal participation in addition to participation of the heart, the mind and the spirit. All of these comparatively new developments must be seen as real and valid, bringing with them new forms of the *Magic of Theatre*. They cannot be ignored, and will be so only by those caught in the *trap of sentimentality*, who feel they may lose the old and the established if they acknowledge the new. Their anxiety is exacerbated by the fact that much of the new is still comparatively untried, still in "the scribble stage," still with a long way to go to begin to fulfil its potential. Nostalgia clouds the issues. Above all, where Children's Theatre is concerned, nostalgia tends to make us want to foist on to children and young people what we ourselves have best loved, and so overlook the possibilities that new doors and windows can open onto experiences, which are as exciting though fundamentally different.

In practical terms, perhaps the worst feature of the sentimentality trap arises when theatre groups with inadequate stage facilities and shoe-string budgets try to ape the staging of large scale productions from Broadway and West End successes, and merely highlight their inadequacies rather than exploiting their potential through imagination and selectivity. Where Children's Theatre with audience participation is concerned, the keynote is *ingenious simplicity*. Whether we are considering scenery, props, costume, lighting or sound, that keynote remains: ingenious simplicity. Harness this to the needs of the play itself and to what is appropriate for the age groups and numbers of youngsters and the environment within which the play is staged, and problems begin to be solved easily, though probably in a quite different manner from that of tradition and custom. Before considering each of these technical areas separately and in some detail, however, let us be quite clear that ingenious simplicity is not synonymous with shabby substitution. So often one sees inferior products thrown together haphazardly at the last minute on the grounds that "simplicity" is important for children and young people. Too often tatty, unironed costume relics, badly made props, scratchily recorded sound-effects or music, unrehearsed lighting cues, slovenly painted scenic-effects masquerade under the banner of simplicity. Ingenious simplicity must have the fullest integrity of aesthetic taste combined with selected artistry of imagination, and the product must be executed with maximum skill and care. Nothing less is worthy of an audience of children and/or young people. Today it is also fashionable to blame economic factors for all tatty technical shortcomings, whereas it is, in fact, often economic necessity that can lead to the most ingenious simplicity, without ever falling short of the most exacting standards. The borderlines of the problems involved can become fuzzy unless carefully thought through from the beginning of a production. Perhaps the following example in many ways exemplifies the point. A production group was confronted with a play in which the final scene takes place in "a magnificent ballroom." The plans for the setting involved a large number of flats, columns, arches, etc., all of which were beyond the resources of the group. The designer came up with a second idea, a brilliant example of "ingenious simplicity," the use of nothing except one large hanging crystal chandelier. With exciting lighting, the effect would be equal to, if not better than, the building of a full set, and the cost of renting the chandelier would be less than that of the set. All agreed. Then, at the last moment, somebody suggested that it would be most economical to use, instead of the crystal chandelier, a cardboard cutout, painted chandelier. Whatever was achieved economicallo, the result was a change from ingenious simplicity to shoddy substitution, and an ultimate letdown for the production group as well as the audience.

At the other end of the economic scale, the story is well told that "in the old days" theatres used to paint burlap (or hessian) to make it look like cloth of gold. Now they paint cloth of gold to make it look like burlap!

Without in any sense attempting to make this chapter one of "How to Make and Do," let us consider separately, from the philosophical and practical viewpoints, the place of scenery, lighting, costumes, properties and sound in Children's Theatre with audience participation.

Scenery

I was sitting behind some teen-age lads at an in-the-round performance of **Oliver Twist.** There was no scenery as such, just a few rostrum blocks at either end of the acting area. As Act One ended, one lad turned and said to his friend: "What do you think of this business of no scenery, then?" His friend replied: "I like it, 'cos what you sees in yer 'ead is better than what they can make for you to look at."

The statement succinctly sums up another factor of audience participation, that of a full, rich use of the imagination.

In **On Trial,** for the 10 to 12 age group, two simple rostrum blocks are set about 12' apart in an oval arena, about 14' wide by 20' long. The audience sit on either side of the oval, with an aisle at each end for the actors' to use as entrances and exits. *(See diagram 13 on page 75).* Mention has already been made of the exciting scene in this play where 20 members of an expedition cross a deep ravine. They do so by means of a primitive rope bridge, where they hang on to a top rope with their hands, and use another rope for their feet. The ravine is several hundred feet deep. In fact, there are no ropes, no ravine — nothing! Nothing except two rostrum blocks that are 15" high, 18" wide and 3'6" long, separated by about 12' of bare floor space. Nothing else, except the *imagination* of the participants and of the audience. Probably the most consistently exciting paintings I have seen resulting from a Children's Theatre experience have been based on this one incident from **On Trial.** The paintings have come from the audience as well as the participants. A selection of the pictures would make an almost filmic strip-cartoon, with a wide variety of camera angles: close-ups of hands gripping the rope; anxious faces; long shots looking down into the yawning ravine, or looking up from the bottom of the ravine to the match-stick figures crossing the rope bridge, silhouetted against the sky. And there was nothing there in the play itself except two rostrum blocks, and *imagination.*

In **The Three Musketeers,** originally written for and produced on a proscenium picture frame stage, there is a permanent set made of rostrum blocks and builder's scaffolding with some of it reaching right out to connect with one of the audience areas and then with ropes down to stage level. The play contains many different scenes in different locations: an attic room in an old house, the Queen's throne room, the quay-side of a harbor and so on. But the scenery never changes. The mind's eye, the imagination, makes whatever detailed change may be necessary at a given moment in time.

In a proscenium stage production of *Macbeth*, the first scene of the witches invariably takes place in a green spotlight with the witches gathered around a smoking or steaming cauldron. In an open stage production of the same scene, in a bare school gymnasium, in broad daylight, the same scene has to be approached differently — with *ingenious simplicity*. A few permanently set rostrum blocks; powerful music; the witches themselves involved in an exciting and purposeful dance drama in which every move has purpose — finding the right "place" for setting up their evil, clearing the place of all positive or good spirits, summoning-up evil spirits and atmospheres and then making their mixture and spell. Finally they summon Macbeth and Banquo to their chosen and prepared place. No scenery, no cauldron, no smoke or steam, no lighting — just characterization, movement, music and the imagination of the audience.

In **Pinocchio**, on the proscenium picture frame stage, a permanent set: a flight of steps on either side of an eight-foot high bridge. Flats flank each set of steps. Half way up each is an open door. On the one side the door has a sign over it simply saying "Mr. Gepetto," and on the other side a sign over the door saying "Mr. Fire-Eater's Puppets." No more. The set is permanent. The curtains are open as the audience arrives. Each of us in the audience has the opportunity to become familiar with the setting. When the action of the play starts we already know that setting, which we would not if the curtains had been closed and then suddenly opened. Because we know it, we are not distracted. We concentrate on the action, rather than being distracted by the scenery. And because it never changes, we are able to follow quite simply all the different locations by use of imagination. *(See Photographs on pp 52 and 53)*.

In the same play, the simplest use of only rostrum blocks because the play is now produced in the open stage, the half-arena. But we still know when and where we are, even with many changes of location, for the actors, as part of the play, have told us. *(See photo on p 54)*. What we see in the mind's eye is different for each one of us, because what we see comes from our own imagination, and imagination is highly individual. We see only what we need to see at a particular moment in time. We are not disturbed by somebody else's detail. We are not distracted by the materialism of scenic effects. We live with the characters and their adventure in life.

In a mixed avenue-arena plus full use of picture frame stage production of **Oliver Twist**, our imagination is fired in many different ways. On the stage itself there are two very detailed locations. One half is Fagin's den, the other is Bill Syke's house. The scenery is detailed, with its filth and vermin, its decadence and criminality. The designer has filled in the detail for us. But suddenly we are in the street. There are only rostrum blocks and space, and many different locations. Now it is a bookshop, now part of a courtroom, and now the countryside just outside London. No detail is supplied except by our imagination, which quietly and unobtrusively fills in any details we need for each moment of the action. Our full concentration meanwhile is given to those involved in that action. Suddenly, we are concerned with the farthest end of the avenue arena — the end opposite the stage — and there is Rose Maylie's home. There are a few rostrum blocks and a delicate filigree of trellis pieces. They give us the *feeling* of delicacy and refinement, a complete contrast to Fagin's den and Bill Syke's room; yet there is no detail of setting, just sufficient to set light to the imagination.

With all of the above examples, and many others that could be quoted, the concept of scenery has arisen from the following considerations:

   i.   what is valid for the particular form of staging;

  ii.   what seems most appropriate for the audience of children and/or young people;

 iii.   what is most stimulating, rather than stifling, to the imagination, so that there is enrichment and enhancement to the action of the play, rather than distraction from it.

Ingenious simplicity has been the keynote. The construction, painting, etc., have been carried out with infinite care. There is nothing shoddy or make-do. The actual amount of scenery used is obviously less for productions in the open stage, particularly when the audience surrounds the action, than it is on the proscenium, picture frame stage. Even with the latter, there is economy rather than profusion, representation and symbolism rather than total realism, the suggestion rather than the actuality of detail. Fundamentally, *the play's the thing*. Priority is given to the action and the dialogue. Embellishment is second to the enrichment of imaginative stimulus.

The function and place of scenery, however, cannot fully be considered without an equal concern for lighting, or its total absence when performances are given in daylight, or for costume and sound. So, although this chapter is divided into specific sections, reference must constantly be made from one section to another, because the function of one aspect often complements another very precisely. Let us consider an example of this complementary factor from a production of **Pinocchio** that uses the picture frame stage, *plus* the auditorium (the whole theatre used as a space in which anything can happen), *plus* lighting, *plus* sound, and with the stage having a cyclorama or sky-cloth backing to a setting comprised mainly of different levels of rostrum blocks. The scene is one already mentioned. Bird (the Fairy in disguise) is helping Pinocchio to fly.

The action starts at the center front of the stage. Bird says to Pinocchio:
       "Stay very close to me, Pinocchio, and then you'll be able to fly."
Pinocchio: "Fly?"
Bird: "Yes. Like me."
Pinocchio: "But how? How can I?"
Bird: "Magic. Magic that works as long as you keep very close to me. Now — try it. Go on, try."

The stage direction continues: "On the stage area, Pinocchio, keeping very close to the Bird, flaps his arms and gradually finds that he can fly." Let us add to the potential of the staging described above, lighting, a cyclorama, the use of music, and different levels created through the use of rostrum blocks. Now the scene, without losing its simplicity and primary dependence on the two actors, might develop as follows: As Bird says the word "Magic," so music begins very, very slowly to fade in, gradually growing as the scene progresses (e.g. part of Ravel's *Daphnes and Chloe).* At the same time, the lighting begins to change, cross-fading with the music. All light slowly drains away, except for a deep blue coverage of the cyclorama or sky-cloth, and a single spotlight on Bird and Pinocchio. Very gradually, Pinocchio masters flying, with both he and Bird improvising dialogue in almost an awed whisper,

Bird constantly encouraging, Pinocchio with growing amazement that the magic is working. Their synchronized movement grows with the music, at the climax of which they "take off" and start to fly. As they do so, the spotlight on them fades out so that they are now just silhouetted against the sky. They swoop upstage and on to the different levels of rostra. Now and again they stop, hovering, searching for Mr. Gepetto. Each time they are still, a spotlight comes up to about half-full, the light catching their fingers and arms and faces, perhaps touching the satin of Bird's wings. And away they swoop again, once more silhouetted against the sky. Bird, with them both caught again in a spotlight, and the music momentarily fading down for the dialogue, says: "We must go and ask all the other birds and the fishes whether they have seen your Pop, Pinocchio. Keep close to me." As the music comes up, they set off on their journey again. Now they swoop down off the stage and into the audience area. We, the audience, have been forewarned by Bird's line as to how we can help. Bird calls to Pinocchio: "You ask the birds and fishes over there, and I'll go in this direction." They separate. Music has faded down. Houselights have come up to about half, sufficient for us to see Bird and Pinocchio and for them to see us. Without losing any of the atmosphere, they talk to groups of us as birds and fishes, and ask our advice. Maybe we can help. Maybe we are unable to. Soon Bird calls Pinocchio, and together they fly back to the stage area, with the music coming up and the houselights fading out. Back into a single spotlight, and Bird tells Pinocchio they must search and search and search. Away they fly, silhouetted against the sky, with the music bringing the scene to a final crescendo and ending as the light fades.

In this scene, a simple setting with lighting, music, costume, all blend into a moment of symphonic production harmonized with the acting and the movement. Each technical factor is complementary to each of the others. But, ultimately, all are fundamentally an enrichment to the acting. The proof of this lies in the fact that exactly the same scene can be done *in daylight*, without the use of the proscenium stage and the sky-cloth, and without any lighting. It can be done simply with the aid of the music and that space in which anything can happen, using rostrum blocks.

Whether on a conventional stage or on the open-stage, whether with lighting or in broad daylight, the *rostrum block* has been constantly referred to, possibly as the *basic* necessity in Children's Theatre. So, before further consideration of lighting or sound, costume or props, let us consider these blocks in more detail.

Rostrum Blocks

The principle behind the use of rostrum blocks is more quickly *accepted by audiences,* particularly in the open stage, than by directors and actors who themselves are more accustomed to the use of detailed scenery. A simple form of logic underlies one major use of rostra, and is unquestionably acceptable to all audiences, particularly those of children and young people. The logic is again linked to imagination. Let us consider an example of this. From time to time, all human beings, whoever they are, *sit down*. If we are in the throne room of a palace, the king and queen will sit on *a throne* or *thrones*.

(For those who feel that the king and queen image is too closely associated either with "Fairy stories" or "classical theatre," let us include within the symbolic potential: "the big fella and his associate;" "the boss and his assistant;" "the hero and heroine;" or "the space leader and his controller." In each case the symbol of power remains and whoever the people are, they will have their equivalent of a throne or thrones.)

Now, what if the king and queen are on a journey, and pause for rest in a forest? Perhaps they sit on *tree stumps.* What if they are captured and put into a dungeon? Perhaps they sit on a *hard bench* or *stools.* And if they are rescued and we see them on board ship returning home? Then perhaps they sit on *packing cases* or *benches.* On a later stage of their journey, they stop at an Inn for refreshment — what then? Perhaps they are sitting on *stools* or *chairs.* As the journey resumes, their coach is attacked, and they hide under the arch of a bridge — then, perhaps, they sit on *rocks* or *on the river bank.* They move from one hiding place to another: in a cave they sit on *boulders;* in a farm worker's cottage they sit on a *rustic bench;* in the barn of another farm, on a *bale of hay;* then on *the steps* of a church, a *pew* within the church, on *chairs* within the pastor's simple lodging...and so on, until perhaps their adventure returns full-circle and they are restored to their palace where they again sit on the throne(s). In *every* case, they *sit down.* The play in which any and/or all of the foregoing can happen is a poorly written play if the author has not made clear to us *by words* what each location is. And if we know what the location is, then we do not need an *illustration* of that location. We see it in the mind's eye, the imagination. Certainly we do not need exact detail of all the furnishings, such as the places on which people sit. If they need to sit and do so, then our concern is with *their need,* not the detail of where they sit. A simple rostrum block, or blocks — *the same block(s)* — can serve all of the above places for sitting, and be completely acceptable by the audience.

This is the logic that supports the *emotional* factors of a play, rather than tracing its intellectual pattern. The logic underlies the picture, not the diagram. Once the logic is accepted at so simple a level as that of the need for people to "sit down," it is swiftly assimilated at all other levels of human action, so that the necessity for detailed scenery becomes less and less, and the rostrum block becomes more and more significant in its *functional simplicity.* "What yer sees in yer head is better than what they can make for you to look at."

This book makes no pretensions to being a treatise on any part of the psychology of acting, but perhaps it is pertinent to consider the simple function of the rostrum block in relation to *the actor* as well as the audience. From the actors' point of view it is fascinating to comtemplate the question: "Which is easier to achieve, an imaginative acceptance of painted flats, back-drops, etc. as some kind of meaningful reality, or the full imaginative creation of location, of furniture, etc. through the use of the totally simple?" Experience suggests that, just as a simple block can be a stimulus to the imagination of the audience, so too can it be to the imagination of the actor. More than that, it can also supply a necessary and immediate *fulfillment* to that stimulus in a simple, straightforward manner — one that is not complicated by the additional imaginative act necessary to make real for himself the detailed painted scene. Without scenery, the actor becomes *confidently dependant* on his own intuitive-imaginative capacity. "We are the players. We have come to play a play." "We are the audience. We have come to see the players play their play." No pretences at false realism. We know that the *actor* playing Laertes has not really killed the *actor* playing Hamlet. Laertes kills Hamlet, that is what is important. We know that our hall or gymnasium or even theatre is not really the palace at Elsinore. But we *feel* that it is, because of the people, the characters, and their actions. *They* will convince us far more than *painted displays.* Our act of participation of the imagination embraces their action far more than it can embrace the painted external of the place of that action.

Making Rostrum Blocks

Basically, a rostrum block is quite simply a box, made of timber, canvas and painted. The size and shape of the box should be determined by its intended use, and can include: the square, the rectangle, the triangle, and various segments that together make up even a full circle. If there is adequate storage space, then a large number of different blocks can gradually be accumulated, and then selected according to the needs of a particular production. If a production is moved from one venue to another on some kind of tour, then limitations will probably be imposed by available space in transport. In such cases, or wherever there is a problem of storage space, then it is useful to make *nesting blocks*, rather in the manner of children's building bricks, so that the space taken up by several blocks is only that of the largest of the nest.

There are many ways of making the blocks, and below is a simple example of one approach:

Many experiments can be made regarding the color of these blocks. The more concerned one is with the "scenic aspect," the more one tends to want to use many different colors, perhaps even linking these with some kind of symbolism. In the first open stage production of **Pinocchio** six different blocks at different levels were used, each painted a different color. The intention was to use, symbolically, the appropriate color for particular scenes. Thus, Mr. Gepetto's "home" las based on a brown rostrum, Mr. Fire-Eater's, a red; the field of miracles was green, the night scene, where Pinocchio and Gepetto go to sleep, was deep blue, and so on. However, the more the intention was studied in practice, the less and less relevant were these factors found to be for the youngsters in the audience. It was difficult to be consistent in the intention, and many of the far more exciting uses of *color in costumes* were nullified by contrast with the blocks. Eventually, all the blocks were painted the same color, a simple, warm, medium gray, and this proved most successful. The gray is serviceable in terms of not getting dirty with footmarks, and is helpful to all colors in costumes. It in no way detracts or distracts from either production or acting. I have personally continued with the use of gray ever since.

The construction of rostrum blocks must be painstaking and accurate, especially for use in the open stage, where faulty workmanship is clearly visible to an audience that is close to the action. Canvassing must be done carefully so that no bubbles form under the canvas. Otherwise toes or heels are likely to catch in these and tear them open. It is also wise to use some kind of rubber stud at each corner and, on large blocks, every few feet. This will help keep the block even, and prevent it from sliding on the floor, or from scratching highly polished gymnasium or hall floors.

The dimensions of each block is of course always related to function. Several small blocks are useful for sitting or standing on. In the open stage, where *young audiences* are sitting on the floor, experiments lead to the conclusion that *13" is the best height for sitting*. When lower than that, the knees of the actor tend to stick up in a rather ungainly and uncomfortable manner. If higher than 13", then, while the sitting positions can be fine, the height becomes too much for standing on, both in terms of towering over the youngsters and also in terms of stepping on and off with ease. With *older audiences,* sitting on chairs in relation to the open stage, 13" is, however, too low. Because the normal height of a chair is 16", when the actor sits on a 13" rostrum, he tends to disappear below the head-level of the majority of the audience. This, of course, has a positive value when there is a long scene in which some of the characters have little to do or say — the lower level solves masking

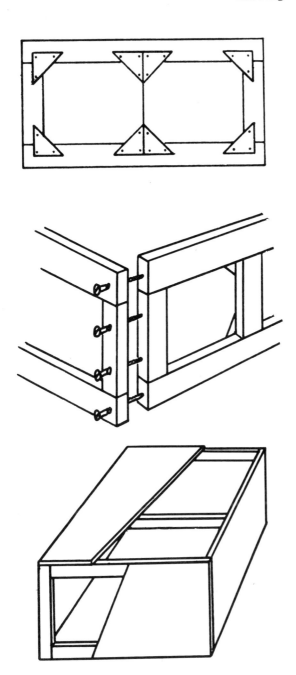

problems and yet keeps the characters within the main orbit of the action. A positive solution to any disadvantage of the 13" high block is to place it on top of another of the same height, but larger in length and width. Thus a 13" high x 15" wide and 18" long rostrum can be placed on top of another that is also 13" high, but is, say 4' wide x 5' long. This combination provides the 13" level of the larger block for sitting or standing, and the smaller block perhaps only for sitting, but now 26" above floor level. According to need, the smaller block can be placed in many different positions on top of the larger: in the center, or in the center of one side, or in one of the corners. The combination makes for many interesting groupings of characters, sitting or standing.

With the nesting blocks mentioned above, there are many different possible combinations, though experiment suggests that a variation in height, width and length of 2" per block makes for both comfortable and compact nesting. Thus if the largest block is 15" high by 4' wide by 5' long, then, in a nest of three, the next would be 13" x 3' 10" x 4' 10", and the smallest would be 11" x 3' 8" x 4' 8". Of course a fourth could be added as the smallest (i.e. 9" x 3' 6" x 4' 6") or as the largest (i.e. 17" x 4' 2" x 5' 2"). Again, the needs of any specific play, together with problems of storage and perhaps of transport, govern final decisions. Blocks can be arranged in many different shapes, from the intentionally formal and symbolic *(See photo on p 166)* to the intentionally asymetrical *(See photo on p 167)*.

One of the most useful size and shape of block is that of the *rectangle,* 15" high by 18" wide by 3' 6" long. Two of these blocks were all that was used for the whole of the play **On Trial**, including the journey across the ravine on a primitive rope bridge. But one of these blocks is also useful as a higher level when placed on another of, say, 13" high by 3' 6" wide by 4' 6" long. This combination was used for the throne for Gertrude and Claudius in the *Hamlet* Crowd scene.

An entirely *circular* rostra, made in exactly *four quarter sections,* can also be extremel useful. Each section can be used separately, or two sections can be used for a half circle or for a kind of S-shape. Cut a circle out of a piece of cardboard and then cut the circle into four equal quarters. You will quickly discover a whole range of potentially exciting different groupings. Of course, the circle can be cut into 5 or even more different segments, increasing the range of groupings, However, as soon as the circle is cut into more than 6 segments, then the sharp end of each segment begins to be less and less useful, as it becomes too narrow either for standing or sitting.

Blocks of whatever size can also be useful when turned *upside down,* so that people can get into them as boats, spacecraft, time machine's, whatever is necessary. They can also be effectively used on their side for some scenes as, for example, in the graveyard scene in *Hamlet,* when four blocks were placed on their sides in a rectangular shape. Within these, the two grave diggers played the scene on their knees, so that only their heads could be seen above the edges of the rostrum blocks.

If one is turning blocks over completely, or using them on one side, care must be taken to give as complete a finish to the inside of the block as to the outside. This can be achieved very simply with the use of thin plywood or several layers of canvas and then painted the same color as the rest of the outside of the block.

The actual positioning of the blocks within the acting area needs very careful consideration, both in relation to the text of the play and of the characters to the audience. For example, it is often very useful to place a block in an aisle, to facilitate strong entrances and exits. But if the block is too far down the off-stage part of the aisle, then it is not sufficiently *within the acting area* to be felt as fully part of it. A useful general rule is to make sure that a little more than half of the block is over the line that would complete the circle, square or rectangle of the acting area. The moment an actor passes the half way point on that block, he is in the acting area, but if, for example, there are circumstances in the play that make the character apprehensive of others in the acting area — reluctant to join them — then the whole feeling is enhanced by the character staying on the off-stage end of the block until such time as he overcomes his reluctance and decides to enter.

When young children attend performances in-the-round, it is wise to keep about 15" between them and any blocks that may be used on the outer periphery of the acting area. 15" enables an actor to move between the blocks and the audience, or to sit on the block without overpowering those closest, thus allowing the child's view of the rest of the acting area.

Such points may seem fastidious, but they make an ultimate difference in the finesse of the acting, the production and the fullest sharing with the audience.

Perhaps some directors interested in the use of rostrum blocks in open stage theatre would find it useful, as I have always done, to acquire a number of different shaped pieces of wood, all on the same scale. I use 1" thick planed timber, taking my scale as 1" to the foot, and cut up all sorts of shapes and sizes which I keep together in a box, just as children do with building bricks. With these, I constantly try out different groupings and combinations, not necessarily with any particular play in mind, but simply in order to get the feeling of the immense variety possible. When a production of a play is due, I invariably find that something in the back of my mind is thrusting forward for consideration.

Lighting

In over my thirty years of theatre for children and young people, if the work had *depended* on the use of lighting I doubt that more than about 5% of the performances would have been given. This is because a high proportion of those performances were given in schools during school hours, in halls without any kind of blackout facilities.

I make no complaint about this. In terms of *appropriateness* of the work to young children particularly — also to the environment — there is neither expectation nor wish for lighting from actors or audience. There is neither worry nor disappointment. The acceptance of the situation is total. Indeed, with the youngest audiences, lighting in the open stage is quite unnecessary and when used sometimes even bewildering.

I quote again from the many varied experiences of **Pinocchio**, which, apart from touring schools, has been performed both in open stage and proscenium theatres. I have already described how, at the end of Act I, Pinocchio and Gepetto go to sleep in full view of the audience, and remain asleep during the interval. In a performance using lighting, as the act was drawing to a close, light very slowly drained away creating an exciting feeling of sunset and night on the sky-cloth. Gepetto finally turns to the audience and says: "Why don't you go to sleep, too. I'll wake you up in the morning. And if I don't, the rooster will. He crows incredibly loudly round these parts. Off to sleep you go, then. Goodnight." He settles down next to Pinocchio to sleep. Music swells, and slowly the lights fade to blackout. A pause after the music ends, and then the

Audience Participation

house lights are put on. Immediately, the majority of the young audience are awake, making rooster-crows and greeting the still sleeping Gepetto and Pinocchio with calls of: "Good morning!" "Wake up," etc. etc. There was no concern for, interest in, or any real awareness of the end of the Act I *lighting effects.* Either there was light or there was no light. In this sense, the houselights were as appropriate to the action and the scene as were the complex fading of spotlights. (Another example of how, in genuine Children's Theatre, we must study what is really appropriate for the youngsters and be prepared to lose some of our own specially loved moments of theatre.) This factor of the inappropriateness of lighting seems to be true for youngsters up to about the age of 9 or 10 years, when, as we have considered before, their own awareness of conscious creation of theatre begins to grow more strongly. From that age onwards, I have no doubt at all that lighting can be a tremendous enrichment to the experience of theatre. I have long been sorry about the lack of black-out in school halls and gymnasia because of the partial limitation of that richness, and because of the consequent lack of possibility in making sufficient experiments with mixing other media. Nevertheless, I accept the limitation as partial. Even in broad daylight, much richness is still possible, as has been described in previous chapters.

Granted the enrichment, what kind of lighting is most appropriate?

Lighting, like so many other factors in theatre, may ultimately be a question of the personal preference and interest of the director — not to mention the practicality of available equipment. There is no simple yardstick for theatre for young audiences, any more than there is for any other kind of theatre. My personal preference and interest is in lighting being used first and foremost for *emotional enrichment* rather than mere illumination. But if one is in a large theatre space, especially if scenery is involved, then one cannot altogether ignore the problems of illumination. When little or no scenery is involved, or if one is working in a small and intimate theatre space, proscenium or open stage, the illumination factor is correspondingly minimized. The open stage, with no scenery at all, limits the problem to one in particular: that of using light on the actors and their actions as there is nothing else *to* light. When we are confronted with this situation, then the important factors become those of *mood* and *atmosphere* rather than place and location. Darkness becomes as important as light, shadow as definitive as substance. Balance and contrast are poetic in their potential, and especially so when light is used in conjunction with sounds, words, footfalls and music — as for example in the earlier described flight of Pinocchio and Bird. In these terms, light becomes a very real part of the "Magic" of theatre, and can do so without intrusion, without theatricality for its own sake.

The most useful single piece of equipment for an approach to lighting that is more concerned with feeling than with illumination is the focus spotlight. This is true both for proscenium and open stage theatres. The floodlight and the ground-row have, of course, great use on the picture frame stage, particularly for illuminating such factors as a sky-cloth, but are very seldom useful in the open stage. There are, naturally, exceptions. For instance in a play in avenue arena where, in a scene in hell, the main lighting came from discreetly placed floodlights under the chairs of the front row of the audience and the silhouettes and shadows against the stark red light, together with grotesquely moving masked figures in a frenzied dance drama to powerful music, made an electrifying impact on the audience. This was partly due to the fact that the floods lit up not only the acting area but the audience as well —

212

the main reason for normally *not* using such equipment in the open stage.

I am constantly surprised at how much effective lighting can be achieved in the open stage with very few pieces of lighting equipment. Indeed, for an area of 20' x 15', even 20' x 20', only a dozen 200-250 watt spots can be wholly adequate, particularly if each spotlight can be on its own dimmer, rather than paired. The wattage, of course, depends on the length of throw of each lamp, which in turn depends on the height of the ceiling and/or on other means of hanging the lamps. Incidentally, I personally find the hard edged spotlight (leko) more useful than the fresnel with its softer, more diffused light, which tends to be more difficult to keep off the audience. The starkenss of the hard edges of the focus spot can always be diffused, if necessary, with a frost. For both the hard edged and the fresnel some form of iris is always useful, particularly for keeping light off the audience. "Barn doors" also serve a useful similar purpose. The actual rigging of spotlights in the open stage, particularly in spaces not built as theatres (e.g. gymnasia), often brings forth many problems that need careful early planning to overcome. Spotlights are most serviceable when the angle at which they throw light on to the acting area is approximately 45°. Less than this angle, the spots tend to light mostly the tops of the heads of the actors; more than 45° and it is most difficult to avoid lighting at least the front rows of the audience. But to achieve the angle of 45° often means that many of the spots need to be hung *over* either the audience or the actual acting area, whereas the normal tendency, often based on simple practicalities like existing brackets for hanging, is to position the spots on the walls. In a small hall, this might well prove to be ideal. In a vast gymnasium, it invariably means that the angle of throw is far too wide, and the length of throw so great that even a 500-watt spot is inadequate. The ideal solution is to have some kind of frame over the acting area, either suspended by chains from the ceiling, or else free standing on its own uprights. Where this is either physically impossible or too expensive to achieve, then much ingenuity is called for, with many possible different solutions. For example, I recall several school halls where it was forbidden to use nails, screws, screw-eyes or bolts on any surface — floor, ceiling or walls. Problems of lighting were solved partly by not only the use of the highest available extension stands (18') but also by lashing tables on top of each other, and then lashing a 20' length of 2" x 2" to one corner of the tables, and attaching the spotlight to a metal bracket at the top of the post.

It is not possible to cover these technical problems in great detail in this short section of a single chapter. Perhaps it is sufficient to say that I have never known such problems not to be overcome, *providing* they have been thought through well in advance, rather than left to a last moment panic when makeshift and inadequate solutions become inevitable.

Every consideration must be given to *safety* as part of these plans and preparations. Safety laws and regulations tend to vary considerably from one area to another, but must be uniformly stringent in the minds of all production groups. Every spotlight must have its own safety-chain. All cable and flex must be above audience reach, or, if snaking across the floor, must be firmly anchored and perhaps covered with lino, carpeting, or heavy canvas. The whole production team, not just the stage management or technical crew, must be familiar with the location of fire extinguishers and exits, both emergency and regular. (For touring groups, this familiarity can even be made part of limbering!) One golden rule on safety might well be: "If in doubt, contact your local fire officer in good time. Better to know all the problems before hand than to be confronted with impossible adjustments at the last moment.

It would be invidious to suggest that lighting the open stage has advantages and enrichments over and above lighting the proscenium stage. Nevertheless, I would claim the singular advantage — one that possibly belongs less to the actual factor of lighting than it does to production as a whole — is that the actors and audience are sharing the same physical and psychological space together. The very nearness and intimacy create advantages for lighting as they do for the spoken word, the subtle look or gesture, the intimacy of contact between characters in the play as well as between characters and the audience. Nearness allows for a greater intimacy of sharing, which in turn calls for different basic concepts and styles in both forms of theatre. When adherents to one style or another can grapple to their hearts the idea of "difference" rather then "better," than the two forms of theatre can exist side by side without unnecessary dichotomy. Where theatre for children and young people is concerned, then we have again to take into account the additional factor of what is *observed* as most appropriate for them, and much of this book has been concerned with observations that the most appropriate form of theatre for children and young people is the open stage. At the same time, I have been painstaking in suggesting methods of approach in conventional theatres, even with fixed seating, because available environment is yet another feature that has to be taken into consideration.

The already described journey of Pinocchio and Bird owed much of the vividness of the experience to the moments of silhouette against the sky-cloth, moments that cannot be achieved in the same manner with theatre in-the-round, simply because there can be no sky-cloth in such theatre. However, the journey itself, in a different style, can still contain many equally vivid moments. Again, comparison is of the *difference* not of which is better or best.

In *Christopher Columbus* (a three-sided arena production, with only two rows of audience around a 15' x 15' area), the playwright, Louis MacNeice, brilliantly covers a time sequence of the endurance of Columbus' voyage, through a sequence of entries in his log. The play was written for radio, and as such these log entries, spoken by Columbus as he is writing them, work superbly. Something else seemed necessary, however, when the play was translated to live theatre in an intimate arena. So, between each entry in the log, and with a background of music entirely suiting the mood of suspended waiting — patience and impatience, fear and uncertainty — a sequence of single spotlights gently faded in on the activities of different sailors. The light focused on each for a few seconds, and then cross-faded to another light on a different sailor or sailors. Momentarily we were with one sailor, staring fixedly into space; then to another, quietly whittling a piece of wood; then to another, writing a letter; another cleaning some ship's brass, and so on. Nothing was taken away by these additions to the original radio script, much was possibly added. But in this case, the whole sequence depended on the closeness of the audience to the actors. The same scene could not be done in the same way on a proscenium stage with a large audience, because the intimate detail of contact would have been missing.

In **Grindling Gibbons and the Plague of London,** produced in avenue arena with the forestage used as Gibbon's house (the rest of the stage seating two rows of audience), there is no scenery, only rostrum blocks. Gibbons tends a friend of his, who has contracted bubonic plague. Light in his home is dim, and lighting is confined only to the forestage. Gibbons tells his friend he is going to the apothecary for some medicine. He opens an imaginary door to the street outside. At once light changes, flooding the whole avenue arena with sunlight in the street, and going out altogether from the forestage and Gibbon's home. The *feeling* of the change of location was total, a moment that was close to film, and would need to be approached in a quite different manner on the proscenium stage.

As previously mentioned, **The Three Musketeers** was produced on a proscenium stage with a permanent set made out of rostrum blocks, scaffolding and builders' planks. The set was in two parts, left and right, joined by a 2' high rostrum behind which was a wide and deep opening with only the sky-cloth beyond. In one section of the play, there is a protracted chase of the three musketeers and d'Artagnan by their enemies — on horseback! No attempt was made to use any props in the way of hobby-horses for the chase. The protagonists, separated by several feet of space, were caught by a crossing pin-point spot of light, catching only their heads and shoulders as they moved with the rhythm of desperate horse riding. Behind them, filling the sky-cloth, was the movement of clouds from a cloud machine. Accompanying them, the sound of horses hooves and exciting music. Totally simple, but highly effective. Again, the same chase could not be done in this manner in the round because of the lack of sky-cloth. It would have to be done in an entirely different manner, or perhaps an early decision would need to be made that avenue arena plus proscenium stage would be a more appropriate form of staging, and accommodate all eventualities including this chase.

The first ever production by Theatre Centre was of Dorothy L. Sayers' radio play *The Man Born to be King*. The small studio allowed two rows of audience, seating about fifty people (half the number in the cast), on three sides of an open playing area about 20' x 15'. There was in addition, a narrow balcony at the end without audience, and black drapes were hung across the whole width of the balcony, leaving a space of about 4' to 5' between the drapes and the balcony rail. The production, lasting three-and-a-half hours, used twelve spotlights, each on its own dimmer. There were over 2,500 changes of light, the basic style and intention being that there would never be light except on people, and then often only on hands and faces. The balcony was used for the Last Supper. Christ and the 12 disciples stood in a straight line across the width of the balcony. Two pin-points of light cut across them, one from each side of the balcony. They spent a long time mastering their body weight, so that with the slightest leaning forward, faces and only faces would come into the light. A slight move backwards, and they had gone again. Nobody could be seen on the balcony unless they leaned into the light, or, as at some moments (e.g. the passing of the sop) there were just two hands in the light. Again, the whole effect was cinematic, a series of close-ups, but in this case only possible because of the extreme intimacy of the staging in relation to the audience.

Opening Plays on the Open Stage

Many people quite naturally feel that one of the greatest advantages of the proscenium stage is the use of the front curtain (or even an additional upstage tab-rail) for the opening and ending of acts and even scenes. The open stage has no such advantage, so that many directors feel the need to use lighting as a kind of replacement of the curtain. It is a delicate matter, and requires a great deal of trial and error, and preparedness to make changes, even from one performance to another, in order to find the ideal for each set of different circumstances.

One of the greatest bogies of all — and, in fact, this applies to the proscenium stage as well as to the open stage — is the fact that almost invariably *if the houselights fade to blackout* before any lights come on to the acting area, there is always *a strong vocal reaction* from the audience, ranging from blatant cheering to stifled sounds of embarrassment. The reaction is often stronger in Children's Theatre than in adult theatre.

In many proscenium theatre productions, we are used to the fact that spotlights focus on the front curtain before the houselights fade. This provides a moment of readiness and final shuffling in the audience, but takes away the reaction when the houselights do go out. Similarly, if a little light comes on to the open stage acting area before the houselights fade, so again the eye has something definite to focus on, while the mind adjusts to the factor of beginning, and again the reaction is obviated. I experimented with this opening problem in an in-the-round production of *Hamlet* (at the Globe Theatre, Regina). The production opens with the sound of a loud and prolonged roll of thunder, lasting about 15 to 20 seconds. At the moment the sound starts, the houselights begin to fade down, and almost at the same moment the opening light for the first scene begins to fade in. By the time the houselights have gone out, and with the thunder still rolling, the eerie night light of the battlements is fully established, making a full focal point for the eyes of the audience, with a continuation for the ears as the thunder slowly rolls away into the distance, and an expectation and readiness for the action to begin. When the timing of such fades and cross-fades (especially when linking sound and light) work to perfection, there is none of the above mentioned audience reaction.

But in many plays the problem of openings on the open stage goes beyond this factor of audience reaction to sudden darkness. What, for example, does one do in a play where the playwright's opening stage direction is: "As the curtain rises we see, center stage, a young woman who is alone, broken hearted and sobbing?" "How," quite naturally the director asks, "does she get there?" The obvious answer is the one discussed above: fade the houselights to blackout, have the character in question come on as swiftly and quietly as possible, give her a moment to settle, then fade in the stage lights. Of course, this can work, and may often be the only solution. Even if there is "audience reaction" to the darkness, it will not be for long, and the few moments provide more time for the actress to settle. Music can also help, by setting the mood of the opening scene and bridging the moments of audience reaction during the blackout.

There is, however, another approach that is worth considering, and certainly works with many such situations. It is also a way that I do not believe many playwrights would look on as an intrusion or alteration to their opening intention. With the proscenium stage, the author selects *a specific moment* in the time/life of a character for the action to begin — at the very moment the curtain is going up. In the open stage, what happens if we set the clock back 15 seconds, thirty seconds, even a whole minute, before that moment decided by the playwright? If we follow through the example mentioned above, the young woman who is heartbrokenly sobbing at center stage, we can contemplate the fact that she has not been there for *all time*. Indeed, we may have no indication at all as to how long she has been there. So, *let us see her go there*. Thus: there is music and the houselights begin to fade. Before they have faded completely, a spotlight focuses our attention somewhere on the stage area. As the houselights completely fade, the young woman walks slowly into the spotlight on stage. She reaches the point at the center of the stage, and breaks down, sobbing. The music fades down and away, under the sobbing. At this moment we are at the point in time originally selected by the playwright for the beginning of the play on a proscenium stage, the moment when the curtain rises. I do not believe we have lost anything by this extension of the opening. We may actually have gained, in terms of a longer time to identify with the woman's feelings, and also to take her in visually. The actress, too, has possibly gained, in terms of time for getting deeply into character, feeling and action. Certainly it is worth trying, and, in my experience, invariably works.

Another problem that can arise for some directors in relation to some plays and audiences is that the open stage may be a quite *new experience* for a large percentage of the audience, as well as possibly to some of the cast (unless they have a fully accepted, regularly performing local open stage theatre.) If the experience is new to the audience, or to many of them, the *sudden nearness* of the characters and the action can be no less than a tremendous shock. Indeed, I know of some members of the public who have been forever put off by the idea of the open stage because of the shock of that first experience. As directors, it is a point we must constantly consider. It is necessary and wise sometimes to think about the *gentlest* way of leading them into this experience, without worry or embarrassment or moments of self-consciousness. None of this will arise with young children, but will more than likely do so with some teen-agers, and almost certainly will with adults, particularly with those who are established theatre-goers with a full experience of only proscenium theatre, and its accompanying barrier between actor and audience.

To quote again from the experience of *The Man Born to be King*. I was confronted not only by an audience *the majority of whom had never before experienced the open stage,* but also by the fact that we were performing in a very small, intimate studio, and, almost the greatest of considerations, the fact that the play was based on the *Bible* and yet performed in *modern dress*, with the person of *Christ portrayed by an actor*.

If any one of us is in an audience and suddenly confronted with such experiences, what is it that we are to expect? To be shocked? To be indignant? To be amazed? To be uncertain? To be uncomfortable? What? There was an obvious need to break through very, very gently.

The solution seemed only to lie in the use of music, light and space. In very faintest light, as far from the audience as possible, two fishermen are seen, working on their nets (mimed). Then, at still the farthest possible point away from the audience, in the dimmest of light, is seen the figure of a man, still and quiet, looking at the two fishermen. They sense his presence, turn and look up at him. Through the music, he says, very simply and quietly: "Follow me." As they do so, with the music, light that is still faint but just a little brighter, cross-fades to pick out another person, a few feet nearer to us. Again, another light picks up the figure of Jesus, again a few feet closer to us, within a slightly brighter light, making him a little clearer to us all. Again he makes his simple command. Again the figure follows him...again the cross-fade to other figures *nearer* to us, more brightly lit, still with the continuity of the music, welding all together in an emotional wholeness. So there are many calls, until all the disciples have been summoned and have followed. The last of all is in the *center* of the acting area, so that both he and Jesus are closer to us and more brightly lit than hitherto, though even now light is no more than three-quarter strength.

This whole opening lasted 4½ minutes, during which time both the intellectual and emotional (and I hope the spiritual) readiness of the audience had been very slowly, gently and sensitively helped to some form of readiness for what was to come. I gathered from colleagues who were very carefully monitoring such points that for the majority it worked.

Technician or Artist?

Tradition, custom and practice have tended to divide theatre people into *technicians,* including prompters, stage managers, property and scenery people, lighting people, etc. on one hand, and *artists,* including actors, designers and directors on the other. In some senses, this has always been an inevitable form of specialization, which today is perpetuated by unions at one extreme and technology at another. This is no place to go into the whys and wherefores or the pros and cons of such a system. However, I am harnessed to a belief that the more each person in theatre knows about every other aspect of theatre the better it is for all concerned, and I still believe deeply that, praticularly for Children's Theatre, actors always benefit from exposure to and experience of stage management and other technical aspects of theatre. This may be a very personal and old-fashioned prejudice, based on the fact that I learned all I know about theatre not from a formal training, but from an apprenticeship that gave me experience of every function in theatre from loading three 60' railway trucks, via every aspect of stage management, to a reasonable amount of acting, directing and administration. There is not one single aspect that I would have avoided, none that has not been subsequently useful, and, above all, none that I cannot see in some simple way as *an art form in its own right.*

The point that is important to consider here, in relation to the type of complex lighting and its link with sound, as mentioned previously, is that the technician must be seen as *an artist.* It is not a question of asking artists to debase themselves by doing technical work, but of helping them to see that intricate technical work is part of artistry, often demanding as much sensitivity, imagination and control as is necessary in acting. Yet again I must quote from the production of *The Man Born to be King.* There were over 2,500 changes of light! None of these was written down on paper. Indeed, cues came so thick and fast that there would not have been the slightest opportunity of following them in the normal prompt-script, and certainly no time to follow "warning" and "go" cue-lights. Instead, the two people in charge of lighting were present at the majority of rehearsals, deeply imbibing the play as a whole, and then working with the utmost sensitivity to the lighting needs. Their final act of *polished and controlled intuition* was as creatively and artistically essential to the play as any of the work of the actors. Indeed, in every sense of the word, they were part of the whole team. There was no division. This is no isolated example. I have personally always felt both the necessity and the value of having technical staff involved in all creative aspects of a production, from as early in rehearsal as possible. Without exception, I have found this to be of all-round benefit. It is both profoundly valuable and absolutely necessary in all forms of Children's Theatre involving audience participation. Technicians help in terms of performance to performance adjustments to such aspects as length of a journey, possible cutting of a scene, actual time on any sequence of participation before returning to the scripted scene, also in terms of precise and exact use of the volume control of a record player or tape recorder, and the intensity of spotlights — often in relation to movement and sound.

Apart from questions of *end product* in the form of production, the training of actors cannot but benefit from their prolonged exposure to the practical working of all aspects of technical theatre. In terms of voice alone, the whole richness of modulation, color tone and so on has vital parallels in the experience of feeling the control of light or sound under one's fingers. So, too, with sensitivity to other actors, to the play as a whole, to mood and atmosphere and to all aspects of ensemble work. Far too many actors are being trained today, in my view, with an almost total dichotomy between technicians and actors. Quite apart from loss of the features mentioned above, there is also a tendency for such actors, particularly when young, to develop an unhealthy arrogance towards technicians. Theatre itself suffers.

To Hide or Not to Hide?

Should lighting and sound equipment and their operators be hidden from view or left plainly exposed for all to see? I have no personal doubts as to the answer for any kind of theatre, but particularly for all forms of Children's Theatre and open stage theatre: *Expose everything. Hide nothing.*

Until recent years, the proscenium theatre tended to hide everything. Nothing was to be allowed to interfere with the creation of illusion. Today there are some differences. Although many theatres still use borders and all sorts of other paraphenalia to cover up lighting battens, little or no attempt is made to hide front of house spots, etc. (Musicals are the main exception. They usually leave everything fully exposed).

The major difference in all new theatres, however, is that the old "prompt corner," from which light and sound were not only controlled but often actually operated, has been moved to the *back of the auditorium,* so that the technicians have an absolute view of what is happening on the stage. This direct view has undoubtedly helped all visual cueing. Systems of intercom from stage to control panel are equally accepted to help audio cuing, and no doubt work very well when the cue is an exact word at the end of a scripted sentence. In my view, however, the quality of most intercom systems, together with the dark "secret" glass in front of the viewing panel, makes the front of house technical control system almost as remote as when everything was tucked away into the prompt corner. If the reader would kindly take the trouble to look back on some of the examples of the use of light and sound quoted in this chapter, he/she will find that over and over again the person in charge of those technical arrangements has to be so fully and sensitively *at work with* the actors that they *must* all be in the same room together, literally on the same sound and light wave lengths. So, although their positioning at the back of the auditorium may be the most effective venue, they must strip away all hiding facilities and *expose themselves to the needs of the play.* The fact that they are also exposed to the audience means little or nothing. Adult audiences will take one curious and cursory glance, and then ignore them. So, too, on the whole, will children and young people, and because this book is primarily concerned with such audiences, let the final consideration of experiences rest with them.

Let us consider these young people simply in relation to sound. The moment there is music in a play, they turn to look for either the loud-speaker or the operator. If both are invisible, they then start on a full, albeit surreptitious, examination. Usually they spot the loud-speaker first. They then start to trace leads from the speaker, hoping to follow them back to the base. By now, they have probably enrolled a few equally curious peers. They go on searching until either they are successful or else totally frustrated. The majority will refuse to allow that frustration to be total, and from time to time will follow up new thoughts and ideas. What happens, however, if everything is visible? The moment they hear music they look for its source. They see the speaker and are satisfied. They then wonder who is making the music, and again as soon as they see the operator, their curiosity is satisfied. By and large, they now take no further notice.

"We are the actors, we have come to play a play. We are the audience, we have come to see your play. We are not going to pretend it isn't a play, so please don't bother to try and kid us that this is real life going on. We accept everything."

Sound

In open stage theatre for children and young people, the factors regarding sound are almost more important than those regarding light, for it is almost impossible to know precisely the volume of sound unless the operator is in the same room as the action of the play. Take **On Trial**, for example. As already described, this play contains many sequences of journey, including the "crossing of the ravine" sequence. Throughout many of these sequences, the volume of the backing music can be as dependent on the acoustics of the hall as is the volume of the actors voices. Furthermore, many times the actors are speaking or calling *through* the music. It is thus almost impossible to plot the music volume. Volume "5" in one hall may be inaudible in another, and an impossibly loud sound in another. If the operator is in the room with the action, he can modify according to precise needs, just as he can change from visual to vocal cues, or *vice versa*, for the fade-in and fade-out of cues.

Perhaps the following anecdote in a small way suggests some of the potential for actor and sound operator to work together as a team. Recently I was looking after sound for an experimental school's tour of this same play, **On Trial**. The "ravine" sequence had been more than usually exciting. When the play was over, I went back to greet one of the involved actors with the words: "I hope I didn't make life difficult for you in the ravine sequence, but it was so exciting I simply had to bring up the volume." He was astonished, and said: "Gee, I wanted to say how great it felt when you brought up the volume in the ravine sequence; it somehow brought things out of me and the scene I've never experienced before."

Which comes first, the chicken or the egg? Or does it really matter?

Audience Participation and Houselights.

Constantly throughout these pages has been the idea of the stage being "a space where anything can happen." The space includes aisles as well as playing area, even when part of the main action happens on a conventional proscenium stage. Close connections have been drawn between the use of such a space and the factor of audience participation. When lighting is used, the same connections must be followed. Audience Participation that is logically written into a play must not be diminished or minimized in any way for the sake of lighting, no matter how effective or exciting that lighting may be.

Let us return to **Pinocchio** again for some typical examples. At the opening of the play, even on a proscenium stage with fixed seating, it is suggested that all of the theatre be used for the entrance of Fire-Eater and his puppet troupe, and that the link to the main stage be via the entrance of Mr. Gepetto who, like ourselves, has come to find out what all the excitement is about. For quite a while the main action stays in the auditorium. During such time, whatever use is made of lighting on the stage area, *the houselights must remain on.* The auditorium and those of us within it as audience, are all part of the action at this time. Later, Fire-Eater's troupe go on to the main stage to enact their preview. As they do so, the houselights can slowly fade down and out, so that our full attention is focused on the stage area.

When the chases of Fox and Cat take place through the audience area; when Gepetto and Pinocchio are washing and having breakfast, with all of us joining in; when the circus advances through the audience; when Pinocchio and Bird come into the audience to ask all of us, as "fishes and birds," if we have seen Mr. Gepetto; and when Pinocchio swims to the sandbank to rescue Gepetto from the belly of the monster — at all of these times, the aisles and the audience area are again used, and, whatever else is happening with main stage lighting, there is the possible need of at least *a partial* use of the *houselights*. There is no rule of thumb either about the moment to use them or the degree of light that should be used. Basically, if the actors, by coming into the *darkness* of the auditorium set up a barrier between themselves and the audience, then there is need for some use of the houselights. Obviously, the problem is eased when the houselights are on dimmer control, and more so still if the controller can be the same person controlling all of the lighting. But this is not always possible. Fortunately, most *houselights* go on in banks or limited circuits, so decisions can be made in advance as to which section(s) to use for each particular sequence of participation, with, if necessary, a separate operator working in close conjunction with the immediate needs of the play (as well as with the central lighting operator).

In the open stage, particularly in small and intimate spaces, there is often sufficient spill or reflected light for aisles to be used without addition of houselights. Few problems arise if this thought is kept uppermost in mind: the stage is the *whole* theatre, not just the main acting area.

Lighting in Theatre for Young People is often helped by keeping in mind the art of film — the director shows us what he wants us to see, and the moment he wants to show something different he *cuts* to that. In this way he focuses our attention from one moment to the next. This can be a most serviceable view of lighting for children's theatre, particularly in the open stage.

Costume

Ingenious simplicity is possibly as pertinent to the art of costume design and making in Theatre for Young People as it is to scenery. Whether a production is on the proscenium stage or the open stage or a mixture of the two; whether it is fully or partially lit or in broad daylight; whether it is for a wide family age-group in large numbers or a controlled age-group in small numbers — whatever the conditions, costume is likely to make a significant contribution to the production. The contribution is aesthetic, is an adjunct to the actors' characterization, and is a help to the audiences' awareness, understanding and feeling for the characters and their relationships. To find the balance of these three factors is the art of costuming in children's theatre. At risk of boring the reader with repetition, let me again emphasize that basic *attitude* is all important, including a detailed study of what is appropriate for youngsters. (Let me again dispense swiftly with the "anything will do for kids" syndrome, from which comes nothing but tatty and tawdry bits and pieces, the spindrift of granny's attic and the filigree of ancient dressing-up boxes — often dirty, always crumpled and usually without rhyme or reason. Such attempts at costuming are as great an insult to the purveyors as to the audience.)

Let us consider the two extremes of the problem: the tendencies to *over-costume* or to *under-costume*. Over-dressing often arises from the best of intentions, particularly in the open stage when there is a conscious or subconscious anxiety to compensate for the absence of other visual experiences in

221

the form of scenery. The intention is laudable, but the effect is often both over-whelming and distracting. In my experience, there are two main sources to this approach. One is where the designer has not contemplated that children's theatre, particularly in the open stage, may indeed have a different set of prin-ciples of design from problems of adult theatre on picture frame stages. The other, usually arising at Universities, is when either:

(a) costumes for children's theatre are taken from "stock," or

(b) a student of design is invited to use a children's theatre production as a "project," to carry out some particular and immediate theory of costume design and without sufficient reference to the precise condi-tions of that production, or who it is for. (An example of this is when a designer has never before met theatre in-the-round, and is skillful and adept at decorating the *front* of costume for proscenium stage produc-tions, but does not realize that *backs* are as important as front in the open stage).

Concern for detailed *accuracy of the period* is one part of the problem. In fact, there are few people in the majority of even *adult audiences* who are suffi-cienty knowledgeable about the clothes of different periods to verify accuracy. Meanwhile, many (yes, even *adults*) can be quite non-plussed in terms of know-ing "who is who," and what the character is really like, or does, and so on. These are factors which are definite distractions from the play itself, no matter how aesthetically exciting the clothes may be in themselves. The factor of distraction can often be well tested by producing certain period plays in modern dress. (I am not about to suggest that all period plays *should* be per-formed in modern dress, although there can be made a strong case that, for the audience's maximum enjoyment and affinity, many plays would be helped by an approximation to clothing *we understand*).

Here are some examples arising from early experiments at Theatre Centre with productions intended for adult audiences and students of senior high school age.

The first concerned *The Man Born to be King*, already mentioned in terms of lighting. I had seen the play done twice on proscenium stages, and subse-quently have seen the same story — the Life of Christ — several times on film or television. All of these productions have been in the costume of the period, and possibly gave some "flavor" of the period. However, all had in common the same disconcerting factor at many moments in the unfolding of the drama, namely that I was wholly confused as to who exactly was who. Yes, of course one soon knew the principal characters and certain highlights of the story, par-ticularly when only two or three characters were involved in a long scene. But, for example, when many of the disciples were gathered together, all in similar robes; though perhaps differentiated by color; all or the majority wearing similar long beards and hair, then confusion was rife, no matter how much one was being given the "flavor" of the period, no matter how accurate the costumes and other adorments. One found oneself longing for moments in the dialogue when people were called by name, so that there was some chance of identification.

It was for these reasons that, with the fullest approval of the playwright, Dorothy L. Sayers ("after all, I wrote it in the modern idiom") that the play was produced at Theatre Center in modern dress, with costumes designed by Margaret Faulkes Jendyk, who subsequently designed the majority of costumes for Theatre Centre's theatre for children and young people. The im-pact on the audience of this modern dress approach was, in the best sense of the word, startling. There was no shock or offense when, to mention but a few of the characters, Christ appeared in immaculate grey flannel trousers and a neat white, open-necked shirt, or when those disciples who were fisherman appeared in roll-necked sweaters, seamen's trousers and sailor's rubber boots, or when Matthew, the tax-collector, was seen in a shiny blue serge suit and a "loud" necktie. There may have been surprise, but no offense and no shock. Above all, each character was recognizable and easily remembered. Costume was an adjunct to, not a distraction from the unfolding drama.

Theatre Centre's second experiment — one that was to affect many approaches to Shakespearean work in secondary schools some years later — was with *Sir Thomas Moore*, a play of rarity value, with an apocryphal scene by William Shakespeare, and seldom produced outside of a few Universities. The play is Elizabethan, and Theatre Centre's experiment, partly in association with Richard Southern and the Society for Theatre Research, was to give four performances in Elizabethan costume and four in modern dress. Theatre Centre had the good fortune of access to the extensive collection of Elizabethan costumes owned by Sir Donald Wolfit, who had commissioned the production. One interesting lesson was learned from the use of these costumes; no matter how splendid they might appear on a proscenium stage, in the intimate open stage every "darn and patch" was clearly visible. The main point, however, is that the majority of the actors felt far more comfortable and at home in the modern dress, and a large proportion of the audience, who saw both versions, found the play more absorbing and "easier to follow" in modern dress. Again, characters were more easily identifiable and remembered. Now, if it is true that even adults can be puzzled or nonplussed by costume, how much greater must the problem be for young people (for many of whom all clothes later than the day before yesterday are "old-fashioned"), particularly the problem of distraction from the play itself? For the majority of young people, period plays already contain a problem in terms of the language — not only just in Shakespeare — and the problem is *compounded, not solved* by dressing the characters in the costume appropriate to the period. For the young person to see, for example, a butcher or a baker in modern dress leads to immediate identification, and if the character talks in period language the young person may well ask: "Why does that butcher talk like that?" But, if in addition to talking period language the butcher is dressed in period costume, the question is more likely to be: "Who's he?" The lack of identification, because of costume, carries the youngster one step further *from* an experience of the play.

Any company concerned with presenting period plays to young people will find this problem exacerbated by teachers and educators who are anxious that the young people should be exposed to the genuine flavor of the period through costuming. A compromise has to be found, so that these interests are served as well as the overriding consideration of the young people themselves. Ingenious simplicity can often reveal many different approaches to solving the problem.

Even in a truncated version of Dumas' **The Three Musketeers**, the story line is not easy to follow, and becomes almost impossibly complex if the audience is not consistently aware of character and relationships. The dilemma is hardly eased by the fact that the 3 central characters, Porthos, Athos, and Aramis — not to mention for the most part of the play d'Artagnan as well, are *all dressed alike*, because they are in the uniform of the King's Musketeers. Of course, they vary in size and other physical characterisitics, they have personality differences, and each has his own specific part in the story line. Nevertheless, there can be confusion, particularly in the early part of the play before these differences in story line are established.

One solution, in the adaptation of the play as well as the costuming, was to start all in a modern setting, using modern dress. In this manner, it was possible for all of the characters, and especially these four, to become well-known and fully established before they were seen in costume — and a large part of the costuming itself actually takes place in front of the audience as part of the action. Many young people, and adults, stated how much this had helped them to overcome problems of identification.

Theatre Centre experimented with many different ways of overcoming these problems in its sequence of Shakespeare programs, some of which are written about in detail in the chapter on *Audience Participation and Teenagers* (Chapter 6). One way was again to have the company, at the beginning of the program, either in a basic modern costume (trousers and shirt) or a basic Elizabethan costume (doublet and hose). After the characters had been introduced, the company then added, in front of the audience, other embellishments toward a full or nearly complete Elizabethan costume, depending on the intention of the scene or scenes that were to follow. If there were several scenes from different plays, then the final costume might be partial. If there were a continuity of scenes with the same characters from only one play, then the costume would more likely be complete. Either way, the process of identification was helped, which in turn helped the young peoples' experience of the play. In some productions, a clothes-rail was brought into the acting area to facilitate this costuming in front of the audience. On one occasion, before some scenes from *Twelfth Night* in which all the characters wore a ruff, the curtain of the stage, which was being used as a dressing room, was opened to reveal the actors in a long line, tying on each others ruff. The scene was partly concerned with sharing "a day in the life of an actor," but the humor of the moment itself was a great "icebreaker," and helped the understanding of relationship of the characters to the dress of the period. Incidentally, in these experiments, when the basic costume for the actors was simply doublet and hose, it was always helpful to be able to explain to the audience that this was indeed modern dress of the period in Elizabethan times, just as trousers and shirt are modern dress in our time.

The aim in all these experiments was to try to increase the potential for intuitive experience of the play by removing intellectual barriers caused by not knowing anything about costume of the period — a removal of the distraction. Sometimes this was done without starting in modern dress, particularly when the period is less distant from our own as, for example, in **Oliver Twist**. Costumes of this late nineteenth century period do not give rise to confusion regarding the *who and what* of character. Nevertheless, the clothes are, in the youngsters' words, "old-fashioned and rather comical." We knew there would be many audience reactions to and whispered discussions about costume, and were anxious that these moments should be "fulfilled" or "drained-off" as early as possible, particularly as there are twenty-seven scenes in the play, and, with a numerically small company, many of the actors were doubling, trebling and even quadrupling parts. The sheer pace of the unfolding drama could not allow time for getting over each new costume experience. So the play, performed in avenue arena, opened with a street scene, lasting five to six minutes. A street organ-grinder played an imaginary barrel-organ (the music was real), with an imaginary monkey on his shoulder. Little by little, the whole arena filled with different characters from the play, in full costume. Some of the characters appeared only briefly, and then went off swiftly to change costume in order to return as another character. Every kind of costume, the poor and the wealthy, the scruffy and the elegant, and those in between, was on view during the street scene. Little concern was for identification with specific characters, but simply to reveal that the people in the play would be wearing clothes different from those we are accustomed to. Throughout the five or six minutes of the scene, there was constant chatter and laughter from the audience, aided by the music of the barrel-organ. This was precisely what we had expected and what we hoped would happen. Once the play itself started, with the crowd drifting away leaving only Oliver and the Artful Dodger, there was an almost total acceptance of the costumes and no further worries — no distractions.

Color as symbol is another whole area that was explored in terms of costume, particularly in **The Struggle** (a free and modern adaptation of John Bunyan's *Pilgrim's Progress*.) In the play, the characters of modern young people become many other characters, but each with similar characteristic traits carefully followed through by use of color. No overt attempt is made to emphasize the similarity of characteristics but, at an unconscious level, the color themes maintain the continuity.

Costumes and young audiences.

For plays presented in primary schools or for the 5 to 11 age group, the problems of costume are no less important but are simply different in kind — especially when the whole wide age-range can be separated into at least two separate groups, say the 5 to 8 and the 9 to 11. The difference is one of sophistication, and related to the content of the plays. For the younger half, and for the whole age range in Family-type plays, fantasy may well be predominant. For the older half, there begins to be gravitation toward more realism, even though the reality of adventure may be very different in time and place from the actual reality that is part of the youngsters' own experience. Aspects of the styles of differing periods can be mixed in plays for the older age-groups without "offense." For example, in **The Island**, for the 9-11/12 age group, the young native girl in the story can be in a sarong, in contrast to the rather stuffy officer's wife who can be in a costume that is *almost* Victorian. *Almost* is the important factor, for it is only the stuffiness of the era that one wishes to indicate, not the full and accurate picture of a Victorian. The play is not set in any special time phase; it is left entirely to the audience to decide whether the story happened a long time ago or is quite modern. In the same play, there is a military major and the "Headman of the Island." The major needs to be dressed in military uniform, but not one that is identifiable in terms of either country or time — and certainly not in some strange and fantastic musical comedy Ruritanian costume that belongs to operetta. The "Headman" can be dressed in a simple, peasant like tunic, decorated for the status, but not to the point that suggests a "musical fantasy." The breadth of imagination in design for such plays is tremendous, but the caution, for both this and the young age-group, is to beware of *cliche*.

Costume *cliche* is part of what I have called the trap of sentimentality. We see it particularly in the realm of fantasy. We see it in Kings and Queens, with their heavy cloaks, gold chains and crowns; we see it in witches, especially the pointed hat; we see it in peasants, with their pastoral tunics; we see it in the black caped villain, together with pointed black beard; we see it in the rustic, the soldier, the sailor; we see it in fairies and elves; we see it in clowns and almost every kind of comical character; we see it in characters that possess magic powers, for good or ill; and we see it in the heroes and heroines. Of course, of course, of course, it goes without saying: there is a *symbolic entity* belonging to all of these characters that has existed throughout the history of Mankind. But a symbolic entity is one thing, a conventionalized *cliche* is quite another. The variety, subtle as it may be, of possibility within the symbol, is the challenge to the designer of costumes for Children's Theatre. Here, indeed, is a case when a costume that is *not* immediately recognizable as a *cliche* character can be an enrichment for the actors, the play and the audience.

Over-dressing for young children is also an important point to take into consideration. There are no golden rules, but on the whole nothing goes wrong when line and cut are clean and straightforward, colors are bright and related to character, and trimming or decoration are kept to a tasteful minimum, without false economy. No distractions!

Under-dressing in the form of *partial costuming* tends to arise with younger age-groups more than with older groups, and often in the name of *simplicity*. There is much to commend the idea of *partial costume* — of donning these in front of the audience, even oh taking the necessary "bits and pieces" from some kind of dressing-up box or rail. But the "bits and pieces" must be thought out with enormous care, and looked after with equal care. There must also be readiness to mix styles rather than anchor to the singular approach. Where an exactly right hat may do for one character, it is possible that a hat *plus* belt or cummerbund may be more appropriate for another; a hat *plus* tunic more so still for another; and a hat *plus* fur-lined gloves for a fourth. The conception of simplicity has here been based on the idea of "hats," but the additions have added further enrichment without in any way spoiling the original notion to use only partial costumes.

At the symbolic as well as the decorative level, color is of course always important, and a book of this kind cannot possibly go into all the necessary details. But at the most basic levels it is perhaps worth considering the relationship of:

Red, with power of many different kinds;
Light blue, with spirituality and positiveness and innocence;
Deep blue, with royalty, strength and integrity;
Green, with all pastoral things, but also with forms of magic;
Brown, with the earth, and rustic, simple people;
Yellow, with the sun, the gods, heroism and triumph;
Purple, with pomp and circumstance, ritual and ceremony.

There are many mixtures of these, both in blending and in contrast. There are also all the shades of grey from near-white to near-black, and white and black themselves.

Once again, there are no golden rules. But, significantly, experience suggests that the younger the children the closer we need to keep to bold primary colors. Tones and shades develop with the growth of sophistication, both in the content of the plays, and in the youngsters themselves.

One tremendous responsibility of costuming in the open stage is that *all* costumes must be superbly made in every detail, because of the nearness of the audience. (Safety pins and repairs with the wrong colored threads stand out like the candle Portia sees in the *Merchant of Venice* —"a good deed in a naughty world!") As I have remarked before, the history of Children's Theatre all over the world is the story of theatre on a shoestring budget. Nevertheless, all of the companyies I have worked with have been most painstaking, both in the making and the maintenance of costumes, and in the everyday care by ironing and careful hanging. Each has achieved a reputation for the quality of its presentations, based on their own philosophy that every performance must be as smart, neat and tidy as the first. I was delighted to be present in a school when the principal said to the company: "I hadn't realized you were touring so extensively. I thought you were playing just this week. And certainly all your props and costumes looked as if they were made especially for us and this one performance." The company had just completed its eighty-fourth performance on tour!

Beards, Wigs, Make-up, and Other Forms of Disguise

No actor in children's theatre, for any age group, and particularly in the open stage, can depend on costume as a substitute for his acting. Less still, especially in performances in daylight, can he depend on make-up. His body, his face, his hair, are the basics of characterization, not externals like clothes and wigs, beards and make-up.

Beards and wigs can, of course, be a most important adjunct, and often very necessary when an actor is playing two, three, four, maybe even more parts in one play.

The major problem today surrounds the cult of personality-acting, recently strengthened by television, but probably originating with film. If it is necessary to have an actor to perform the part of a small man of forty, a large man of fifty, or an impish geriatric, then the right person will be found for *each* part. Not so many years ago, one actor, a "character" actor, might be asked to perform all three parts in succession. This was one of the fascinating challenges of acting. Today, the face is the fortune (or not, as the case may be!) and there are fewer and fewer actors prepared to "pull or distort" their face, rearrange their hair style into many different styles, or change their physical self in broad or even subtle manners. Theatre does not lose, because there are so many exactly "right" actors available. Actors, however, do lose. They lose both opportunity and creative adventure. The one form of theatre that almost invariably still has both to offer is theatre for children or young people.

For an actor contemplating such an opportunity, again with special reference to open stage productions in broad daylight, it is sometimes worth recalling how make-up ever came into being in the first place. In a nutshell it is quite simply this: Theatres are places of darkness, which thus necessitate artificial light. That light removes all pigments from the face. Make-up replaces the pigments and adds shadows and highlights in a remoulding of the face. A beard or a moustache or a pair of spectacles are further adjuncts to more detailed disguise.

In the open stage, the wig, the beard, the moustache — or any combination of the three — will help the factor of *disguise*. So, too, will spectacles. But make-up in itself adds nothing. Acting is the root of characterization, not make-up or costume. An exhilarating thought.

Properties

In London's Tottenham Court Road are many shops which sell seemingly thousands of bits and pieces of television, tape-recording and video-tape sets. The bits and pieces are spares for repairs, or even basic units for making your own set. Into one of these shops walked a member of one of Theatre Centre's Children's Theatre companies. Solemnly he browsed around, seeking here, seeking there, thumbing this, that and the other. A curious assistant eventually moved over to him: "Can I help you, sir?" asked the assistant, politely. "Well, I'm not sure. I'm making a machine for blowing up the world. Wondered if you might have something useful here." His face was absolutely dead-pan and serious. But the assistant matched him.

"Well, sir," he said, "let's see if I can help..."

I tell the story because it underlies one fascinating aspect of Children's Theatre in the Open Stage: the occasional making of exciting and imaginative props.

Once again, ingenious simplicity is the keynote. The "machine that blew up the world" was eventually made. It comprised a rectangular box, covered with dials and knobs, curling wires and flashing lights; it was on wheels, with a handle to push it by. It was imaginatively exciting. Indeed it was so exciting that it had to be gauged against the very exacting test: enrichment that is necessary, or distraction that is disposable?

In this particular case it *was* necessary, and it was possible to save it from being any form of continuous distraction because the character using it was able to do so entirely on his own for some minutes. Consequently, the youngsters in the audience became completely familiar with it before the main dialogue and action of the play continued. He spent some time taking it to various parts of the acting area, trying to assess exactly where to place it. He constantly turned knobs and switches, so that lights flashed and buzzers hummed — all as part of this same personal ritual. Had he not spent time in this manner, and walked straight into another scene and got involved in a dialogue with others, then the machine would have been a distraction. The youngsters would have had eyes and ears only for the machine, and would have ignored the dialogue.

This fact underlies a basic principle regarding props, similar to that already discussed regarding scenery and costume: the principle of distraction. Over and over again this principle has to be our guide, both in the choice of props, in the making of them, and in production.

In another play, **The Opposites Machines**, there is a similar but less ambitious machine. But in this play, it would have been wholly inapprorpiate to have a *real* machine — a really grave distraction — so the machine and its whole operation was totally mimed.

Some people are worried by the bareness of an open stage, with only a few rostrum blocks, and are relieved if there is one elaborate property. In **The Bell**, for the 5 to 7 years old, Tom, the Maker and Seller of Bells, has a cart on wheels. The cart is brilliantly decorated, and from its center rises up a post, from the top of which extends a brightly colored umbrella. Many arms of different lengths stem out around the pole, and on each arm hang two or three bells, so that there are many bells overall: Chinese, Indian, Swiss, Javanese bells, ships bells, ceremonial bells, dinner bells and so on. There is no doubt that the youngsters are charmed by this gay cart, and again steps must be taken in production to make sure that it does not become a distraction. This will be achieved if for the first few minutes of the play, which open with the arrival of Tom and his cart into the market place, ample opportunity is given for everyone to look at the cart in detail, from where they are sitting. Part of this is scripted: Tom talks to us about himself and his work as he cleans some of the bells. Part depends on production moments, such as Tom at the very opening moving the cart from one place to another in the circle, trying to find the best place for it in the market place. With this kind of care, we all become familiar with the cart, and it ceases to be a distraction. (Even so, with very young children, there will be moments when one sees them just staring at the cart, discovering and taking in new details they had not noticed before.)

What has already been said about skill in making, and constant care throughout many performances, is naturally as applicable to props as to costumes, and very particularly so to small hand-props such as *Books of Spells* or *Instructions*. If a character is reading from such a book in a small and intimate circle, the chances are that many of the youngsters will be able to see what is being read, so that detail inside the book must be as carefully thought out and created as the outer cover—all of this from the *viewpoint* of the character who owns the book. For this reason, I have often found the actors themselves interested in creating their own book, rather than leaving it to the property department. In **The Mirrorman,** both the Mirrorman himself and the Toyman, of whom the Mirrorman is the reflection, are identically dressed in every respect, and possess identical books. "But they are only identical from the *outside* — the insides are quite different," explains the Mirrorman. Indeed they are. The Toyman's book is partly filled with names and addresses of customers, a kind of Order Book. Another part may contain "How to Make" details about various toys. But it is possibly quite mundane compared to the Mirorman's Book, which is filled with all kinds of magic spells, and on every page are magic signs in many different colors. The playwright mentions only those spells used as part of the action, but these are at different places in the book, so that all the other pages need to contain different spells, perhaps created by the actor himself. These need to be as seriously thought out as those contained in the script, just in case the book should, at some point in the play, fall open when lying on the floor beside some curious youngster in the audience.

Much thought needs to be given to the use of *Crowns*. In childrens' own play, they will swiftly make a crown from a piece of paper, with the help of a little glue and gold paint. These are often made with haste in order to get on with the action, and they are absolutely appropriate for that need. Indeed, it would be inappropriate for an adult to interfere, and to suggest greater elaboration. But in the presentaton by adults of a play to a child or familo audience, then elaboration is important. The crown needs three-dimensional body, and careful and imaginative decoration — sometimes filling in the top with rich velvet material in purple, royal blue or gold can make all the difference.

In many of the plays for the younger or family age groups, there are animal characters, e.g. the bird, the bloodhounds and Fox and Cat in **Pinocchio.** These often at once stimulate the idea of *masks*. Over and over again, experience proves that it is wise not to go beyond the *half mask*. The golden rule is: Leave the actors' face free; the expressions of the face are what make a rich experience for the audience. The full mask is rich only in the first few seconds of our seeing it. Thereafter it becomes a dead and expressionless thing, or, if some fixed expression has been made on the mask itself, then it belies the many different feelings that arise in the character wearing it. Sometimes the problem can be solved by the costume department. For instance, the full bloodhound costume (with tail) can include a close fitting headdress (with ears) that fit closely under the chin like a balaclava helmet or hood. The whole face is free and the actor needs only, with make-up, to put on a simple brown or black nose. Fox and Cat, in the same play, can be approached in a similar manner. Of course, there are short periods in some plays where masks are used as deliberate stylization, often including the overt disguise of a character, as for example in the ritual "Carnival of the Seasons" in **Adventure Faces,** or the masked accusers in such plays as **On Trial** or **The Struggle**. Here the full or very nearly full mask is appropriate, a quite different circumstance from the use of a mask for basic characterization. But even with the fuller masks, I would recommend trying to keep the mouth free from cover to help the actors' speech work.

Property Themes, Particularly for Older Age Groups

The final sentence of the first paragraph of this chapter on *Part of the "Magic" of Theatre* reads: "The paramount demands are on taste, economy, imagination and selectivity." These are very precisely the qualities that need to underly property selection and making in plays for older age groups. Especially in the open stage, it is important not to become obsessed with *realism*. In certain kinds of theatre on the picture frame stage it has become essential for all props to be real. Kettles must boil, sausages must sizzle, decanters of port must — must what? *Be* real, or *look* real, in terms of color perhaps? Of course the port cannot, must not, be real. No one wants drunken actors whirling around the stage, possibly forgetting lines and bringing in new business. So, what of the kettle and the sausages? "We have come to see the players *play* their play."

Whatever the necessities of tradition and convention in proscenium theatre for adults, it behoves us to reconsider many questions in terms of Theatre for Young People, and this is made abudantly clear the moment we move into forms of open stage, even if such forms include a partial use of the proscenium stage. Our processes will be questioned by the audience if too complex, and it is wise not to have that questioning take place *during* the play, as, for example, "Is Shylock's knife real or not?" Alternatively, the *convention* of process that we set-up overtly from the very start of a play will be totally acceptable, and remain so if we remain consistent. Economy and selectivity are the root of the convention-setting. Taste and imagination, including stimulating the imagination of the audience, are the process. Linked throughout is concern for what is *distracting*.

To quote again from **Oliver Twist**, as produced either wholly in the open stage or with a partial use of the proscenium stage. Hours of sifting and selecting, trial and error, led to the final decision that the only properties necessary were those directly concerning Oliver himself — "Oliver's theme." Thus, in Fagin's den, it was important to have the *wipes* (handkerchiefs) and other items taken from Fagin's pockets during the pick-pocketing practice. But all other props *in the same scene*, everything to do with "supper", frying and eating sausages with plates and knives and forks and so on, were entirely mimed. "Oliver's theme" remained consistent as a basis of prop selection for the rest of the play.

One more example. In **Grindling Gibbons and the Plague of London**, again performed in the open stage plus the use of only the forestage of the proscenium (the rest was taken up by two rows of audience), the props were based on "Gibbon's theme." The story, a swash-buckling adventure set in London during the Plague and Great Fire of the seventeenth century, concerns the early life of one of the world's greatest wood-carvers, destined to help Sir Christopher Wren with St. Paul's Cathedral and many of London's most famous churches. "Gibbon's theme" of props concerned his own carving, from the earliest whittling of a lump of timber through to its completion as a carved pot of flowers, and to his greatest triumph, the carving of wood into a Tintoretto cartoon, which won for him the coveted prize of being appointed "Carver to the King." No other props were used, all other's mimed. A doctor appears in many scenes concerned with the plague. He carries and uses a "doctor's bag" as a symbol of office, but all medical instruments and medicine taken from it are mimed. A young friend of Gibbon's becomes a great violinist. We often hear the music of his playing, but the instrument is mimed. The convention of "Gibbon's theme" was established at the outset of the production, and wholly accepted by the teen-age audience.

One main exception to this "property theme," which is by no means a golden rule, — perhaps it is more a reminder to ourselves of how much the materialism of theatrical paraphernalia can interfere with inner experience — concerns the question of *guns.* If a gun is to be used, then it must be a real prop, a functional prop. Yes, even including the old blunderbuss used in **Oliver Twist.** It must be able to be fired on the open stage as well as the proscenium stage. It cannot be faked, with the sound coming from off-stage. One must always be ready, however, for the *emotional reactions* of the audience. These generally take the form of stifled screams or of laughter, and are a perfectly natural emotional outlet. If the cast is ready for the reaction, then they will not be disturbed. Needless to say, in the intimacy of the open stage, it is vitally necessary to make sure the gun is fired well away from any of the young audience. It shoud be fired in the center of the acting area, rather than close to one side.

The "magic" of the Theatre: taste, economy, imagination and selectivity in the material sphere of scenery, costumes and props. This plus deep sincerity and believability in the acting. And for theatre for children and young people, an occasional integrated extension of participation of the heart, the mind and the spirit, which includes active participation of the voice and the body.

Plays by Brian Way

Plays for Family Audiences

A CHRISTMAS CAROL
OLIVER TWIST
PINOCCHIO
PUSS IN BOOTS

SLEEPING BEAUTY
THE STORYTELLERS
THE THREE MUSKETEERS
TREASURE ISLAND

Plays for Audiences in Kindergarten through Third Grade

BALLOON FACES
THE BELL
THE HAT
MR. GRUMP AND THE CLOWN

THE MIRRORMAN
THE RAINBOW BOX
SOS
THE WHEEL

Plays for Audiences from Grades Four through Six

ADVENTURE FACES
THE CLOWN
CROSSROADS
THE DECISION

THE ISLAND
THE KEY
THE LADDER
THE LANTERN

ON TRIAL

Plays for Audiences in Junior and Senior High School

ANGEL OF THE PRISONS
DISCOVERY AND SURVIVAL
GRINDLING GIBBONS AND THE PLAGUE OF LONDON
SPEAK THE SPEECH I PRAY YOU
THE STRUGGLE

Plays with Similar Themes for Audiences of Different Ages

Theme: Faces
ADVENTURE FACES (5 & 6)
BALLOON FACES (K-3)

* MAGICAL FACES (3 & 4)

Theme: Key
(5 & 6) THE KEY
(3 & 4)* THE OPPOSITES
MACHINE
(K-3) THE RAINBOW BOX

Theme: The Clown Who Lost His Laugh
THE CLOWN
MR. GRUMP AND THE CLOWN
* THE VALLEY OF ECHOES

* These plays are not listed under the grade categories as they are expressly intended for grades three and four.

All the plays mentioned above are available from

BAKER'S PLAYS, Boston, MA. 02111.